No Shame in Love

By Maggie Pierson

No Shame in Love

Copyright © 1997
Rimrock Enterprises
First Printing 1997

Library of Congress Catalog Card Number: 97-76096
ISBN: 1-57502-672-4

Published by: Rimrock Enterprises
            PO Box 450067
            Atlanta, Georgia 31145-0067

Printed in the USA by

MORRIS PUBLISHING
3212 East Highway 30 • Kearney, NE 68847 • 1-800-650-7888

Dedication:

For Liz

Acknowledgments

For their inspiration, patience, support and friendly criticism, I owe many thanks to my family and friends.

To: The Best Editors an author ever had:
Mayo and Alan

To: Benjamin, wherever you are.
I Pray that You Find Peace and Happiness.

Chapter 1

Charlotte Hamby had been hiding in her room ever since her mother, Peggy, had informed her of the impending arrival of Mason Burns. Mason was another unattached male seeking a wife. Charlotte was content to remain single, but her mother was determined to rid herself of her twenty-seven-year-old daughter. Peggy Hamby was certain that this gentleman from the south was the solution to their problem.

Peggy selfishly had arranged a loveless match under the guise of saving Charlotte's reputation. Her mother had been willing to pay a depraved man to marry her only child to satisfy her own pompous desires. Charlotte would learn to love Mason Burns, after all he came from a fine family recently plagued by reduced circumstance. Feeling the pinch of their personal recession, it had been agreed that Mason would journey North seeking a bride.

Mason's mother, Nola Burns, and Peggy Hamby had been school friends before Nola abruptly eloped. Nola had given birth to her son Mason shortly after her marriage to Jim Burns.

Charlotte was told to expect their guest about six o'clock for dinner. She prayed he wouldn't be just another one of those rough two-fisted drinkers her mother was famous for bringing home.

Charlotte's quiet life had become chaotic for Peggy, the very merry widow of Henry Hamby, had made every effort to rid herself of her old-maid daughter. Charlotte felt that the front door should be replaced with a revolving door due to the steady stream of marriageable aged men for her approval.

Henry Stafford Hamby, a highly respected scholar, was loved by all, but his superficial wife, Peggy. Their only child, Charlotte was the apple of his eye. She had stood by helplessly as her beloved father slowly shriveled from the chronic deficiency of a diseased heart. It seemed as though it was only yesterday when Charlotte had rushed home from work to find that her father had passed away.

"Papa, I'm home. You'll never believe what I found buried in a bunch of old boxes in the back of the bookstore. Do you hear me? Papa, it's a first edition of *David Copperfield*. Can you imagine?

We'll have some supper and then I'll read...."

Charlotte never finished the sentence. She was standing in her parents' bedroom, where her father Henry Stafford Hamby lay white as chalk and stiff as a board.

Charlotte was horrified to find him laying face down on the floor. Her father's legs were tangled up in his bed covers as he dangled helplessly over the edge. He looked as though with his last breath he had struggled to get out of the bed.

Charlotte couldn't leave her father laying so precariously, so she gently moved him back onto the bed.

"Oh Papa, you're so cold. You've been gone for quite a while. Mama, where are you?" Charlotte called out. "Mama, are you all right? Have you called the doctor, the paramedics, somebody?" The house remained quiet except for Charlotte's unanswered questions.

She tiptoed around the room from habit as to not disturb her sleeping father, but it was unnecessary for he was now abiding in eternity with the angels. "Papa, did you die alone? Where is my mother?"

Charlotte knew her Mother was a silly thoughtless little thing, but she wasn't callous enough to let him die alone. Charlotte must learn the truth, so she sat by her dead father and waited.

"Oh, Papa. I remember when we sat in the park and you read to me. First we read books about ponies and fish. I suppose my favorite was "The Little Puppy." I loved the golden books collection. Papa, I still have them," Charlotte talked to her dead father as though he could hear her every word.

"Remember my twelfth birthday you surprised me with a copy of *Jane Eyre*. I've read it so often it's almost worn out," Charlotte stroked her father's hand. "Papa, I won't cry now. I will drink in your face, every feature. I'll remember only the handsome face of his youth, not the tired, wrinkled face, ravaged by disease," Charlotte said with surprising calm.

Charlotte had been sitting with her father about half an hour when she heard the rattle of the front door opening.

"Henry, I'm back. I hurried as quickly as I could. I hope you haven't been worried," Peggy called. "Charlotte will be home soon and we'll have a lovely dinner. She started a roast in the crock pot before she left for work this morning."

Peggy Hamby ran up the stairs into their bedroom to find their stony faced daughter sitting by her father.

"What happened?" Peggy asked Charlotte softly.

Tear stained eyes glared accusingly into her confused mother's face, "Papa's gone, Mother! Where were you?" Charlotte asked in cold monotone.

"Henry, what's happened? I slipped out for a minute. I wasn't gone long." She ran over to their bed but shrank back in horror at the sight of her dead husband.

"He's been dead a long time, Mother," Charlotte's tone was cold and as brittle as her father's corpse. "Where have you been? Papa died alone, Mother. I'll ask you again, where have you been?" Charlotte demanded.

Peggy stood wide-eyed as she refused to meet her daughter's accusing stare, "I wasn't gone long, Henry. Charlotte, he was sound asleep. I had to run an errand."

"Mother! Why didn't you call someone to sit with him, if you were forced to leave? You know how sick was," Charlotte pressed on.

"Caring for a sick old man gets tiring. Don't look at me with that contemptuous expression. I do have a right to a life."   "Well, while you were out, living your life, My Father died alone." Charlotte snapped.

Peggy muttered something inaudible as she suddenly dropped to the floor into blissful unconsciousness far away from Charlotte's accusations.

Charlotte wouldn't get an answer today of her mother's whereabouts. She only knew that in the moments of her father's greatest need her mother was gone.

Charlotte walked to the phone, and called Dr. Phillips, her father's cardiologist.

"Dr. Phillips, please."

"He can't come to the phone," the receptionist stated, "Dr. Phillips is with a patient. May I take a message?"

"This is Charlotte Hamby. Would you have Dr. Phillips send help? My father Henry Hamby has died." Charlotte did not wait for a response as she hung up the receiver.

"I'm sorry, Miss Hamby," the receptionist attempted to reply as the telephone line went dead.

Charlotte placed a damp wash cloth on her unconscious mother as she heard a siren in the distance announcing the urgency of its mission. There was the screech of brakes and the loud banging of heavy fists on the front door. Dr. Phillip's receptionist had called the police and paramedics.

Charlotte trudged down the steps to open the door for the rescuers. She sadly realized that their help came too late.

"My father is upstairs." Charlotte's lip quivered from stress.

"Miss, I'm Officer Stanley. Did someone call for assistance. Can you tell us what happened?"

"Yes! It's my father. He's had a heart condition for sometime. He's dead," Charlotte said quietly.

"Take us to him please," the paramedic replied gently as her and the others of the rescue group followed the solemn young lady up the stairs.

"Pete, I'll wait downstairs for the other," Officer Stanley stated.
"Thanks, Stan."

"He died several hours ago. Rigor mortis has already begun to set in," Charlotte volunteered.

"Let us check him out, miss."

"He's been quite ill for several years. We've been expecting it. Did Dr. Phillip's office call?"

"Miss, would you care to wait downstairs?" the policeman asked.

"No thank you, I'll stay. Papa never hurt me in life, why should he hurt me in death?" Charlotte replied as she stared into the peaceful face of her father. "The doctors have been trying to get me to put him in a nursing home, but that wasn't for him. He wanted to die in his own bed."

The paramedics moved quickly past Charlotte to check for vital signs. There were none.

"Joe, you look after the lady," the paramedic spoke to his partner.

Except for the cloth on her forehead, Peggy Hamby remained on the floor in a heap.

"Sure Pete," the second paramedic answered as he brought what appeared to be smelling salts under Peggy Hamby's nose. She shook her head and sputtered from the pungent aroma of ammonia.

"There's nothing we can do for him," the paramedic stated as he turned to Charlotte. "Sorry miss."

"What uh? Oh, no Henry," with an outburst, Peggy cried as she attempted to crawl into the bed beside her dead husband.

"Steady ma'am. We ought to take Mrs. Uh..," Joe turned to Charlotte.

"Mrs. Hamby, Mrs. Peggy Hamby," Charlotte answered. "She's my mother, and he's my father, Mr. Henry Hamby. Professor Henry Stanford Hamby." Her tone softened as she spoke his name.

"Mrs. Hamby, would you like for us to carry you to the hospital?" Joe asked.

"Yes, that would be nice of you," Peggy fluttered her eyes. She never missed an opportunity to be coquettish.

Pete stood up and walked over to Peggy, "Mrs. Hamby, I'm sorry to inform you, but your husband, your husband has gone."

"Gone where?" Peggy asked, in a confused muddled tone.

"Your husband has passed away," Pete rephrased his statement, attempting to help Peggy understand.

"Oh yes, You have been so very kind. Would you young men care to stay for dinner? Our daughter Charlotte prepared a fantastic roast. Charlotte where are you? Henry will be upset if you're out late again," Peggy rattled, as she looked about the room.

Charlotte's anger was replaced by concern. She had never seen her mother so disconnected. Peggy Hamby rejected the horror that had suddenly engulfed the household. She rambled on as though nothing had transpired. Henry was alive and well, and would forgive her tardiness as he had so many times in the past.

"Mother, it's all right. I'm here," Charlotte spoke to her mother.

"There you are, dear. I've invited these nice young men to dinner."

"Yes, Mama, I heard. Why don't you go to the hospital with Joe and Pete? I'll take care of things."

"Charlotte dear, take care of things until your father gets home. Make sure his coffee is ready. You know how he is about his coffee-extra cream, no sugar," the loquacious Peggy babbled on, as the paramedics assisted her down the stairs.

Charlotte had forgotten about the police being in the house until Officer Stanley spoke,

"Pete! Joe! You know better than to assist anyone from leaving the premises. This area must be secured," Officer Stanley stated.

"Jim, look at this woman. She's out of it. Babbling her head off. You can see she's no help to anybody. The hospital will keep her under isolation. Send a man to keep watch, if you like," Joe stated.

"Okay, we'll talk to her later on," Jim Stanley replied.

"Miss Hamby, this area must be kept secured. Please stay seated on this couch. Touch nothing until the supervisor arrives. The coroner will have to determine the official cause of death."

"The coroner, why the coroner? Papa was terminally ill. Why all the questions?" Charlotte asked.

"It's procedure, miss," Officer Stanley answered.

"When were your father's prescriptions refilled, Miss Hamby?" Officer Stanley suddenly asked.

"Let me think. I am sure 's prescriptions were refilled three days ago. Excuse me. What do you think you are doing?" Charlotte demanded.

"What am I doing about what, miss?" the officer asked.

"What are you doing with my father's prescriptions?" Charlotte snapped.

"Miss, uh. This was an unattended death. We must bag and identify all potential evidence," the young officer appeared to be uncomfortable.

She could have sworn that he was embarrassed to be answering her accusing questions. For a split second as the officer let his guard down, a crimson color rose on his face.

"He's embarrassed; I know he is. I see it in his eyes," Charlotte thought.

"Your father passed away at home. We must collect all of his medication, for examination," Officer Stanley replied as he cleared his throat. He returned to his professional attitude.

Her eyes were so big, and her face was so sweet. Did she have any idea the affect she had on a person? Jim Stanley would have to be careful in his dealing with Charlotte Hamby.

Breaking through his wanderlust, Charlotte cried out as a tear trickled down her cheek, "In other words, I wrapped emotionally in cotton. I kept alive, fretted over him day and night. Then I went nuts and murdered him, most foully."

The officer refused to respond to the accusation. He made a few notes in a small black book for what seemed an eternity. Jim Stanley finally looked up. "Miss Hamby, you stated that you refilled your father's medication three days ago."

"That's correct. I am careful about dispensing his medication. That prescription is digitalis," Charlotte said in a perplexed manner. She watched as Officer Stanley examined a prescription bottle through the plastic bag.

"Digitalis? Three days ago?" Officer Stanley repeated, as he busily wrote in his notebook.

"Yes, that's right. Digitalis. Three days ago. Why?"

"Because, Miss Hamby, this prescription, the digitalis, that you claim to have refilled three days ago, and should be almost full, is empty." The word "empty" dropped out of his mouth as though it were a cymbal falling on a library floor.

"I don't understand?" Charlotte whispered. "There should only be a three day supply missing from each bottle."

"Exactly where did you find your father?" Officer Stanley asked.

"Papa was hanging off the bed face down on the floor. He appeared to have fallen while trying to get out of bed. The doctor had told him to be careful. He lacked the strength to move about unassisted."

Officer Stanley walked out of the room, picked up the phone and dialed.

"Homicide," the voice said.

"It's Officer Stanley. Who's the senior man?"

"Dempsey."

"Let me speak to him."

"This is Lt. Dempsey."

"Lt. Dempsey, this is Officer Stanley. I arrived with the paramedics at 445 Parkview Place. The resident Mr. Henry S. Hamby, 63 year old Caucasian, has expired. Decedent was terminally ill with heart disease."

"Is the area secured? Anything unusual?" Dempsey asked.

"Yes, sir. I secured the area. We may have a possible homicide. A man terminally ill appears to have received an overdose of digitalis. Daughter admits to moving the body."

"Digitalis, you say?"

"Yes, sir," Officer Stanley.

"Anything else?" Lt. Dempsey asked.

"The mother, Mrs. Peggy Hamby was out of control, so the paramedics took her to hospital."

"We'll have to get a statement from Mrs. Hamby. I'll send somebody over to the hospital as soon as possible. I'll bring the lab boys with me. Good job, Officer Stanley."

"Yes sir."

Officer Stanley hung up the receiver and returned to the young woman's side.

"Miss Hamby, Lt. Dempsey, our superior will be joining us in a few minutes. He'll have a few questions for you. Please continue to wait here until his arrival."

Officer Stanley, needing to clear his head, left Charlotte with her father's body and walked downstairs to await the arrival of his supervisor.

He was startled by the sudden chime of the doorbell. He continued down the stairs to determine the cause of the alarm.

Instead of his supervisor, he found the Hamby's next door neighbor Mrs. Weinstock who was fidgeting on the stoop. She was accompanied by her faithful French poodle, Brandy. Instead of falling into step behind her mistress, Brandy treated herself to the luxury of a final leak on the Hambys' formerly pristine steps.

Mrs. Weinstock ignored Brandy's lapse of etiquette as she entered the house. "Oh, I was afraid something was wrong when I saw the police car. Is Charlotte all right? May I be of help?" She frowned at the policeman as he attempted to block her way.

"Charlotte, where are you, dear?" Mrs. Weinstock called out as she barged into the room.

"I'm upstairs in Papa's room, Mrs. Weinstock. Don't touch anything. If the officer looks startled, he probably thought you were his boss, a Lt. Somebody," Charlotte replied. She could not suppress a laugh as Brandy bounced into her lap jealously keeping the two women separated.

Charlotte sought the comfort of her black furry friend as Brandy gave her a flurry of wet doggie kisses.

"I'm sorry, dear. It's been such a long uphill battle. Where is Peggy?" Mrs. Weinstock frowned.

"The paramedics have taken mama to the hospital for observation, I suppose. Papa is gone, and there is so much to be done. Would you believe it? That policeman is collecting his medications. They probably think I murdered him. How could they be so cruel? I loved him so. Oh Mrs. W., I've dreaded this day for so long," Charlotte buried her face into the dog's soft fur. "Gee you smell good, Brandy," Charlotte whispered, forcing herself to think of a more pleasant subject.

"I know it is difficult, dear, but Henry is in a better place. He's suffered so long. His poor tired body just wore out. Henry hated the idea of being hooked up to the damnable machines."

"I know, but it hurts worse than I expected. I must keep a cool head about me and call the funeral home. Mother's in no condition to handle the arrangements. We'll have the funeral in few days, whenever the police will release his body."

"Remember Charlotte, I am always close by." Brandy bounced into Mrs. Weinstock's arms as he responded to the sound of her voice. "Oh ho! you little minx. You think I'm talking to you. Not this time precious. Our Charlotte needs our help. Be a good doggie." Mrs. Weinstock could not suppress laughter.

"Miss Hamby," Officer Stanley interrupted the two women as he returned to the bedroom. We would appreciate your assistance. If you feel up to it, will you check this plastic bag, see if this is all the medication your father was taking?"

"My father is finally been released from his tortured earthly shell, and you want me to discuss his medications?"

"Routine miss." The young officer shifted from one foot to another. No other woman had ever affected him in such a way. She was so sweet and honest. Under other circumstances he would have asked her out.

"Routine. What's routine?" Charlotte looked at Mrs. Weinstock with confusion.

"Dear," Mrs. Weinstock said, "when a person dies, and he's not in the hospital. Well," she paused as she took Charlotte's hand, "they collect up all of his pills. They'll also have to do an autopsy."

"Oh, great. I've cared for my father for the last three years. I kept him away from all unpleasantness and stress, and now I'm suspected of murdering him." Charlotte began to cry. "This is too much, more than anyone should have to bear." She permitted Mrs. Weinstock to comfort her.

"I can tell them what a good daughter you were. You have taken care of your father's every need," she turned her attention to the policemen. "Charlotte's also taken care of her mother, if you boys in blue are interested," Mrs. Weinstock added.

"Sorry ma'am, you understand it's the law." Officer Stanley was examining the bottles carefully. He stared intently at one particular bottle.

"Of course, Officer Stanley, I suppose you know best. If we touch nothing, may Mrs. Weinstock, stay with me?" Charlotte whispered.

"I'll be glad to my dear. If the officer doesn't mind?" She joined Charlotte on the couch.

The young officer decided it would be simpler to keep the area secure if he kept the two women on the bedroom couch until his superiors arrived.

The officer stood quietly as he waited with the subdued Charlotte for the arrival of his supervisor, the investigators and the ID technician.

Fifteen minutes later, Officer Stanley left the women upstairs to answer the door bell's ring. Charlotte's anger increased for this interloper who acted as though he were the master of this domain.

"Lt. Dempsey, the women are upstairs."

Officer Stanley led his superiors to the bedroom. "This is Miss Charlotte Hamby. She is the daughter of Mr. Henry Hamby, and her neighbor Mrs. Weinstock. The paramedics have taken Mrs. Hamby to the hospital for observation."

"Thank you, Officer Stanley. Ladies, we'll be with you in a moment." Lt. Dempsey turned to Officer Stanley. "Escort the ladies downstairs and stay with them. Do you have a preliminary statement from Miss Hamby?"

Several officers entered the bedroom as the young officer conferred with his superior.

"Yes sir," was all the officer said as he turned to Charlotte and Mrs. Weinstock. "Please follow me, ladies," he said as he shepherded the two women out the door.

"Bag, tag and photograph everything," Lt. Dempsey stated while pulling on a pair of rubber gloves. "All right men, let's go over this room with a fine tooth comb."

"I am sure that the family will co-operate while you look around the master bedroom," he called out to the departing woman, "Miss Hamby, you have no objections if my men look around, do you?" The lieutenant asked as though any objection would go unheeded.

"No, Lt. Dempsey, you and your men go right ahead. Ask them not to make anymore mess than necessary. I'm not wealthy and can't afford a maid. I'm a working person, just like you," Charlotte stated with a frown.

"You heard the lady. Don't make a mess," Lt. Dempsey replied to Charlotte's request.

Lt. Dempsey and his men searched the room from one end to the other. They photographed every inch of the bedroom. They bagged up the address book, stacks of bills, credit cards and an empty bottle of vodka.

Lt. Dempsey was in deep conversation with one of his men as another officer pulled a piece of paper from behind the night table, and placed it in a plastic bag.

"Now we'll go downstairs to the ladies and get down to business," Lt. Dempsey stated as he left the bedroom.

He joined the women who were waiting in the living room. "First, Miss Hamby, I'm terribly sorry about your father. I am sure that he has suffered for years and that suffering is over now."

"Thank you, Lt. Dempsey. Is anything wrong with?" Charlotte could not bring herself to say death. "You are all acting so strange? Do you suspect foul play?"

"Lt. Dempsey, I have lived next door to this little lamb for the last twenty years. If you think she could harm a hair on her father's head, you are wrong," Mrs. Weinstock interrupted the officer before he could respond.

Facing the agitated neighbor, Lt. Dempsey asked, "Have I stated at any time that we suspected Miss Hamby of doing away with her father?"

"No sir. You cops do tend to get funny notions," Mrs Weinstock snapped.

"Well Mrs. Weinstock, someone could have assisted him out of this world," Lt. Dempsey stated.

"How can you say such a thing? Everyone loved my Papa," Charlotte protested.

"Someone may have helped him, out of love," Lt. Dempsey continued.

"That's murder," Charlotte protested.

"Don't get excited, Miss Hamby. Let's not jump to conclusions. After all we've just begun our investigation," Lt. Dempsey turned as one of his officers handed him a plastic bag containing a piece of paper.

"We found this piece of paper behind one of the night tables," the officer stated.

Lt. Dempsey read what was written on the paper without removing it from the protective plastic bag. He turned to face a nervous Charlotte. He handed the plastic encased paper to Charlotte which she then read aloud.

"Charlotte, I am taking the coward's way out. Your mother is still young and deserves a life of her own. Please forgive me." Charlotte stared, face white as chalk, at her father's last words.

"Is this your father's handwriting, Miss Hamby?" Lt. Dempsey asked, as he took the note from her hand.

"Yes, I think so, lieutenant. That appears to be Papa's hand. I don't understand. He never gave me a clue No not , I don't believe it."

Charlotte cried, falling into Mrs. Weinstock's loving arms. "That's not at all like . I don't care how much he suffered. He had too much respect for the value of life."

"It's all right, baby. We'll find out what really happened. You've always been a strong girl. We've gotten through bad times, my lamb. We'll get though this," Mrs. Weinstock crooned, stroking Charlotte's hair.

"I know, but this is impossible. Papa wouldn't have killed himself. Not Papa. If the authorities pile tons of evidence in front of me, I'll never believe it. Oh, I'm all alone now. You know mother is no help. She will be a basket case," Charlotte whispered.

"We'll have to take your father to the hospital, to have him officially pronounced dead. Then the coroner will perform an autopsy, and we'll go from there, Miss Hamby," Lt. Dempsey stated.

Charlotte watched helplessly as the paramedics took the last remains of her father, Henry Stanford Hamby, Professor of Literature, down the stairs to the ambulance.

Charlotte lunged at the Gurney carrying the body of her deceased father for one more touch of this precious man.

"Papa, no," Charlotte cried out, "not yet, I'm not ready."

"Sorry sugar. They've got to carry him out," Mrs. Weinstock said, pulling Charlotte close. "You'll see him again, I promise."

"Sorry, Miss Hamby, we'll be going now," Lt. Dempsey stated. "We'll be in touch. I'll let you know as soon as the coroner's office makes the determination of the official cause of death. Mrs. Weinstock, will you be staying with Miss Hamby? If not, we could transport her to the hospital until she's stronger. After all, her mother is already there. I imagine she will want to know how her mother is doing."

"No, no thank you. I've an aversion to hospitals. I'll be just fine with Mrs. Weinstock next door. Thank you for your courtesy, lieutenant," Charlotte said, remembering her father's words as she escorted the officer to the door. It matters not, in triumphant or in adversity Charlotte, strength and courtesy distinguish us from the animals.

"Lets go into the kitchen and have a bite of some of that meal your mother kept bragging about to the officers. I'll set the table, dear," Mrs. Weinstock said as she made every attempt to aid her young friend.

"Brandy is hungry enough to eat a very small horse, even if we aren't," Charlotte laughed, scooping up the bouncy ball of fluff.

"Mrs. W, could you do me a favor. I need to find out about mother, and I just don't think I can stand to call the hospital just now. Would you call for me?" Charlotte's shoulders sagged as she slipped into a kitchen chair for she was unable to bear another stressful encounter with her mother.

"I'll be happy to, my dear. You just sit here at the kitchen table for a few more minutes, and I'll find out how Peggy is doing," Mrs. Weinstock went into the living room to use the phone.

She returned in just a few minutes with the information. "Your mother is okay, Charlotte. They decided to admit her. The doctor administered her a strong sedative and she is sleeping. I've jotted down her room and telephone number. We'll check on her tomorrow. The floor nurse does not expect her to awaken before morning."

Charlotte emptied her plate unaware that she had been famished. "Thanks for your help, Mrs. W. I really appreciate it. I'll do the dishes later. Thanks for everything. I don't know how I could have gotten through today if you had not been here. See you in the morning." Charlotte hugged Mrs. Weinstock as she showed Mrs. Weinstock out and locked the door.

Wondering when the next shoe would drop, Charlotte dragged herself up the steps and to bed. The stressful times never seemed to end. What next?

Charlotte became more restless as she paced about her room.

Unable to sleep, she took out her dog-eared copy of *Jane Eyre*, and tried to concentrate on her favorite passages. In no time the sun, ushering in another beautiful day, was shining through her bedroom window.

Charlotte was in the kitchen, preparing a cup of coffee, when Mrs. Weinstock peeked into the back window.

"Come on in, Mrs. Weinstock," Charlotte said, as she opened the door.

"My dear, I've been tossing all night long not knowing what to do," Mrs. Weinstock stated.

"What has you so upset?" Charlotte replied.

"I'm upset because I am sure you are right. Your father, God rest his poor soul, never committed suicide."

"But, Mrs. Weinstock, what do you believe happened? You saw the note. It had to be papa's handwriting."

"Maybe not. I hate to tell you this, Charlotte, but I suspect foul play. Your mother has been sneaking out with a nasty little man named Howie Cramer. Local gossip is, he's a small time hood. Some folks believed he wanted to get rid of your father so he could help Peggy spend his insurance money."

"Are you sure, Mrs. Weinstock?" Charlotte whispered. "I've never heard of this Howie person. Are you sure? Of course you are," Charlotte's voice cracked with disgust as she dug her fingers into her trembling flesh.

"I've seen them together a couple of times. I saw them once, here in the kitchen, with your poor papa upstairs so ill, and them going at it on the floor like a couple of dogs in heat," Mrs. Weinstock stated as she turned up her nose in disgust.

Charlotte's face turned crimson with the realization of her mother's adultery. "Mama and another man. That explains many of her strange comings and goings. My poor papa, I hope that he never knew," Charlotte frowned as she hugged her numbing arms.

"I know, my dear. It's a difficult situation. What will you do? You don't plan on discussing this matter with the police?"

"No, Mrs. W., It's too painful, too humiliating. Papa's gone. Nothing would really be served by exposing this situation. Papa was

a private man. I could not bear to see him made a laughing stock,"
Charlotte stated.

"Do you want that piece of trash to get away with murdering
Henry?" Mrs. Weinstock anguished, "I suppose you are right.
We've no real proof, but watch your back."

"I will, I promise. Thanks for caring, Mrs. Weinstock."

"My pleasure, little one."

Charlotte spent the remainder of the day alone, drowning in
painful thoughts. Peggy Hamby wasn't much, but she was
Charlotte's mother. She had no real proof of anything but her
mother's probable indiscretion. Charlotte would bide her time.

Peggy Hamby was released from the hospital that evening
accompanied by none other than Howie Cramer.

"This is your Uncle Howie, Charlotte," Peggy smiled brightly to
this small dirty little stranger.

"We're all aware had no siblings. Have you got another brother,
Mama? Grandma always said you and Uncle Charlie were her only
children, so this man can hardly be my Uncle Charlie," Charlotte
replied as she raised her head with an air of aloofness from the
situation.

"Oh sweetie, of course, he's not your real uncle, but he is too
close a friend for you to call Mr. Cramer," Peggy sputtered as she
nervously twisted a loose curl.

"How do you do, Mr. Cramer," Charlotte stated in a prim cold
voice.

"Nice to meet you Charlotte. I've heard great things about you.
Your mom is real proud of you." Howie caught her off guard and
planted a wet slippery kiss on her full ruby mouth. He held her
hand, imprisoning her fingers in his steely grip. "This kid of Peggy's
is all class. She's got a great pair of jugs too," Howie thought as he
licked his lips.

"Really! Great things, huh," as she freed herself from his grasp,
the startled Charlotte replied, "Interesting since I've heard nothing
about you, such a close friend of my mother's. By the way mother,
we've got to finish the arrangements for Papa's funeral."

"I'm sure, Charlotte, loving your father as you did, everything you have chosen will be fine. She's all torn up, Howie. She and Henry were so close. Charlotte could all but read Henry's mind." Peggy shot Charlotte a piercing glare, as she turned to Howie. "Forgive Charlotte's abruptness, we've suffered such a loss."

"That's all right sweetie, she's just tired. Why don't you go upstairs and change clothes. I'll take you girls out to dinner. Do you like anything special, Charlotte?" Howie asked, squeezing Charlotte's hand. She snatched it away as though she'd been bitten by a rattler.

"I'm not hungry, thank you, Mr. Cramer. Go ahead without me. As you said, I'm tired. I'll go upstairs and rest." Charlotte walked away.

"You don't expect your Mama to leave you home alone. You gotta eat sometime, and I told you, call me Howie," He frowned in Charlotte's direction.

"Now Charlotte, that's not the proper attitude. Here's Howie, all ready to pay for your dinner, and you're not hungry. If you hadn't just lost your papa I'd smack your face and make you go," Peggy stated.

"You and what army, Mama?" Charlotte glared at Peggy. "I'm going upstairs to my room. You two do what you please." Charlotte climbed the stairs feeling as old as time.

"Come on, honey. When you talk like that and get so uppity, you sound like your grandmother. Be nice," Peggy pleaded.

"Hey Peg! Why do we have to starve just because your kid's not hungry?" Howie playfully whacked Peggy on the butt.

Taking Peggy's hand, Howie Cramer led her out of the living room. "Howie, don't be mad. She was so close to her papa."

"Sure, baby, sure, nothing personal." Howie's face darkened at the obvious snub. "I'll put you in your place. you little bitch," thought Howie.

Chapter 2

Charlotte nervously scanned the obituary section of the Baltimore Sun looking for the official notice of her father's death. She stared at the upper left corner of the page where the paper had inserted a news article: Henry Stanford Hamby, Scholar, Educator dead at age 63 after a lengthy illness. Professor Hamby taught at Goucher College[1], formerly Woman's College of Baltimore, for more than 20 years until he was stricken with heart disease... The article continued, but Charlotte's mind seemed to go blank. Her stomach knotted up as a thick mucus choked in the back of her throat and a wave of nauseousness spread over her body. Three hectic days later Charlotte sat next to her mother, with Howie Cramer looming over Charlotte's shoulder, as her father was laid to rest. There were people present from the academic world as well as friends of the family. Many onlookers were present because there were few suicides in the city.

The chapel was bare instead of the usual abundance of flowers. The neighbors sent a floral spray of large white chrysanthemums. Charlotte had the florist place a blanket of red roses atop the dark casket. The nurses from Dr. Phillips' office sent a potted plant with pink blossoms. There was also a pot of yellow tulips from Nola and Mason Burns of Charleston, S.C.

Charlotte sat in shock trying to listen to the words of comfort from the Reverend Cresswell.

"I will read these words of comfort from St. John 14:6,7. Jesus saith unto him, I am the way, the truth and the life: no man cometh unto the Father, but by me. If ye had known me, ye should have known my Father also:," Reverend Cresswell continued, adjusting his glasses. "Blessed are they that mourn: for they shall be comforted. If we believe that Jesus died and rose again, even so

---

[1]   Goucher College was established in 1895 by the Methodist Church. It was formerly the Women's College of Baltimore.

them also which sleep in Jesus will God bring with him."

"Mother, how dare you flaunt that man at my poor father's funeral?" Charlotte thought. "How can you permit him to sit on the front row as though he were family?"

"Henry Hamby was a lifetime citizen of Baltimore, Maryland. He was educated in the city, where he married the lovely young Margaret Campbell after graduation. They had their only child Charlotte Bethesda Hamby."

"Big mouth," whispered Charlotte. "I could have lived a lifetime without your blabbing that dreadful name to the world."

"He loved our rolling green hills, and his family told me that his fondest dream was to own a horse farm. This was not to be his lot in life. He became an educator, respected by all." Reverend Cresswell shuffled his notes.

"Professor Henry Hamby taught for many years at Goucher College until stricken by heart disease. He and his helpmate have suffered greatly the last three years."

Reverend Cresswell looked down at Peggy Hamby, seated unashamedly clinging to Howie Cramer.

"Uh, huh, uh," was all that came from his mouth. "It is particularly difficult to preach Professor Hamby's service because we were too close, Henry and I. He was--"

Reverend Cresswell's supposed words of comfort were lost to Charlotte for she was deep in her own thoughts.

"He's a great man, good friend."

"You hypocritical jerk," Charlotte thought, "remember the day I called your office requesting communion in our home for my father. You told me he wasn't a regular member. Yeah! No regular. Now you tell the world you had the greatest respect for him. You fraud! What kind of Christian are you? Papa was better off without you."

Charlotte was bolted back to reality as the reverend went on and on, "I am sure that God forgives Henry Hamby for his weakness. Taking ones life had to be a difficult decision. To leave his beloved wife and child in such a manner. We know not what he was thinking, but he surely was weak of mind to take out of God's hand the decision to end his life."

"What's that fool saying?" thought Charlotte. "Papa was no coward, nor feeble of mind."

"In closing, I will read this scripture from The twenty-third Psalm."

"What do you mean by 'in closing'? We just got here." Charlotte pouted. "Say something about the real ."

"The Lord is my Shepherd; I shall not want. He maketh me to lie down in green pastures: he leadeth me beside the still waters. He restoreth my soul: he leadeth me in the paths...."

"He was always happy with his life. He was a fighter, not a quitter." Charlotte thought she would explode.

"Yea, though I walk through the valley of the shadow of death, I will fear no evil;" Reverend Cresswell continued. "And, thy staff they comfort me."

"Comfort, what comfort? You came the first year. Papa took too long dying. You never came around when needed comfort. Well, what comfort are you today?"

"In the presence of mine enemies," Reverend Cresswell droned on.

"My enemies are around me. Sitting next to me, preacher."

"Mercy shall follow me all the days of my life; and I will dwell in the house of the Lord forever. Let us pray."

Charlotte moved away from Howie to greet several late arrivals, but Howie managed to slip his hand under her skirt, for a quick squeeze.

Howie smirked triumphantly, as he challenged Charlotte to complain.

"Charlotte, are you alright, sweetie?" Peggy asked. "It will be over soon."

"I'm fine, Mother." Charlotte shot a glare in Howie's direction.

Charlotte felt the greatest sense of loss as the casket moved forward to the crematory area. Mama was having her father cremated. She felt that any minute she would faint. I can't appear weak in front of the enemy. I must be strong. I'll think of happier times with . What's occurring I will put out of my mind.

Howie Cramer sat next to mother so cocky just as though he

owned the place. Why can't Howie keep his hands off my mother, and ME? This isn't the time or place for such shenanigans. Oh, how I hate my mother. She never loved . Stop it, Charlotte. Hate eats you up. Forget it, Papa's out of all of this mess." Charlotte wiped a tear.

Charlotte loved her father from the first day he held her in his strong arms. She loved his endearing stories of the many times that he had sneaked into her room, and he picked her up and danced to imaginary music. She had always felt secure with this man that everyone respected. He seemed to possess all of the manly virtues. He was tall, lean and, in spite of his obvious intellect there was a touch of mischievousness in his eyes. Henry Hamby frequently wore a smile that suggested that he knew something others didn't. One could never be quite sure what he was thinking.

In spite of the circumstance of the occasion, Charlotte found herself smiling, remembering the love and security they had shared.

"Oh ," Charlotte thought, "remember our peaceful days in the park enjoying our favorite books, *Moby Dick*. Oh, I always loved the hunt for the white whale. *Treasure Island*, by Robert Louis Stephenson. Old, Pegleg, himself. I always love pirates. But, , I still love *Jane Eyre* the best."

After the service, Howie approached Charlotte.

"How are you doing, Charlotte honey?" Howie attempted to hug the girl.

Pushing him away, she said, "I'm all right, Mr. Cramer."

"How many times, little darling must I say, call me Howie?" he said as his eyes wandered time after time across her bulging breasts.

Howie followed Charlotte into an alcove and attempted to kiss her.

"What the hell do you think you're doing? This is my father's funeral. Isn't it bad enough your publicly flaunting yourself with my mother?" Charlotte growled with exasperation.

"Just keeping it in the family," Howie laughed. "Get use to it, baby girl. I'll be around from now on."

"Get away from me. Are you nuts? I can't stand your hands on me. My father's just been laid to rest. Don't you have any decency?

Let go of me," Charlotte exploded.

Howie held on to Charlotte's arms crushing her back into the solid wall. She tried to push him away, but he held her in the strong vice like hands. His kiss made her sick at her stomach. She was aware of the hardness of his manhood, straining through his suit pants longing to be united with Charlotte's body. His tongue had penetrated her tiny mouth, almost eating her. She wanted to cry out in horror, but her voice died in her throat. Charlotte could only submit to the humiliating assault.

"What's wrong with you baby?" Howie looked confused. Nobody had turned him down in years. "I ain't been this het up over a piece of tail in years. Relax, I won't hurt you. We can have fun, you and me."

"Please don't." Charlotte felt terrified wrapped in the arms of this ugly octopus. He had more arms than any man she'd ever known. She was repulsed by him.

"You act like some frightened---Are you telling me you're never done it before?" Howie laughed with surprise. "That's it, baby. You're a virgin. I had me one of them years ago in the eighth grade. Milly Potter was her name. You remember your first." Howie ran his hand up her thigh provocatively. Charlotte struggled as his arms tightened round her waist. There was no one about, only the distant sound of mourners leaving the funeral home.

Charlotte stared in disgust. This man is standing in a funeral home. Her very own father was just being cremated, and this disgusting animal is trying to seduce her. What is wrong with her mother? Was she blind? How could her mother bring such a sleaze around her family? Around her daughter?

"Where is my mother?" Charlotte asked, finding her voice, hoping there was still decency in him.

"Easy baby, easy. It won't hurt. I want you, baby. You want your mama? You don't need her help, we're doing just fine," Howie whispered against Charlotte's hair. "I want you bad. Been watching you, so soft and sweet. Why should I want that old cow mother of yours when I can sample your fresh milk." He ran his hand across her buttock. "You're just tired. Been stressed out over all of this sickness. We'll relax together. I'll slip into your room, and we'll get better acquainted."

"Look, Mr. Cramer. I don't know where you were raised, but where I come from you don't attack the deceased's daughter in the funeral home."

"What's the matter with you, you frigid, or something? Your mama's real hot between the sheets. Surely you don't take after your balless old man? What a waste," Howie laughed, stroking Charlotte's cheek, catching him off guard she jammed her knee sharply between his legs.

Howie leaned against the wall grimacing with pain.

"You kicked me in my balls. What did you do that for?" Howie whined.

"Can I be of any assistance, Miss Hamby?" a sedately dressed man appeared in the doorway.

Charlotte turned apprehensively to find the funeral director approaching. Howie Cramer released her.

"We appreciate your concern," Howie replied, recovering from his earlier pain. "Miss Hamby is having a difficult time, as I am sure you will understand."

Stepping away from Howie, Charlotte faced the newcomer. "Thank you for your concern. I'll join my mother." Smiling her gratitude, Charlotte glanced in Howie's direction.

"If you try to touch me again, Mr. Cramer, I'll uh... Just stay away," she stammered as she walked quickly through the exit. Charlotte's face was haggard showing the strain of the last few minutes.

Howie thought, "God! You're gorgeous. If her mother only knew what I wanted to do to her kid, she'd take a gun and blow my dick off. But here you are, right in front of me, young, tasty, not all used up like Peggy. A fresh cherry, ripe for the picking. I love being a fresh fruit picker, and I'm gonna use my special tool to pluck that sweet young thing. You're scared right now, but old Howie's gonna change your mind."

As though Charlotte read Howie Cramer's mind she sped up her departure. Charlotte thought, "If he tries a stunt like that again I'll tell Mother. Just because she's available to trash like Howie Cramer, doesn't mean I am. I must speak to Mrs. Weinstock. I'll be safe at her place tonight."

Howie watched Charlotte in flight. "She's all class, that one is. Peggy is so rough in spite of her family background. I'd better watch myself. She might tell her mama. If I play my cards right, she won't believe the kid. After all, Peggy thinks we're in love." A rumble of laughter deep in Howie's throat electrified the situation.

Charlotte rushed into Mrs. Weinstock's arms. "What is it darling? You look so pale. Shall we sit down?"

"Mrs. Weinstock, I've got to get away from that man. If he touches me one more time, I'll kill him," Charlotte whispered.

"Hush, sweetie, hush up such talk. Killing that man will in the long run hurt only you. Those kind aren't worth shooting."

"Please, I can't sleep with that man in our house tonight."

"Peggy," called Mrs. Weinstock. "Charlotte is so nervous with her loss. I'm next door. You can't object to her spending the night with me."

"Well, uh, Mrs. Weinstock," Peggy began as she looked around at Howie. "I suppose, yes, it would be alright. My Charlotte's been under so much strain. I'll be fine, if not, I can always holler over the fence," Peggy said brightly.

She'd have Howie to herself tonight. After a proper mourning period they would go public. No need to sneak around with Henry gone.

Charlotte, defeated, and suddenly rudderless walked away from the funeral home, arm and arm with Mrs. Weinstock.

"You got away for now, you cold fish. I'll get even with you for refusing me. You'll be sorry," Howie thought, as he watched the object of his lust escaping his clutches, for now.

Charlotte felt safe and sound in Mrs. Weinstock's home sipping tea and eating English muffins. Afternoons sitting in the bright yellow kitchen of her friend, Mrs. W, was one of Charlotte's fondest memories.

"What are you going to do with yourself, Charlotte?" Mrs. Weinstock asked.

"Oh, I don't know. For now I'll continue working, and as soon as I can save up the money, I'll get a place of my own."

"Have some marmalade, dear. You worry me. You're so pale."

"I'll be fine, Mrs. W." Charlotte attempted a smile.

Monday morning bright and early Charlotte returned to the Mitchell's Bookstore. Her employers were kind to her as always.

"Charlotte, how are you, dear?" Mr. Mitchell asked.

Mrs. Mitchell hugged Charlotte tenderly, "It wasn't necessary for you to come in so soon."

"Thank you. You have been so kind. Thank you for attending Papa's funeral service."

"My dear, Mr. Mitchell and I love you. You have been the greatest joy of our lives, my dear," Mrs. Mitchell, brushed a curl out of Charlotte's face. "We're just a lonely old couple with grown children living far away. We rarely hear from them and our grandchildren, Tammy and Jamie, never call or write."

"I'm sure they love you. It's difficult to keep in contact with the busy schedules of the young today," Charlotte reassured the older couple.

"We're happy you chose to be with us. If we can be of any help please let us know."

"This is a beautiful shop," Charlotte said, as she glanced toward the rows of book lined shelves.

A tall faded step-ladder rested against wall. An entire section of the store had been constructed for long-play records. The Mitchell's loved the classics.

Books and newspapers were stacked everywhere, causing chaos to the otherwise neat appearance of the store.

"Why do you work in this little shop, Charlotte? With your education you could pick and choose a career, yet you appear to be content with a clerk's job."

"I don't intend to make a career of selling books, but for now I enjoy living my life among my best friends, my books." Charlotte said sweetly.

Six o'clock sharp, Charlotte Hamby strolled down the street that led to her home. She turned the corner and found herself face to face with a ugly, dirty hulk of a man who had an obvious aversion to soap. His dark, long, and smelly hair was tangled in the crucifix he wore about his neck.

The heavy footsteps behind her sent alarms clanging in her senses. Charlotte was afraid to turn around for fear of what might be behind her. Where could she run? Furtive glances to the left and the right confirmed her worst fears. There was no clear avenue of escape from the worst nightmare she could conjure up. One of the men smiled through ominous, terrifying eyes. His cold steely stare caused Charlotte to tremble uncontrollably. The pungent odor of old sweat, cheap wine and tobacco made Charlotte's stomach heave threatening to regurgitate on a massive scale. One had several missing teeth, probably causalities of fist fights. These were violent men aching for no good.

"Hi pretty girl. Where are you going?" one man sneered, smiling through his green and yellow teeth.

"Hey, don't walk away. We just wanna talk," the ugly hulk was saying, smelling Charlotte's fear.

"Yeah, we just wanna talk. You got some cash? We're broke," another said.

"I'm sorry. I don't have any extra with me," Charlotte said cautiously.

"How about a sip?" the third one asked.

"No thank you, I'm not a drinking lady. If you gentlemen will excuse me my family's waiting for me." Charlotte walked away.

"Hey bitch, think you're too good to have a drink with us," a slurred voice bellowed.

A terrified Charlotte picked up her step.

The short man tried to slip his arm about her waist. Her body stiffened as Charlotte walked faster.

"Please leave me alone. I've never done anything to you," Charlotte cried as she tried to get away.

He turned her roughly and pushed her against the wall. Charlotte gazed around for help. She was crying hard and her body was shaking uncontrollably.

"Come one, we just wanna play."

"Yeah, let's have some fun. What's wrong; don't you like fun?" another drunken voice behind her muttered. The stink of his breath caused Charlotte to gasp.

"Wish we had a place soft to lay your weary little head, but we're ones that make do," another man laughed.

A hand moved and cupped Charlotte's buttock, giving it a tight squeeze as Charlotte closed her eyes and prayed.

She was being pushed to the right and then to the left. Fingers groped and pinched her virginal flesh.

"I get her first," one man rasped, his voice hoarse with desire.

"No, I seen her first. I get first crack," the larger man crowed.

"What do you mean you seen her first. I saw her coming out of the bookstore," one of the others bellowed.

"Come on baby. Tell us you're ready. We won't hurt you none."

"No, we just want to play some. You'll like us; we're friendly folk."

"Please leave me alone. I've never done anything to you." Charlotte whimpered through her cascading tears.

"Don't cry little lady. I promise you'll be glad when we're through with you," the shorter man promised.

"Yeah! Just relax. Have a drink," Charlotte heard one of the men cajoling.

"I don't know!" Charlotte's tone changed as though she sought her avenue of escape.

Misunderstanding Charlotte's sudden docile behavior, the smaller man loosened his grip as she appeared to be considering their evening's entertainment.

There was no help insight. She was watching them closely for the right moment to bolt.

"I don't even know your names. How can we party? Strangers, you understand." Charlotte tried to sound interested. "I must keep calm," the terrified Charlotte thought.

The first man actually was introducing himself to his victim. He touched Charlotte's skin roughly. His hands were like two large hams, callused from years of abuse. He placed his lips on hers, whispering. "I'm Leo, little princess, and do you think we're that nuts. You just want our names so you can turn us into the police."

"Why would I turn you into the police for wanting to have a good time?" she asked innocently.

"Yeah, Leo! Why would she tell the police just because we want to party?" grumbled one of the men.

"You, fools! She'll turn us in the first chance she gets. She's some bloody ice princess, too good for us," Leo stated, spitting on the ground.

"You don't understand. We're strangers, and you're so big. You might hurt me," Charlotte said. "I'm no ice princess."

The thin man placed a suffocating kiss on her mouth as he fumbled inside her blouse. "God! You sure feel good. Hey! She's got great tits," he laughed loudly.

Charlotte remained quiet submitting to his fondling and tobacco stinking breath, biding her time for the chance to escape.

"Come on. You're name is Leo. What's yours?" she said as she turned to the thin man, feigning interest.

"Folks call me, Mouse."

"Why do they call you Mouse?" Charlotte asked. "Because of your soft voice?" she continued.

"Oh Hell, No!" Leo joined the others in laughter. "We call him, Mouse, because his dick ain't no bigger than a mouse's."

"Yeah! Mouse won't hurt you, baby. You'll never feel it when he has his time."

"Now, I'm called, Bull. You wanna know why?" Bull laughed as he unzipped his pants. "Biggest pecker you ever saw, right?" He displayed his maleness.

Charlotte looked at the ground, shamefaced at the sight of that enormous red appendage.

"When old Bull gets through with you, you'll never want nobody else," he roared.

"Let's cut out the crap, and get down to business," Leo interrupted. "I go first. Drop your drawers lady and get ready for the ride of your life." Leo grabbed Charlotte by the arm, as he attempted to drag her to the ground.

It was now or never. Charlotte came up with her knee striking the man between the legs with such force that he dropped his pants around his ankles as he crashed to the ground. This caught the thugs off guard, allowing the terrified girl her moment of escape.

Charlotte began to run for her life with the swiftness of a gazelle. She didn't look back for she knew the five frightening men were in hot pursuit. She ran through the dark streets of Baltimore. Where was everybody? There was no help insight as she ran to escape her would-be attackers. It felt as though she had run a hundred miles, but it had been only several blocks.

Charlotte suddenly became aware that she had been running in the wrong direction from her home. In total exhaustion she leaned against a crumbling wall attempting to make herself invisible. She listened as the sounds of their boots passed and grew dimmer.

Charlotte screamed as a pair of massive hands grabbed her from behind.

"Hi Honey!" Leo laughed. "Now that was great exercise before we party. Don't you agree fellows?"

"Sure we do," The chorus agreed.

"Now that we have had all of that good exercise, give me a kiss," Leo grabbed Charlotte, gagging her as he pressed his tongue into her small mouth.

Charlotte started to regurgitate from the assault.

"Scared of snakes, baby," Bull laughed.

"Yes, there are snakes, and there are snakes," Leo laughed, cautiously unzipping his pants. He was suffocating her with his kisses. She pushed away as hard as she could. "You can't get away this time, missy," Leo took great pleasure in Charlotte's terror.

Leo pushed her into Bull's waiting arms.

"Come here, baby," Bull bellowed, his hands groping under Charlotte's skirt, pinning her against the wall.

"Let go of me. Let go, you sorry SOB," Charlotte screamed, shocked with herself, for she never spoke in such terms.

Bull looked up, "Naughty, naughty. Such talk from a refined lady."

She squirmed, turning her face to avoid his mouth.

"If you keep wiggling, so sweet lady, we'll figure you're all hot and ready for us," Bull's words were like cold water in her face.

The time of her deflowering had come and there was no hope of rescue.

"Please, don't do this," Charlotte's voice was pitifully inaudible that Bull almost took pity.

He waited for her next move, but she laid against the wall frozen in time waiting for something, she knew not what. She felt the erection, his member pressing against her skirt. She heard him emit a raw animal tone, as her skirt was ripped from her body. There was no place she could run.

The group held her to the earth as Bull steadied himself for the first plunge. She cried out in pain as the ugly red member tore it's way into her body.

"No! Please! Charlotte moaned." The unspoken question, "Why?" reverberated in her brain, as he moved back and forth inside her bleeding body.

"God, Leo! She was a virgin," Bull moaned in dismay. "Oh, poor baby. I hope old Bull wasn't too rough on you, being your first time, and all."

"Get out of the way," yelled Leo. "Her being a virgin, I should have done her first."

"Hurry up, Leo," complained Mouse. "I'm ready, if you're not."

"I'm always ready," laughed Leo. "Better watch her, she's tricky, might try to escape." He crawled on to do his worst.

Charlotte lay in great confusion, not even knowing her name. Who were these men and why were they hurting her? She only knew she ached in every joint of her body. Why was she covered with blood? Where were all of those grunting sounds coming from? She knew she must get away. Feeling something hard near her right hand, she picked up a brick and began striking out at her attackers.

"Oh, ouch. She's got a brick," Mouse complained.

"Watch it. Grab her hand." Leo yelled.

"Hey, I'm bleeding, she hit me in the head. That's what I get for trying to be nice. So much for you lady," Bull screamed, as he began kicking Charlotte with his heavy work boots. The others joined in the assault, and for Charlotte, blissful oblivion.

The yellow rays of the sun danced through the thick white clouds streaming across her battered face. Charlotte Hamby, another victim of urban violence awoke the next morning in an alley stripped naked, moaning incoherently.

Chapter 3

The same morning rays awoke Peggy Hamby. She lay safe and sound in her warm bed with eyes closed. She sat up hearing an abrupt knock at the door, "Charlotte, did you forget your key? You finally sneaking home. Who have you been out with all night?" Peggy called out. The knocking continued. Peggy opened the front door. It was a young police officer.

"May I help you, officer?" Peggy asked. "Would you care to come inside?"

"Thank you. Are you Mrs. Henry Hamby? I'm Officer Graham. Sorry to disturb you so early in the morning, but have you heard from your daughter?"

"Charlotte, no she's never stayed out so late. It's so unlike her. Something wrong, officer?" Peggy inquired.

"If you will please accompany me to the Baltimore hospital, there is a badly beaten young woman in the emergency room. Her identification says that she is Charlotte Hamby."

"Is she alright? What happened to my child?" Peggy inquired.

"The lady has been attacked by what appears to be a group of thugs while on her way home from work last night. She knows her name, but she doesn't appear to remember what happened last evening."

"She's lost her memory?" Peggy asked.

"One of the neighbors walking to work this morning found her and called us. We found her in an alley on the other side of town, severely abused. Will you come with me?"

"Give me a moment to change," Peggy dashed up the stairs.

"Oh God! I'm gonna gag," Peggy Hamby thought as the officer led her down the long dirty white hospital corridor to an awaiting nurse. "Oh I hate these smelly places with the weekend drunks puking their guts out all over the floors. The last three years stuck here on at least thirty separate occasions with Henry. Now Charlotte. At least Henry was really sick. Charlotte, oh, Charlotte. It was probably your fault. You were in the wrong place at the wrong time. Nobody could be turned on by such a dried up prune like Charlotte," Peggy thought with disdain.

"Ma'am, are you alright?" the nervous officer asked.

Peggy deep in her own thoughts did not respond. "During his illness Henry had suffered multiple congestive heart failures, three MI's and two strokes. I became used to that, but look at the shame Charlotte has heaped on my head."

"Are you the patient's mother?" the nurse whispered.

"The patient? Yes, uh, I'm Peggy Hamby," was all Peggy could bring herself to say.

"Thank you officer for bringing Mrs. Hamby so quickly," she nodded as he walked away.

The nurse turned, giving Peggy her undivided attention. "Please follow me, Mrs. Hamby."

Peggy was escorted into the room by the soft spoken dark-haired nurse.

She found her only child naked, lying on a bed half covered only by a thin sheet. Charlotte's face was battered beyond recognition. She was black and blue all over.

"They treated her brutally. Mercifully, she remembers nothing of this evening. Mrs. Hamby, I've worked here for years and this is one of the worst..," the nurse stopped. "She's got bloody teeth marks gouged into her breasts, and one of her nipples was almost chewed off." She raised the sheet for Peggy to see the extent of her only child's injuries.

"What have those animals done to my baby? Your clothes, where are they? Where in the hell were our great city's police, the supposed protectors, of the young and innocent? Oh God," Peggy Hamby moaned, "They've stolen your virginity. You weren't much to look at and now with your innocence taken, who will marry you?" Peggy screamed for everyone to hear.

Charlotte was in critical condition oblivious to the many tubes running out of her mangled body, but somewhere in the deepest recesses of her subconscious, she heard her mother's cries. Her body jerked involuntarily as though she was reliving her night's ordeal.

"I'm sorry, Mrs. Hamby," the nurse attempted to offer comfort, "but you will have to be strong to be able to help your daughter. This has been a terrible shock for both of you. She's sustained broken ribs where several of her attackers kicked her with heavy boots. They also beat her about the head which is why she was unconscious. Charlotte must have fought as though she were a wild animal. Unfortunately, she was outnumbered. Please come with me. The doctor would like to speak with you," she said as she led Peggy to the doctor's office.

"Mrs. Hamby, this is Doctor Peters." she left Peggy staring dumbfounded at the young doctor.

"Please, be seated." Doctor Peters gestured to an uncomfortable chair across from his desk. "Mrs. Hamby, I am sorry to inform you that your daughter Charlotte has been raped multiple times, by at least five young toughs. Her face is so battered that she will require plastic surgery."

"Is she going to die? I don't know what to do. My husband has just died, I'm all alone except for Charlotte," Peggy whined.

"Your daughter could die. The long term threat is more from the emotional trauma of the attack, than from the physical injuries. She did sustain life threatening injuries, but we have those under control. I am more concerned that when the police found Charlotte, she was praying for death. She seems to have lost all reason for living. We are concerned that due to the brutality of the attack, Charlotte might will herself to die. She needs everybody's support," Dr. Peters said.

"Yes! yes! I'll do what is necessary, after all she is my flesh and blood," Peggy muttered as she looked blankly about this Doctor Peters austere office. "I want to get out of this place. I want to be with Howie and feel his arms about me. I want him to do the delightfully wicked things with his hands," deep in thought Peggy could not suppress a smile.

"Mrs. Hamby, do you understand what I have been explaining to you?" Dr. Peters shot Peggy an disgusted glare. "Does this woman care about her daughter? She appears to be bored and obviously wishes to be elsewhere. Maybe she is in shock, and I am judging her too severely."

She left the hospital as quickly as she could extricate herself from that well meaning doctor. It's a shame he's not my type. Oh the things I could teach him," Peggy laughed aloud.

The flighty Peggy Hamby was undecided what she must do with the latest tragedy.

"I'll have to talk to Howie," Peggy spoke to the stars as she walked home.

On the other side of town a fidgety Howie Cramer sat by his phone. His hands were clenched into fists which made his knuckles turn white in sharp contrast against his sunburned skin.

"Howie? It's Peggy. Did I wake you?"

"No, I was still up."

"Howie, you'll never believe it but a group of toughs attacked my Charlotte. They've nearly killed her. She was beaten to a bloody pulp."

"Oh no, sweetie. I'm sorry. Will she be alright?" Howie asked.

"They don't know. Howie, my baby girl looks terrible. They raped her, and she was a virgin. I'm so thankful her papa isn't alive today. The neighbors think I'm a lousy enough mother, especially that snoopy Mrs. Weinstock. Just wait until they hear about the attack," Peggy groaned.

"Stay calm, Peg. Tell the neighbors, especially Mrs. Weinstock that after all of the stress from her father's death you sent her away for a rest."

"Good idea, Howie. Will you come over tonight? I don't want to stay here alone."

"Nonsense, you'll be okay. Early in the morning, baby, call Mrs. Mitchell. Tell her that you have been concerned about Charlotte's health so you sent her to visit friends."

"I will," Peggy answered mechanically. She hung up the phone, and went straight to bed.

Howie sat back in his chair dialing the telephone.

"Hello yourself, You stupid SOB. You dumb shit, I wanted you to scare her. Have her come running to me. I didn't plan on your nearly killing her. Just wanted to teach her a lesson. Not to be so snooty, share some of her goodies with me." He threw the receiver across the room. "Peggy better not find out about this, she'll turn me into the cops."

The next day Peggy visited her daughter. The rules of the ICU limited all visits to no more than 15 minutes. Peggy spoke quickly to Charlotte as soon as she was admitted to the room.

"I haven't told anyone except Howie what happened to you. I told everyone that you were visiting with friends. After all of the stress over your father's illness and death they were glad to hear about your little vacation." She seemed to be talking more to herself than her child.

"Mrs. Weinstock agreed. She felt you needed some rest." The half consciousness Charlotte could hardly follow her mother's prattle.

"Oh yes, my self-sacrificing daughter. Everyone's sweet little innocent Charlotte. Little do they know," whispered the snide Peggy Hamby.

Charlotte's jaw had been broken, and the jaw was wired shut. Charlotte really couldn't speak. She tried to mumble a few words. "Mama, please. I'm sorry. Maybe it was my fault. Maybe I should have let them kill me."

"Don't be so melodramatic, Charlotte. The doctors say you will require plastic surgery, and I don't know where we'll find the money. We have spent everything on your father's medical treatment. Those drugs were unbelievably expensive. We should have been investing our money in, pharmaceutical companies, that's it, drug stocks. That's where our money should have been going. All of those years with your papa squandering our money on books, for nothing. I'm so glad Henry's dead so we will not have to keep buying those heart drugs," Peggy said sarcastically.

"I'm sorry, Mother," Charlotte said softly through her closed jaw.

"I am sorry, too, Charlotte, but you have been my cross to bear since your birth. Your delivery ripped me so I could never have another child. The trauma was so great I lost the sight in my right eye. Yes, I suppose we'd have been better off if you had died."

"I know, Mama. You have reminded me so often."

"Your father and I were happy traveling around the country whenever we wanted. Your birth stopped all of our good times. I guess I've never been very maternal, but your father, oh yes, he thrived on fatherhood," Peggy continued rattling on not caring about the emotional pain she was causing.

"I guess I've always been jealous of the relationship between you and Henry. I always seemed to be the fifth wheel. You two were always content in your own little world of books." Peggy left Charlotte's room after delivering her stinging barrage.

The silent Charlotte, began to sob, finally reacting to the violent assault. The harshness of her mother's recriminations was more than she could bear. Charlotte felt life would never be the same. How could she face people? Everyone would know what happened eventually. How could she face the people that worked with her at the Mitchell's Bookstore.

After four weeks in the hospital, Charlotte was ready to go home. The family had to be given an explanation for Charlotte's continued absence. Peggy told friends and family that Charlotte, while resting from her father's death had been in a minor automobile accident thus explaining her cuts and bruises. It never occurred to Peggy Hamby that the truth of Charlotte's assault was all over town.

Charlotte returned to work several weeks after being released from the hospital to the tender care of her employers.

One Wednesday afternoon Charlotte came home from work to check on her mother. She had stopped in the kitchen to prepare a hot bowl of soup, for Charlotte feared her mother wasn't eating properly. She placed the bowl on a tray with a lovely yellow rose from their garden. She put as much into the presentation of the food as she did it's preparation. Charlotte's father use to tease her saying she was a secret oriental, because she cared so much for beauty in all things.

Carrying the tray up the stairs, Charlotte heard giggling voices coming from her mother's bedroom. She almost dropped the tray as she overheard snatches of a disgusting conversation coming from inside.

"I've got to forget about that night and think about my latest project," Peggy said to Howie. They were in bed together for some early afternoon maneuvers. "If Charlotte is smart, she'll get some out of town man to marry her and take her away where nobody knows about my personal tragedy."

It never occurred to Peggy that her embarrassment was minuscule to the emotional scars Charlotte would carry to her grave.

"I don't understand your haste in trying to send our Charlotte so far away from those that love her," Howie stated.

"Your constant defense of that wicked girl astonishes me. She can't stand the sight of you," Peggy replied.

"Why did you keep me waiting? What took you so long, Howie? It was late morning when you arrived. It's not smart to keep me waiting when I need a man. It would serve you right if I took my goodies down the street," Peggy said in her infamous pouty voice.

"I am sorry, Peggy," Howie replied, "but I've got other things to do than run over here. When are you going to tell your brat about me anyway. Don't you think it's about time I moved in with you?"

"Howie, don't nag. I've still got to live in this town. Can you imagine how many eye brows would be raised with Henry so soon in the grave." She threw her arms around his neck and he kissed her.

"You don't give a tinkers damn what the neighbors say. Besides, I like you like this. Begging for it. Keeps you in line. And as for your crack about taking it next door," he stopped, placing his big rough hands around Peggy's pale white throat, "I'd kill you, first." He placed his mouth over hers.

She giggled, "I need you. My heat is up and I'm in bad need." Peggy's giggle changed to a pleading tone. "He's been dead for three weeks and my puss is hurting bad."

Charlotte was shocked as she lay against the wall listening to her mother pleading for sexual satisfaction. She was appalled with her mother's callous activities with her father not cold in his grave.

It was obvious that Peggy Hamby, the impatient widow would wait no longer. Charlotte closed her eyes as the bed hummed with the motion of two lovers satisfying their needs.

Peggy was drugged by the scent of his maleness. Her breasts were pressed against his body as she surrendered to his intoxicating kisses. Peggy Hamby couldn't get enough of this vigorous man.

Her eyes roamed over his. Oh, how she craved his body. She needed this crude and vital man. With Henry gone, nobody could complain or judge.

Charlotte, eyes wide, watched in fascinated horror like a snake charmer mesmerized by a cobra. She could not help remembering her night of torture, and her feelings quickly became a sensation of revulsion and disgust.

Watching Howie on top of her mother, Charlotte remembered the slobbering mouths on hers, digging their nails into her flesh. She caught her breath as she remembered the man attacking her nipple. Oh the pain, the blood. Charlotte felt sick.

"Kiss me, Howie," Peggy begged, her voice raspy with desire.

Peggy moaned as he captured her mouth, his tongue licking its recesses. He stroked her lips and cheeks. Howie was driven to the edge of insanity with the aroma of lovemaking juices secreting from her deepest recesses. His fingers were flicking her mother's sensitive folds and occasionally penetrating her. Her velvety juices sent out signals that she was uncontrollably hot with sizzling desire.

Shamelessly, Charlotte continued to watch as she felt a stirring in her lower parts. A sudden gush of moisture trickled along her thighs as Howie and Peggy, bodies sleek and wet in ecstasy rolled together entwined as one.

"Are you ready for me, Sugar? Oh my lord you're wet and ready," Howie moaned.

Peggy's body wreathed with heated passion. She wiggled, twisted, and moaned under the ministrations of her lover.

Charlotte watched as Howie's member stood tall and straight as if at attention, prepared to impale the impatient Peggy.

Eventually, Howie lay back spent and temporarily exhausted by the energetic Peggy. Suddenly, the room became silent as the floundering on the bed ceased.

"Exactly how much did that husband of yours leave you? Wasn't there some life insurance?" Charlotte overheard, Howie ask.

"No, not really very much. I'll become a pauper if Charlotte stays," Peggy replied.

"What will we do?"

"I've been hinting to dear Charlotte that she should find her own place. Seek independence, that sort of thing, but she thinks I need her," Peggy moaned.

"We could start bringing some eligible men around the house. You know, get some started courting her. What do you say, old gal?"

"Good idea, but pass me another beer, I'm as dry as sawdust," Peggy muttered.

"Here, I'll share mine," Howie replied. Peggy grabbed the bottle and chug-a-lugged half of Howie's beer.

"Hey Peg, Now I'll have to go downstairs for another six pack."

"Not now, sweet man," Peggy, quickly forgot her thirst for drink and concentrated on her other thirst.

Charlotte staggered down the stairs, left the tray on the kitchen counter, and raced out the door. She was horrified, and she needed to clear the cobwebs from her thoughts.

"She wants to get rid of me," Charlotte whispered as she left the house, while upstairs the lovers continued with their plans.

Charlotte walked for about an hour. She allowed the cool evening to wipe the scene from her mind.

"Who is that?" Charlotte asked. Charlotte felt such terror that she began to remember the night she was raped. Those hands, those slobbering mouths. The men who caused her young body such pain. "Oh Dear God in Heaven, why am I out here alone?"

Charlotte began to quicken her pace, and then she was running, racing down the street like a mad woman just escaped from a psycho ward. She slowed her pace only when she was surrounded by the familiarity of her own home.

An exhausted Charlotte slowly climbed the stairs to her private world, her bedroom. She changed into her gown, falling across the bed in complete exhaustion. The blissful oblivion of sleep quickly engulfed her.

"Oh God, I want you," a strange voice moaned. She felt hands moving over her body, tearing at her gown. She could feel the evening breeze blowing on her bare skin. Fingers were stroking between her legs. She must be dreaming, but the sensation was so real.

"What?" She jerked away from the fingers, her mind cloudy from sleep. "Stop it," Charlotte attempted to get away. The hated intruder was lying beside her fondling her breasts.

"Good God, why have you been keeping this beautiful body hidden from me all of these months?" he asked slowly.
Charlotte was suffocating from the smell of liquor on his breath as he came closer. She saw the look in his eyes as they slowly narrowed.

"I want you, baby. You're a raving beauty. That body--"
"No, Howie!" Charlotte fought back from his evil purpose. Before she could scream for help his vile sticky lips covered hers.

"I beg you don't." She attempted to say, but it came out as a choking whisper, it was no use for he had become a man possessed by lust.

Charlotte struggled, beating him with her fists until she fell back exhausted from the struggle.

"Relax, baby. It won't hurt. God, you're the prettiest thing I've ever seen."

He ruthlessly tore her gown from her body. He kissed her, his mouth covering Charlotte's, stifling her so she gasped for breath.

"Come here to your Uncle Howie. You're so sweet and wet." His eyes shown more of lust than the alcohol. "I have to see you naked. I have to feel your skin against mine."

"Please let go. Don't hurt me," Charlotte whispered.

He moaned grasping her hand, demanding, "Touch me, baby. I'd never hurt an inch of your delicate creamy skin." Howie continued. "Do it to me," his penis poking her belly. He forced her hand around it, his ragged breathing, "Do me," Howie begged.

"No, get away from me, Howie," Charlotte fought as he held her wrist imprisoned in his vice like grip. Howie Cramer, out of control with passion moaned incoherently as he forced her hand to move down his stiff member.

Charlotte shook with terror as she closed her eyes and fought back vomit.

"Faster," he urged. She attempted to jerk her hand away, driving him into a greater frenzy. He moved on top, the weight of his body pressed her into the bed. His weight was so heavy that she felt her spine would snap.

He pinched her rosy nipples as he parted her thighs sending a shock wave through her body. That ugly red thing was inside her, moving back and forth, and Charlotte was dying inside. She fought this mad man violating her tender body, but he ignored her protests.

"I'll never rest until I have you. Can't sleep thinking about you. You're so young, there's so much to learn," Howie moaned.

He withdrew from her. Then he forced her to turn over and to kneel. He would have rammed himself into her quaking body from behind, but Charlotte's pitiful pleading stopped his amorous advances.

"Howie, please. Don't. Mama will find out. What if I get pregnant?" Charlotte was stalling for time in hopes her mother would hear the commotion.

Howie smiled wickedly. "I'll do you until you are. It would be great to see your belly swollen with my kid." The prospect drove him to farther insanity. "As for old Peggy, she's had too much beer to care about any little noise." He stopped moving inside her as he ran his hands across her stomach. "I get real wet imagining your belly heavy..." Howie moaned with excitement.

Charlotte tried to crawl away. Howie grabbed her ankle.

"Get back here and hold still, or in that provocative position another tender area might be in danger," Howie bellowed.

He moved back quickly anticipating another release of his juices.

"I'm gonna fill you deep. You're gonna carry lots of seed from a real man. Not those wimps that got to you first."

Suddenly the bedroom light came on.

Peggy staggered in Charlotte's room, "What the hell is going on in here?" She managed to mutter through alcohol thickened lips.

Howie withdrew from Charlotte as his semen shot all over her backside and her bed.

"Shit!" was all Howie could say.

Howie suddenly rolled away from Charlotte with a groan. He staggered into Peggy's direction.

"He raped me. This animal that you take to your bed has raped me!" Charlotte screamed at the top of her lungs.

"Peggy, what's going on? Where am I? Oh God, Charlotte, I'm sorry," he turned to Peggy, "Baby, I'm sorry. Drank too much tonight. Thought it was you, honest, Howie muttered innocently."

"Charlotte, you're not hurt are you? He didn't hurt you, did he?" a confused Peggy asked.

"Mother, where are your senses? This man just raped me. Look at my gown," Charlotte demanded, "look at my bed covered with his inferior seed."

"He said he was drunk. He said he was sorry. He thought it was me," Peggy whined, "go back to bed, no real harm done. It's not like he's your first."

"How stupid can you be, Mother?"

"Get some sleep, sweetie. We'll talk this over in the morning," Peggy pushed the naked Howie out of the room.

"I'm sorry sugar. This will never happen again. I love you," Howie Cramer moaned. Looking over her shoulder, Howie shot Charlotte a smirk of satisfaction. He had been inside her and if he had his way he'd sample her charms again and they both knew it.

Charlotte stood up, and walked to the vanity mirror. She wanted to see if she looked differently after their aborted encounter, but she only saw the sad eyes of Charlotte Hamby staring back at her.

"I've got to get out of here. This can never happen again," still in shock, the naked Charlotte crawled back to her bed.

During the next few months, as though the hellish occurrence with Howie never happened, Peggy introduced Charlotte to what seemed to be every male in the state of Maryland. She had avoided her mother and Howie as much as possible since the unfortunate encounter.

Peggy Hamby became unusually excited with a letter she received one afternoon from her dear childhood friend. "Howie," She picked up the phone. "Charlotte's at work. Get over here. I got a letter from Nola Burns and it's got great news."

Twenty minutes later Howie came charging up Peggy's steps.

"Okay, what's all of the excitement," he stated as he pushed open the door.

"Don't I get a kiss," Peggy replied.

"I'll kiss you after I hear why I had to beat it over here so fast."

"Okay. Do you remember my telling you about my school friend, Nola Burns? The one that got knocked up and had to leave school." She began waving a letter in Howie's face, "This letter is from Nola. I wrote her last week."

"How is dear Nola going to help us?" Howie asked, failing to make the connection.

"Her son Mason is two years older than Charlotte. He's never married. Something about trying to get little girls to pull down their panties for him."

"Oh great! A depraved sex fiend."

"Not a sex fiend. Nola assures me that he is better. They've had no recurrence of that little problem in years."

"Little problem. You call attacking children, a little problem," Howie yelled.

"Well, Nola wrote me several years ago that the police snooped around for a while. Brought Mason in for questioning, but he was never indicted. If you've got a better idea for a husband for Charlotte, you just let me know," Peggy demanded.

"Okay, okay. Maybe if you invite him for a visit we could check him out," Howie replied.

"Well, honey," Peggy didn't continue.

"Well honey, what? Anytime you call me honey that way, I in deep shit. What else, Peggy?" Howie challenged.

"Howie, don't get excited. They have been having some financial problems, and uh..I promised to send them $10,000 to assist them in paying bills," Peggy replied.   "Damn it, Peggy. That's almost all the money we've got left."

"I told them that once Mason and Charlotte were married she could be put to work," Peggy pleaded.

"All right, But, what makes you think Charlotte will go along with your scheme?" Howie asked.

"Those southern men. They are full of charm and bullshit. If he's anything like his daddy, it will take him no time to get into her britches. And make her like it," Peggy laughed.

"Did you ever meet Mason's father, Jim Burns?" Howie asked.

"I met him once. Nola didn't trust him around any of the girls at school. She was probably afraid someone might steal him," Peggy laughed. "He was good looking, slightly built, with dark hair and a mustache. Nola was so crazy about him she spread her legs on their first date. Couldn't seem to get enough of that stuff, no matter how many times she got it," Peggy roared.

"Miss innocent. You act like you're some vestal virgin. You can't seem to enough of that stuff, as you call it, yourself," Howie replied, squeezing Peggy's waist.

"I'm just hoping she'll take to Mason. She's awfully skittish after the unfortunate incident in her room. I hope Mason can heat her up a might," Peggy said, obviously concerned for the success of their venture.

"Well she is her mother's daughter. She could be taught, by the right man, to like a little tussle in the hay." Howie agreed. "I'd better leave. Can't push our luck and have Charlotte catching me here. She hates my guts, these days. See you later, baby." Howie kissed Peggy as he walked out the door.

Chapter 4

At five thirty, like clock work, Charlotte walked into the door.

"Charlotte is that you sweetie?"

"Who else would it be?" Charlotte replied sarcastically.

"Honey, you've become so hard since died. You shouldn't talk to your mama so," Peggy said pitifully.

"What do you want for supper, Mama? Or are you going out again?" Charlotte's words hit their mark.

"I'm in for the evening dear." Peggy walked over to the sofa. She patted the place next to her. "Come over, sit down. I have some wonderful news for you."

"What have you been up to now, Mama?" Charlotte asked as she sat next to her mother.

"Charlotte, with everything that has happened to you in the last few years. Your daddy, the attack and all, well, you're not quite the marriageable material you once were." Peggy looked innocently into her daughter's eyes. "Howie's drawn to you. I've got to get you out of my house before there's real trouble," Peggy thought.

"What about it, Mother?" Charlotte responded coldly.

"Mason Burns, the son of one of my oldest friends, Nola Burns, will be traveling to Maryland and he wants to come by and meet you, honey."

"Meet me. Why? What have you been up to?" Charlotte's eyes challenged Peggy's.

"Well dear, after you were attacked the way you were, no matter how hard I've tried, no young man has been serious about you. The men around here just don't want to marry damaged goods."

"You're saying I'm damaged goods, and local men don't want to marry me."

"That's right, dear."

"I'm not interested in marrying."

"Of course, every descent girl wants to get married." "I'm not descent, Mama, because I don't want to be tied to a man?"

"Don't get defensive, Charlotte. People's attitudes never change. Women without husbands are looked upon as strange."

"Strange in what way?" Charlotte replied.

"Don't play coy with me, young lady," Peggy replied.

"What are you talking about, Mother?"

"People think you are a lesbian. Hating men, you know," Peggy whispered.

"Oh Mother, where do you get your notions?" Charlotte laughed.

"It's not an unreasonable notion. Do you remember that evil girl years ago trying to touch you in private places?" Peggy growled. "I put a stop to her. You are not going to be thought of as one of those funny people. Do I make myself clear?" Peggy continued.

"What evil girl are you talking about?" Charlotte turned to face her mother. "My heavens, I was twelve or thirteen, just learning about life. I sure couldn't get any information from you. I asked you once where babies came from, and you told me that you found me under a gooseberry bush."

"Well young lady, descent women never discussed those subjects with their daughters." Peggy was exasperated.

"Right, I had to get raped to find out about sex. I never should have learned it the hard way, Mother." Charlotte complained bitterly.

"I am sorry, dear. We must put the past behind us, and move on."

"Move on to where, Mother?" Charlotte asked.

"You will never find a man to marry you in Baltimore with your track record. I have written my friend Nola Burns. Her son has broken his engagement to his childhood sweetheart. She wants him to come up north while his broken heart mends."

"Why did he break off his engagement?"

"Oh Charlotte, I don't know. Nola only said that she was not a proper young lady, nor was she appropriate for her family," Peggy smiled brightly.

"Not good enough? What are they, royalty? Do they own the town?"

"No, they don't own the town. They come from a fine southern family. Genteel in every way. They had a plantation before the civil war. Now their circumstances are not..... Well, lets simply say that they have fallen on hard times."

"All right Mother, if he comes to town, I'll be nice."

"Charlotte, you will be more than nice. Mason Burns is your last hope. Down south they don't know about your past, and I am not planning to tell him," Peggy stated flatly.

"Mother, I don't know. There are few prospects left for me in Baltimore. I'll have to give it some thought," Charlotte said as she sought the peaceful serenity of her room.

Peggy Hamby had the determined sound that Charlotte knew meant business. She and Peggy were sitting in the kitchen consuming their meal of chicken soup and ham sandwiches. Charlotte listened again feeling the rapier slashes of her mother's tongue. Peggy considered the verbal barrage dinner conversation.

"I feel, Charlotte, that Mason Burns will be an excellent prospect. He is a genteel man and kind in every way," Peggy returned to their earlier conversation.

"Have you met him, Mama?" Charlotte asked, without looking up.

"No dear. I know only that any child of my beloved Nola would be special. He's from good stock."

"Mother!" Charlotte exclaimed. "You sound as though you are discussing breeding stock. I'm not some brood mare about to be put out to pasture with a stallion."

"Well, sweetie," Peggy giggled, "marriage is something like that, no matter how distasteful you find it. Farmers pick the best bull for their cow and chances are that if parents did the same for their children, their grandchildren would have superior genes."

"What if I mix my genes with those of some reject? I could have intellectual vegetables, correct mother," Charlotte replied.

"Your only experience with men has been disgusting, my dear. When you have a loving relationship, and if you are lucky, when your husband takes you to the marital bed, you will find the ultimate of ecstasy," Peggy stated with great resolve.

"Ecstasy, huh. I'll have to think this through," Charlotte said to the soapy dish pan.

"Charlotte, you are my little book worm, and you need advice on this subject. Have you not read that royalty and better class people have arranged marriages?"

"Yes, I have read about such matters. You're not telling me that the Burns' are royalty, just to get me to agree... really, mother!"

"Just think about what I have said," Peggy replied as she left the kitchen. "Night dear," Peggy called out as the door swung shut, leaving Charlotte to ponder her thoughts.

Alone in her room, Charlotte talked to her father. It seemed so long since Henry Hamby had passed away.

"Daddy, What am I to do? If you were only here when I needed you, my life would have been so different. I'm so glad you died never knowing what those animals did to me. Maybe this time mama is right. Get out of this town. If this Southerner is fairly respectable and not a half-wit, maybe I'll marry him and start over. I'll go south with Mason Burns and have my own family," Charlotte stated. "I must be strong like my heroine, Jane Eyre."

Tired from pacing her room, Charlotte fell asleep dreaming of her favorite storybook heroine, Jane Eyre and Jane's, Edward Rochester.

Charlotte, defeated from her life's tragedies, succumbed to her mother's demands. Charlotte was sure that changes in her life could only be improvements over the present state of affairs. Mason Burns couldn't be too bad; he hadn't been in jail, as far as she knew. He was the son of her mother's oldest friend. Charlotte supposed that was a plus. Her grandmother had known Nola and hadn't run her off.

Now, everything in her life was too much for her to handle. Peggy's whining, Howie's suggestive remarks, and the semi-imprisonment that she had imposed on herself to avoid Howie or a situation where she might be caught alone with him or any strange man.

She no longer felt that she must help her mother. Anyway, if she were out of the way, Howie would take care of Peggy. Charlotte was tired of her mother's sneaking around, and she wished to be free. Charlotte laid down on her bed and let her thoughts drift over the image of a life that she would like to live.

Charlotte heard the doorbell, and rising from her bed as though in a dream, walked to meet her destiny. Charlotte noticed as she passed the clock that it was only 5:00 in the afternoon. This man, this Mason Burns, was too eager. She shook uncontrollably as she straightened her collar and walked towards the staircase.

Standing in the shadows on the landing, Charlotte could hear her mother fawning over this stranger from the south.

"Oh Lord, please help me," Charlotte whispered. Glancing down at the sounds coming from the foyer, Charlotte Hamby couldn't suppress her surprise and pleasure. Mason Burns wasn't that handsome, but he had bright twinkling eyes that seemed to challenge you.

He was almost six feet tall, dark skinned with wind tossed brown hair. Peggy looked dwarfed in comparison. He listened patiently as she prattled on about childhood memories of her and Nola. He had the quiet dignity expected of a gentleman of the old south. She hugged her arms together as a sense of both anticipation and foreboding caused a shiver to run down her back. There was still something strange in his countenance, but she was sure she must be over reacting.

"I was traveling through your area, ma'am," Charlotte heard him saying, "and I knew my mother would skin my hide if I didn't pay my respects. She'd never forgive me if I didn't deliver a proper report on how her oldest friend was doing."

"Mason, we are so pleased you dropped by. How is my dear friend Nola?" Peggy asked innocently.

Peggy pretended that she and Nola had not been in communication, let alone that the childhood friends had made the decision to see their children wed.

"Here's my daughter, Charlotte," Peggy crooned as she motioned for Charlotte to join them. "Sweetheart, come down and let me introduce you to Mason Burns, the son of my darling friend Nola. You remember the stories of my youth. Come on down," Peggy's voice changed to her usual grating tone. "Didn't you hear me? Get down here. Now!"

"There's no hurry, Miss Charlotte, we've got all the time in the world," Mason said while smiling up at the nervous young woman.

Not a bad looker, for an outsider, he thought. She does have the
biggest blue eyes I've ever seen on a woman. They were the color
of blue star sapphires, brighter than those he had seen in the
Smithsonian Institute.

A pale Charlotte slowly descended the stairs and was face to face
with her destiny. Mason Burns took her hand and squeezed it
tenderly.

"It's a beautiful afternoon. Would you care to show me around the
neighborhood. I rarely get this far north and I do enjoy the
differences in the seasons."

Charlotte continued in self-imposed silence as she picked up her
purse and allowed herself to be led to the door.

"You two have fun and remember dinner will be served at 7:00
sharp. Have fun. Bye." Peggy sounded very pleasant as she closed
the door behind the couple.   "We could take a walk in the park.
The trees are breathtaking this time of year. We even have
dogwood trees just like you do back home," Peggy heard her
boring daughter as she suddenly came to life.

Peggy raced to her telephone.

"Howie, it's me. Yes. He's here. Seems better than we
expected."

"Hope the little fool doesn't blow it, baby. I'm tired of sleeping in
this broken down flea bag motel," replied Howie.

"If she does I'll put her to work paying me back the $10,000 I
invested. Mason and his mama were anxious to start a business.
They were happy with our suggestion of a little green stuff to assist
the couple down the road to happiness."

"If it had been left up to me, I'd of thrown her out when all that
mess happened," Howie replied.

"Don't talk like that, sweetie. It really wasn't her fault. Those
boys really messed her up."

"I know. She sure didn't attack them. Real frigid, that kid of
yours," Howie said flatly.

"And how would you be knowing that?"

"Don't get your hackles up, doll baby. You know how she always
acted better than everybody else. Well, I'm sorry they hurt her, but

they sure put her in her place. Showed her who was boss."

"Talk to you later. Let you know how things go. I've got to finish supper. We're having steaks. I even pulled out my lace tablecloth and that china my mother left me."

"Don't think I've ever seen the china. Why are you wasting that fancy food on those two when I'm eating hot dogs. You're sure showing off for that "reb". Dragging out all of those fancy schmancy things. Where you been hiding them?" Howie pouted.

"I keep them boxed up. They are white with small blue flowers in the center. Mama loved those silly things because my papa gave them to her on her fifth anniversary. It's about all I've got left from her, and I'm not risking their being ruined. We haven't had anybody around lately to entertain. I've got to run along now. I need to rest awhile before Mason returns. Charlotte's been no help. She doesn't care if we make a good impression. Oh that girl."

"What's the need to keep me out of the house? This Mason Burns seems to have you, not Charlotte all in a flutter. I don't see you putting anything fancy out when I drop by. You just toss me a can of beer. Can't I come by after the girl goes to sleep. My feet get cold without you next to me, keeping them warm. Besides, my balls feel heavy as lead," Howie whispered suggestively.

"We'll see. Bye." Peggy placed the receiver in its cradle and returned to the kitchen.

This night's entertainment could change their lives forever. She was tired of having that daughter hanging around. Peggy considered herself young, almost an ingenue, and she wanted to have some fun before it was too late. Howie Cramer eased her heat when her time came around, but it was difficult to get romantic with an old-maid hanging around the house.

The end of the day found Charlotte and Mason walking through the park enjoying the fragrance of the fall flowers. The leaves had begun to turn their exquisite reds and golds while from somewhere in the distance came the aroma of burning leaves.

"Let's sit on this bench and enjoy the late afternoon," Mason said, as he drew Charlotte to his side.

"I hope I don't sound to much like a tour guide, but I love living in Baltimore. I wish I could always stay here. I hate change," Charlotte rambled nervously.

"Give me the grand tour, please ma'am," Mason stated as he ignored her reference to disliking change. "You just lead, little one, and I will follow."

"This area is filled historical sights that played an important roll in the birth of our nation. Are you much of a history buff?"

"Somewhat."

"Well, let me test you just a bit. Charles Carroll of Baltimore signed the Declaration of Independence for Maryland. Who signed from South Carolina?" Charlotte asked. "I don't have the slightest idea, but for you I'll find out," Mason smiled.

Charlotte pointed out the landmarks in which she felt any visitor should be interested.

"We've got lots of Colonial buildings. Do you want to see any of them?" she asked pleasantly.

"I sure do. We don't have many back home. If you'll forgive my impolite reference to the former unpleasantness between the North and the South. General Sherman sure did cost us a lot of our history. That's what you get when you let a bunch of Yankee soldiers play with matches," Mason laughed.

Charlotte rose and looked around, "I could spend my entire life enjoying our parks. I love the wisteria vines entwining around the boughs of the trees. They cling together like lovers in a last embrace. There are trees with green, gold, and red autumn leaves blazing in contrast against the deep blue of the sky. You'll have to return in the spring. The dogwood trees and azaleas dot the landscape like a painting, God's handiwork at its finest."

"Listen, Charlotte," Mason said pointing towards a tree, "those birds are serenading us. I don't know much about our feathered friends, but I'll bet they are singing celebrating our meeting. It's destiny our being together."

"Mason, please don't be in such a hurry. We really don't know each other well enough to discuss the subject of marriage," Charlotte laughed. "The little ones are finches. The loud one is an Oriole, our state bird. They are singing because it's a lovely afternoon."

"You think your way, I'll think mine," Mason continued as he ignored Charlotte as she attempted to keep the subject on safe ground.

The joyous laughter of children could be heard everywhere. A group of squealing small boys were happily enjoying a game of kickball.

"How do you spend your days, Charlotte?" Mason said, attempting to draw his quiet companion into conversation.

"Mostly, when I'm not working, I read and take walks," Charlotte replied as she attempted to read his thoughts. "Please, Mason," Charlotte whispered as she touched his arm, "You must listen to me. We know nothing of each other."

"I know you are the daughter of my mom's dearest friend. You are physically attractive, and you are obviously intelligent and well educated. So far, I'm enjoying being with you. Isn't that enough for starters?" Mason smiled brightly. "Lets just take it slow and easy on a day to day basis. We've all had problems. When dad was alive, we lived in a big house. Things are different, now."

"I remember cutting my teeth on tales of mother's adventures with her dear Nola. I know every story by heart," Charlotte giggled.

"Yes, those two were a pair. Mama still talks and talks and talks of her childhood memories of her and Peggy," Mason laughed."Well back to current events. Dad secured mama a housekeeper. We went through several housekeepers because my sister Gladys and I were impossible children."

"I was not aware that you have a sister."

"Had a sister," Mason corrected. "Gladys passed away when she was ten. Miss the little brat."

"I'm sorry, you must have been close."

"We were, but it was a long time ago. Where was I? One day we had servants, and then we were broke. Dad didn't believe in insurance, so we were forced to sell everything. I work as a framing carpenter helping build houses when there is work in the area. My greatest passion is car repair, but there seems to be more need for carpenters. I plan to begin my own business. Something small, at first, and then I'll enlarge things as the business grows. I will work out of the house, make the estimates, collect the money, and leave the physical labor to my employees. We all have our own dreams. Oh well, enough rattling on about me and our fall from grace," Mason said, as he attempted to change a subject that was obviously painful.

"Mason before we go further I must tell you. One evening a year ago my world fell apart. I enjoyed sitting in the park enjoying the beauty of the flowers and watching the children play. Mother claims I am a health nut, always walking. I loved the change of seasons. Now I hide out in the house. I can't bring myself to enjoy again." Charlotte's voice cracked as she looked at the darkening sky.

"Parks are for the young," Mason said, ignoring Charlotte's change of mood. He watched the children at play. "Fresh air, exercise, and love, especially love permit them to thrive. Children are like these flowers, when properly tended they bloom. Don't you agree?"

"Yes, I do, Mason," Charlotte's eyes flew open with surprise. This man feels as I do about a family's importance.

"You told me you enjoyed reading. What do you read, Charlotte?" Mason continued.

"I usually prefer the classics, and my favorite book is *Jane Eyre*," whispered Charlotte. "I suppose I tend to compare my life with that of Jane."

"A day dreamy sort of book, wouldn't you say?" Mason Burns looked down into Charlotte's eyes. "I don't have time to read much, but maybe after we are married, you'll introduce me to some of your favorites."

Charlotte jumped at Mason's latest reference to their marriage. "Aren't you presuming a lot?" Charlotte snapped. "I don't recall agreeing to marry you or anyone else, for that matter."

"My dear, you ought to be married. Don't you agree that you should put the past behind you and proceed to a bright new future? I think our mothers may have already set the date. I like to make my own decisions, but in this instance, from what I have seen already, this may well be the best decision mother ever tried to make for me."

"Oh I don't know," Charlotte said as she avoided Mason's big eyes, as she glanced at her watch. "It's time we were going. Mother will be impatiently waiting to find out if we can get along."

Mason took Charlotte's hand. "What's the rush? We've just arrived, and the park is lovely."

Mason's matter-of-fact statement startled her, for Charlotte was unwilling to commit her life to a total stranger. Everything was moving too swiftly. Her mother, Mason and Nola Burns were pushing just a little too hard.

Papa had always warned her that if something sounded too good it usually was. Slow down Charlotte, tread lightly. You know so little of this formerly aristocratic family.

"Please, listen. This whole thing is not fair to you. You must be made aware that of the assault on me last year. I was gang raped," Charlotte whispered. "Shush, I know, and it's not important to me. I only see what you are. What happened was not of your doing," Mason sounded sincere as he squeezed her hand tightly.

"Before we can discuss a lifetime commitment, you must know what happened. It's not a pretty picture, and anyone thinking about marrying me has every right to know the entire story. You may not be able to forget or forgive," Charlotte said imploringly with her eyes downcast as she refused to meet Mason's steady gaze.

"I am aware of the incident, my dear, so discussion is unnecessary. Back home those bully boys would have been taken out and castrated. We take better care of our women folk than that," Mason said as his face darkened with anger.

Charlotte was impressed. Mason Burns had deep compassion. Maybe this man from the south could become her friend. Maybe she could develop a relationship. Maybe she could learn to love Mason Burns. He seemed to be man enough to deal with the knowledge of her attack.

"I know it is a great deal to ask. It takes an exceptional man to be able to forget that kind of incident," Charlotte pressed on.

"Oh, my poor girl. You were a victim of animals. You are a strong woman to have survived such an attack upon your sweet young body." She's hooked. Say the things she needs to hear. I'll get her back home where Mama and I will beat some sense into her. That money almost makes the acceptance of damaged goods palatable.

"I need to tell you about that night, so you'll better understand what occurred. It was the closest to being in hell I've ever known," Charlotte looked straight into Mason Burns' eyes.

"I told you little girl, it's not important. Try to put it out of your mind. In time, you'll forget."

"I hope so. I'm haunted by the memory. I wish I could blank out the memory of that night."

"I can't imagine anything worse happening to a lady. Try to remain calm. You're safe now," Mason said supportively.

"I begin to remember, and now, every time I shut my eyes, I remember that awful night. I ran through the dark streets of Baltimore trying to escape those animals. I'd never been so afraid. I had never felt so helpless."

Charlotte continued, "I was walking home from work. I worked for Mitchell's Book Store. About three blocks away from the house, five dark men stepped out of the shadows and demanded money. I told them I didn't have any, but they told me I was lying. They told me they knew I had plenty of money. One tried to grab my purse, and I ran for my life," Charlotte stopped, gasping for breath, as the memory of the night of horror threatened to overwhelm her.

Charlotte placed her head in her hands as she continued, "It seemed like I ran a hundred miles, but it was only several blocks," Charlotte raised her head as she faced the startled Mason.

"Unfortunately, I had been running in the wrong direction, away from home instead of towards it. I leaned against a wall attempting to make myself invisible. I listened as the sound of their boots passed and then grew dimmer."

The shaken Charlotte relived her story for Mason. "I've told this story to nobody except for the young policeman that found me. Everything was so fuzzy. I remember shivering on that metal Gurney covered only by a single sheet. I remember thinking, somebody ought to turn on the heat. I could hear a voice behind me reassuring me. It's all right, miss, he kept saying. Take it slow. You've got plenty of time. Just relax and try to remember."

The officer was kind, and he spoke softly. Even so, I had a hard time talking to a man. I'm afraid that I begged for a lady police officer. I'll never forget his embarrassed response. Sorry miss, the only female officers on the force are meter maids," Charlotte sighed as she continued.

"He was the only officer assigned to interview the victims of rape attacks and, in retrospect he was pretty good at it and very kind. He told me that he knew how difficult the situation was for a lady like me. He did take things slowly and easy. The officer said they wanted to catch those animals and put them away so they could never again attack me or any other woman. I was the only help they had. He told me to do my best," Charlotte's face turned pale as a tear slipped down her cheek. I said I would try. Actually, the only thing that would have helped was for him to be a woman, but a woman couldn't have been any nicer."

Charlotte drew out a handkerchief as she wiped away her tear. "Where was I?, Oh yes. I was hiding, trying so hard not to make a sound when suddenly they turned around and chased me into a dead-end street. They circled me like, uh, you know, in the movies when Indians attack settlers in their covered wagons. They taunted me as I cried and pleaded with them to let me go. They kicked me with heavy boots, you know, like construction workers wear."

Charlotte remembered her interview with the officers as if it had taken place yesterday. "The police stared at me as if I were some bug under a microscope. My torture was multiplied in several ways. Talking to anyone had been excruciating. My broken jaw made my words unintelligible. My broken ribs made each breath a nightmare. I suffered from the worst fear, a sudden panic attack whenever a man came into view. All of these feelings contributed to my torture. The only man I wished comfort from was my father." Charlotte's memories took over her mind.

She continued talking to Mason, an unconscious action. While her mind relived the night of her rape, over and over again, like a horror movie.

Charlotte remembered developing a nervous cough. The young police officer asked the nurse to please get some water for me. I took a drink of water and tried to compose myself, he continued his questions, "Where were we?"

Charlotte wiped her forehead with her damp handkerchief and continued her story. "They yelled, spit on me, and ripped at my clothes. Why don't you make it easy on yourself? Why don't you give us money? That's all we wanted?"

"Yeah! We just want money," a voice behind me laughed.

"Miss Burns, was that their reason for attacking you? Your refusal to give them money," inquired the officer.

"No. I think it was just an excuse. They probably would have attacked me even if I had given them the money. They had tried to stop me, asking for some change. Then they demanded all my cash. I just couldn't give them my money. I didn't have very much. My mother was counting on me for my contribution to our living expenses. It was mortgage day. So I ran."

"Then what?"

"Two of them finally caught me by the arms and held me while the others stripped me naked. I tried to clench my fists, striking one of the men in the face. He screamed."

"Hey, you hurt me bitch."

"I began to fight for all I was worth. There were too many of them and they were too strong. They held me down and beat and raped me. I believe the one I hit went first. After he was through, the others took their turn. Before leaving they beat, stomped and kicked me until I was incoherent. My head ached, my vision was blurred, I couldn't think. When they were finished, they chased me naked into the street. My attackers disappeared into the holes that the rats crawl out of."

Charlotte became aware that Mason was asking her a question, and the horror movie in her mind disappeared and she was in the present.

"That is appalling. Did they catch the scum?"

"No, I was finally told that mine wasn't the first attack of its kind, and the perpetrators would probably never be caught."

The couple continued their in silence until they reached the water's edge.

Charlotte attempted to brighten the afternoon by replacing the memory of her attack with one of happier times. She pointed to a statue in the nearby square, a larger than life statue of a horse and rider.

"When I was small, my father told me this was my own personal magical horse."

"Your magical horse?" Mason asked, raising his brow.

"Oh yes, mine," Charlotte giggled like a school girl. "Papa told me the horse and rider were magic, and when things became unbearable I was to clap my hands, and with the proper words the rider and horse would come to life and rescue me."

"What were the proper words to bring them to life?" Mason smiled as he gazed at her great rider and steed.

"Close your eyes, repeat the words, Bim-Bam-Alakazam, and clap your hands three times. Sadly enough when the need to be rescued arose, I was too old to believe in magic."

"I'm sorry, Charlotte."

"Yeah! Me to, but thanks anyway."

"Well I still believe in magic," Mason stood facing the statue. "I'll close my eyes, make a wish, and clap my hands three times. Well the statue did not come to life, but maybe I'll get my wish anyway."

"Your wish?" Charlotte asked.

"Yes, my wish is that a certain little gal will put her troubles behind her and think of me as her rescuer, her Shining Knight in Confederate Gray, and ride off into the sunset with me back to South Carolina. It's the land of milk and honey. You are aware of that, aren't you?" Mason smiled confidently at his suggestion.

Attempting to change the subject, Charlotte said, "Being from Charleston, I know you enjoy living where so much history occurred."

"I don't know too much about the local history. Been too busy earning a living for Ma and me," Mason seemed to complain. "I did learn about the civil war in school. Fort Sumter is in Charleston Harbor, our back yard, so to speak. Stuff like that."

Mason did not wish to sound ignorant to Charlotte, but work had consumed most of his time. After a day of construction work, you were just too tired to have a hobby or do anything except get some rest. This girl's expectations of what a man should be like included an education and an appreciation and knowledge of history. It wasn't going to be as easy to convince Charlotte to marry him as his mother had stated.

"I respect a man that cares for his mother. It's more important supporting ones family than accumulating a lot of useless information," Charlotte replied.

"That's true. I've never been a dreamy sort. Dreamers are difficult to employ," Mason said with a tone of disapproval.

"You surely don't believe that statement?" Charlotte asked.

"Yes, I do. But a dreamer in a man's life doesn't hurt," Mason smiled.

"What do you and your family do for fun in Baltimore?" Mason asked.

"We have a clam bake," Charlotte smiled. "Have you ever gone to a clam bake?" She continued.

"No, I'm afraid that I haven't. Just what does one do on a clam bake?" Mason asked. "I'm sure if you enjoy them, I would."

"You first secure a clam rake."

"Secure? a clam rake, did you say? Why secure one?" Mason questioned.

"Well with Uncle Charlie around the rake must be hidden or bolted down," Charlotte giggled. "He borrowed a clam rake, not for a clam bake, but to mix cement for a flagstone walk to his pool. Father had to retrieve it, and it never was the same," Charlotte laughed.

"I would imagine your father was none too thrilled with your Uncle Charlie," Mason joined in the merriment.

"The teens would take their boats out into the bay, while the older folks dug a pit in the wet sand and built a bonfire."

"What did the ones in boats catch?"   "They would put out crab and lobster traps with bait; fish heads, chicken necks or livers. I never enjoyed that part. I left the smelly part to the guys,"

Charlotte turned up her nose. "They could locate the traps by buoys made from floating milk jugs, or sometimes they used big corks. More adventurous folks used hand nets to catch shrimp in shallow water along the creeks."

"Okay, everybody is fishing or building fires," Mason encouraged Charlotte to continue.

"Right, when the traps are full and there are enough crab, the nets have caught enough shrimp, and the fire is going full blast, you boil the water to cook the catch. Those on shore wade out to the clam beds with rake and bucket and rake up the clams. Also you must bring along pocket knives, small wooden hammers and lots of paper towels."

"I suppose everyone brings along beach blankets. The younger ones might sneak away to do a little necking. That's a universal hobby, wouldn't you say?" replied Mason as he attempted to appear romantic.

"Then you bake potatoes in the fire after they are wrapped in aluminum foil. The corn is soaked in water and roasted in the coals while still in the shucks. Sometimes it is covered with wet seaweed. Everybody eats to his heart's desire. The most common implement is their fingers, incidently."

"What do you drink?" Enjoying the picture Charlotte had painted Mason laughed.

"There are iced-down tubs of beer and soda, and sometimes we put a pot of coffee on the coals for the older folk."

"It sounds wonderful. Sorry I don't have time to enjoy one of your special clam bakes. Maybe we can host one sometime when we return to Charleston?" His reference to Charleston brought the conversation back to the issue of marriage.

"Maybe." Charlotte didn't seem willing to give an inch.

"Let's go back to your place. It would be down right inhospitable for us to be late on the first of many meals we will share together." Mason took Charlotte's arm and allowed her to lead him back to Peggy's and the waiting special meal.

"How can you pick out which house is yours?" Mason asked. "All of the houses, in rows, just alike, with the same number of steps. It would make me crazy worrying about finding the right one. You would have to have enough light to read the number."

Charlotte laughed, "One evening, several years ago, Mr. McDougall had been celebrating Saint Patrick's Day a little too much. He was so sotted that he attempted to go into three wrong front doors before he found his own home."

Mason and Charlotte were still laughing as they walked into the Hamby house.

Charlotte hardly recognized their dining room. Peggy had washed the chandelier, polished the furniture and had placed an elegant lace tablecloth on the dining room table.

Charlotte remembered the china and silver as her grandmother, Peggy's mother.

The menu consisted of a twelve-ounce filet mignon, baked potatoes, broccoli served with a cheese sauce on top and a tossed salad. Hot steaming rolls lay in a wicker basket.

"Everything is simply wonderful. I feel like the prodigal son returning home," Mason smiled as he stuffed a chunk of steak in his mouth.

"Just consider this meal one of many to come, SON," Peggy put great emphasis on the word, son.

"Thanks. You make this poor old southern boy feel like part of the family."

"Please consider yourself one of us. Maybe.." Peggy never finished her remark as she indicated where the young couple were to be seated.

Charlotte quietly listened to the conversation until she felt it was necessary to interrupt her mother's unbridled tongue.

"Mother, this meal is very lovely. One of the nicest we've had since father's death."

"What did you two young people do this evening?" Peggy asked.

"We strolled through the town. I met Charlotte's favorite statue," Mason said.

"Yes, that fool statue. Has it come to life yet?" Peggy butted in.

"No, not yet, but I asked our dear Charlotte to permit me to become her rescuer."

"Now I consider that an excellent suggestion. Charlotte you need a rescuer, a hero. Wouldn't you say, my dear?"

"Possibly, Mother," Charlotte stated sharply.

"I also heard about clam bakes and Uncle Charlie mixing cement for his flagstone walk with your husband's favorite clam rake."

"Yes, Henry became hysterical at the sight of dried cement all over his favorite clam rake," Peggy laughed.

"Charlotte told me. I love family stories."

"I'll tell you one Charlotte doesn't know."

"Oh Mother, please," Charlotte moaned.

"Hush Charlotte. This happened before you were born. Do you want to hear, Mason dear?"

"Oh course, mom," His reference did not go unnoticed.

"Well, let me see. It was the night I went into labor with Charlotte. I was a professor's wife," Peggy tilted her nose slightly. "There was little money to afford a car. Poor Henry had such dreams. He wanted to buy me the moon. Since the moon was unobtainable he saved every penny towards a prime piece of land west of Baltimore. Oh yes, where was I?" Peggy frowned.

"You were in labor with me, MOM," Charlotte answered.

"Oh yes, Henry called your Uncle Charlie to drive us to the hospital. Charlie arrived with your grandmother who was determined to come along. After all you were her first grandchild. I always believed that she intruded because she was afraid of missing something. Mother was always nosy. She loved sticking her nose in where it didn't belong."

"Good grief!" Charlotte interjected. "Granny and Father were like oil and water. Two loggerheads ready to fight." "Yes   dear, Granny and your father were a pair."

"A pair of what I never figured out."

"Now dear, let's be charitable, they are both in heaven. Remember, it's not nice to speak ill of the dead."

"Oh pooh. That's just silly old wives tales. Go on with your story, if you must."

"Granny pushed her way into the house ahead of Uncle Charlie." Granny said, "She's my daughter, and it is my duty to attend to her."

"I think that's sweet," Mason said.

"Sweet, my eye. She'd refused to come near me my last month because she said one of her dearest friends had to deliver her own grandchild, and it had been a nightmare. Well it would never happen to Mother, she just stayed away," Peggy laughed and Mason joined her.

"While driving to the hospital, my mother and husband got into their usual argument about everything including which street to take, and the fact that Henry wanted a girl. He wanted to name her Charlotte, after Charlotte Bronte."

"Papa always told me I was named for Charlotte Bronte, but I do not recall ever hearing this story," Charlotte was suddenly showing interest.

"Oh yes, that was a day I'll never forget. Because of what happened next, Mother refused to put in an appearance in our home for six months, grandchild or no grandchild."

"Granny never could stand to be around anybody that was ill," Charlotte said. "I know she was your mother, but how in the world could you stand her constant interference."

Peggy laughed, "She made it difficult sometimes. Charlotte, hush, I'll lose my train of thought. Mother and Henry were arguing. I was having terrible labor pains and their incessant bickering was making me a wreck. We were two blocks from the hospital," Peggy continued.

"Henry," I said, "will you and mother please put a stop to the arguing. Mother, this is our baby. We'll name her what we choose," I said in an irritated manner.

Mother found your Uncle Charlie's umbrella and began to whack your father about the head. Henry had all he could stand.

"Mother, can't you behave? Put down that fool umbrella. Act your age, not your shoe size," Uncle Charlie said.

"Charles, I am your mother. You will not talk to me in such a manner."

"I know who you are, and don't try to high hat me. You have never intimidated me the way you have my sister. Sit down and behave," Charlie demanded.

"Even your poor Uncle Charlie couldn't shut our mother up.

"Charlie," Henry snapped. "Stop the car."

Charlie pulled the car to the curb and Henry got out. He rather unceremoniously pulled mother out, pointed her in the direction of the hospital.

"Mother Campbell, Peggy and I have had all of the nonsense out of you we can bear. If you wish to be part of the blessed event, you may walk." Peggy was laughing so hysterically tears were streaming down her face.

Mason and Charlotte were also laughing uncontrollably.

"I have never seen your poor father so angry, but my pains were three minutes apart and I was in no mood to be Miss Congeniality."

"Now that was some night, the birth of a new baby and being beaten up by an old granny," Mason stated with amusement.

"That's only the first part," Peggy continued. "Would you care for another cup of coffee, Mason dear?"

"No thanks, what happened next?" Mason asked.

"Oh you two. Don't rush me, I haven't thought about that night in years." Peggy smiled.

"Okay Mother, don't tell us the rest. Just run us crazy wondering."

"Oh yes. Your boring, silly old mother is finally worth listening to," Peggy pouted.

"Oh Mother, I've never called you boring or silly." Charlotte spontaneously hugged Peggy. "What happened next?"

"You were not born immediately. Always slow aren't you Charlotte. The nurse came out to discuss the situation with your father."

"Mr. Hamby," the nurse said, "your wife is doing just fine. Her contractions have slowed up, but there is no cause for concern. This is not unusual. I'll let you know, if there is any change."

"Thank you," Henry said, and returned to the waiting room.

"What's wrong with my child?" Granny demanded.

"Nothing! You're not a grandmother yet. Peggy's contractions have slowed down. They assure me this is not unusual."

"My poor daughter. Laboring to bring new life into the world.

Oh, but for you men and your animal desires. It is all your fault, Henry Hamby," Granny snapped at her exhausted son-in-law.

"I hope so, Mother. They are married. So pipe down, and sit down. Henry doesn't need your theatrical commentary. We all know where babies come from."

"Charles. I never," Mother said indignantly.

"Well you must have at least two times, or you wouldn't have had me and Peggy." Charlie faced the expectant father. "Have you noticed two extra stars in the east, Henry?"

"Charles, don't be vulgar and please don't blaspheme."

Granny resumed the argument about the naming of her first grandchild.

"I wish my grandchild to be named after Great Aunt Harriet Hornsby, Harriet Bethesda Hornsby."

"Good lord, Mother. That's a hell of a name to hang on a kid."

"We have told you a thousand times, Peggy and I have chosen the name Charlotte," the exasperated Henry stated.   "Are you so crazy about the name Charlotte?" mother asked with an exaggerated drawl on the name Charlotte. She could always pronounce a word in such a manner that made your flesh crawl.

"If the baby's a boy, what will you name him, Henry Hamby, Jr.?" Charlie asked.

"I don't care for the name Henry," Mother stated.

"Mother, hush, it is not your baby, therefore not your decision," Charlie retorted, amused with the situation.

"You won't find it so amusing when you start your family, Charlie. What makes you think you are exempt from her interference?" Henry asked.

"Interference? How dare you accuse me of interfering. Margaret, after all, is my only daughter," Mother sniffed.

"Get off your high horse, Mother. You play the role of martyr so badly," Charlie said, enjoying Henry's discomfort.

The discussion became so loud that the head nurse came out.

"If you don't quiet down, it will give me the greatest pleasure to have you thrown out of this hospital."

Mother replied, "You and whose army."

"You and whose army? My darling little granny said that? I had forgotten she used that phrase when she was good and riled. Did they throw them out of the hospital?" Charlotte asked, still giggling over the situation. "Poor father, he must have been mortified."

"Yes he was. But his quick action kept them from being tossed out into the night. He found a vending machine with bags of peanuts, and every time granny opened her mouth to complain, he popped a peanut in her mouth."

Peggy, Mason and Charlotte laughed and laughed over the story of granny and Henry Hamby and the birth of sweet Charlotte.

"It took granny six months to cool off. Maternal instincts or just plain curiosity got the better of her so she showed up unannounced one afternoon. Oh well, for six blissful months there was peace and quiet in the Hamby household. THE END."

"Why have you never told that story? You have been so unfair, keeping the best stories to yourself," Charlotte pouted.

"How is my dear Nola?"

"Just the same," Mason laughed.

Peggy joined Mason in laughter as though they shared some private joke. Charlotte's heart skipped a beat at the tone of his voice in merriment.

"She has not changed, Huh!"

"No, ma'am. She never changes, but Ma has intriguing things happening when you least expect them. Strange happenings," Mason replied.

"I remember dear," Peggy giggled.

"I'm sure you do," Mrs. Hamby.

"Not Mrs. Hamby, dear boy. Call me, Peggy," Peggy Hamby purred in her familiar coquettish manner.

"All right, Peggy," Mason smiled.

"I remember when we were in school, Nola and I decided to dye our hair. Come on you two. Let's find more comfortable chairs to continue this story." Peggy gestured for the young couple to be seated on the couch as she settled into her favorite chair. "Now where was I? Oh yes, we were dying our hair."

"Oh Mama, you didn't?" Charlotte sputtered as she regained her voice.

"Yes, we did! We were modern women. Unfortunately we did not use the proper ingredients. Our hair turned pink. Our parents put us on restriction for two months. Next, Nola and I also tried cigarettes," Peggy laughed remembering that particular misadventure.

"My, my, I haven't thought of that in years. I turned a dreadful shade of green and threw up all over Papa's new car."

"How ever did you explain the uhh... stuff in his automobile?"

"I told that it must have been the cat next door," Peggy chortled louder as she remembered that poor cat with her papa in hot pursuit. Peggy remembered the blood in his eyes as he swung an old broom at that innocent cat as he chased it about the yard."

"I felt so bad about the cat that I finally confessed. Papa tore up my britches. Wow! It was the worse spanking I ever received."

"Mama, you really were a dreadful child. Poor Granny Campbell, you must have driven her nuts," Charlotte laughed.

"Nola and I found that cat snoozing on the neighbor's back porch so I put him in a box. We painted him pink and returned him to the porch."

"Mama, that's terrible. The poor cat, he must have been a mess," giggled Charlotte.

"Oh yes! he was mad as a hornet. It took a large container of turpentine to get that messy stuff off that squirmy varmint," Peggy squealed. Mason, that mother of yours played it so coy as though she had never been involved in the cigarette or pink cat incident." Peggy laughed, but Mason and Charlotte seemed to laugh the loudest.

"Peggy, without you around mother has lost interest in completing anything. She knits, she paints, and she gardens, but she never finishes. She's been working on a shawl for three years. My dad use to say, watch mother especially when she is fiddling in the kitchen."

"Kitchen, what harm could she possibly do to a kitchen?"

"Ma has always been forgetful. She would put butter in the frying pan and forget to turn down the burner. One afternoon the butter melted black, and caught fire. The next thing we knew the curtains were ablaze. That time dad had to call the fire department. Fortunately, we were insured. That's my Ma mess it up or not finish it," Mason laughed, remembering his mother's antics.

"That's my Nola. The only reason she finished with you, old boy, is babies once planted cook until they are ready." Peggy laughed as she slapped Mason on his knee.

Peggy served the dessert, hot apple pie with vanilla ice cream and coffee. After the great granny story, the trio sat around making conversation while attempting to stay awake.

"I'm tired, you two. I'll do the dishes in the morning. Good night. See you later Mason."

Peggy did not look back as she climbed the stairs to her soft warm bed. She felt exhausted, but happy. She had done her part; the rest was up to Charlotte.

Mason prepared to leave for his hotel just before midnight.

"I had a great evening Charlotte. You never told me your mother was so funny. I'll call you tomorrow."

"Yes, I'm just finding out for myself. Good night," she said as she closed the door behind her.

As Charlotte skipped up the steps to her bedroom her mother called out to her. Peaking into her mother's room, she found Peggy sitting at her vanity, face covered with some kind of white pack.

"Well! What did you think about Mason Burns?" Peggy asked smiling, cracking the creamy mass on her face.

"He seems all right, I guess," Charlotte said cautiously.

"He's all right!" Peggy replied. "He's better than either one of us had hoped for. You bet your life, sweetie. Mason Burns is more that all right. Best thing that's walked into this house in years," Peggy laughed. "Did you get a load of that bulge in his pants? Looks like he'll give you a good ride, sweetie," Peggy roared.

Charlotte's face turned a deep crimson, "OH MOTHER! Must you always be so crude?"

"Crude, because we're talking about what's really on our minds. No need to hook up with a bull unless he is well hung," Peggy giggled. "You don't want to be short changed, do you?"

"Mother, all you seem to think about is sex," Charlotte complained.

"Sex is everything, Charlotte. You can forget about all the rest of the stuff, if you've got good sex." "Mother, you've become so uninhibited since father's gone."

"Uninhibited, me. I've always been like this. You're just being introduced to the real me. And as for your sainted father, you don't suppose you were an immaculate conception, do you? Hardly. If you are too scandalized to ask, your precious was great in the sack. In the beginning, we use to wear each other out. Man was your father hung," Peggy stated, hugging her arms. "I miss him, especially on a cold winter's night."

"What about Howie? Doesn't he satisfy you, Mother?"

"Don't be so mean. I'm young, and I still have the need of a man in my bed."

"Obviously," Charlotte stated primly.

"If you weren't so straightlaced, you'd enjoy a big stick, just like the rest of us females."

"Mother!" Charlotte growled.

"Since I am offending your delicate sensibilities would you mind if we change the subject? I need your advice."

"You want my advice, or do you want me to agree with you?" Charlotte asked.

Ignoring Charlotte's remark Peggy went on, "Do you remember Myrtle Goldstein? Her husband Horace Goldstein passed away the year before Henry."

"Yes, I remember the Goldsteins. You went to school with Mrs. Goldstein, didn't you, Mother?"

"Yes, from grade school all the way through high school," Peggy smiled, remembering her youth.

"What about Mrs. Goldstein?" Charlotte asked.

"Their daughter Sarah is getting married in three months. If they are waiting that long, Sarah must not be pregnant."

"Must you always be so judgmental, Mother. Get to the point," Charlotte stated in an irritated manner.

"We received an invitation to the wedding. What should we do?"

"What do you want to do, Mother? She is your friend, isn't she?" Charlotte asked.

"Not exactly. When Horace passed away I sent a card. I did not attend the service. I heard months later that Myrtle was telling our friends that if I couldn't attend the service, the least I could have done was send flowers."

"Why didn't you attend? What were you doing about that time?"

"That was during the terrible time with your father in intensive care. He had a massive heart attack. That was the time we almost lost him."

"I remember, Mother," Charlotte stroked her mother's hair. "It was a terrible time in our lives."

"Yes dear," Peggy whispered.

"Don't stay away because of a misunderstanding. If you want to attend the wedding, go," Charlotte stated.

"You think so. Maybe she just wants a gift for that kid of hers. I don't care, Myrtle is just a big-mouth broad," Peggy laughed.

"You do care, mother. If not, you wouldn't be bothered by her remarks."

"I know, what shall I do, baby?"

"I wouldn't wait. I would call Myrtle and tell her that you were thrilled to hear of Sarah's impending nuptials. Tell her you'd like to visit with her. You want to hear all about her future son-in-law. Suggest you take her to lunch?, to get her out of the house. Tell her you're sure she needs a break from all of the wedding preparations. Bring the subject around to Horace's funeral, and refresh her memory about our stress during her own personal loss," Charlotte said.

"Well aren't you the smart one."

"Not smart, mother. You know what's right. Just use your adorable little horse sense. That's all you have to do. Night. I'm going to bed."

"Sweet dreams. What are you going to do about Mason Burns?" Peggy called.

"I don't know. See you in the morning."

The next few days the couple ate together and talked together.

They were inseparable. Mason courted Charlotte at a slow pace.
He must not spook her. She'd had a terrible experience. At the end
of the week, Mason came by the Hamby house.

"Mason!" Charlotte was surprised to see him on her door step so
early in the morning. "Come on in. Would you like a cup off
coffee."

"I'd enjoy a cup of your wonderful coffee." Mason smiled brightly
as he followed Charlotte into the kitchen. "Sweet girl, I must return
home," he stated as he took the coffee cup that Charlotte prepared
for him. "I haven't wanted to rush you but, if you will marry me in
the next few days, you can accompany me to Charleston. I don't
have the money to carry on a long distance courtship. What do you
say?"

"I'm not sure," Charlotte replied hesitantly. "I hate being rushed
into important manners involving the rest of my life."

"It will be another year before I can return to Baltimore. We
could be having our first baby, by then," Mason smiled cajolingly.

"Mother, can you join Mason and me in the living room?"
Charlotte called out.

"What is it Charlotte? Mason, what a surprise. How long have
you been here?"

"Just a few minutes." Mason kissed Peggy on her cheek.

"Mother, Mason says he must return to Charleston, and he wants
me to leave with him."

"So soon? I thought he'd be in town longer. What will the
neighbors think? They might think you have to get married. Don't
you think Mason could return in a few months?" Peggy rattled
intermixing statements and questions.

She forgot about Howie's attraction to Charlotte as a sudden
wave of protectiveness consumed Peggy. She felt as if she were
walking into quick sand and that she was pulling her only child
down, down into a dark black hole of uncertainty.

Mason shot Peggy a warning glare.

Charlotte, frozen by her mother's barrage found her tongue. "This
marriage will be right for me, and I don't care, what the neighbors
believe," Charlotte snapped. "All right, all right. Keep calm, dear.

I'll go along with what ever you to wish. After all my dear, it is your life," Peggy whimpered.

Charlotte became surprisingly quiet so Mason said, "We'll be married at once. Right Charlotte. I could never transport a single young lady across the country without benefit of matrimony."

"Charlotte, how do you feel? It is up to you. You know how I feel about you and Mason," Peggy said as she toyed with Charlotte's emotions.

Pretty Peggy found herself torn between the feelings she had for her child, and her animal instincts. Charlotte must be separated from Howie. If she sent her daughter to Charleston with Mason Burns, Peggy could keep Howie to warm her bed.

"Mason, dear, please excuse us while we have a private discussion in the kitchen."

Mason paced back and forth in the living room, feeling like a criminal awaiting the jury's verdict. Mason's future hinged on Charlotte's decision. Her dowry would permit him to start a business. He had hated the humiliation of the lean years he and his mother had suffered.

The two smiling women joined him. Mason Burns was now confident of Charlotte's answer.

"I'd be honored to become your wife and return to Charleston with a handsome new husband. I adore you, Mason."

Mason Burns drew her against his chest. Charlotte's face was radiant as the evening sunset. Her lips opened slightly as she gasped for air between his wild and passionate kisses.

She stood gazing up into the dark eyes of her future, for better or for worse, Charlotte Hamby knew she would wed this strange man from the old south.

Mason interrupted her thoughts as he brought his mouth down upon her's, at first with feather like softness and then his kisses became more demanding and more fiery. Her frozen mind and body came to life as her blood thawed as it raced through her veins like molten lava cascading down a mountainside. Her mind whirled as Charlotte was swept along in this moment of ecstasy.

His arms slowly tightened around her slender body. Charlotte leaned against his strong, hard manliness and basked in the pleasant sensations running through her being. A brilliant spark suddenly ignited between the pair and reassured the frightened Charlotte.

Charlotte's face turned crimson as she remembered her mother's presence.

"Oh mother, I am so happy," Charlotte sighed.

"I know, my child." Peggy could not suppress a smile. "I feel a celebration is in order."

"I am sure we should celebrate," Mason replied as he placed a possessive arm about Charlotte's waist. "I'll take you both out to dinner. How does that sound?"

"Great!" Charlotte giggled.

"Go on upstairs and get your jacket. You have plenty to celebrate," Peggy giggled as she wrapped her arms seductively around Mason's neck. She placed her rosy red lips upon those of her startled future son-in-law.

"Okay you two. Cut it out. I'm the bride-to-be, somebody should be hugging me," Charlotte giggled, her face flushed with excitement.

"Okay, you old wet blanket," Peggy said. "Get out of here. Go celebrate. A lady does not get engaged to her prince charming everyday. Scat, you two, go on before I cry."

"Mother, you don't think we're going without you? You were our matchmaker. You're responsible for everything. Come on get your coat and mine. I'm happy, but starved."

Charlotte felt a shiver run up her spine. She impulsively hugged her startled mother. Charlotte shook her head as though she were releasing unsettling thoughts. This was not the time for unpleasant memories. She and Mason were about to embark upon a bright new life. Charlotte smiled, thinking of her father. It's all right . I'll be just fine.

Charlotte was called to the world of reality when she heard Mason say, "mom, come along. We are family now. Get your coat."

"Charlotte, will you get my coat while I have a private word with your intended?"

"Don't say anything interesting until I get back," Charlotte called out as she raced up the stairs.

"What did you say to her, Peggy?" Mason turned Charlotte's mother around.

"I simply reminded her that before you, she had been lonely. How would her life be improved with you gone?"

"Thanks, MOM," Mason squeezed Peggy.

"Don't hurt my Charlotte. She's really a sweet person, not like you and me. We're just two users," Peggy sighed.

Peggy thought Mason was ignoring her remark until he raised an ominous brow, "we'll celebrate tonight, but when do I get my money. I have expenses, you'll remember."

"You'll get your $10,000, after you have said "I Do". Not one minute sooner," Peggy whispered.

Charlotte returned to find Peggy and Mason in deep conversation.

"Hey you two, no serious discussions tonight. This is my engagement party. The best conversation is the right restaurant for the celebration."

"How did you guess?" Mason said as he took Charlotte's arm, leading the way. "Come on mom, Don't dawdle, my bride says she's starved. Are you girls in the mood for a good thick steak?"

"Sounds great, Mason. Don't you agree, mother?" Charlotte asked.

"It sure does, sweetie." Peggy sounded strange, but in Charlotte's excitement her mother's strained voice went unnoticed.

During the engagement dinner Peggy ate in uncharacteristic silence.

"What have I really gotten my child into? Wonder if I should back out of the deal before it's too late," Peggy thought. Oh she'll be all right. I'm just overacting, thought the foolish Peggy. "She'll be able to handle that insignificant wheeler-dealer from the old south."

Mason's body stiffened as his dark eyes appeared to read her every thought. He shot Peggy Hamby a ominous warning as he silenced her lips. Maybe Charlotte could learn to handle Mason

Burns. Peggy had been handling men for years. She wished she had taken the time to teach her unsophisticated child a few tricks.

"Yours was an excellent suggestion, Mason, having a vegetable, not hash browns," Charlotte sighed oblivious to the electricity in the air. "This evening is the most relaxed I've had been in years.

"Thank you, my dear. We're use to eating a variety of vegetables. I'm not use to the stuff you serve up here. Miss my grits," Mason protested.

"I would imagine in the twentieth century you could find grits somewhere in the state of Maryland," Charlotte responded primly.

"Not just any grits, good grits!" Mason continued. "The true south is the only place in the world you can get good grits. I'll teach you once we get home."

"I can not cook grits, Mason," Charlotte confessed.

"That's okay, Little Lady. My ma will teach you the proper way. We don't want you to start off your new life with any bad habits," Mason teased.

"Mother, is anything wrong?" Charlotte turned to her quiet mother.

"Yes, MOM! Is your steak too tough?"

"No, it's fine, dear. I just realized I may never see my baby girl again."

"Oh! that's nonsense, MOM! We'll get our business going and come back for visits every summer," Mason reassured.

Charlotte nestled her shoulder on Mason's.

"Champagne is in order for this special occasion. A man doesn't get engaged to the most beautiful girl in the world, everyday." Mason motioned to the waiter. "Waiter, champagne all around."

Charlotte giggled like a school girl. "You are so thoughtful. Life will be wonderful with you."

"We'll party tonight. When we get home money will be tight for a while, but for now what the hell. We only live once."

The waiter brought three glasses and poured the bubbly liquid.

"To Us. One family. Good luck, good health. Everything good." Mason toasted.

Peggy kept her thoughts to herself. Mason might make a helpful friend, but she was positive he would make a formidable enemy.

Two days later everything was ready for Charlotte's minister, Reverend Tolbert Johnson, to marry the happy couple in the Hamby's living room. Peggy's earlier concern for her child's safety and happiness had given way to the importance of getting some distance between Howie and Charlotte. Howie was much too interested in Charlotte, and if she didn't play her cards right Peggy would lose her man to her daughter. With Charlotte out of the house, Howie could devote more attention to her.

Peggy Hamby flittered around the house attempting to make the tiny wedding as pleasant as possible.

Charlotte wore a white street length dress with baby's breath adorning each side of her hair. Mason was wearing his best Sunday blue suit.

Mr. Mitchell, owner of the bookstore, agreed to be Mason's best man. And dear Mrs. Weinstock loaned Charlotte two wedding bells saved from her daughter's wedding. Years of living in the same community with her neighbors had helped Peggy secure the necessities for a proper wedding. Mrs. Mitchell brought over her silver punch bowl which had been passed down through several generations of her family. The church secretary happily provided the plates, forks, knives and napkins.

Peggy ordered a single layered cake from the local German Bakery. Bobby Peterson, family friend and amateur photographer, volunteered to make a set of wedding pictures as his gift to the happy couple. The dining room table sported Mrs. Mitchell's silver punch bowl now filled with fruit juice and an inexpensive champagne. There were assorted nuts, mints and small sandwiches.

All was ready for the arrival of the minister and the several guests Peggy had hastily invited for the occasion.

At one o'clock in the afternoon, Peggy excitedly exclaimed, "The photographer is late. I hope he hasn't forgotten the appointment. You can't have a wedding without pictures."

Just then the door bell rang which sounded the arrival of the minister and his wife. Bobby Peterson and his camera were right behind them.

"I told you not to worry, Peggy. I would never miss an occasion as important as our Charlotte's wedding," Bobby Peterson exclaimed. "You will have copies of photographs of this occasion by the time you arrive at your new home."

Charlotte, while hugging Mrs. Johnson quietly said, "Come in Reverend Johnson. Let's get on with the wedding before my mother has a nervous breakdown," She smiled brightly to her friend and minister.

Earlier in the day, Charlotte, being sensible, had slipped upstairs while her mother and friends were decorating and setting everything up for the wedding. She had gone to her room, taken a Valium, and laid down for a short but quiet nap. She was aware that this wedding would not be the social event of the year, but they would attempt to survive the happy occasion with as little trauma as necessary. The tranquillizer and nap now allowed her to appear calm and collected.

The ceremony was brief, and the couple were toasted by those assembled. Charlotte opened the small stack of wedding gifts.

"Oh Mrs. Weinstock, a lace nightgown. Thank you, dear lady," Charlotte smiled, hugging her elderly friend.

"You are quite welcome," Mrs. Weinstock replied. "Wish it could have been more."   "I will miss you terribly," Charlotte stated, wiping a tear from her eye. "South Carolina is so far away."

"Nonsense, we'll write. You will certainly come back home to visit your mother."

"Yes, I know."

"What's in the next box?" Mrs. Mitchell asked.

Peggy passed the subdued bride the next gift. A severe rainstorm had moved into the area halfway through the celebration, "An omen of dark things to come," Charlotte thought.

"This box is heavy." Charlotte giggled. "Who is it from?"

"Read the card, dear," Peggy replied.

"Mother, it's from you. You've been so busy with all of the preparation. How did you find the time? Thank you for whatever it is," Charlotte smiled.

"Open it. I hope you will be pleased," Peggy said.

"I'm sure I will mother."

Peggy watched nervously as Charlotte opened the gift.

"Oh, it is china. Granny's china with blue flowers." Charlotte squealed, as she hugged a plate to her breast.

"I'm glad you're pleased. She loved you so," Peggy smiled, "Open the next gift."

"Oh Reverend and Mrs. Johnson, how exquisite. A white bible."

"Yes dear," Mrs. Johnson replied, "I'm happy you're pleased. I took the liberty of writing your names and today's date inside. You'll have to fill in the names and dates of your children."

"We're in no rush about children," Charlotte laughed, bestowing Mason with a loving expression.

"That's right. But we do want a house full," Mason's statement pleased those assembled.

"You'd better get busy, you're not as young as you use to be," Mr. Peterson said, suddenly joining in the merriment.   "We'll notify you when we have our first blessed event," Mason's words brought a redness to his bride's face, but continued, "I am sure that you will understand when I say we must end the festivities. Our bus leaves at six in the morning, and we still have much to pack."

The merrymakers understood the grooms desire to be alone with his new wife, so they ended the polite chit-chat and departed. Mason spend the next two hours packing the rental car for the drive to their honeymoon love nest. In a few days Peggy had agreed to send the larger items by UPS.

"Thank you, Mama, for the lovely ceremony. I'll write as so as we reach Charleston," Charlotte stated as she picked up her small cosmetic case.

"Yes, I'm sure my brand new bride will be dreaming of nothing but writing home," Mason replied with merry but crude undertones.

"We'll spend tonight...." Charlotte's voice trailed off. "Mason, you never told me where we're spending our honeymoon night," Charlotte laughed.

"It's been my secret. I've been so confident that we would wed, I booked a pleasant room at Moody's Bed and Breakfast. They cater to honeymooners."

"That will be wonderful, Charlotte," Peggy's words dripping with honey. "The Moody's run quite a place. I never could get your father to take me. Oh well, happy marriage." Peggy kissed her daughter goodbye.

"Please treat her right, Mason," Peggy whispered as she attempted to kiss his cheek.

"I'll treat her the way she deserves." Mason's face darkened. "Goodbye, Mother." Mason walked over to his bride who was giving her final farewell to Mrs. Weinstock.

"If this marriage isn't what you hope, call me, darling. You can always come back home to me," Mrs. Weinstock hugged her little friend.

"Don't worry so, Mrs. W. Life with Mason can't be any worse than it's been with Mother and Howie," Charlotte attempted a laugh. She handed her bridal bouquet to her neighbor. "Put these on Papa's grave, Mrs. W. Mason's in such a hurry," Charlotte whispered.

"I will darling," Mrs. Weinstock replied, taking the small bunch of flowers.

"Come on Charlotte. I don't like driving a rental car when I'm so tired. Remind me to leave the car keys at the hotel desk. The car rental company has agreed to pick it up at the hotel." Mason said.

"Of course, my husband." Charlotte replied as she smiled happily at her new bridegroom. "Goodbye everyone. Thanks for all you have done for us," Charlotte called.

"We'll ship all of your wedding gifts later this week," Peggy stated happily, waving to the happy couple.

"Thanks Mama. Take care of yourself," Charlotte walked out of her childhood home, and into an uncertain destiny.

Chapter 5

Charlotte and Mason drove off into the night to spend their first night as a married couple at the Moody's Bed and Breakfast. They would board the bus the next morning for South Carolina and his waiting family.

Mason proudly ushered his new bride into Moody's Bed and Breakfast.

"Good evening, may I be of assistance?" the grey haired lady behind the desk asked.

"Yes," smiled Mason, "we are Mr. and Mrs. Mason Burns, and we have a reservation for tonight."

"Oh yes. Mr. Burns. You and Mrs. Burns are honeymooning with us this evening. I'm Annabel Moody. My husband and I run this place, so if you two need anything special, just let me know. Please follow me."

Mrs. Moody smiled as she directed the newlyweds down the hall.

"I hope you enjoy the room. I selected one of our finest room. I call this our John Paul Jones Room. My husband and I spent our first night as a married couple in this very room. Maybe it will bring you extra good luck," Mrs. Moody rattled on as she tenderly touched the vanity and bedspread, seemingly lost in the past.

At last they were alone in their room. The proprietor had built a crackling fire in the fireplace. His wife had placed bowls of flowers around the room and rose petals between the sheets gave a romantic atmosphere for the honeymooners.

There was a chronometer placed on the center of the mantel, with ship models on either side.

"Mason, look at the ship on the right. It is a replica of John Paul Jones ship, the Bon Homme Richard. Isn't it thrilling to be in a place so steeped in history?"

Mason did not speak until the proprietor left. Mason yanked off his coat and turned to the smiling Charlotte and began grabbing for her blouse.

"Mason, what is wrong?" asked a confused Charlotte as the smile drained from her face.   "I'm not interested in a history lesson.

I've waited on you long enough. It's not as if you're a virgin. Come here you bitch, don't play coy with me. You are mine now. It's legal. Don't bother to cry out. Nobody will come to your rescue. They'll all just laugh at the nervous frightened bride being gored by her stallion bridegroom."

Charlotte faced a stranger. All of Mason's tenderness had gone. His face was red and he was making ugly gasping sounds.

"Mason, please, you told me we had a lifetime. Can't we proceed a little slower?"

"Proceed slower," he mimicked her sarcastically. "I've had a hard on since I met you. I'm not first, but I've got the biggest. You've only been with a bunch of little boys. Tonight you'll find out what a man can do," he bellowed, as he grabbed at her undergarments. His fingers caught in her bodice, and he yanked downward, destroying her slip. Next he tore off her bra and tossed it on the floor.

"You said I had been their victim. You said you understood," she cried in anguish.

"Understand what, Whore? A descent woman would have killed herself rather than live with your shame."

"Please, if you feel that way, let's end the marriage right now. Keep my dowry. I'll leave and you'll never be bothered by me again."

"Oh no, you harlot. You're my wife and you need to pay for your wantonness. Come here, you unspeakable..." He reached for her panties as he snatched her to him.

Mason, held Charlotte's wrist in one hand and with the other he slapped her on the cheek, then he flung her naked body to the floor. Her mind whirled back to the first rape when those disgusting men drug her into that dark alley. They had taunted her, abused her, and ignored her pleas in the same disgusting manner.

Breathing heavily, he repeatedly slapped her body and kicked her in her groan. Charlotte moaned and prayed for the oblivion of unconsciousness that refused to come.

"You stupid cow, stop it. Stop your whining. I'll show you what a man can do for you."

Charlotte attempted to reach the sanity she hoped still existed in

Mason. Charlotte said as gently and quietly as she could under the circumstances. "Please wait. Go slower, I promise I am curious about what it's like to be with a real man. I'm so sorry about the others. I wish you were my first."

Mason, in a crazed frenzy stepped out of his pants. She was startled that he wore no underwear. Charlotte was staring at his engorged member. "You have teased me long enough with your maidenliness. Your time has now come."

He leaped astride her and flopped forward onto her stomach, knocking the breath from her body. Then he supported his upper body by holding on to her throat. His violent actions inflicted large bruises on her neck.

"How do you like this, Whore?" He held her down on the bed and jammed his monstrous, red, throbbing member into her. She would have screamed but he had his hands wrapped around her neck. The pain was so unbearable that she blissfully fainted.

After what seemed an eternity, he rolled off her mutilated body. Holding her breath, feigning sleep, a devastated Charlotte thought, "This man is an animal. If this is marriage, what in heaven's name have I gotten myself into. I must escape at the first opportunity."

As though reading her very thoughts, "Playing opossum are we. How did a real man stack up against your other lovers? Don't even think about running away. If you do I'll track you down, and I'll kill you. Since we're both awake lets do it again. Come here." Mason pulled Charlotte into his arms and kissed her until she had no breath.

"I'll be nice from now on. I've never blown my stack like that before, sorry kid. Stop looking at me like that. Ask my girl back home. She always said I was the greatest stallion in bed." "Why didn't you marry your girlfriend back home."

Mason laughed, popping her playfully on the bottom, "She didn't have the money your mama had. Don't worry, I won't be worrying you much. I'll be visiting my local lady when we get back."

"You plan on continuing to, -uh see her, now that we are married?" Charlotte asked in a confused manner.

"Southern ladies are known for having the phony fainting spells. I was hoping a little gal from Maryland would show a little more life, but you're as frigid as an arctic iceberg. I'll just bother you when I want to make a baby. The rest of the time I'll be visiting my little Janie Sue Parker. At least she's honest. She's not a lady, and doesn't pretend to be."

Charlotte smiled with relief. Mason Burns could visit Janie Sue for the next fifty years as far as she was concerned. She would bear his child and keep it separate from his depraved world.

Sometime during the night Mason began to kiss Charlotte, and he was surprisingly tender, but with his arousal kindness was quickly forgotten.

"You know what I want. Roll over," Mason laughed. "Smile, Mrs. Burns, you'll get use to it. Don't look so shocked. We'll do it again, and any other time I decide."

Every searing thrust was worse than before. She hated sex with Mason, lying spread-eagled, under this rooting pig as he forced himself inside her.

Mason finally released Charlotte, rolling away with his hairy naked back to her. She hoped that she could convince him to wear pajamas. The mere thought of his hot sweaty body draped over her caused a wave of nausea to sweep over her.

"Where are you going?" Mason growled, as he felt her movement to leave the bed.

"I'm going to clean up. There's blood everywhere." Charlotte had wiped a finger between her legs finding a bloody discharge. "Why blood? You ain't no virgin," Mason replied. "Probably happened because you've finally had it done by a real man, not little boys. Night."

When she returned from the bathroom, Mason lay face down on the mattress, snoring loud enough to wake the dead. She slid in beside him, careful not to disturb him and sobbed herself to sleep.

Marriage, this goring, this nightly ritual of male dominance. She had dreamed of this night. The night of unspeakable beauty. The joining of two bodies, two souls for eternity. Forever. What a joke. She had read romantic stories and poetry of romance with men. But, what an obscene joke.

The honeymoon ended as quickly as it had begun.

The tedious journey from Maryland to South Carolina on the bus afforded Charlotte no privacy at any time. He tried to molest her when the lights were out and the other passengers were asleep. His hands roamed familiarly under her blanket, and he was angered by her lack of cooperation.

"Please, Mason, wait until we have privacy. What if someone saw us? I'd be so embarrassed. Can't we talk? We really know little of each other," Charlotte attempted to change the subject.

"We don't know each other well?"

Mason laughed as he attempted to slip his hand between Charlotte's thighs. "Okay! okay! What do you want to talk about?" He scowled.

"Tell me about your mother. Mine always thought so much of her. She felt Nola was the strongest, most resilient person she had ever known."

"As a young woman, Ma was always happy-go-lucky. She had planned a life of travel and adventure. Married to dad she thought she had caught the gravy train, but it did not workout that way. Dad had the name and social position. Unfortunately, my grandfather had lost all of his money. He was in business with unscrupulous men and they stole him blind." "Oh Mason," she squeezed his hand, "that must have been dreadful for your family. Did he go to the police and have the scoundrels arrested?"

"No! It was all political. You know how it is, Charlotte. With grandpa's money gone the local authorities turned their backs on him and he died penniless." Mason's face turned crimson with anger.

"Your parents must have been devastated," Charlotte whispered with deep concern.

"Ma was a real trooper until dad's death. She really fell apart."

"I was terribly sorry that mama...that we were unable to comfort her more."

"You did more than most. I remember the pink flowers and your letter of condolence meant so much. Ma cried and hugged the flowers, they seem to give her strength," Mason frowned as he remembered.

"How did she handle the funeral service? I remember when my

father passed away I had my friend Mrs. Weinstock to comfort me." Charlotte became pale.

The memory of her flighty mother sitting in the small chapel holding hands with Howie Cramer was branded in her brain forever.

"The funeral was a nightmare. One minute I thought she was going to be alright until they began to lower his casket. Ma suddenly staggered and let our a blood curdling scream. She attempted to dive into dad's final resting place. I found myself holding her about the waist upside down as her arms flailed about. Charlotte, I never felt so helpless in my life," Mason's eyes were filled with tears as he finished painting the picture of his poor mother's mental deterioration.

Filled with the well of overflowing compassion, Charlotte moved closer to comfort her husband as she held both his hands, kissing them tenderly.

Mason grabbed his bride, all thoughts of pain had disappeared from his face as he rained kisses down her neck.

"Please don't do this," Charlotte pleaded, "not here. Wait until we reach home."

"I've told you before, stop complaining. It's legal," Mason responded. Charlotte's color darkened as the couple received a knowing look from a passenger across the aisle.

"I'd like to get some sleep," Charlotte said as she attempted to turn away from him.

"We're newlyweds, and you're acting as though we are strangers. I expect a little intimate tickling. You're acting as though you were my maiden aunt."

Charlotte didn't respond as she feigned sleep.

"Shit," was all she heard from her bridegroom's lips as she drifted off into the land of nod.

During the daytime, Charlotte entertained herself by daydreaming of the south of a hundred years ago. She pretended she was a lady from a plantation traveling down river on a steamboat, the Mississippi Queen. She had a fine stateroom that she and her handsome bridegroom rarely left. They were the talk of the boat. Her groom was tall, dark and handsome. Every woman's dream.

He was a fantastic lover, and just wicked enough to be an excellent gambler. While she rested in the evening, he would go upstairs and win enough money to buy her another pretty diamond bauble.

While waiting his arrival she would stroll the deck. The passengers would all marvel at the elegant couple. They all agreed that they had never seen two people more suited to each other. She waited impatiently for her dream man to walk up behind her, taking her into his arms, and kissing her breath away. She was frequently embarrassed when, with his urgency for her, that he would sweep her into his arms and carry her to their stateroom. They received knowing smiles from the other passengers as they understood the blissful state of the happy lovers.

In her fantasy world, the honeymooners on the steamboat joined the other passengers for their meals. There were Negro attendants assisting in the service of excellent meals. There were exceptional singers and musicians to entertain the passengers, but the lovers always managed to make their excuses to return to their cabin.

Charlotte loved the boat's whistles signaling her arrival at the landings. Many of the town's people, upon hearing the signal would rush to the dock to see the rich and pretty people who traveled on the steamer.

Oh, how she longed to give her beloved husband a child, an heir, to eventually inherit their plantation and wealth. Back to reality, there was no boat whistle. No rich handsome lover. Only Mason Burns. Charlotte was back in the present and the only sounds she heard were the squeaks emitting from the air-brakes.

Charlotte gazed out the window as she enjoyed the beauty of the fall season. There were yellow leaves the color of lemons floating alongside leaves that were as bright as red apples, and brown one, a reminder that winter was not far away. With a gust of wind orange leaves would combine with the others to make a collage of extravagant beauty.

Charlotte could not suppress laughter at the sight of a squirrel perched on a limb chastising local farmers busily working their fields.

Charlotte cracked the window to enjoy the aromas created by the rustling autumn wind, blends of the mother earth, the fallen leaves, fresh cut fields with the black smoke from a farmers chimney curling toward the light grey sky. The warm sun, relaxing sounds, the gentle breeze blew softly across Charlotte's face as she drifted into the land of pleasant dreams. A noise from the rear of the bus woke Charlotte.

Charlotte returned to enjoying the glorious views that stretched for miles as they basked in the beauty of the region. She enjoyed the wildflowers that spread across the valleys and slopes. Charlotte caught her breath at the sight of the pristine rivers and lakes. This was truly God's country, Charlotte thought, as she saw crystal clear waterfalls, with white caps. There were grey-green streams and azure lakes. Charlotte woke with a start as she returned to the land of reality. She turned up her nose with disgust as she remembered the last few days. Mason had changed. He was no longer gentle and kind. He had a cruel side. He hurt her, cried, apologized and suddenly he was tender again. She never knew what would set him off. He had promised to break it off with his home town girl friend. Charlotte was unsure that he could be trusted.

Mason was a vigorous husband, and she feared he would impregnate her on their honeymoon. She wished she had brought some form of birth control she could use without Mason's knowledge. She hadn't had a period since his arrival, and eagerly anticipated its return. What she always considered an aggravation would be a Godsend. There was no chance that a pregnancy could help things just now.

Chapter 6

The bus pulled into the final station. The end of one journey and the beginning of another.

"We're in the real south now, Charlotte. I expect you to act the lady. We do things different, and at a slower pace. You'll catch on, my little girl," Mason guided her off the bus.

Two strangers stood holding oversized luggage, each with their own trepidations of the new live they had begun.

Nola Burns reacted to the marriage of her son with great excitement. Peggy's daughter would bring with her a dowry and several antiques to adorn their home. This marriage would allow them to return to the standard of living they had once enjoyed.

"Welcome, daughter, welcome to your new home. How was the trip? Come here sonny and give your mother a big hug. You're a naughty impetuous little boy to marry this stranger so fast. Some people will think you had to." Nola hugged Charlotte tightly. Charlotte caught her breath as she pulled away, stepping back to get a better look at her mother's beloved friend.

All Charlotte had known about Nola Burns was that she was her mother Peggy's oldest friend. She was the widow of Jim Burns a lawyer from Charleston, South Carolina. She had been the rage of Charleston society.. Thirty years ago men had fought for her favors. But here stood this short woman who must have weighed at least 250 pounds. Time had not been kind to her. Nola had the angry look of a bulldog. She had short hair which had originally been strawberry blonde, but now was half gray and half pink the result of bad dye jobs.

Her teeth had a greenish touch due to infrequent brushing. She was as crude as a used corn cob with a well ingrained unpleasant attitude the result of a lifetime filled with disappointment and envy. She felt the good life had passed her by. She married anticipating being treated like royalty. Jim Burns had promised her the world, but he had failed her, failed himself. Nola Burns' face was a map of hate, envy and malice toward all. You could read life's disappointments in her vacant eyes.

Nola dominated her family. She could become outrageous and totally out of control if it served her purpose. Jim Burns had stood by helpless as she ripped Mason's spirit from his body. She used mother-love and concern as her whip to control. Nola Burns ruled her family with fear, and if that failed, intimidation.

Nola had been a self centered beauty in her youth. She had been spoiled and indulged by her father, husband and then her own son.

Gone was the beautiful tyrant, the princess beloved by men. Charlotte thought sadly that there was no resemblance left of the young Nola from the tiny faded picture that Charlotte's mother had so lovingly carried for a lifetime.

Charlotte frowned, her senses whirling, "This can't be mother's darling friend. She certainly isn't heaven bound, and as for hell, she'd be too much competition for the devil."

"Mason," Nola turned to her son, "Peggy did send the $10,000?, the dowry, uh... We need a little extra. You took so long courting this gal that we'll lose the property. We can keep the land if we can come up with another $2,000. Peggy will send the extra, won't she."

"No, I'm sorry the $10,000 was all mama could scrape together," Charlotte answered, hanging her head.

The humiliation from the rape of her body was nothing compared to the humiliation of the rape of her pride, her dignity. This woman, her mother's childhood friend, this Nola Burns was airing her dirty linens in public. She was discussing the private family business for every stranger to hear.

"No more money. Well what good are you to me. We'll put you to work, somewhere. You do work, don't you?"

"Yes, uh mom," Charlotte attempted a smile.

"Don't you mom me. You are the greatest disappointment in our lives. Did you bring along any personal affects? Jewelry, china, silver? Something we could sell or pawn," greed written all over the older woman's face.

"No, Mrs. Burns. I have a few clothes, but the other things will be sent in the next few days. I'll call mother tomorrow and see if she can get another $2,000." If you remember, I am to get a job. I am accustomed to carrying my weight," Charlotte looked around the town. "I am a strong woman from good Yankee stock. I can keep house and hold down a job without any problem," she said proudly.

"Sure, sure. You're going to clean my house and keep a job. When will you be doing all of this work. If Mason runs true to form he'll be keeping you on your back, in bed," Nola laughed in a vulgar manner that Charlotte would soon learn to despise.

"Mason, in the morning when you are through with your gal, uh your wife," Nola bellowed, "send her off to get a job. She's not going to lay around in bed when there is money to be made. If she's good enough in the sack, you could rent out her little patch," Nola changed the subject, "Mason dear, have you seen my knitting? I'm working on a sweater."

"Not that ugly blue thing? Ma, you've been working on that fool sweater for a long as I can remember. I was about eight when you started it. At this rate you won't finish it in the next hundred years."

Charlotte turned her back on the arguing mother and son. She felt complete revulsion at Nola's suggestion. Prostituting herself was unthinkable. She walked blindly to the awaiting car.

Charlotte Hamby Burns was far too submerged in her own pain to enjoy her first sunset in Charleston, South Carolina. She became aware of her surroundings when she heard several birds squawking and twittering at intruders disturbing their nest on the high branches of a large oak tree.

Charlotte smiled in spite of herself, and settled back to enjoy the scenery. There was a dimly lit cottage reminiscent of by gone years. A gray-haired wiry little man with a scarred face stood up and waved to the traffic. He returned to his work planting annuals as he fought a battle against the descending twilight.

The car turned onto Battery with exquisite homes carefully restored to their former elegance. Street lights were reflected in the nearby water. They turned off Battery to find moss covered oak trees lining the road.

The car finally turned onto a street filled with smaller houses that remained untouched by the city's restoration project.

The Burns home was an old two story frame weathered by time

and in great need of repair. Here and there a board no longer lined up the way the builder had intended. The screened porch had large enough holes that the resident mosquitoes could fly in and out without obstruction. If ever a house needed painting this house was the one.

Charlotte quietly walked into the drab house and into her destiny.

Chapter 7

Mason demanded that Charlotte wait about employment until she had time to clean and organize the Burns household. There was much to be done for it was apparent that Nola never cleaned up her house. There were stacks of newspapers and mildewed magazines all over the place. Charlotte began her days scrubbing down the house, and her nights on her back submitting to Mason's lewd attentions.

Long cat hair clung to the furnishings. Charlotte would never forget her unceremonious introduction to Nola's cat, "Precious". It was hate at first sight. Charlotte, upon entering her new home was terrified as Precious leaped upon her shoulders scratching her flesh and ripping at her clothing. The spoiled feline ruled the house and was giving notice that there would be no interference. The clutter was a perfect breeding ground for all types of vermin.

Charlotte began to concentrate on their bedroom. She took down the ugly twisted blind that hung over their only window, and restrung it with a vengeance.

"Damn it, Precious. Get off my bed," Charlotte shouted.
The cat glared at the intruder as she jumped to the floor. Precious sneezed as a cloud of dust sifted down her coat.

"Scat! Take a nap on Nola's bed. She likes you, I don't."
Charlotte returned to her assault on spider webs that appeared to have come with the house. She cracked the window filling the room with damp fresh air.

Charlotte tiptoed down the stairs in search of a pine cleaner. Her spirits soared as the odor of dust and old age began to disappear. She rearranged the chest of drawers, and dusted every inch of the dingy room.

Charlotte felt a great since of accomplishment as she reveled in the fruits of her labor.

Charlotte's routine was to rise early before her screaming family. She delighted in the quiet time as she sipped a cup of tea. It was during the times she reflected on her existence. She spruced up the place as she tiptoed around her constant companion or guard, Precious.

She would sit by the kitchen window reading her tattered copy of *Jane Eyre*. Why had her life been so difficult? Charlotte thought of herself as another Jane Eyre, suffering in silence as she permitted herself to be bullied and abused by those around her.

"Am I crazy, Precious? What sane person would stay in this marriage? I must be nuts, I'm asking a cat," Charlotte laughed. "Maybe in time Mason will soften," Charlotte smiled as she stroked the fur of her arch enemy.

Time did not soften Mason's mean streak for he derived pleasure in taunting Charlotte. His laughter caused a physical aching inside Charlotte. Resenting her confinement, Charlotte knew that now was the time to approach Mason about a job.

Until the day of her release she would continue to make improvements in the house. Charlotte made new curtains for the kitchen windows, and put a fresh coat of paint on the dinette set. The Burns' had no money to paint the walls so she used a small amount of her own.

Mrs. Burns had screamed bloody murder when she found the receipts for the Clorox and a quart of paint.

"My poor sonny works his fingers to the bones, and here you are squandering what's his on useless frills."

"Nola, the money I used is mine," Charlotte snapped.

"Now that you are married to my son all of your personal effects belong to him. You must defer to Mason about any financial decisions," Nola replied as she appeared to soften her tone. Charlotte's reward for wasting money, fixing up the kitchen was another slap across the face from her loving bridegroom.

Charlotte was miserable in her isolation. All of her family and friends were hundreds of miles away. She was away from all that was familiar to her. At first she tried to break through the strange barriers to make friends with her husband and his mother, but they rebuffed her every effort. Charlotte would have to make her own life. Someday, Charlotte dreamed, she would have a baby and her baby would be her world.

Charlotte sipped the warm tea as the sun shone brightly through the window. She could hear them moving around upstairs. She had better put down her book and prepare their breakfast.

"Charlotte, where the hell are you?" Mason bellowed.

"I'm in the kitchen," Charlotte replied from the bottom of the stairs as she waited for an angry reprimand. "What do you want to eat this morning? It's cold outside, oatmeal would be good. What do you think?"

"You know all I have for breakfast is a cup of your damn coffee. Get your ass up here, quick," he replied as he ignored her discussion of breakfast.

Charlotte walked quietly into the bedroom carrying a hot cup of coffee.

"It better be coffee, not that fancy tea you insist on drinking. Put that cup down you know what I want. Strip bitch."

"Mason, please, you'll be late for work."

"What makes you think I care about work. I might call in sick. You've been avoiding me too much lately."

"When have I avoided you. We made love three times last night."

"Sure we did. And we've done it enough for your belly to be swelling?" He looked at her strangely. "You aren't pulling a fast one on me, are you?" Mason jerked her against his chest.

"Mason, please you are hurting me."

"Answer me, are you using anything not to get pregnant?" His eyes flashing angrily. "I have no money. I'm not permitted out of the house. How could I have gotten any birth control protection?"

"You'd better not be hiding anymore money," Mason bellowed.

"I'm not! You took it all."

"You better not be lying to me, girl."

Charlotte tried to pull away, but he pushed his hands inside her panties and began to stroke her thighs.

"Drop the drawers, bitch. I need a woman."

"Why haven't you visited Janie Sue?" she replied without thinking.

"I have been, you fool. I'm still man enough to service at least two ladies. Come on don't make me mad."

"I hear you two in there," yelled Nola, as she banged on her wall. "Charlotte, leave my boy alone. Let him get some rest. He's got to be as tired as I am. You kept me up most of the night with those bed springs squeaking."

"Shut up, ma. I'm busy," Mason rammed his member into Charlotte's poor weary body.

After he was finished with his wife, he slapped her buttocks. He lay on his side resting from this morning's exercise, as he loved to call it. "Get my breakfast, bitch. Fix me some eggs, not your gooey oatmeal."

Charlotte's face revealed none of her disgust as she pulled away from him. Deep down inside she cursed herself for her weakness for staying with Mason as she suffered every indignity. As usual Mason was wrapped up in his own feelings, his own needs. Mason Burns gave no thought to what he put his wife through, showing no concern for any pain he caused.

"Remember breakfast. Hurry, you don't want be late to work," Charlotte quickly slipped into her clothes and dashed down the stairs.

Charlotte was frying eggs and bacon when Mason and Nola came staggering down the stairs. Fresh toast popped out of the toaster as Nola screamed, "Butter that toast before it gets cold, Charlotte, stop dawdling. When you finish the dishes, start the laundry. The rain must be coming, my rheumatism is acting up. I'll stay in bed until you've get my lunch ready. See you this afternoon sonny."

Nola Burns whined as she picked up her toast and coffee and climbed the stairs slowly dragging her right leg. Charlotte thought, "she's faking. Her leg was fine when she charged up to the table."

"Remember what I told you. When you are outside hanging the laundry, stay away from those people next door." Mason reminded Charlotte with a menacing look. "Scram Precious, you stupid cat. This is my chair, not yours." Mason snapped.

"You've never told me Mason, what's wrong with the people?" Charlotte responded, raising her brow in confusion. "They appeared pleasant enough. But, since you have lived near them for years, you obviously know more about them. My dear, please don't get excited, you know that I always abide by your wishes."

"Wishes! Wishes! I've warned you before. They're peculiar, that's enough said. I won't have strangers mixing into my business. Do you understand me woman?"

Charlotte's short time in the Burns' home had taught her to quickly retreat within her own private world when he was acting totally irrational.

"You will never, and I mean never, go near those people. Do you hear me, Charlotte."

"Yes dear, of course, anything you say." Charlotte turned to her stack of dirty dishes not wishing to trigger his wrath.

She had received little welcome in her husband's home, so she saw little reason to obey unreasonable demands. Perhaps she might have listened to him had he not shown his penchant for violence so early in marriage.

Charlotte's father had been a gentle, quiet educated man. He had taught her the art of discovery as he probed her mind, stimulating it with stories of adventure and romantic dreams. Charlotte had been devoted to her father and she was lonely without him.

Charlotte prayed that one day with patience and kindness she could change the atmosphere of the Burns' house. For now, she was alone among people of different customs, values and virtually penniless. She was unprepared to deal with the reality of her situation. Mason and his mother had made her a servant, isolated from those around her who could give her friendship. It had been discussed on several occasions, but Mason had steadfastly refused to allow Charlotte out of the house long enough to secure employment. She desperately needed to obtain a job or she would surely go mad, mad as her mother-in-law, Nola.

Charlotte enjoyed the solitude of the late morning as she washed the dishes, then she did the laundry. There were few dirty clothes for she tried to run a load each day.

This morning she was feeling unusually tired, occasionally sensing perspiration dotting her forehead. Charlotte attempted to overlook this minor problem, which might be a sign of unwellness. Charlotte ignored the giddiness as she enjoyed the fresh air.

Charlotte busily hung out the morning wash. She was eager for them to dry before the afternoon rains. She continued to feel unusually tired even after a full nights sleep. She would sneak in a nap after she finished hanging out the laundry, she thought, but suddenly, her ears began to ring. She felt as if the surroundings were beginning to move around her. A wave of dizziness threatened nausea. Her peripheral vision narrowed to just what was in front of her and then even that faded into blackness.

Charlotte's eyes flickered in confusion. Where am I? she attempted to raise herself from the supine position, but a gentle voice said, "Careful, not too fast."

Charlotte saw the face of a strange woman.

"Wha.., what happened? Where am I? How did I get here?" Charlotte asked while she was looking about nervously.

"My dear, you fainted. My brother saw you lying on the ground and attempted to draw the attention of someone in the house. Since no one answered, we brought you to our place."

"Thank you," Charlotte whispered.

"Sure sweetie," replied the older woman. "Here, try a small sip of water. I'm Shelley Branson, your neighbor."

Charlotte bolted straight up. Here I am in the house of the forbidden ones. Mason's words rang in her ears. "I order you. Never speak to those perverts." As usual, he had done so in his godlike manner. Mason never bothered to explain his reasons.

Shelley Branson appears to be concerned about my health. She looks fairly normal. She has no cloven hooves or a forked tail. And, as for now, I haven't been attacked by some ferocious creature skulking around in the closet, Charlotte thought as she smiled lying back on the pillows, assisted by her neighbor.

"Thank you for your assistance. I can't imagine what's wrong with me. I must return home. Thanks again."

"There's no hurry, just rest for now. I sent my brother Tom over to your place to tell your family where you are and about your fainting," Shelley told her softly.

Charlotte scrambled out of the bed. "That wasn't necessary, I'm fine now. I'd better get back and start dinner. My mother-in-law has been under the weather and mustn't be left alone.   Bye."

   She looked quickly about noticing the beautifully decorated room and the wonderful aroma emitted by an incense candle burning on a table near the window. The Branson house didn't have the feel of a place where untouchables resided.

   Charlotte had reached the back door when a small hand touched her shoulder. Looking back she heard her neighbor say, "Before you leave won't you tell me your name. You are Mr. Burns' new bride, aren't you? You were so confused when you came around you may not remember, but my name is Shelley Branson. I live here with my brother, Tom.

   "I'm sorry, my mother-in-law isn't feeling well today and I must check on her. My name is Charlotte Hamby," Charlotte laughed as she nervously darted for the door, "Charlotte Burns, yes, I'm Mason Burns's bride. Nice to meet you," she extended her hand to this stranger. Charlotte rushed through the screen door bumping into a man.

   "This character you just bumped into is Charles Allgood, our boarder. When you have some free time, please drop by for tea."

   Shelley Branson waved as Charlotte raced down the path joining the two houses.

   Through the kitchen window Shelley heard fragments of conversation. She felt a sickening disgust as the insults of an ignorant drunk floated through her window on the evening's breeze.

   "Charlotte, you slut, I couldn't believe that after we had cautioned you so often that you were actually in those people's house," screamed Nola Burns. "You just wait until I tell Mason. That man, that pervert knocked on my door and told me you were next door inside their house," she was pointing an ugly finger in Charlotte's face.

   "I'm sorry, but lower your voice, Miss Branson can hear you," Charlotte wanted to add, tell Mason, who cares. But as usual, Charlotte was too cowed to respond. Finally, regaining her voice, "I was ill and the Bransons were kind and took me into their house for some cool water. That was all."

   "Yeah, likely story. I thought Mason told you to stay away from trash like that. Besides weren't you bragging about being from healthy Yankee stock. All you do is lay about all day, what's made you so sickly that you've taken to fainting? Don't tell me you're pregnant?"

"I don't know. I haven't had a period since our marriage," Charlotte replied.

"Oh my God!" Nola Burns moaned as she dramatically threw her hands over her face. "My baby boy, being forced to accept damaged goods into my family and now you're trying to palm off somebody else's bastard off on me. I knew you were too good to be true."

"Please, Mrs. Burns, don't talk in such a way."

"You tricked my boy. You saw he was easy prey. You knew he'd always been good to his sick old mother and you trapped him to make yours and your bastard's lives easier," Nola moaned in self-pity. Mason came through the back door.

"You two arguing again." He went to the refrigerator for a beer.

Ignoring Mason's remark, Nola continued, "my boy never would have married you, if he had known you were pregnant." Charlotte stared at her mother-in-law in disbelief. "We got a pig in the poke, a pregnant pig in the poke. We've been tricked," Nola continued her tirade.

"That is not true," Charlotte protested fiercely. "Why would I treat you so cruelly? Why do you think the worst of me? I've never done anything but try to make your son happy."

Nola placed her knitting in her bag as she motioned for Mason to follow her from the kitchen, "Sonny, I think Charlotte's pregnant. If so, do you think it's yours?"

"Hush, Mama. My wife is such an iceberg, if she's pregnant, it's mine," Mason stated proudly.

"Ma says you've been sick today. Fainted did you? Do you think you might be pregnant?" Mason grinned from ear to ear, quite pleased with himself. "Mason, I haven't thought it possible so soon. I should see a doctor. Don't you agree?" Charlotte asked.

"It's sooner than I expected, but since I never used any protection, it was bound to happen. I've been expecting you to get caught." Mason smiled in such an arrogant manner.

Why do men get so puffed up? They've never done anything important. They simply get their wives pregnant. That's easier than falling off a log.

"Sonny, if she is pregnant, maybe you ought to see she gets rid of it. Better make sure it's yours."

"Shut up ma. I've told you before, if she is, it's mine."

"But how can she get a job. We need her paycheck."

Finally including Charlotte into the conversation, "Don't pay my ma no mind, sweetie. We'll see the doctor tomorrow."

"If you two go to the doctor, make him tell you just how far gone she is. You've got to make sure the baby's yours. We won't support her bastard," Nola said accusingly.

"I'll handle my wife, ma. Don't worry your little head. I told Charlotte what I'd do if she tried anything funny."

"Did she tell you that she was hanging around with those queers next door?"

"What is Ma talking about, Charlotte? I ordered you not to set foot on their property. Have you forgotten what disobedience of my laws will bring?"

"No Mason, I have forgotten nothing. Your mother didn't bother to explain that I passed out in the back yard. When Shelley and her brother attempted unsuccessfully to get your mother's attention, they took me to their house. They were really quite sweet."

"Who the hell is Shelley?" Mason screamed.

"Shelley and Tom Branson are our next door neighbors. I never met Tom. He must have been the one I ran past in the yard. I met a boarder, Mr. Charles Allgood. Shelley sat with me until I regained consciousness. She is very nice," Charlotte winced as she tried to explain to her irate husband.

"Nice, those kind of people, you are calling nice?" Mason continued his tirade. "Charlotte, those people are queers. Queers, do you hear me? Did your mother teach you nothing?"

"Mason", Charlotte whispered, "what are queers?"

"Queers are the worst kind of trash. weirdos..weirdos."

"What kind of weirdos. What makes them weird?"

"They are women that prefer women, sexually, understand. I've never known anybody so dumb. Didn't your mother warn you to be careful of those kind of people? They try to force themselves on stupid people like you. They attack women, try to turn them into weirdos," Mason lectured.

"What kind of attacks, Mason? What do they do to women?" the confused Charlotte asked.

"I don't know exactly what they do, but they cast spells on women and do unspeakable things to them. Worst of all, they turn women against men. Can you imagine, giving up men?"

Charlotte smiled. That was an interesting question. She had enjoyed her first twenty-seven years without a man to boss her or bother her. It certainly was an interesting thought.

"Let's stop all of this talk about those queer neighbors of ours. Ma, call Dr. Manley. I'm taking Charlotte to see him as soon as we can get appointment."

Nola had attempted to keep herself out of the way. Mason was in such a foul mood. She had returned to her knitting but quickly put it down as she responded to her son's orders.

"Good grief," Mason thought. "She's still working on that same silly sweater. She was working on it when dad was alive." Mason laughed as he watched his mother as she replaced her knitting into its bag and waddled toward the phone. "Ma, when are you finishing that piece of junk? I've never known you to finish anything."

Nola joined Mason in the kitchen after calling Dr. Manley's office this evening.

"Sonny, Dr. Manley said we should let poor, helpless Charlotte rest while he saw his last three patients, and then bring her to his office. He gave me impression that we've probably been working her too hard," Nola growled.

"Nonsense ma, you're imagining things. And as for Charlotte, she's a strong girl. She's said so herself, plenty of times. Now Charlotte, go upstairs and take a nap until we're ready to go," Mason crooned, insincerity dripping from his lips.

"Before I go upstairs, may we talk. I've been thinking that with another mouth to feed that now would be time for me to get an outside job. Don't you think?" Charlotte approached the subject again.

"Sonny, if Charlotte is pregnant will she be able to take care of the house and hold down a job?" Nola asked so innocently that butter wouldn't melt in her mouth.

"Oh, Mrs. Burns, I can handle them both."

"Rest, my dear wife. If you are okay, and if the doctor gives you a clean bill of health, tomorrow, you can look around for a job. But remember, stay away from those strange people," Mason said as he smiled his most frightening crocodile smile.

"I'll rest in a few minutes. Think I'll take a stroll in the yard, and get some fresh air," Charlotte whispered.

Mason replied in a sarcastic manner, "Okay, but make your stroll, short."

Charlotte enjoyed the afternoon breeze. The buzz of the bees, birds chirping. She would do anything to get out of that house. She spotted Shelley Branson resting on her back steps.

"Hello Shelley, may I join you? I wanted to thank you for your assistance. I've never fainted before in all my life."

"Think nothing of it. I'd of done it for anyone, well almost anyone," Shelley responded as her head nodded in the direction of the Burns house.

"Well I am appreciative, no matter what they think."

"Where are my manners? Charlotte, please sit down. I'm sorry. Here you are a brand new bride and I'm criticizing your new family."

"That's all right, Shelley. I knew little of Mason, we met and married in two weeks. I had never met his mother. Mrs. Burns was a childhood friend of my mother. This marriage was arranged. My mother thought he was my best hope, and Mason seemed a sympathetic person. So here I am, miles away from my home in Baltimore, with no friends, and possibly pregnant," Charlotte blurted out as she surprised herself revealing so much to a complete stranger.

"It can't be as bad as that," Shelley stated as she forced a smile.

"I am a long way from home. I am just tired, and I haven't been feeling myself. Everything will work out. It's just that I have had little outside contact since my marriage," Charlotte laughed. "You have no idea how I have longed for the sound of another's' voice. I sincerely want you to know how I appreciate kindness."

"You mean you are not afraid of contamination. Yes, I've heard your husband on the subject of weirdos. It's dangerous talking to the evil ones. We might soil your reputation."

There was something sad about this older woman for she appeared to be accustomed to rejection. Charlotte felt Shelley Branson could be a good friend and ally.

"I was taught by my papa to treat others the way I'd wish to be treated. I attempt to like others until they prove that I am wrong about their character."

Shelley blinked with surprise, "Would you care to come in for a cup of tea?"

"No, thanks," Charlotte watched Shelley's expression change, so she added quickly, "later, I promise to come for a long visit. I've a doctor's appointment in a short while, so I must run along."

"You're alright, aren't you? Or am I being too nosey?" Shelley smiled down at Charlotte.

"No, As I said earlier, I afraid I might be pregnant. It's much too soon, but if I am..." Charlotte paused, "I'll have somebody to love."

"Good luck, see you later," Shelley called, as she watched the younger woman slowly returned to her home.

Shelley returned to her cheerful kitchen to find Tom and Charles enjoying mugs of tea. "That poor thing," she muttered to herself. I hope she's not pregnant. A baby is the last thing she needs."

"Who are you talking to? The walls, or the two of us?" Tom said.

Shelley glanced up, "Tom, that girl next door, her mother married her off to a man she hardly knew. She's miserable. You can see it in her eyes."

"You can't rescue the world, Shelley," Charles responded.

"I can't rescue the world, but it is my prayer that that child, Charlotte Burns, isn't pregnant," Shelley cast a worried look out of her kitchen window. Shelley felt a strange sense of protectiveness for this young stranger.

It was six o'clock when Nola, Mason, and the reluctant Charlotte arrived at the doctor's office. Charlotte was pale and feeling nauseous.

"Doc, I'd like for you to meet my wife, Charlotte Burns," Mason said.

Charlotte stared at the blurred faces as her breath became an unsteady wheeze. She squeezed her eyes closed as the outdated calender on the dingy office wall appeared to move.

Dr. Manley took Charlotte's hand saying, "Charlotte Burns, how do you do? You are much too pale. Mason, " Dr. Manley turned, "I can tell you without examining your wife that she isn't getting enough rest, " He stated with concern as he continued to hold Charlotte's trembling fingers.

"How do you do, Doctor?" Charlotte replied.

"Pleased to meet you ma'am," he answered in the slowest, honey-dripping southern drawl she'd ever heard.

Dr. Manley was a thin grey-haired man that smiled through the horn-rimmed glasses. He reached inside his vest pocket, retrieving a watch as he proceeded to check his new patient's pulse.

Charlotte permitted the doctor to lead her into his examining room, where she disrobed. She had expected to fall in love for life, but here she was married a couple of months to a monster. Charlotte wanted children, but she was not sure by Mason. What would she do if she were pregnant? Could she run away?

She laid on the examination table praying she was barren, but she was afraid there was a tiny bud of life growing inside her body. She hoped for a girl.

Mason's lips were tightened white with anger as the two walked out to join him.

"What's the verdict, doc? I'm a father, right? What's happening? You two are chattering like old friends," Mason complained.

"Make yourself comfortable in my office while I check some test results. It will take a few minutes before I'll know if you are gonna be a papa. Sit tight, you two."

Charlotte's silence wasn't missed on Dr. Manley. Mason paced the room waiting the verdict. His mother was still, but she too was nervously waiting for the announcement.

"You'd better be pregnant. I'll not have my mama think I'm

shooting blanks," Mason snapped at the silent Charlotte.

Dr. Manley returned to his desk continuing to study the results that could change Charlotte's life forever. He looked up from the mass of papers.

"Sorry Mason, Mrs. Burns. I have the lab tests before me. I had them run a second time. My dear, I had cautioned you not to get your hopes up this soon. You are not having a baby."

Dr. Manley turned as he smiled in a fatherly fashion to the agitated Mason. "My boy, what's the rush. You two just married. There's plenty of time. There is no reason to assume there is a problem."

Mason did not respond as he glared angrily into the kind eyes of his doctor.

Dr. Manley continued, "Mason, don't get yourself into such a state. These things happen."

"What do you mean there's no kid? I do her every night. She hadn't had her period since our marriage. My mama will think I'm not a man?" Mason responded indignantly.

"I'm sure you've done your homework, Mason my boy," replied the compassionate physician. "You're a virile man, I'm sure."

"What's wrong, why's she not pregnant?" complained Mason.

"Calm yourself, my boy. Your wife is sensitive. When you've been uprooted from everything that is familiar to you, and then abruptly deposited into another culture, what do you expect? You understand jet lag, don't you? Well Charlotte is suffering from a short of jet lag, but it's a culture shock."

"Culture shock! What does she think is wrong with people from Charleston anyway?" Mason growled.

"May I suggest that you encourage her to make friends. Get a job. Outside activities would be good for her. But, it is most important that she stop worrying. A baby will appear when you least expect it. Good luck, you two," the doctor said as he escorted the Burns family to the door.

"According to the doctor it's that simple. If she gets a job and makes friends, then I'll have a baby. Nuttiest notion I've ever heard, but I'm game. Thanks, Doc. Come on Charlotte, lets head home,"

Mason guided her out of the door.

"Thank you, Doctor," was all Charlotte could bring herself to say.

"Can the silly nonsense. I'm taking you home and screwing your little brains out. I've got great juices and I'm going to use them on you. I'll become a father or you'll be sorry bitch," Mason said, ignoring his startled wife.

Charlotte, head downcast remained subdued as Mason dragged her to the family car. She sat motionless as she watched the gentle current of the Cooper River as it guided a large ship towards the sea.

Charlotte walked into the Burns' house in abject misery knowing her husband meant every word he said that he intended to see to it that she becomes pregnant.

The moment their bedroom door closed, Mason was all over Charlotte. She began to scream as he tore the sweater off her trembling body. Charlotte was embarrassed knowing that Nola could hear her screams.

Sexually drained, Mason fell asleep.

Charlotte was so horrified with another night of mistreatment that she crawled into the bathroom and vomited up the entire contents of her stomach. Next, she stood in the shower attempting to scrub his scent and feel from her body.

Returning to her bed, Charlotte finally drifted off to sleep.

She rose earlier than usual for Charlotte didn't intend to give them any excuse to force her to stay at home. Ten o'clock finally arrived and an excited girl was ready to embark on her latest adventure, job-hunting.

"Don't be disappointed if no one hires you today. Remember you're from the Maryland and our people are suspicious of strangers. Thought I'd see you off. You run along, let my Sonny sleep, he had a late night," Nola sneered.

Disgusted with Nola's incessant whining Charlotte slammed the backdoor as she left, "You're from another part of the country. Our people won't hire you. Pooh, A good worker will be hired no matter where they are from," mocked Charlotte as she ignored Nola's glare.

Charlotte looked forward to a quiet, peaceful afternoon, seeking employment, hopefully making new friends.

"Hello, again."

Charlotte looked around to see Shelley Branson walking a few steps behind her.

"Oh hello, Miss Branson," Charlotte smiled brightly.

"How are you feeling, this morning?" asked Shelley.

"I'm much better, thank you." Getting out of the house helps, was what she almost said.   "After yesterday, that fainting spell and everything. You were terribly pale, Shelley asked in a motherly manner. "Don't you think you should wait about shopping?"

"I'll assure you that I am much better. Just a touch of jet lag, you might say," Charlotte smiled. "I'm out job hunting."

Charlotte noticed for the first time that Shelley Branson was a small woman, with large brown eyes, about 40 or 45 with masses of dark brown hair with sprinkles of grey. Curls blew about in the wind obscuring her vision.

"Oh someday, I threaten I'll cut this mess. In my business, all it does is get in the way," Shelley yanked at her flowing tresses.

"Your business, what do you do?" Charlotte inquired.

"I work for a local fashion shop, Madame Lorraine's. Do you sew? You say you're looking for a job," Shelley remarked.

"I sew very little," Charlotte frowned as she stepped back suddenly.

"What's the matter, sweetie. Afraid to work near me? That husband of yours warn you off?" Shelley laughed.

"Well, he does have his opinions, I've mine. As for sewing, I never learned much, but I could help you with your hair. My total career experience is working in bookstores," Charlotte frowned.

"Oh I'm sorry Charlotte. I shouldn't embarrass you in such a manner. You love Mason Burns and you're a brand new bride. Tom says I open mouth before engaging my brain. As for this stringy head of hair, please help," Shelley laughed as she forgot all about Charlotte's crude husband.

"How can you call that beautiful mane, stringy? It is beautiful. And please forget what Mason thinks, forget it. I'd love for you to introduce me to your boss. Thanks, but I'm not sure what I can do in a fashion shop, sales, maybe."

"Come on and never fear. I don't bite, not at our first meeting," Shelley's laughter was contagious

"Maybe I should be concerned, it's our second meeting. I can't believe I said that." Charlotte giggled as she placed her hand over her mouth. "Come on, Charlotte Burns, I'll take you to see Madame Lorraine," Shelley smiled happily as she took the younger woman's arm.

Madame Lorraine's shop was in the middle of Market Street. The back work room was piled with all types of fabric and colors. Charlotte followed Shelley behind rows of filing cabinets and desks. The area wasn't particularly neat, Charlotte thought.

"Messy, huh," Shelley read her mind. "But wait until you see Madame Lorraine's line of clothes. They're fantastic," Shelley said enthusiastically.

"Hi, sweetie," called a voice from behind a bolt of fabric.

"I've brought someone to meet you." Shelley stated.

"Our neighbor, Mrs. Burns, I see. How are you feeling, my dear?" Charles Allgood asked.

"I'm fine, thank you," replied a confused Charlotte.

"Nice to see you again. I'm Charles Allgood, Tom Branson's, uh, renter. I came home just after you took that dreadful spill."

"Oh, I see. Nice to see you again," the startled Charlotte shook Charles's hand, and looked around the room. "When do I meet Madame Lorraine."

"You just did, minx. Well half of her," Shelley squealed.

"I must have missed something," Charlotte replied amid the laughter.

"Please ignore our apparent rudeness, my dear. You are new in town, and there is no reason you would understand," Charles Allgood stated. "I'm Madame Lorraine, or half of her. Shelley's brother Tom is the other half."

"Really!" Charlotte replied.

"That's right," Charles smiled. "Women loved being clothed by women, not men. Tom and I met in school, and we devised the plan to become Madame Lorraine." "Charles, you and Tom could always use another expert hand. Why not hire Charlotte?" Shelley said in a cajoling manner.

"Mrs. Burns, have you ever worked in the rag trade?"

"I'm not sure, what is the rag trade? And please call me Charlotte, and may I call you Charles?" Charlotte asked.

"At least she's honest about her training. And yes, Charlotte, please call me Charles," he replied gently squeezing her hand.

"Give her a chance. She has a lot on the ball, and I want to help get her out of that house," Shelley stated firmly.

"Okay, take her upstairs and introduce her to the others. We'll give her a trial period and see where it goes." Charles walked away as he turned to work.

Mason and his mother would have strokes that Charlotte had secured a job, but she would be able to spend her days in quiet learning, and maybe the evenings of rough talk and violence would be the more bearable.

Madame Lorraine's workrooms were on the second floor, above the salon. The well lit workroom was where the patterns were cut and fitted and the connecting door led to the sewing area. Rows of machines hummed in the largest room.

"This is our world during the daytime," Shelley stated. "During the night we go our separate ways. Let me introduce you to our fellow workers. Miss Amy Brackett, Miss Harriet Kennedy, may I present to you our latest recruit, Mrs. Charlotte Burns. She will be joining us tomorrow."

"Hello, I'm so thrilled to be working with you," Charlotte smiled happily. "I hope I can learn quickly."   "Don't worry sweetie, if I can learn, you can learn. Have you met Madame Lorraine, yet?" asked Amy Brackett.

"Hush, Amy. It's not polite to bite the hand that feeds you. Back to work ladies. See you tomorrow," said Harriet Kennedy, returning to her table.

Charlotte's eyes were large, filled with admiration for the two women as their slender fingers moved over the patterns cutting and gathering the dress materials on the big table in the workroom.

"Shelley, watch those scissors and needles fly. I could never do that," Charlotte gasped.

"Sure you can. Anyone, if taught properly can learn to work in the garment industry. Just do as you are told and you'll catch on fast."

"I hope so," Charlotte laughed.

Charlotte waltzed into the Burns house. "I'm pleased to announce that I have obtained a position working four days a week at Madame Lorraine's Shoppe, an exclusive women's boutique. I am going to be a trainee, but I'm being paid to learn."

"What you? A job your first time out? I can't believe it. Did you fuck somebody already, or is it just a promise?"

"Must you always be disgusting, Mrs. Burns? You'll believe I'm employed when I bring in my first pay check," Charlotte stated as she attempted to ignore Nola's disparaging words.

"Mama, knock it off. She's just trying to help." Charlotte could not believe what she was hearing. Mason was actually defending her. "Sweetie, what if you get pregnant?"

"We'll work it out if I do. I told them about the possibility, and they seemed unconcerned," Charlotte replied.

Charlotte worked hard each day, and came home to her second job, cooking and maintaining her husband and Nola. After the dishes were done, Charlotte retired for the evening. She stood combing her hair glancing thoughtfully out the window towards Shelley's house when Mason barked in a voice which split the air like a bolt of summer lightning.

"Come back here. I cannot talk to the back of your head."

She turned immediately, and walked back to the bed. He gestured for her to join him, patting the spot where she was to sit. Charlotte couldn't force herself to make eye contact with her husband, instead she looked over his shoulder and out of the window, thinking of a saner life.

"Get out of that gown. You know how I like you, naked. Strip bitch, now," Mason commanded. "Baby, I'm sorry I sound so rough on you sometimes, but I want you so bad. I love you, sugar," Charlotte stared in disbelief as Mason's tone changed.

"Mason, what do you want of me?" she asked.

"I must have a son, now," Mason declared.

She paused for a moment, searching his face for some sign of love, but she saw none. Charlotte fought back the tears as she closed her eyes bracing herself for the inevitable. She clenched her teeth so Nola would not hear her cries.

Mason moaned as his hand cupped Charlotte's milky white breast as his tongue tickled and enticed her rosy nipple. He wanted a eager woman tonight, but all he got was an unresponsive wife.

Suddenly his fingertips traced the valleys and peaks of her silken body. He slid his hands up his wife's tiny back to pull her closer. Charlotte was startled by her reaction to his caresses.

Mason moved his fingers to awaken the dormant juices that lay hidden in Charlotte's deepest recesses. She felt a moistening within her triangle. His deep laughter shocked her. Who was the man lying above her? He certainly was not the crazed man she married.

Mason lowered his head capturing her mouth. He penetrated her dark cavern with his tongue. Charlotte's mind and body were being seduced by a masterful lover. Their bodies spoke of their urgent need.

Charlotte moved against Mason's rigid manhood whispering inaudible tones of desire. Charlotte was drawn into a spinning whirlpool of emotion. She had never known such primeval passion.

Mason's body captured her wet velvet triangle, sliding slowly, and then pushing, his hard hot manhood into her body. He grasped her hips and pushed himself deeper inside Charlotte as she expelled a loud gasp and arched herself against him to receive his seed.

Her legs were wrapped tightly around his perspiring, writhing body. Mason abruptly jerked away, rolled off the bed as he looked down at his love drugged wife.

"Well shit! You are human after all," Mason laughed as Charlotte stared through love sotted eyes.

"What? What did you say?" Charlotte replied, as she drew up the covers concealing her nakedness.

"Janie Sue told me that if I was to get a baby out of an icicle like you, I'd have to make you do some major thawing out. Worked, didn't it?" Mason chortled as he dressed to leave.

Charlotte wept into her pillow until she fell asleep. She had never felt such revulsion. Mason Burns were cruel and evil through and through.

Charlotte's only pleasure would be working with Shelley and Charles at Madame Lorraine's. She dreaded the end of the day, and being forced to return a house filled with physical violence and humiliating verbal assaults.

Chapter 8

Charlotte strolled down Market Street as she enjoyed a peaceful afternoon. The temperature must be at least one hundred, and the humidity sent streams of moisture cascading into her bra. Charlotte was sure she would die of heat prostration.

"Charlotte, must you always race home each afternoon?" Shelley approached her friend and co-worker.

"I must do the laundry before Nola and Mason return home," Charlotte frowned at the thought.

"Where is that loving family of yours?"

"They are spending the day with a distance cousin of theirs. They won't be back until midnight."

"Come on, no need for you to mope around that old house. Let's get a bite of supper, and then we'll think of something."

"Oh, I don't know," Charlotte said with a tinge of sorrow.

"You've been working like a slave for months now. I'll bet you haven't had time to enjoy the sights," Shelley challenged.

"No, I've been quite busy, settling in. You understand what it's like, everything is so new."

Yes, Shelley understood more than Charlotte imagined. She had seen those bruises that her young friend had unsuccessfully attempted to hide.

"We'll get a bite to eat, and then we'll tour the city. I've got a friend in the business. Think of it, you can tour with a group of sweaty strangers or you can rent my friend's carriage for a small amount and have a private tour."

"Okay, okay, you've sold me. Let's go."

Strolling along Church Street, Shelley and Charlotte enjoyed the sounds of Irish Music emanating from Tommy Condon's.

The two women ordered Shepard's pie, and shared a big tasty flowering onion.   "We'll have a little bit of everything. It has taken me such a long time to drag you here. I promise you'll be wild about the she-crab stew if you add a touch of brandy."

"I haven't been out in months so I am at your mercy," Charlotte stated.

"Your marriage isn't what you expected. Is it?" Shelley stated firmly.

"It is difficult when you wake up married a stranger."

"What ever made you marry Mason Burns? You are so attractive. You could have had the pick of the crop in Maryland," Shelley exploded.

Charlotte watched as Shelley's eyes grew black with anger as she listened somberly to the terrifying account of Charlotte's life.

She held Charlotte's hand tightly fearing she might bolt and run for the door. Depraved men had attempted to crush Charlotte by the worst type of attack.

Charlotte was beginning to feel the slightest bud of emotion growing inside her. She had not known such protection since her father. Charlotte looked away from her young friend as she trembled. She realized the delicious attraction she felt.

"I have never heard anything so degrading. Mason doesn't treat you any better," Shelley broke the silence as she tenderly brushed a loose curl out of Charlotte's face.

"Life was kinder when was alive, sometimes I wish I could have died with him," Charlotte whispered.

"Nonsense, you're with people that love you."

"I'm not sure I know the meaning of love, anymore. I feel lost."

"I'm the best lost lamb finder in town. Tom accuses me of suffering from what he calls the stray cat syndrome," Shelley laughed.

"I've been comfortable with you since we first met," Charlotte smiled.

"Charlotte, if you keep looking at me with such trust, I might embarrass the both of us," Shelley stopped. "What?" Charlotte looked surprised, as her face began to darken.

"Don't worry. I don't force myself on disinterested persons. I prefer women, but I'm content for us to remain friends. For the moment."

"I'm aware that I appear unworldly, I'm not dumb."

"Okay friend, let's go. Have you ever ridden in a carriage, oh worldly one?" Shelley laughed.

"Of course," Charlotte joined in the merriment. "We do have carriages in Maryland."

"Not quite as many as Charleston. The city is in the tourist business. There are more carriage businesses per square foot than anywhere else."

"Well what do you expect? You live in a town where so much of the past has been preserved."

"I know, but constantly stepping over all of the tourists gets to be an aggravation. Charles says not to complain. Tourists bring in all of that nice green stuff that keeps us going," Shelley laughed as she took Charlotte's hand. "You now live in the ancestor capital of the world, sweetie."

They walked down the street swinging their hands like a pair of giddy school kids.

A brisk five minute walk found Charlotte and Shelley facing a rickety black carriage with a red chestnut horse. Charlotte watched quietly as Shelley walked into the arms of the young man who had been leaning against a small shade tree.

"Matt, this is my friend Charlotte Burns," Shelley introduced the young man to Charlotte.

"Matt, I was pleased to find you were available this evening."

"My lady," Matt replied as he bowed at the waist. "I am always available to you. Charlotte, any friend of Shelley's is a friend of mine." Matt took her hand.

"Nice to meet you Matt."

"Are you ladies ready to see the sights?" Matt asked.

"We most certainly are," Shelley replied. "This, my gentle steed is Rusty. The most gentle horse in the town."

"Hello, Rusty," Charlotte said, stroking Rusty's velvety nose. "You are a real beauty." The horse neighed in response to her tender attention.

"Enough with the fondling of my great steed. Shelley, you and Charlotte climb into this magnificent surrey and off we'll be off." Matt flicked the reins as Rusty pranced toward Bay Street.

"Now that I have enticed you out of the house, the next treat will be the beach," Shelley stated.

"We'll see. Let's just take one day at a time." Charlotte smiled.

"The Market Street area was nine and a half feet under water during Hurricane Hugo. It was one of the most frightening time of my life. It was hell trying to get my Rusty boy out of the city safely," Matt stated.

"I'm happy to know Rusty was rescued from the storm," Charlotte crooned.

Rusty, neighed happily, responding to the gentle sound of her voice.

"Cut it out, Charlotte. Some people think animals are dumb. Well this old horse of mine is as bright as a penny. He knows you're talking about him, and he'll be impossible to live with after your attention," Matt laughed.

"Now, you just ignore that old grouch, Rusty," Charlotte crooned, as Rusty began to strut with the pride of a young stallion.

"Charlotte, can you see the bolts in the houses?" Matt asked. "They are earthquake bolts installed after the big earthquake of 1886. It tightens the frames on the houses so they will be safer to live in. Somebody just forgot to waterproof them," Matt laughed.

The carriage was gently swaying as Charlotte edged forward on the seat, enjoying the scenery. "Oh, look at the colorful houses."

"This is called Rainbow Row," Matt stated. "Dorothy Leg painted her house pink to encourage her neighbors to paint theirs. They were becoming slums. Well it worked. Everybody got into the act, hence, Rainbow Row."

"The homes are beautiful. I'll bet they are gorgeous at Christmas time."

"We had more Spanish moss before Hurricane Hugo raised all of that havoc in September, 1989. We took quite a beating, but we're strong and we've bounced back. I suppose greed is the best motivator."

"Greed?" Charlotte asked.

"The city's fathers had to rebuild and paint the damaged buildings as soon as possible, for tourists won't part with their money to look at a dump. We were blown to pieces," Matt's voice was raspy as he replied.

"That's so sad."

"Don't let him sound so tough, Charlotte," Shelley joined in the conversation. "Matt was one of the brave ones that stayed behind to help in the rescue efforts. He's a real hero."

"Hush, girl. I did no more than the others. We Charlestonians have to take care of each other. On your left is the Sea Wall," Matt attempted to change the subject. "They made it wide enough so two of our southern belles could stroll together without their hoops popping up betraying their maidenly modesty."

Shelley and Charlotte squealed at the mental picture of two women in extreme distress with their hoops over their heads.

"The gardens are exquisite, Shelley."

"Yes, they are," Shelley responded, smiling warmly into her friend's face.

"The wealthy merchants trimmed their homes with roped molding, denoting wealth. One of the mansions front doors are made of solid walnut, weighing two hundred pounds each," Matt continued his lecture.

"I have enough work to do. I'm glad I don't have to dust those great big houses," Charlotte said.

She thought how difficult it must be for Mason to live so near the E. Battery with all of its obvious opulence while living a few blocks away in a area that felt like being on another planet.

"Charlotte, if you like the homes so much, several permit tours inside," Shelley said.

"Oh Shelley, that would be wonderful."

Lumbering back to the barn, Rusty was excited with the prospect of a bag of oats after a long journey.

"Thank you, Matt. Your tour was wonderful as always," Shelley kissed his cheek.

"Yes, it was a great treat," Charlotte chimed in.

"It has been mine and Rusty's profound pleasure, ladies," Matt replied.

"Night." The two women walked quietly back toward their respective homes each engrossed in their own thoughts.

Charlotte stopped short at the sight of the Burns house, her hands clasped in fists as the color was suddenly drained from her face.

"Charlotte, what is it? You're hands are cold as ice," Shelley pled.

"Oh my God, how I hate the prospect of going back into that hell hole."

Shelley pulled Charlotte to her as she impulsively placed a tender kiss upon her lips. Charlotte jumped as though she had been bit by a rattler. She swayed, and then she steadied herself with a hand on Shelley's chest.

What am I doing? thought Shelley. Don't ruin a perfectly good friendship this way, but I want more, damn it. "Sorry, sweetie. I didn't mean to do that. It's just that you looked so.." Shelley never finished her apology.

"Charlotte, that you? Where the hell have you been? Working late? We sure as hell can use the extra money," Mason Burns bellowed. "Get in here, girl, you've got work to do."

Shelley slipped away into the shadows as Charlotte, looking as old as time, trudged into the Burns house.   Shelley ran up to her room, throwing herself into her bed. "What in the world was I thinking of? Everything was going along just find. Why do I have to mess things up?" She cried to the four walls.

"Talking to yourself again, sis?" Tom asked, poking his head in her door.

"I've probably blown it with Charlotte."

"What in the world did you do so despicable, sister of mine?"

"I kissed Charlotte and she looked so, disgusted," Shelley cried..

"Did she say so?"

"No, that jerk she married bellowed at her and she ran into the house."

"Give her some quiet time tomorrow, then to her."

"Tell her what? Tell her that I've got the hots for her and scare the shit out of her. You didn't see her face. Her husband treats her bad enough, so the last thing she needs is for my desire to be added pressure. Charlotte told me she was all alone except for us, and leave it to me to let it get out of hand."

"Doesn't that tell you something? Calm down. You two can

work it out tomorrow," Tom responded, patting Shelley on the shoulder. "Get some sleep, things will look better in the morning. Sweet dreams, Shell."

The birds were chirping as the sun burst through Shelley's window heralding another bright and shiny day. She had gotten almost no sleep, dreading her first meeting with Charlotte.

"Shut up, you fool birds," Shelley shouted as she threw a pillow toward the opened window. "I've wrecked everything, so who are you to be so chipper this morning?"

"Well, my dear, waking up on the wrong side of the bed. Attacking our fine feathered friends so early in the morn. Shame, shame," Tom chided.

"Oh go soak your head, Tom. I'm in no mood for your witticism. Go away, please," Shelley moaned.

"Get any sleep?" Tom asked with concern.   "No, I didn't. Tom, what am I to do? I couldn't stand it if I drove her away. She's so important to me."

"I know," Tom stated as he reached for Shelley's hand. "Go to work, and talk honestly to Charlotte. She may understand your feelings better than you suspect. I've seen her watching you when you weren't aware."

"Watching me, when?" Shelley face filled with doubt.

"Take my word. Charlotte is wrestling with feelings that she might not quite understand."

"Okay, I'll give it a try not to fall apart. I have to face her, talk to her."

Shelley, exhausted from sleep's brevity, dressed slowly for work. The last thing she wanted was conversation with Charlotte. She wished only to erase the unfortunate happening of last evening. The kiss. The kiss had not been unpleasant for Shelley. She had loved before, but until Charlotte, Shelley hadn't realized how much she could need another human being. The taste of Charlotte's lips, so honey and sweet sent shivers of shame and delight through Shelley's body.

The south was experiencing the worst heat wave in years. The heat compounded by the tension caused a nervously exhausted

Shelley's feet to drag through the streets as though trudging aimlessly through a soggy marsh.

Reaching the shop, Shelley sought out Charlotte.

"Morning," was all Shelley could say, in the presence of other staff members. Her private conversation with Charlotte would have to wait.

Shelley busied herself with the day's correspondence, occasionally sneaking a glance in Charlotte's direction. She was deeply worried over Charlotte coolness.

"Charlotte, come into my office," Shelley stated in a businesslike manner.

Following Shelley, Charlotte stood motionless until the office door closed behind the two women. "I didn't get much sleep last night. I am afraid I owe you an apology. I hope I haven't damaged our friendship. I feel like such a fool," Shelley said, unable to raise her eyes to meet Charlotte's.

"I was warned about the abnormal attraction that wicked people like you had for little lost lambs like me. I never thought I'd meet somebody like you so soon upon my arrival in Charleston," Charlotte replied, eyes twinkling.

Shelley startled by Charlotte's words looked into a guileless face.

"I know I frightened you. Can we still be friends?" Shelley asked as she searched Charlotte's face for the answer.

"Oh course, we're friends. Everybody makes mistakes. Don't worry I was caught off guard, never thought of you, that way."

"You are not offended," Shelley smiled.

"No, I was more startled than offended. I felt something I didn't understand. A strange feeling ignited inside me, but Shelley, I'm not ready for a...another relationship."

"Then, we'll start over?" Shelley asked as she took Charlotte's hand.

"But please be warned you drive me crazy with your nearness," she had wanted to say. Raw emotion filled Shelley's face. Go slowly. She's content to remain friends. Shelley's features tightened as her hand dropped away.

"No, not start over, we'll continue to build a lasting friendship,"

Charlotte whispered in a reassuring manner.

Shelley stammered as her uncontrolled feelings threatened to surface, "Alright, friends. True friends for life."

Shelley feared that Charlotte would bolt and run if she was threatened with the possibilities of the awakening of another side of her sexual nature. Last night, the kiss they shared. Charlotte had been kissed before, but never had she been affected so profoundly. She savored the memory of the aborted contact. Had Mason not called out, what would have happened next? Charlotte's mind was dallying in an area unfamiliar to her. Where in heaven's name would this relationship lead? She was disturbed by the new feelings overtaking her. Would she be plummeted into some immoral, forbidden ecstasy?

Charlotte expelled a despairing gasp.

"Shelley, I've been drawn to you since our first meeting. The thought of your friendship makes my morning brighter," Charlotte said as her voice trembled with emotion.

Shelley turned her back on her young friend as she attempted to disassociate herself from the situation.

"Take it slow," thought Shelley, but she was overcome by the nearness, the smell of Charlotte. Shelley could only dream of the wonderful day when:

Charlotte would stand in the center of the office trembling as her icy control melted. She would lean against Shelley's desk as she heard the door's lock click shut against intrusion.

Shelley's fingers would run freely through Charlotte's hair, as she would cradle her head. Charlotte would surrender completely to the soft lushness of Shelley's kisses. Shelley would carry Charlotte on a magical carpet ride into a paradise beyond belief.

Sheer physical need drove Shelley. Months of denial demanded release. Her experienced fingers would stroke Charlotte.

"Why did you do that?" Charlotte would ask, her voice raspy with passion.

"I need you Charlotte," Shelley would reply.

Shelley could smell Charlotte's womanly scent. She could feel the curve of her body beneath her clothing. Shelley swallowed hard as she took Charlotte into forbidden territory. Shelley was suddenly jolted back to the present.

"Charlotte, we'd better get back to work or Tom will fire both of us," Shelley said as she tried to cool her ardor.

"You are so right. Nepotism doesn't bother that brother of yours. See you later," Charlotte smiled as she turned and left the office.

Chapter 9

Charlotte had her own daydreams that with patience and kindness she would change the atmosphere of the house. Nothing she tried worked. She was alone, except for Shelley. She lived among people of different customs and ideas. Her new family kept her isolated and penniless, so Shelley encouraged Charlotte to open a small local bank account for a rainy day.

Charlotte had not been prepared to deal with the reality of her new life. Mason and his mother had made her a virtual slave, and they had isolated her from those that might help. She had obtained a job with Madame Lorraine so she didn't become as mad as her mother-in-law.

Charlotte was uncomfortable with sharing the knowledge of her terrifying existence with her co-workers. She had already told Shelley the truth of her home life. The others could wait until she know them better.

Today, for an hour or two she would forget. She would spend a quiet time with her friend.

Charlotte and Shelley planned a quiet picnic lunch. They spread a red and white checkered table cloth under a majestic oak tree in the park close to Madame Lorraine's. The heat of the noon sun danced through the trees as the girls dressed in their favorite summer attire spread their lunch.

"Oh the picnic is wonderful. All of this fried chicken, potato salad and fruit. You remembered I adored fruit," Charlotte spoke, almost in a childlike tone.

"What did you take on picnics in the Maryland?" Shelley asked.

"Mother never liked eating outside, so we never had a picnic. We dined occasionally on the patio on a hot summer's night. She could occasionally be persuaded to participated in a night time clam bake."

"A clam bake sounds enticing. We'll have to have one sometime. But it is so sad to know that you have had such a deprived life. Imagine what you've missed. You haven't lived until you have experienced a good old southern picnic. Including a few fat ants," Shelley laughed as she removed a chubby ant from their table cloth.

"The sunshine is too warm and compelling to have to stay cooped up inside. I feel like racing through a meadow, walking barefoot along a gentle gurgling brook, and even catching a fish."

Shelley laughed, "Fishing? Yuck! I've never been fishing. Can't stand the smelly uncooked things."

"You've never been fishing? You've not really lived until you have drowned a few worms. On Chesapeake Bay, and I spent many peaceful hours catching fish. You've never been fishing?" Charlotte watched her friend shake her head in a negative manner. "Your education has been sadly neglected. Someday, I'll teach you. Tom and Charles, if they like. Papa was a avid sportsman."

"I'll look forward to the day," Shelley replied as she enjoyed the quiet afternoon. "What did you do with your time back home, in Baltimore?" Shelley inquired.

"I enjoyed working at Mitchell's Book Store. In the evening I read to my father. He was ill for many years, so we spent many pleasant hours together reading. Our favorite book was *Jane Eyre*. Shelley, I felt so helpless watching him lose interest in the outside world."

"Yes, I can know. I cared for our mother until her death. Watching and waiting is the worst of it. I've always enjoyed *Jane Eyre*." Shelley attempted to change the subject back to a more pleasant topic. "I suspect you are better read than most of the folk with whom you work."

"I don't know, but my life has been so different than I planned. I tend to dwell in my books," Charlotte replied.

"What type of picnic would Edward Rochester have prepared for Jane Eyre?" Shelley giggled.

"First of all Edward Rochester would have ordered a beautiful afternoon, and they would have ridden horseback to a secluded spot," Charlotte said pausing to dream. "He would have dismounted first, and rakishly lifted her from her saddle. He would have boldly remarked about her tiny waist, fitting perfectly in his two hands."

"Wow! Charlotte, he even makes me drool. Then what would he do, that wicked Edward Rochester," Shelley prompted as she enjoyed the sound of Charlotte's voice.

"He would have been very practical, having his chef pack the perfect lunch for two hungry lovers."

"Perfect lunch?" Shelley giggled.

"Oh yes," Charlotte joined in the merriment. "They would have caviar, assorted cheeses, and grapes. Grapes are the nectar of the gods. Of course they would have champagne, and for the main course, they'd have had leftovers, something that the chef had kept aside for emergencies," Charlotte finished as the two women broke into childlike giggles.

Charlotte suddenly grew quiet, and she turned toward her companion, "Shelley, I haven't found marriage to be what I expected. I don't understand Mason. Sometimes he can be so vile," Charlotte whispered, as she nibbled on a fried chicken leg.

"I know little of your husband, except his bigotry. Maybe you expected too much of a mere man." Shelley reached over and touched her friend's arm.

"He is insensitive." Charlotte frowned. "He is obsessed with getting me pregnant. He talks about making babies in such a filthy manner. I'm just around for breeding purposes."

"Maybe you have misunderstood. Maybe marriage is too new to you."

"I wish it was a misunderstanding. A man can not possibly do such despicable things to the woman he loves."

"I'm sorry, I am so glad that you feel free to tell me about your life." Shelley tried her best to keep her tone soft and comforting. "You really ought to consider getting out of that marriage before you do get pregnant, unless you love your husband?" Shelley raised an eyebrow as if she were asking a question. "No, I don't love him. He talks about everybody with such hate, such contempt."

"Me, for one," Shelley replied.

"He talks about all of you, you know. He says that you are all queers. He said you were not content to be a biological female. He said you are angry that you were not born with a penis." Charlotte tried to explain Mason. "He's probably afraid that you women would make better lovers than men like him."

"His silly narrow nonsense does not make you afraid of me, does it? Have I attacked you, Charlotte?"

"No, oddly enough I feel you are my best friend." Charlotte gazed steadily into Shelley's eyes.

"Thanks," Shelley responded.

"He seems to spend a lot of time worrying about what women do to women? He thinks women like that are unspeakable creatures."

"Women like me."

"Yes," Charlotte whispered.

Shelley squeezed her arm with encouragement. She was positive that Charlotte had not been able to talk freely with another person since her father's death.

"Let me tell you about what happened back home, the night of the rape," Charlotte took a deep breath.

Shelley continued resting her arm on Charlotte's aware that this was an evening that was difficult to relive.

"My mother was embarrassed the night I was attacked. Her greatest concern was that the neighbors might have seen the police came to our house. I believe that at that moment she wished me dead."

"Poor baby. It must have been dreadful. I got beat up once, by the big brother of a friend of mine, but never raped," Shelley said.

"Maybe it was my fault, Shelley. Do you think, it was? Maybe I should have fought harder? Mason says that a decent woman would have died before allowing herself to be raped." "Silly goose. Did you want those guys? Did you enjoy getting hurt? How badly were you messed up?"

Charlotte replied, "The doctors had to do plastic surgery on my face and nose," Charlotte stared at her friend with great big eyes. "Those beasts shattered my ribs, my pelvic..."

Shelley feigned a smile, "That's enough, I get the idea. Well I don't know what your original nose looked like, but this a cute nose," she said as she tweaked the end.

"Do you really think so?" Charlotte asked as she touched the tip of her nose.

"Yep! It's a great little nose. And as for that other thing. Mason's a fool if he thinks you should have let those creeps kill you," Shelley growled.

"You will never know the horror of my introduction to sex. First those guys attacked, and then, Mason on our wedding night. His force was more degrading then the first attack. His kind of attitude can really turn a woman away from men," Charlotte confided as she searched her friend's face for disgust.

Charlotte had not bared her soul to anybody since her teens. She found herself telling Shelley things she never could have told her father.

Shelley began to tell Charlotte more of her life's history.

"I was born the way I am. I'm the queer that your husband hates so much. I suppose that's me. Being with a woman is the most natural thing. Have you ever thought about girls instead of guys?" Shelley pursued into dangerous waters.

"Not really. I experimented with my friend Alice. Just childhood curiosity. At a spend the night party, we played strip poker. One day I touched her breast, she touched mine. Mother caught us, and she chased Alice home. She called me a slut, that I was warped. She never let Alice near me. Mother overreacted. We were young, learning about bodies."

"Have you ever even held a woman before?" Shelley inquired.

"I kissed my friend Alice. We were so lonely after Mother ran her off. We would meet in the school rest room, and we would hold each other. She'd kiss me; once she got so excited she pushed her tongue into my mouth. It felt so strange. It never happened again," Charlotte whispered so softly as if she were afraid someone might hear her. "Did you date much in your teens?"

"No, not really. I dated a couple of boys. One in particular was such a clumsy oaf. He was always trying to make me lie down on my folks sofa with him. He kept trying to run his hand up my dress and touch me." Shelley said as she attempted to share more of her private thoughts.

"Good grief! Didn't you hate the youthful gropers"

"Yes," Shelley giggled as she remembered.

"My teen years were so miserable. I felt so out of step so I lived my life through my books."

"Don't I remember those awkward years. You felt so uncoordinated, so clumsy. You were sure nobody understood."

"I know," Charlotte joined in the laughter. "How did we ever survive the mating rituals?"

"I felt different from other girls. I had a girlfriend, Marty, when I was about sixteen. It felt great every time we were together. We enjoyed touching each other. You know what I mean?"

"Yes," Charlotte replied.

"We'd hide in the cloak room and kissed. We shared a sense of physical attraction that neither of us understood. Of course there was nobody that you could talk to. Taboos, and all of that."

"I have tried to hide from life, but it caught me. I've always be such a coward. Mama said I was afraid of my shadow." Charlotte's eyes were big as saucers.

Shelley continued her story. "We were concerned about being discovered so we found an abandoned building where we could be alone. We tried everything. I can still remember the feel of her small breasts. The taste of her rosy red nipples. We were so decadent that we experimented with marijuana cigarettes. Those were wonderful days," Shelley smiled as she remembered Marty's sweet face. She would always remember the smell of Marty's hair as its long strands dangled tickling Shelley's face.

"Anybody ever catch you."

"Yeah, a teacher. She had a fit. She turned me in to the principal. It was all over school within a day, and they made my life miserable. Marty's folks sent her away to live with her aunt. I always wondered what became of her. She never wrote," Shelley said sadly. "I was treated like a curse by my friends and family. I have other stories, but those are for another day."

"Strange being a leper. My mother said Alice was the spawn of the devil and she would teach me dirty things. Mother was so mortified," Charlotte grinned.

"I tried to explain to my family that I was unhappy with my identity," Shelley continued, "Everybody laughed at first when I told them I was so unhappy. I terrified everyone but Tom. I'd have gone crazy without my big brother."

"Shelley, what I never understood, if parents loved you why didn't they try to understand your feelings?"

"Oh sweetie, I made them nervous. I was different. At an early age I knew I was different. I tried to explain that I couldn't help it, it was biological. I'll always remember Mother's reaction," Shelley continued.

"This whole thing has nothing to do with biology. Society has announced it's all right to be flakes, kinky, and they have encouraged your being different. People like you are just using their endorsement as a license to be weirder," mother screamed at me.

"I'm sorry, Shell," Charlotte replied. "It must have been dreadful."

"One was bad enough. You should have heard their reaction when they found out that Tom was gay. He was supposed to be a man and carry on their genes. They really went nuts. All of their hopes of being grandparents went out the window in one fell swoop. They went crazy, and they ordered us to leave the house," Shelley said sadly.

"I remember the night as vividly as if it were yesterday. Our father screamed at Tom, "nobody, but nobody in this family is a wimp. Get out! Both of you. You are no longer a member of this family. Never contact us again. Never contact us again."

Shelley continued in a strained voice, "We never did. The saddest part was when our parents passed away and we tried to attend our uncles asked us to leave. They told Tom and me that we were not fit to live around descent people. One of our cousins informed us that due to lifestyle we caused their deaths. Another uncle said that they never could face the community after we left. He said they died from embarrassment and disappointment."

"It must have taken a lot of courage to go public. I suppose I am a fraidy cat. I couldn't buck the system." Charlotte stroked Shelley's hair as she attempted to soothe her friend, "Your hair is so soft. I love the feel of it. Mine is such a limp nothing."

"You are so wrong. You're hair has quite a lovely texture," Charlotte stroked her arm.

"Has Mason ever taken you to Savannah?" Shelley attempted to cool her own flaming desire by changing the subject.

"No, This is the farthest south I've traveled," Charlotte replied as she admired every feature of her companion.

"Someday, we'll go. There is the sweetest little bookstore on Jones Street in the historic section which specializes in historical writings. It would be your cup of tea, I suspect."

"We enjoy the same things. I'll look forward to that trip."

"We'll eat at Careys Grill. Lots of atmosphere. Tom and I ran into a couple of big named stars having breakfast there not too long ago. They are such a sweet couple."

"Movie stars in Savannah, Georgia?" Charlotte asked, obviously impressed. "Oh, yes. They were making their latest movie. Georgia is famous for extending Southern Hospitality to the movie makers."

"I never knew that," Charlotte replied.

"Oh Charlotte, you'd love Savannah. We could sit on the balcony at the Radisson. It over looks the river."

"The Savannah river, the town? What's so special? I love Charleston."

"Oh yes, what is special about the town?" Shelley replied dreamily. "The city of Savannah is not like anywhere else. Life moves at a slower pace. Charles and Tommy took me years ago as a surprise birthday gift. We had this gorgeous suite overlooking the river. I sat on the balcony early in the morning, eating fresh fruit, and watching the ships go by. We ate lobster bisque on River Street."

"I personally love blue crab," Charlotte laughed.

"They have great hospitals too."

"Hospitals? Why were you visiting hospitals? Charlotte's laughter turned to concern.

"One hospital in particular. St. Joseph's Hospital. I stepped off the curb twisting my knee. It sounded like a fresh twig snapping."

"It must have been painful."

"It was. I thought it would be all right after all I could stand on it, and it wasn't black or blue. Was I ever wrong? The next day I could hardly walk. Tommy insisted I seek medical attention. One of the locals recommended St. Joseph's Hospital. The hospital can pride itself on their employees. They were the most caring group we had ever met."

"Were you admitted?"

"Nope! The emergency slapped on a walking brace and off we went. Savannah is a wonderful place to be wounded." Shelley grimaced as she remembered her injury.

"One care giver stands out in my mind. She was the x-ray technician named Camilla. She was a doll. Camilla was good looking and had a great smile, but at the same time very professional and gentle. Tom might have given up men for sweet Camilla," Shelley laughed at her statement.

"Charles won't appreciate your brand of humor this afternoon," Charlotte laughed as she imagined Charles' displeasure.

"Well anyway, Charlotte, Savannah is really laid back. A great tourist town. We'd have a blast."

"The city sounds exquisite."

"It is! There's much I can teach you," Shelley whispered, brushing a wisp of hair from Charlotte's face.

"How long would it take for us to get to Savannah?"

"We could get there in no time. A couple of hours, or less. Oh my darling girl, there are so many places I'd love to take you," Shelley continued.

"You would love the historic section. Savannah has a wonderful selection of antebellum homes. Speaking of old homes. A sleepy little town further north, Madison, Georgia is one of the few cities, not touched by that pyromaniac, General Sherman, during the civil war."

"I'd never been more than fifty miles from home until Mason brought me to Charleston."

"Stick with me kid, and we'll go places," Shelley laughed.

"Where would we go first?" Charlotte said dreamily.

"Charleston."

"We're in Charleston, silly."

"I know where we live. But if you will let me continue, do you know why the houses are long and narrow?"

"No," Charlotte replied.

"Taxes, my dear."

"Taxes? You're teasing me."

"Nope, Taxes," Shelley laughed.

"What do taxes have to do with the width of houses?" Charlotte asked curiously.

"Why I thought everybody knew about our strange tax system? Homes were taxed, about a hundred years ago, according to the width of the house. That's why they were constructed long and narrow."

"That's the funniest thing I've ever heard. I fell in love with Charleston the moment I arrived. After Savannah, where else would we go?" Charlotte continued.

"Maybe we could sneak off one afternoon when Mason and Nola are visiting relatives."

"We could pack another picnic lunch and have a wonderful time," Charlotte suggested.

"If we had more time, we could drive all of the way to Atlanta and catch a ball game when the Braves are in town. We'll see a ballet at the Fox Theater, and there is always Stone Mountain."

"Seeing the sights in person, not in books, sounds so wonderful," Charlotte said dreamily.

"Time to go back to work. If we keep on going in this direction we'll be late. Can't force Tommy and Charles to have to dock our pay," Shelley whispered huskily.

The couple folded their tablecloth and walked back to work.

Chapter 10

On Friday afternoon, Mason was waiting for Charlotte to bring him her paycheck.

"Where's your paycheck Charlotte? I've got places to go and people to see, and I've got bills to pay, if there's any money left," Mason smirked as she grabbed her check and was out of the door.

"Mason, when will you be back? I'm not feeling well this evening. You be a good boy and hurry back," Nola whined.

"Sure Ma," he replied as he slammed the door behind him. Mason Burns had heard his mother's whine so often that he did not bother with a backward glance.

"He's probably going to meet Janie Sue. Fine with me. I'll get some rest," the exhausted Charlotte said as she slowly climbed the stairs.

Charlotte, a normally a quick-witted woman, felt as if her head was filled with cotton wool. If she could just get some bed rest, she'd be all right.

Saturday morning Mason whacked Charlotte on her buttock, "Get up Charlotte, Ma says I've been too rough on you. She thinks you're not getting enough rest. Call in sick and we will spend the day together."

"I can't tell the Bransons that I'm ill. They've been so good to me, besides I hate lying." Charlotte whispered as an acidic surged bubbled at the back of her throat.

"Mason would you mind if we put off our outing? I'm truly not feeling well this morning."

Charlotte suddenly dashed into the bathroom. She returned to the bed with a cold cloth held against her throat. The bubbling feeling returned, and she dropped to her knees. Charlotte's trembling body sagged against her pillow.

"Listen to me Charlotte, you've been complaining that I never take you anywhere. Well, little lady, today is the day. Get your sweet ass out of bed. Poised in the air in such a provocative manner, I might mistake your position as an invitation," Mason laughed.

Charlotte jumped out of the bed before he carried out his vulgar threat.

"Ma's got breakfast ready, and as soon as we've eaten, we're off," Mason appeared to be in uncharacteristically good spirits.

"You and Janie Sue must have had great sex last night. You're in such a good mood," Charlotte replied under her breath.

"Whatd'd you say, Charlotte?" Mason called.

"Nothing. I don't feel much like eating. Toast and coffee will be enough."

"What's wrong with eating Ma's oatmeal?" Mason grimaced.

"I'm feeling kind of green this morning," Charlotte replied.

"Probably something you ate with those precious weirdo friends of yours," Mason accused.

"Because they are not like you, doesn't make them weird or wrong," Charlotte snapped.

"My, my! Aren't we testy this morning," Mason replied.

"I told you I'm not feeling very well this morning," Charlotte protested.

"Not Feeling Well? Lately you are not feeling well every morning. I don't feel very well either, if you care. Do you see this decanter? This is one of only a few things left of our illustrious family. Generations ago, my family - yes, my family - owned the entire Charleston area."

Charlotte's eyes widened as they continued downstairs where Nola had prepared a sumptuous breakfast.

"Yes, Miss la de dah, educated lady. My family, the Burns side, not Ma's side, once owned everything around here. Thought you'd finally be impressed."

Mason, instead of eating oatmeal, poured and gulped down a drink of whiskey. Charlotte sat down next to Nola, who was buttering a stack of toast.   "Mason," Charlotte whispered. "Isn't it too early in the morning for that stuff? I thought we were going out."

"I'll drink where and when I wish," Mason glowered.

Charlotte picked up a piece of toast and offered it to her husband as she tried to remain calm. "Try a little toast. Maybe some tea. Tea always settles my stomach."

Mason sat down, pointedly ignoring the toast.

"Charlotte's right, my boy. Remaining angry about things that happened before you were born will do you no good," Nola stated as she stroked his forehead.

As gracefully as she could, Charlotte placed the toast back on the stack. Nola sighed and placed the same piece on her own plate. Lost in the past of what could have been, what should have been Mason ignored the entire exchange between the two women.

"I'd like to hear the family story. I've never heard this one. Please go on, Mason," Charlotte insisted.

"Oh yes, now I've got your attention. Money, money, money. That's all you bitches are interested in."

"Hush, Mason. Don't upset yourself. Think about your outing with your wife. Where are you two going, son?" Nola cajoled.

"That's for me to know. You're not invited." Mason almost snapped his mother's head off.

Seeing her mother-in-law nearly in tears, Charlotte said, "Mother Burns, of course you may come along.

Mason suddenly jerked the kitchen chair out from under himself, throwing it across the room. Charlotte and Nola both flinched, but remained in their chairs.

"You bitch about our not going anywhere, Charlotte. What's wrong now? Are you afraid to be alone with me? Want to bring ma along for protection? What's your problem?"

"I'm sorry you two. I didn't mean to start anything. I've got a lot of mending to keep me busy," Nola sounded nervous.

Charlotte noticed her skin had a greyish appearance causing her to suddenly look old and incredibly wasted.

"All settled. Charlotte, get your things, and we'll be going." Mason escorted his wife to their car with the charm and grace he had shown during their courting days.

They were driving north through the city on Highway 17 approaching the bay bridge when Mason said, "Look at the city, my dear. This is all that is left of the south that once was." He gestured ahead to the ships which were now very evident at their moorings. "We're going to Patriot's Point, and we'll gawk and see the sights, just like Yankee tourists." He pointed to a tiny boat in the bay. "We'll even take the 'General Beauregard' for a ride out to Fort Sumter," Mason laughed.

"Oh Mason, it's such a lovely day," Charlotte smiled in spite of her apprehension. "Those boats are extraordinary. Will we have time for a tour?"

"Yes Charlotte," Mason's laughter filled the air as he enjoyed his wife's excitement.

"What did you say is the name of our boat?" Charlotte asked.

"You can read," Mason's change of tone startled Charlotte. "The General Beauregard", one of our local heroes."

"While we're out, might I purchase a souvenir spoon from the fort. I left an extensive collection back home."

"Women, and their fool nick-nacks. I suppose we can spare a couple of bucks."

Mason purchased the boat tour tickets to Ft. Sumter. The couple soon discovered the small tour boat was almost empty.

Mason's face darkened, as he drew Charlotte to his side.

"You didn't believe me this morning when I told you our family, at one time had owned Charleston. Ma doesn't like it when I talk about the past. She's calls me obsessed. I should be in the Sons of the American Revolution. But no, those damned Yankees burned the proof of our families' participation."   "Mason, you have every right to be proud of your ancestry. Maybe we could search out the records in Columbia. The records have to be somewhere. But please go on..." Charlotte smiled reassuringly.

"The Burns had a land grant more than two hundred years ago, so the story goes. My great, great grandfather Burns was rolled after a card game. Some no good scurvy dog stole the deed that Papa Burns carried in a pouch. That piece of vermin cheated us out of our land and our rightful heritage," Mason scowled as he looked out at the rolling sea.

"Couldn't your family have gotten a duplicate copy?" Charlotte asked innocently.

"They were supposed to have attempted to contact the king, but never received a reply. My father tried to sue the city years ago, but everybody laughed at him."

"I'm sorry, Mason." Charlotte touched his shoulder.

"You're sorry. All we've got left is a few acres north of here."

"That's wonderful. Does it have a house? Have you ever considered building?"

"Now that you know that there is property, a small house, now I get a little respect," Mason jerked Charlotte's arm.

"Please Mason, someone might overhear us."

"Overhear us. I don't give a tinkers damn who hears," Mason's eyes were suddenly hot and wild with rage.

"Please Mason, what have I done?" Charlotte was confused. What had she done to trigger such an outburst? The day had been going so well.

"If the Yankees had kept their stinking noses out of our business. Out of our lives, my life would have been so much---" Mason didn't finish the statement. His hands were making fists.

"You would not have had to come begging for a wife with money. Your life would have been much better. That's why you are angry all of the time," Charlotte muttered in a despondent manner.

"Our family had more money than yours before the civil war. My life should have been..Oh how I hate those damned Yankees. We lost so much. You don't understand?"

"Nobody wins in a war, especially a civil war, any war costs everyone," Charlotte responded as she attempted to be the voice of reason in the modern wilderness.

"We had a large plantation over there." Mason cried out as he pointed to an area north of Charleston. "They took our lands, our pride. You take pride in your town's heritage. Our Colonial era buildings. We..the Carolina's would have had more of them too, if it hadn't been for the damn Yankees. The scourge of the earth....not fit to..." Mason never finished his tirade for an elderly couple, concerned for Charlotte's safety, complained about Mason's outburst to one of the crew.

The crewman walked up to Mason and Charlotte.

"Excuse me, sir, ma'am."

"Yes...what do you want?" Mason snapped.

"Is there some problem with the lady? She seems to be ...uh...ill. upset about something," he eyed Mason suspiciously.

"Ma'am. May I be of assistance?" another crew member stepped forward.

"Oh, no thank you," Charlotte replied a little too brightly. "I'm being a spoil sport today. A touch of sea sickness, I'm afraid."

As the crew members walked away, Mason twisted Charlotte's fingers so hard they made a cracking sound. "I tried to give you a pleasant day, visiting historical areas, since you are so nuts about them. Now you've shamed me. You will have to be punished," Mason growled.

Charlotte never purchased her souvenir spoon, she never got to tour the ships, but Charlotte did receive another beating for disloyalty.

That night, Charlotte Burns lay naked in her bed following Mason's orders. She could feel his hands as they wandered slowly over her body. She didn't care much for his brand of sex.   H e moved over her grunting while she lay as unresponsive as a corpse. Why had she been persuaded to marry? Why had she been so weak as to agree? She was responsible for her life in hell.

Finally finished, sweaty with exertion, he rolled off her, taking most of the sheet with him.

Mason was sprawled face down on their bed, his snoring filling the room. He lay exhausted from his violent attack and sexual gratification.

The only light, the candles gave the room a reddish glow as Charlotte cowered in the corner attempting to regain her composure. She shuttered as she looked out of the window feeling dead inside, black and dead as the black emptiness engulfing her heart. Charlotte wished she could become invisible so no one could find her. Here she was alone, cut off from everything familiar to her. She was stricken with terror for she was finally carrying her husband's child.

The next morning Charlotte telephoned Dr. Manley.

"Hello. This is Charlotte Burns."

"Good morning, Mrs. Burns. How may I help you?"

"I would like to see the doctor for a pregnancy test," Charlotte's voice had an exhausted tone.

"How about eleven o'clock in the morning?"

"That's fine. I'll see you then," Charlotte replied and hung up the receiver.

Charlotte dragged herself into Dr. Manley's office precisely at eleven o'clock the next morning.

"Good morning, Mrs. Burns. You are right on time. The doctor will see you immediately."

"Thanks," Charlotte muttered, following the nurse into the examining room.

Dr. Manley had his nurse draw some blood, and then the nurse gave her a plastic cup for a urine sample.

The verdict was quicker than Charlotte expected.

"Congratulations, Charlotte. You are finally expecting a baby. Mason must be thrilled."

"I haven't told him. I couldn't bear another false alarm. Oh, Dr. Manley, I wish I could tell mother first. It feels like a million years, not one since I've seen her."

"You must rush right home, and share your bit of news." Dr. Manley replied as he gave her shoulder a comforting squeeze.

"For once, maybe I've done something right," Charlotte stated without looking back. "See you later, Doctor. Thanks!"

Twenty minutes later Charlotte tiptoed into the kitchen.

"Where the hell have you been, bitch?" Mason bellowed.

"Ma and I were getting ready for the police to drag the river. Where have you been?"

"Mason, I was hoping to talk to you privately, but since that is not possible, I have just returned from a second visit to Dr. Manley. He confirmed my suspicions, I'm pregnant. You're going to be a father," Charlotte, sat down slowly into a kitchen chair.

Mason picked up Charlotte and swung her around the room. "Finally we're having a kid. Ma you're gonna be a grandma. It's great isn't it?"

"Don't be so rough. You don't want to make me loose it, do you?" Charlotte asked.

"Loose my son, don't worry your pretty head about him. Once I stick one in ya, he'll stay stuck until he's through cooking. Told you I was a man. Told you I didn't shoot blanks," Mason bellowed for the neighbors to hear. "Come on up stairs, sugar. We've got some celebrating to do. Excuse us, Ma. You understand," Mason gave Nola a vulgar knowing leer.

Mason carried Charlotte upstairs and tossed her on the bed.

"Strip, you're not playing the long suffering vestal virgin tonight." Mason was dragging off Charlotte's clothing.   "Please don't yank my clothes so hard," Charlotte was unable to continue as Mason's lips savagely covered her mouth.

"We'd have been celebrating sooner, if you'd of taken off your clothes for me more regular," Mason complained.

"Please be careful. Remember, I am expecting. Don't hurt the baby," Charlotte whispered.

"I won't hurt the kid, so get your skinny ass over here. It will be months before your belly gets in the way of our pleasure," Mason demanded as he pulled Charlotte's naked body across their bed. He dropped his trousers and forced her to lie spread eagled, helpless under his attack.

Charlotte closed her eyes. Pleasure, what pleasure, she thought as he jammed that ugly red thing into her body. Over and over again, she fought back the tears and nausea that had become a familiar part of their life together.

When he had finished, he pulled her up on her knees, and mounted her from the rear. As Charlotte began to scream, Mason shoved her blouse in her mouth.

"Shut up, you fool. You trying to alert the neighbors, so they'll call the police. I'll have to hurt you bad now, shaming me like this," he withdrew his penis and jammed it hard and deep into her anus. Gagging on her blouse, Charlotte vomited.

The attack seemed to last forever, but finally Mason was spent and quiet. Charlotte lay violated, while the animal known as her husband, snored peacefully beside her.

She finally summoned the courage to tip-toe to the bath room to inspect her body for damage, and clean his stench from her body.

She returned miserably to her side of the bed, finally sleeping fretfully.

It was just past three in the morning when the phone jolted Mason out of an erotic dream. He and Janie Sue had been performing unspeakable sex acts, and he resented the disturbance.

"Yeah! Who the hell is it? What, okay. That's awful. Yes, I'll tell her." Mason frowned, hanging up the phone.

He laid back on his pillow, drawing Charlotte to his side. "Who's calling so early in the morning?" Charlotte asked sleepily.

In a low voice Mason said, "I've got something to tell you. That was Howie Cramer. Your mother had a severe stroke this afternoon. She died about two hours ago."

Charlotte stiffened in sheer astonishment as she thought, "Mother's dead. While you were doing those things to me, my mother was gasping for her last breaths. Oh, my God," Charlotte prayed, "Dear Lord, please never abandon me."

Charlotte remained stony silence as Mason moved a little closer to her, and said in a soothing voice, "you're not alone, my darling little orphan. I promise, Ma and I will help you get though this awful time. We'll get to your mother's place, and make a quick inventory of her possessions before that parasite Howie gets them."

"Wh.. what did you say?" Charlotte responded from her deep fog.

"Howie wasn't married to your mother, so everything goes to us. I mean you, and as your husband, we'll share. Right, dear," Mason said confidently. "I'll go tell ma. She'll be heartbroken that her oldest friend has gone." Mason slipped out of the bed and headed for his mother's room.

Charlotte knew that no matter how much money Nola Burns shared, the loss of Peggy Hamby would be difficult on her mother-in-law.

Charlotte never questioned Nola valued Peggy's friendship. For Nola, the cold wind of her mortality would be blowing down the back of her neck. The loss of Peggy Hamby would be too much even for her mother-in-law to bear.

Mason returned to their room, "Ma wanted to be alone. She is devastated by her personal loss. She said to tell you how sad she was that Peggy knew nothing of your pregnancy. Ma knew how the information would have thrilled your mother." Mason, in his way was attempting to give Charlotte support.

She said nothing so Mason continued, "I love you, Charlotte. I never thought it was possible to feel as I do. You love me, and what could be more wonderful than our having a child together," Mason stared at his wife unable to understand the reason for Charlotte's continued silence.   "We'll take care of you, Ma and I, I promise.

Charlotte quietly headed for the bedroom door.

"Where are you going? Charlotte, come back here. Where are you going at this time of night?"

"Mason, thank you for your concern. I'll be fine but I need a little fresh air," was all Charlotte could say as she grabbed her robe and headed down the stairs.

Charlotte stumbled blindly out of the house, and found herself at the back porch of Shelley and Tom Branson. To her surprise Shelley was sitting on her back steps in the dark.

"Charlotte, what's wrong. You're trembling so. Please sweet girl. Has that animal hurt you, again?" Shelley asked drawing the young girl into her arms. She stroked Charlotte's back, as she tenderly kissed her tears away.

"He doesn't matter now. We just received a call from back home. Mother died this afternoon, and I'm pregnant, and they are just worried about how fast they can get to her things and spend the money."

"My poor baby. Come on in the house."

"Shell, I had to get out of that house before I screamed. How could I have possibly been so stupid marrying somebody like Mason Burns? He and that mother of his, they are so insensitive. Mother has just died and they are already trying to divvy up her possessions."

"My poor angel." Shelley cuddled Charlotte in her arms. "Come on to my room." Shelley led the way. Closing the door, she slid Charlotte's robe off and laid her on the bed. "Lay down, you look exhausted."

"I've got to get back."

"Shush! stay here until you regain your composure."

"I call them callous and insensitive, but I'm the callous one. My mother died hours ago and I seeking solace in your arms. It's so obscene."

"That's right, you callous monster. How are you seek solace in the arms of the one that cares for you. You are where you should be." Shelley covered Charlotte, as she slid in beside her. She held Charlotte in her arms, stroking her hair and shoulders as Charlotte wept for the loss of her world.

"That's right, little one. Have a good cry, get it out of your system. It will be good for you," Shelley crooned gently to the younger girl. In spite of her pain, Charlotte found herself relaxing against Shelley's strong shoulder.

Charlotte's eyes flew open in great surprise as she responded to Shelley's tenderness.

"Oh, my precious, you make me forget myself for this is hardly the time, but I am wet all over with the need of you," Shelley whispered.

Shelley slid closer as she kissed Charlotte tenderly on the lips, while slipping her hand discretely onto Charlotte's breast. Shelley slowly withdrew her hand. "We've got to go slowly. These feelings are new to you. If they are not right, others could be hurt. We have your unborn child to consider."

Filled with the tenderness of the moment Charlotte responded as she pressed her lips against Shelley's, returning kiss for kiss.

"I don't want to, but I really ought to leave. The funeral. The house. Settling mother's estate. I have dreaded this day, facing those vultures."

Shelley remained silent for speech was unnecessary as the two women gained strength for the coming days ahead.

Tom poked his head in the door, awaking the startled pair.

"Wake up you two. That husband of Charlotte's is tearing the neighborhood apart looking for her."

Tom turned his attention to Charlotte, "You'd better sneak around and go in the front door while Charles diverts them out back."

Charlotte slipped into her robe, and raced toward the door.

"I'll call you when I can. Let me give you Mother's phone number. Don't worry, I'll be fine," Charlotte smiled at Shelley.

"Thanks Tom. See you later."

Charlotte sneaked through the front of the Burns' house and returned to her bedroom. She came down the stairs moments later to meet her husband and mother-in-law in the kitchen.

"Where have you two been?" Charlotte took the initiative. "When I returned nobody was to be found."

"When did you come in?" Nola demanded.

"Oh, I don't know. Awhile ago," Charlotte feigned a big yawn. "I've been so upset about mother. I walked around the neighborhood and suddenly it was light, and I didn't want anyone to see me in my robe. I didn't want to ruin your reputation so I came in and dropped off on the sofa," Charlotte attempted to make her story sound totally reasonable.

"What the hell do you think you are doing? What will the neighbors think you running around in your nightgown?" Mason came charging up to Charlotte as though the devil was in hot pursuit.

"Mason dear, Charlotte is just fine. She's been asleep on the sofa while we were scurrying around like mice looking for her," Nola answered for Charlotte.

"Well I'm glad you're okay. What are you doing about your job? If you go back to Baltimore, will they hold it for you?" Mason inquired.

"If they don't, I'll get another," Charlotte responded. "Are you packed for the trip?" Charlotte chattered. "Will we drive, take the train, or fly?" "We'll fly, dear. Can't leave my poor Peggy alone with strangers," Nola replied. "We won't have time to discuss the pregnancy until after the funeral. Run upstairs and pack."

Mason ignored his mother's orders as he turned to asked, "Ma, can you believe that Charles person actually spoke to me? He asked if anything was wrong, could he help? I've never seen such nerve," Mason complained.

"Oh dear, Mason, he didn't attempt to pick you up, did he? You never know about that type of person, can't even turn your back on them. Maybe he even lied about holding my job for me?" Charlotte replied in a sarcastic tone.

"Don't get smart with me bitch. You'd better not be lying about your pregnancy. If you're not, you remember what I promised. Don't force me to punish you. Your easy life will be over. You've had it too good since you came to Charleston," Mason snapped.

"My life is easy. What easy life?" Charlotte could not refrain from laughter. " I clean the house, do the laundry and hold down a full time job. When does my life get easy?" Charlotte slipped past her startled husband to pack for the long trip home. Her nerves were taunt as steel bands.

Charlotte telephoned Shelley moments before the Burns family left on a Delta flight to Baltimore.

"Shell, hi, it's me. We're leaving in the morning, Delta #1868 due in Baltimore 9:55 am. There's a layover in Atlanta."

"Charlotte, are you all right? You sound so tired." Shelley sounded worried.

"I feel kind of green, but it's probably stress."

"If you feel worse, promise me you'll call the doctor, please Charlotte."

"I will. You shouldn't worry so much, Shell," Charlotte smiled. "See you when we get back. You have mother's number. Bye."

The silver jet touched down in Baltimore at precisely 9:55 am. After gathering their luggage, the Burns' took a taxi to the Hamby house.

The weary Charlotte Hamby Burns returned to her childhood home not as the confident matron with a doting husband, but as an abused wife. She stood on the front stoop, with her old house key in hand undecided about entering when Howie Cramer appeared from nowhere.

"Charlotte, sorry about Peggy," she heard him saying. "She went fast, if that is any consolation," Howie continued, unsure of himself.

Peggy's death had seemed to affect him profoundly, whether due to his personal loss, or the loss of his home and income.

"Thanks Howie. You remember my husband, Mason Burns and this is his mother Nola," Charlotte said as she walked past him to open the front door.

"Everything appears the same," Charlotte spoke as she looked about the living room.

"You know how your mother was. She hated change," Howie replied.

"We brought a copy of Peggy's will. Charlotte gets everything," Mason cut coldly to the chase.

"Well Mason, that's not entirely right," Howie interjected. "My Peggy... she left me $5,000," he watched for any reaction to his announcement before he continued. "Peggy's lawyer has the changes in his copy. Feel free to check with him. Name's George Brady, he's in the book," Howie attempted to leave the room.

"Wait a moment Howie. You surely don't intend to drop that kind of bomb and then walk away. Five thousand dollars is a lot of money," Charlotte replied. "Why so much?"

"You being her only living relative, Peggy wanted you to have the house. Since Peggy and I were getting married, she thought, uh...$5,000...it was my due," Howie snarled.

"Howie, I don't care about the money, but...," Charlotte never finished the sentence.

"What do you mean, you don't care about the money?" Nola screamed at Charlotte, as she turned to Howie. "You two weren't married, not real family. We'll see you in court before you get a penny."

"I thought you might feel that way. Mr. Brady, Peggy's attorney told me that she had the legal right to leave me the money. She was in her right mind, not daft when she wrote, the codicil. That's what it's called," Howie smiled, proud of his new knowledge of law.

"Howie, let's not argue," Charlotte gave Howie the regard she would a roach on the floor. "Where have they taken mother's body?" Charlotte asked.

"Charlotte," Howie wheedled while attempting to stroke her arm. "You've become so cold," his tone brightened as he continued, "we were friends. Don't you remember?" Howie cooed.

"I remember everything, Mr. Cramer."

Charlotte's icy stare and the frigid tone of her voice was enough to send chills up and down his spine and render him speechless. He realized Charlotte had changed, become stronger. Getting the money was not going to be so easy.

"You've become hard girl. Peggy would of died alone except for me; you abandoned her when you went off to South Carolina. It took my poor Peggy's dying to get your interest. Now you are here with the scavengers, prepared to loot all that she prized. Well, she's at the Eternal Rest funeral home. The one where your daddy was taken."

"Eternal Rest," Charlotte kept her thoughts in check as she ignored Howie's tirade. "It's close enough, I'll walk over. Mason, you and your mama stay here. Rest, take inventory, if you like," Charlotte said wearily as perspiration slid down her pale face.

She must get out of this stifling place. Charlotte suppressed the need to vomit as she dashed for the front door.

She took a short brisk walk to the funeral home. The leaves of the trees blazed in the red and golds. Charlotte felt comfortable in her beloved Baltimore, happy, in spite of the circumstances.

"I'm here to see, Mrs. Peggy Hamby," Charlotte spoke to the funeral home attendant.

"Are you kin?" the thin man asked.

"I'm her daughter, Mrs. Burns. Charlotte Burns. Is she ready for viewing?" Charlotte asked.

"Yes, she is. I hope you will be pleased. We did the best we could. She was a pretty lady in her younger days. I remember her well. Peggy and I went to high school together," the undertaker stated as he guided the trembling Charlotte to the viewing room.

"Did you and mama date? She had lots of boy friends. Mr. Uh. I'm sorry I don't remember your name."

"The name's Bishop, Walter Bishop. No we never went out. I sat near her in history, and English. She was always surrounded by boys. She was very popular," Mr. Bishop smiled remembering their school days.

"Mama was the prettiest girl my father ever laid eyes on, he

always said. You have done a wonderful job. Thank you for your
kindness." Charlotte turned from the undertaker to spend her final
moments alone with her mother.

"Mama," Charlotte whispered to her mother's body. "Why did we
never reconcile our differences. You didn't hate me, did you
Mama?" I never understood you." Charlotte stroked her mother's
thin waxen face. "I tried so hard to love you. I hope you have
found peace."

"Charlotte!" a voice startled her. Charlotte turned.

"Mrs. Mitchell. How nice to see you?" Charlotte whispered as
the older woman embraced her.

"Sorry my dear. It's the greatest loss to lose one's mother. She
was a woman with strange ideas. She never should have run you
off. If it is any consolation she lived to regret her hasty actions,"
Mrs. Mitchell stated.

"She did?" Charlotte asked, her face ravaged with pain.

"I visited her several weeks before her death. We talked for
hours. I had never heard her so filled with anguish. She told me she
had driven you away to live with those terrible people. Charlotte,
your mother was spoiled, never grew up. Used to having her own
way. Don't hold it against her. Peggy was not totally to blame.
Your grandfather and even your father catered to her every whim,
overlooked her wild streak. Don't let their foolishness wreck your
life. It can only hurt you."

"Thank you, Mrs. Mitchell. I'm glad you told me. Mama was a
free spirit. That's what attracted to her. The flighty girl and the
stuffy professor, that was what called them."

"I must go dear. I'll see you at the service," Mrs. Mitchell hugged
Charlotte one last time before leaving the funeral home.

"Oh Mama, we missed out on so much. We never had a chance
to be mother and daughter. Circumstance threw us away. Mama
you missed out on the best part, I'm pregnant. You were going to be
a grandmother. Don't worry about me, the baby and I will be just
fine. By the way mama, you wouldn't approve, but I'm in love. In
love for the first time in my life." Charlotte left the funeral home
feeling more peace than she had known in years. She was confident

that she had been loved, and would be able to face the future.

"Charlotte, when did you get back?" Mason came out.

"I've been sitting in the back yard enjoying the flowers and remembering my childhood."

"We went through your mother's papers. Ma phoned a real estate company to put the house on the market and a Mr. Jacobs will be by tomorrow morning for a walk through. We hope to get a good price, it's a seller's market, he tells me."

"Do what you wish, Mason," Charlotte said wearily, walking up the familiar stairs.

"Charlotte, where are you going? There's so much to do," Nola bellowed. "We can't carry all of this junk back home. Sonny agrees with me. We'll have a estate sale and give the unsalable items to the salvation army. What do you think, Charlotte?"

Charlotte ignored her mother-in-law as she trudged up the stairs to her old room. Oh, if only Shelley could be with her. She needed the comfort of her arms.

Charlotte collapsed on her bed. The lavender scented sheets filled her nose transporting her back in time to the glorious years of her childhood. The wonderful childhood shared with her father and their love of books.

Charlotte cried herself to sleep. A sudden noise jolted her into the present. As her sleep filled brain cleared she realized that the sound of the telephone had brought her back to consciousness.

"Charlotte, it's me."

"Oh, Shell. You'll never know how desperately I needed to hear from you," Charlotte's sleep thickened voice whispered.

"Charlotte, who is it?" Mason called up the stairs.

"It's for me, Mason. Someone calling to extend their sympathy," Charlotte replied, irritated with the intrusion of her husband.

"Alright. When you're through we must continue the inventory."

"I'll be brief Mason," Charlotte responded as she returned to the awaiting caller.

"Oh Shelley, it's awful. They are snooping through everything. Nola has managed to search through all of mama's personal effects," Charlotte whimpered.

"Good grief! Stop fretting! Let them do their worst. You can't stop them short of a killing, and they are not worth the bother. Let's speak of better things. I'm here in Baltimore. You did not think I would leave you to the tender mercies of those two vultures," Shelley said.

"You're here? Where?" Charlotte pleaded.

"Get your coat on and meet me at the Baltimore Marriott. Thought you might could use an ally. If they are busy pilfering through your mother's things, they won't notice your absence."

"I'll get there as quickly as possible. I'll make an excuse to get out of the house and come right over," Charlotte responded.

"Mason, I've got to go over to the funeral home to make sure everything is ready for the service," Charlotte darted out the door before Mason could delay her departure.

"Can't I come along, honey?" Mason called out as he oozed with the charm that she had not seen since before their marriage.

"No, you and Nola keep yourselves busy with the inventory. The sale will be upon us before we know it. It's a difficult time, but it is necessary," she called to her husband as she darted out the door.

Charlotte flagged down a taxi, and headed for the hotel.

Charlotte rushed into the hotel. Moments later Shelley opened the door, and the two women fell in a tight embrace.

Shelley greeted Charlotte with a light kiss that spoke more of concern than passion. Shelley discretely placed the "do not disturb" sign on the doorknob, and the two women walked inside.

Two hours later, Charlotte returned to the Hamby house, emotionally fortified to face the greedy Burns family.

"Charlotte, where the hell have you been? I called the funeral home, and they hadn't seen you," Mason yelled accusingly.

"I know. After the arrangements were confirmed I wanted to be alone. This will probably be the last time we come to Baltimore, so I wanted to walk around. Sorry you and Nola were worried," Charlotte replied contritely.

"Okay, okay, enough said. This whole business has got to be hard on you. Speaking of hard," forgetting his former anger, Mason reached under Charlotte's dress. "Feel like a little tussle?"

"I'm so tired, Mason. Could we wait awhile?" Charlotte answered.

"Yeah, yeah. Go on upstairs, but you need to get your cute little ass down here when that real estate man returns. You hear me?"

"When he returns? I thought he was coming tomorrow?" the perplexed Charlotte asked.

"Oh, he called a couple of hours ago. He said he had a cancellation. I told him to drop by. I've never been so insulted in my life." Mason's face turned crimson remembering the confrontation with the unpleasant little man. "I told the man that I was your husband, but he would only talk to you. The nerve of some people. Ma finally persuaded him into taking a look around. He said he was sure he could get us a good price. Now you run along upstairs, and I'll call you when Mr. Jacobs returns."

"Run along now. Go upstairs. What does he think I am, a child?"

Charlotte was awakened when the bedroom door flew open and Nola Burns called out,

"Charlotte, the real estate man is downstairs. Mason said for you to wake up and come down to talk to him."

"Alright, thank you, I'll be right down," Charlotte replied.

"Mrs. Burns, please, let me extend my condolences over the loss of your mother. I never met her, but I understand she was a fine woman," Mr. Jacobs said politely.

"Thank you, sir," Charlotte replied as she shook his hand.

"Now lets get down to business. This is an established neighborhood and as I am sure your husband has informed you this is an excellent time to sell."

"Yes, am I to understand that it is a sellers market," Charlotte responded.

"Yes, that is correct. I do not wish to cause you further strain, so if you ask around you will discover that we have an excellent reputation. Our company has been doing business for over thirty-five years."

"Yes, I remember hearing your jingle ads on the radio when I was a child."

"It's so kind of you to recall, Mrs. Burns. Mr. Burns indicated that you were in a rush to sell and, I uh..hesitate to mention."

"Mention what, Mr. Jacobs," Mason joined in the conversation.

"Our company, when we find a well constructed, well maintained house such as this has been known to take a chance, and purchase the property ourselves.." Mr. Jacobs stopped, seeing the obvious greed on Mason's face. "You do understand that, since we are taking a chance, we have to make an offer under the fair market price."

"How much of a loss will we have to take?" Mason replied.

"Oh, Mr. Burns, I'm not sure. I'll have to go back to my office and discuss the property with my partner. I can return with an offer, if you would wish?" Mr. Jacobs continued as he played the greedy Mason like a hungry trout in a stream.

After Mr. Jacobs left Charlotte turned to her husband, "Please Mason, I won't just give away mother's place. We don't have to sell it right now. We should proceed at a slower pace."

"I want to get my money and get the hell back home. I hate hanging around places where people have died. You'll have to clean up your mother's room. Ma and me don't take kindly to touching things used by a dead person."

"This whole house is full of things used by a dead person. First daddy and then mother. They both lived here, you will recall," Charlotte replied. "I'm tired, I'm going back upstairs."

"Rest, that's all you've done. Sonny, why should I do all of the work?" Nola whined.

"Hush, Ma! It's better if Charlotte upstairs. If we find some money or jewelry we don't have to mention it to my noble wife," Mason smiled as he imagined the wonderful possibilities of hidden money.

"Oh Mason, you're so clever." Nola continued her search.

"Let them haul off the whole place. Both of my parents are gone, so I don't care," Charlotte responded to the four walls of her mother's bedroom.

She lay for hours on Peggy's bed wondering how she spent her last hours. Out of the corner of her eye, Charlotte noticed a white envelope sticking out of her mother's copy of Jane Eyre. Charlotte opened it, and immediately recognized her mother's handwriting.

"Dear Charlotte, I will have left this world, if you are reading my final thoughts. I am sorry I drove you away to live with those people. Please forgive my selfish stupidity. I have placed a codicil leaving Howie $500.00 for all of the good times we shared. See that he gets it. You were always a better daughter than I deserved. Sorry I waited too late to speak of it. Love, Mama."

"Oh ho! $500.00 not $5,000.00. Somebody's been messing with wills, if I am any judge of people," Charlotte smiled, hugging her mother's letter to her breast.

The knowledge of her mother's last message aided Charlotte during the next few days. She blanked out the intruders around her as she went through the painful experience of laying her mother to rest. During the night while she was alone in her room she took out the small note and reread it finding surprising solace in their words. Charlotte kept her mother's letter secret.

The time for reading Peggy's will arrived. The two vultures had assembled with Charlotte in Mr. George Brady's office when a stranger walked in.

"Excuse me, sir. You have wandered into the wrong room. This is the reading of the Last Will and Testament of Peggy Hamby," Mr. George Brady stated.

"I am aware of my location, Mr. Brady. I'm Terry Paxton of Annapolis, Mrs. Charlotte Hamby Burns' attorney.
Sorry I'm late, Charlotte. The traffic was murder," Terry Paxton continued as he closed the office door.

"Charlotte, we're all friends, here. There was no need to call in separate counsel," Mr. Brady stated, annoyed with the change of events.

"Since we're all friends, I'm sure you don't mind if my friend sits in on the reading. I might need some help understanding all of those big legal terms," Charlotte's voice dripping with sarcasm.

"Mr. Paxton is here to help us remain friends," Charlotte said with feigned sincerity.

"Charlotte, I don't know what you think you are doing. I suspect you're trying to screw me, and make me pay for the experience," Howie complained bitterly.

"Before you two go any further, Mr. Cramer," Mr. Paxton squarely faced Brady. "Mr. Brady, I am here to determine if the supposed will of one Margaret Hamby, that you are about to read has been altered in the favor of Mr. Cramer," Mr. Paxton stated firmly.

"What do you think you are doing? How dare you impugn my honor, Mr. Paxton?" George Brady rebutted as a sudden touch of red began to darken his neck.

"Sir, I have been in contact with the President of the State Bar Association. If you read this will as a legitimate unaltered document of the last will and testament of one Margaret (Peggy) Hamby, he is prepared to launch an investigation into your complicity in perpetrating a fraud. If it is proved that you had prior knowledge of a crime, he will bring you up on criminal charges of fraud and begin disbarment proceedings. Do I make myself perfectly clear, Sir?"

"What is this all about, Mr. Paxton? Mr. Howie Cramer brought me a will to read upon Mrs. Margaret (Peggy) Hamby's death. The signature is a true signature. I know nothing of any alteration," Mr. Brady retorted with an indignant tone.

"Mrs. Charlotte Burns became concerned about the amount bequeathed to Mr. Cramer. She contacted the main office of Colony Insurance. She learned that several days before Mrs. Hamby's death, Mr. Cramer brought her into the local Colony agent's office. You'll never guess the name of the Colony agent, none other than our good friend, Mr. George Brady. I spoke to a couple of the Hamby neighbors that work in this building. They informed me that Charlotte's mother was brought in slumped over in a wheelchair. They hardly recognized her," Terry Paxton growled.

Charlotte continued the story as Howie Cramer squirmed about in his chair.

"I spoke with a Mr. Perry of Colony. I was told their files showed that on the day of the visit to Mr. Brady's office, mama changed her beneficiary to Howie Cramer. She had that policy for as long as I can remember. She had some weird notion about having burial money. Something she picked up from my grandmother. Feeling as she did why would she suddenly change her mind," Charlotte frowned.

It was so painful remembering her frail mother looking so small in that large coffin.

"Charlotte Hamby, you are making this all up. You've had a grudge against me for years. She was jealous of Peggy loving me. Always trying to break us up." Howie looked about a room filled with hostile unbelieving spectators.

"Howie, give it up. Mama's gone and I'll see you do not get one red cent. The policy was for $5,000.00 and the co-beneficiaries have always been The Eternal Rest Funeral Home, and I receive the remainder," Charlotte replied, her voice as cold as an iceberg.

"Mrs. Hamby's bank account balance was only $500.00. We are prepared to go to court, and prove that this was the bequest Mrs. Hamby had actually planned for Mr. Cramer," Mr. Paxton challenged.

"This whole business is dreadful. If there has been any alteration of these documents I am not aware. I agree that an investigation may be necessary. Howie, it is imperative that this situation be resolved," Mr. Brady chimed in, "Ladies and gentlemen, I suggest that we delay the reading of this fine lady's last request until we can guarantee its authenticity."

"Howie, you'd better take what you can get. Five hundred dollars is better than nothing. You could be facing a little jail time," Charlotte smiled.

"I'll be seeing you later, missy," Howie glowered as he slammed out of the office.

"Charlotte, if you aren't the clever one. How did you figure out the will was tampered with. We've got that leach on the ropes," Mason smiled as he hugged his wife.

"I found a letter from my mother stating she trusted me to be fair. Mama stated that she was giving Howie $500.00, not the $5,000.00. It never occurred to him that mother would leave me a last message," Charlotte replied. She was at last secure in the knowledge of her mother's love.

"Lets go back to your mother's, pack and head back for home. Mr. Jacobs will sell your mama's house and things, and send us the money," Mason crowed.

"Having your mama's letter in our hands, we don't have to give that trash Howie Cramer anything, do we?" Nola asked.

"We'll let Mr. Paxton determine, what if anything is to be given to Mr. Cramer. I have given Mr. Paxton my power of attorney to settle the estate," Charlotte answered, as she walked out of the sleazy attorney's office.

She did not tell Mason or Nola that there were additional instructions that had been given to Mr. Paxton that would help protect Charlotte and her baby in the future.

"What's wrong with her?" Nola complained, "You'd think she was on their side."

"I'm on my side, Mrs. Burns," Charlotte answered.

Chapter 11

The next few months continued to be difficult. Charlotte worked at Madame Lorraine's during the day, and came home at night to an unbearable environment of nagging pressure and violence. She manage to sneak regular visits to the Branson household for they were Charlotte's only link with sanity.

Charlotte hoped that after the estate was settled Mason and Nola would treat her in a kinder manner, but she became reconciled the absurdity of her dream.

She knew how badly Mason wanted a son. Charlotte also knew if she failed to produce a son, in the eyes of Mason and his mother she would have failed, again. She didn't care, she wanted a daughter, an ally. Her daughter would become her best friend so Charlotte prayed daily for a child to love and nurture, a child to build her life around.

Charlotte having returned to work forced Nola Burns back into the kitchen. She cooked her favorite evening meal consisting of meat loaf, mashed potatoes and green beans. The three sat quietly at the kitchen table engrossed in their own particular thoughts.

Charlotte pushed the meat around her plate as she mixed the beans and potatoes.

As Nola was clearing off the table, she suddenly remembered that she had failed to lock the front door.

"Times have changed. When I was a child it wasn't necessary to lock the doors and windows. Today we could all be murdered in our beds, and nobody would know the difference," the nervous Nola Burns charged out of the kitchen to lock the door.

As soon as Nola was out of earshot Mason turned to Charlotte and said, "Ma tries to hard. Eat as much as you can. I call it the meat loaf from hell. When I was a child she made it with spoiled meat. I vomited all night long," Mason chuckled. "We had to go to the doctor. He told me on the QT that if I hadn't eaten so much I'd of probably died of food poisoning."

Charlotte glanced at his curiously, "If it's so bad, why do you pretend to like it?"

"Ma's a lousy cook, but she's still my mother. If you are still hungry, I'll sneak out later and get you a hamburger."

The perplexed Charlotte did not respond as she observed her husband. He was a strange, complex man, a man of many faces.

Nola returned satisfied that the doors and windows secure from invasion.

"Let me help you, Ma. You've must be tired after such a busy day." Mason stood up and began to help his mother clear away the dishes.

Charlotte was surprisingly touched by the tenderness in his voice.

The dishes done, Nola returned to the table joining her son and Charlotte for a last cup of coffee.

"I know that you feel I am paranoid, but I will remember to my dying day. My father had taken us out to dinner, and when we arrived home the front yard was filled with policemen."

"What on earth? You must have been terrified?" Charlotte asked.

"Father found my piggy bank smashed on the walkway. All of my nickels and pennies were stolen. They never found who broke into the house, but the next day father installed locks everywhere."

"It's such a shame. Nothing seems to be sacred anymore." Charlotte's tone was filled with sympathy.

There was another lull in the conversation. Nola was nervous, Mason sat uncharacteristically quiet sipping his cold coffee as his shoulders slumped, and Charlotte had a great case of the blues tonight. She was annoyed with her life and feeling lonely and a bit sorry for herself. "I wonder what Shelley is doing?" she thought.

"I know you are having a difficult pregnancy, " Nola broke into Charlotte's gloom and continued, "Everybody has got to pull his weight, Charlotte dear," Nola interjected. She recognized the pregnancy blues, that kind of blues Nola remembered, remembered well.

Charlotte looked up at her mother-in-law, her face filled with surprise at Nola's sudden kindness.

"I'm dreadfully tired," Charlotte replied as she attempted a small smile of appreciation.

"You'll feel better once the baby is born. I'll look after it and you will return to work. You'll find once you are shed of your burden work at the dress shop won't be as difficult," Nola stated as fact.

Charlotte stared at her silent husband as a tide of nausea rolled through the pit of her stomach. "What do you mean, an it? It as you call her is a baby, and you think you'll be taking care of my child? Mason what does she mean?"

"Now you know we need your salary, so don't start getting fussy." Nola snapped.

Mason did not move, he did not speak.

Charlotte would have none of this nonsense so without further comment she waddled up to their room. The subject was dropped, for the moment.

That night the rains began. It poured for the next few days as the rivers turned an angry gray. The Charleston area became eerie as the rivers overflowed their banks. The residents, accustomed to sudden changes in the weather cautiously went about their activities.

These dreary days were spent sharing Shelley's passion, china painting. The Branson house was filled with hundreds of pattern of intricate design.

Charlotte complained that she could never paint as well as Shelley. Charles laughed when he said Shelley would paint the entire world if she were ever turned loose with a brush.

During other quiet moments Charles instructed Charlotte in the culinary arts. They made stews, clam and seafood chowders, and her favorite, shepherd's pies. She loved the bit of brandy on its top. She was especially proud of the simple accomplishment, cooking proper rice. Most folks use instant, but she learned the old fashioned way.

Outside the Branson house the dismal weather set the mood of the city, and its inhabitants.

Inside the Burns house the residents were forced indoors and into an unspoken truce.

Fortunately for Charlotte her belly was so swollen Mason didn't bother her much these days, for he spent much of his time shooting pool or with Janie Sue. Charlotte did not care for as long as he was away her unborn baby was safe from his violence.

Charlotte lived for her time with Shelley. She had made the best of her marriage, but the meetings with Shell made all of the difference in her drab and painful existence.

Spring arrived and the earth blossomed as did Charlotte. As months fled by Charlotte sloughed off the inhibitions and shackles of guilt, disregarding societies narrow conviction that non-heterosexual relationships were evil. In spite of the fact that Charlotte was the size of a barn she became closer to Shelley.

Charlotte continued to cook and clean at the Burns house, and work for Madame Lorraine. She no longer accepted the isolation Mason and his mother tried to inflict upon her. In quiet times with Shelley, they lay in the bed taking great pleasure watching her belly grow. The relationship with Shelley had strengthened her backbone. Charlotte never again wavered under the Burns' verbal assault. She had become immune to their venomous tongues as they lost their ability to hurt her.

One quiet afternoon Charlotte was rejuvenating her spirit laying with Shelley. It was their bed, their room, their secret world. The two women had converted this tiny room into a private home where they worked through their loneliness, anger, and their happiness.

"What are you thinking, Shell? You are so deep in thought," Charlotte finally broke the silence.

"I was thinking of how happy I am, here with you in our own private world," Shelley smiled into her lover's face.

"You too. I was thinking what my life would have been if you hadn't entered it." Charlotte stroked Shelley's hair.

"How will our lives be changed when the baby comes? We'll never be able to appear in public as a couple?"

"Shelley, you worry too much."

"I know, I've always been." Shelley raised up on her elbow.

"Silly goose. What do you want me to do, stand up on the rooftop, pregnant as a cow, and shout, I LOVE SHELLEY BRANSON." A giggling Charlotte hugged Shelley as tightly as her bulging tummy would permit.

"I've been thinking about something important in our relationship."

"What's that, Shell?" Charlotte became quiet.

"I want to give you something, a ring that belonged to mine and Tom's grandmother," Shelley stated.

"It's an antique. It's exquisite. No Shelley," replied Charlotte. "Dearest heart, I can not accept this. It is too valuable you must keep it in your family."

"It will remain in my family. You will wear it with your wedding ring, and then when our little Becky is born, she'll wear it. A gift from her mother and me."

"You're determined this one is a girl," Charlotte smiled dreamily as she rubbed her tummy. Her eyes flew open wide, "She hears you, Shell, she just kicked me. She approves."

"May I feel," Shelley placed her hand on Charlotte's bare stomach, sharing the excitement of their baby. "I'd be honored to wear your ring, if Tom approves."

"He does. He gave his blessing. You make me happy, and that's all he wishes. My happiness," Shelley slipped the ring on Charlotte's third finger left hand, and they kissed tenderly.

"You're officially mine now, lady," Shelley popped her on her bottom.

"I've been yours since I opened my eyes in this very bed, and looked into your wonderful adoring face."

A shiver shot through Charlotte's body as a small hand cupped her milk white flesh. She groaned deep with need for after a marriage of violence Charlotte was eager and ready for tender intimacy.

The sound of Shelley's laughter drifted through the open bedroom window as she and Charlotte sank deeper into the softness of the mattress. Beneath trembling fingertips, Shelley's companion writhed under her gentle ministration. She slid her hands up the silken back as she drew Charlotte closer.

Days of separation demanded release. Mutual need drove the women. Their bodies communicated all they needed to know.

Shelley lowered her head, capturing Charlotte's lips. Charlotte closed her eyes as Shelley's tongue penetrated her tiny mouth as Shelley's hands continued to stroke her lover's quivering body.

"I wish I could stay the night, Shell," Charlotte purred as intimate fingers coaxed her body to pleasure.

"Sometime soon, you will," Shelley whispered as she caressed every inch of her body.

Charlotte gasped and arched her back allowing Shelley greater access wanting it to last as long as possible. They moved slowly prolonging their pleasure. Entwined bodies moved in perfect unison as they peaked and collapsed.

They laid back on the bed drained of strength, floating on a cloud of ecstasy , temporarily sated from their lovemaking. The time would come when Charlotte must leave her mate and return to that house of violence. For now, they must be content.

Shelley awoke to a knock at the door.

"Shelley," Tom poked his head into their room. He observed that the two women were naked, and he could not suppress a quick smile. "You must have given her the ring."

Shelley pulled the sheet over her sleeping lover. "Yes," she returned her brother's smile, "she cried, she loved it. I've never known such happiness, but it is making me crazy thinking about her returning to those deviates."

"Deviates, huh," Charlotte awoke abruptly, "Hi Tom."

She realized that her breasts drooped over their covering. She jerked the sheet up, tucking it under her chin before she continued, "Look at my ring. Shell's so thoughtful, isn't she."

"Congratulations, my dear.. I suppose we're really family now," Tom smiled.

"Who's family?" Charles appeared from nowhere. He rested his arm on Tom's shoulder as he admired Charlotte ring.

"It's about time. I'm happy that you have committed yourselves to each other. Our next plan should be how to rid ourselves of those two next door," Charles suggested.

"Scoot, you two. Charlotte's got to dress," Shelley requested. She shuddered as a chill crept down her spine as she wondered what further distress time would bring.

Shelley leaped out of the bed, "ah-ha!" she giggled. Alone at last. You know sweetie, if those two stayed much longer I suppose we would have charged them rent. Shall I walk you home?" Shelley asked imploringly.

"Afraid I might get kidnaped. Never happen. No derrick is big enough to haul me off. I must dress and go ...back."

Charlotte didn't say home, for home was with Shelley. She never felt more alive than when they were together.

"Where have you been?" Nola demanded as she spotted Charlotte lumbering across the back yard.

"I've been taking my afternoon walk. The doctor instructed me to exercise daily for the sake of the baby," Charlotte ignored her mother-in-law's question.

"Where did that come from?" Nola pointed to Charlotte's ring.

"It's a family heirloom. Thought I'd like to wear it," Charlotte walked passed Nola.

"I don't remember seeing it in Peggy's things," Nola continued accusingly.

"Oh, don't you?" she refused to be baited, "I'm going upstairs for a bath, then I'll be down, and cook dinner. What do you think of pork chops?" Charlotte continued her journey.

Feeling refreshed after a long soak, Charlotte prepared dinner in silence, but Nola's tongue never slowed its rapid pace.

"Do you see what your snooty wife is flashing around these days? Claims it's an heirloom. Do you remember seeing it when we were doing inventory?" Nola resumed her earlier tirade.

"Knock it off, ma. Charlotte's mother was very fond of jewelry. Rings were her favorite, weren't they Charlotte. She had so many that even you could have missed a one or two." Mason was irritated with Nola's prattle.

"Charlotte, the food is great. Never get used to all of that green lettuce stuck between my teeth, but the meals look better than when Ma was cooking."

"Thanks, for attacking your poor helpless mother. All your life I worked my fingers to the bone for you. Now that I am old and helpless, this is how you pay me back. Insults, nothing but insults."

"Mason, would you care for a slice of fresh apple pie? I cooked it earlier. Would you like it with some vanilla ice cream on top."

"Sure would," Mason playfully slapped Charlotte's fanny. "This wife of mine knows how to treat a man, and you're just pea green with jealousy, ma."

"Don't be ridiculous, son. I don't have a jealous bone in my body," Nola replied as she continued to shovel in her meal.

Charlotte avoided watching Mason and Nola while they consumed their meals. She should have put large shovels at their plates, not forks. She had often thought that her life would have been simpler if she had built a fence outside and slopped them like the hogs they had become. Any genteel manners that they had been exposed to had long been forgotten, replaced by the return to caveman tactics.

Chapter 12

The Madame Lorraine shop was filled with gentle loving people. Charlotte thrived on the kindness of her friends and co-workers. The word kindness could not be found in the Burns family vocabulary.

"How is your work coming along today, my dear?" Charles asked as he stuck his head in the work room.

"Fine, thank you Charles," Charlotte smiled.

Charles returned her smile, You never complain, even when there is cause. "I've been discussing your situation with Tom. We want you to consider letting us bump you up to bookkeeping."

"Oh!" Charlotte forced a small smile as she replied, "Oh Charles, I don't know."

"You are a fast learner. You are one of our most diligent employees, and you are a joy to all."

"How can I be anybody's joy! I'm so emotional these days. It's probably just the pregnancy. Women get nutty ideas when they are bulged out in all directions," Charlotte sadly replied.

"Never fear, dear heart, we'll all survive the pregnancy and your training period. You have a job with our company as long as you wish."

"Thanks, Charles. I appreciate your confidence."

"You're a smart girl, Charlotte and we intend to use your natural abilities."

"My natural abilities," Charlotte laughed, "I wasn't aware, after my bad judgment with Mason that I had any good natural abilities."

"You'd be surprised. You have greater talent than you imagine, but as for your marrying Mason, well my dear, there's no explaining such choices."

"Isn't that the truth, and as for my talent! Mason complains that I have no talent, that I'm just a dreamer."

"And what's wrong with dreaming?" Charles asked, "Dreamers are visionaries."

"Mason says dreamers are unemployable."

"What does he know? You unemployable. We want to begin

training you on our computer."

"Computer! Charles, I love you dearly, but have you been out of your mind?"

"Not hardly. I love you too, little one, but I am also an excellent businessman. I was at the head of my class, and I also major in good common sense," Charles stated. Her friend, and employer appeared to take great offense with Charlotte's reaction.

"We run a business, not a hobby. We treated you the same way we treat all prospective employees. We ran our usual check, your minister, co-workers, friends, and of course, with your school in Baltimore. You could have been a secret ax murderess for all we knew," Charles teased. "We never realized you had such a well rounded education. Naughty girl, hiding your light under the proverbial bushel basket."

"An ax murderess, huh! Father felt we should be introduced to many areas of learning. Music, art, even physics. I've had them all, but never computers. Those things confound me."

"We confirmed what we already suspected that you were an excellent student and that you did well in academic courses. Tom and I, feel you are wasted in the cutting room. Monday you begin a new career working under our head bookkeeper. You will have a six week training period at your same salary. Then we will see. There could be a raise in your future. You might even consider night school."

Charlotte jumped out of her chair giving Charles a great big bear hug.

"I just love you so much. I'll do my best."

"Enough hugging, young lady. Stop trying to jump up and down, I'm not delivering that baby. Now lets get back to business. In our business we use the Sperry Computer System, IBM compatible."

"Are you sure I can be brought into this strange new world, Charles?" Charlotte whispered.

"Hush brat! You could take business courses that would insure that raise. You can use the money, can't you?"

"Alright, if you're not afraid I'll misplace all of your money, or send it off into infinity," Charlotte smiled.

"If I thought you incapable, no amount of friendship would make me risk my business. It's settled." Charlotte's training began the next day as she began to learn the business activities of Madame's business activities.

As her girth increased, so did her business knowledge, and her piggy bank. She used the shop as a mailing address so that her private business could remain private. Charlotte kept secret the news of her promotion as she continued to give Mason her pay check and deposited the difference in her personal account.

Mason never came to Charlotte's work place for fear of contamination from those weirdos. He knew Charlotte worked with Tom and Charles, but was not aware that they were the owners.

One day, Mason was short of funds, and appeared on the front doorsteps of the business.

"I'm looking for my wife, Charlotte Burns. Where does she work?" he demanded about the time she came waddling out of the door on the arm of none other than Tom Branson.

"Mason, what are you doing here? Is it five o'clock already?" Charlotte attempted to make the surprise visit appear natural.

"No, it is not five o'clock. Why are you holding onto that fags arm? Are you two having a thing, and he's just pretending to be a queer to throw people off?" Mason yelled as he dragged Charlotte out the front door with Charles in hot pursuit.

"Mason, please be careful. The baby, don't hurt the baby," Charlotte cried pitifully as he dragged her down the stairs.

"If it wasn't for the baby, I'd kill you right this minute, you slut. All of these months working here around these weirdos, and not mentioning a word about how cosy you've become."

"Come back inside, let me introduce you to two of the ladies I work with. Please, Mason," Charlotte tried to ignore his ugly accusations.

"I'll ask you again. That man your lover. You trying to palm off your bastard off on me?" "How could you say such a thing?" Charlotte's body shook with terror as she faced her enraged husband.

Suddenly without warning he slapped her so hard that her ears were ringing as she lost her balance and collapsed to the ground.

The shop employees ran to Charlotte's aid. Tom and Charles grabbed Mason's arms to prevent further violence.

"DO NOT interfere between a man and his wife. A woman needs a good smack every now and then to keep her in line." Mason reveled in the uproar he had created at Madame Lorraine's. It was obvious that he took pride in his abuse of his pregnant wife.

"You don't slap around a woman in my presence, especially a pregnant woman," Tom screamed his face red with anger.

"Well pansy, what do into to do about it. Want to fight?" Mason roared.

Charles ignored Mason's taunting as he knelt beside their unconscious friend while inside the office several fellow workers held Shelley at bay. They knew should Shelley's arms be freed that she would charge outside to protect her lover, and their carefully guarded secret would be no more.

"Call an ambulance, somebody please!" Charles called to one of the employees. "Charlotte needs immediate medical attention."

"An ambulance. Who can afford an ambulance bill?" Mason shrieked. "She's not hurt, that bad. Besides, I'm not made of money. Put her in the car, I'll drive my wife to her personal physician," Mason demanded as he continued his complaints.

"As an employee of this company, Charlotte, uh, Mrs. Burns', uh, accident occurred on our property. We are prepared to pay her medical expenses. Satisfied, Mr. Burns?" Tom replied to the insensitive husband.

He knew that somewhere in the building his terrified sister watched helpless to comfort Charlotte. For the love of Shelley and Charlotte, Tom intended to see that Charlotte received proper care for herself and her unborn child.

"Well, that's better. Call the ambulance," Mason agreed, quite pleased that the cost of Charlotte's temporary rebellion would not come out of his pockets.

Hum, he thought, "these people seem real concerned. Maybe they feel guilty about Charlotte's accident. We just might sue them. Ma and me sure could use some extra spending money. These weirdos are prime for a fleecing."

"We called an ambulance minutes ago, Mr. Allgood," the employee ignored Mason as though he were not there.

"We not only work with Charlotte, she is our friend," another employee chimed in.

The small crowd had assembled after the occurrence and were getting restless and hostile.

Mason was becoming nervous about this bunch of jerks getting nasty, they might cause him some trouble, just because he tried to put his wife in her place. He looked about at the angry faces of strangers. Where the hell was that damnable ambulance? What was taking it so long? The hospital wasn't more than ten minutes away.

Mason regained his voice, "If you folks are such good friends, how can you let her, in her delicate state of health wander about in such unsafe conditions? Yeah, you're some friends to let this accident happen. Lousy mortar on the steps. Maybe I'll sue?"

"I don't think I'd try that if I were you. I was looking out the window when Charlotte's--uh, accident occurred." The employee continued, "perhaps we should also call the police."

"Yeah, yeah, you weirdos stick together. You can't be trusted. Call the cops for all I care. Accidents happen everyday." Mason leaned over to his wife. "Are you awake, sweetie? We've called an ambulance, and you'll be right as rain in no time."

"She'd better be or you will answer to me." Tom Branson, leaving Charles to care for Charlotte, turned on his heel, for inside was his hysterical sister. He prayed that someone was caring for her.

Tom found Shelley out in the hall leaning against a co-worker.

"How is she, Tom?" Shelley asked, her face white as chalk.

"She's conscious, and doesn't appear to be in much pain. I'm just concerned about the baby." Tom hugged Shelley as he concealed his worried expression in her long tresses.

"What will we do if Charlotte loses the baby? We've so looked forward to her arrival," Shelley whispered as she received strength and comfort from her adoring brother.

"We'll be there for our Charlotte. Give her all of the love and support she'll need. For now sweetie, the hospital is the best place for her," Tom stated as he watched Shelley leave.

Shelley almost fainted when she saw her beloved Charlotte laying so still on the ground. It seemed like an eternity since the emergency call was made, but in the distance the wail of the siren could be heard.

"Charlotte, it's Shelley. How are you, dear?" Shelley reached for Charlotte's hand.

"What's this damn, dear business? Get the hell away from my wife," Mason demanded.

"She's fine, Shelley. Our Charlotte will be just fine," Charles reassured his friend.

"You act as though you're the only ones concerned about my wife," Mason snapped.

"Of course, we're not, sir. She is a good woman and highly respected. Mr. Burns, Charlotte is a friend to everyone at Madame Lorraine's. She is a valued employee. You know your wife's tender heart," Charles spoke to the mad man.

"That's Charlotte alright. She's a pushover for every stray cat, on two feet or four. Always bringing home strays. Cats, dogs and kids, she's nuts about all of them."

There was a sudden screech of brakes and car doors opening as the emergency crew arrived.

"What's happened?" the EM asked, as he examined the fallen woman.   "Charlotte Burns, my wife, I was picking her up from work, and as you can see she is very pregnant, and she took a fall. Stumbled on some loose mortar," Mason explained.

"Uh huh," was all the attendant said. He had not missed the deep red partial hand print and streak marring the otherwise delicate white skin.

"Mrs. Burns, when's your due date," the attendant asked.
"Five weeks."
"Are you in pain?"
"My back is hurting."
"Where? Upper or lower?"
"Lower. Oh, please help me. It stings so."
"Ma'am, try to relax. Let us do our job."

"Oh no!" moaned Charlotte. "My water just broke. I'm in labor. It's too soon."

"Don't you worry, ma'am. Babies come when they are ready.

"I don't think southern manners are necessary. I'm Charlotte, what's yours?"

"My name is Mike, and I'm an expert at delivering babies. Stay calm, we may have to deliver this one together. Okay?"

"Oooh. Shelley, Where are you?"

"I'm here, honey," answered the frightened woman. "I'm Shelley, her friend and coach," Shelley added.

Shelley took Charlotte's hand and squeezed it tenderly. "It hurts worse than I expected. Oh it's bad, Shell," Charlotte moaned.

"I know. Remember all of those lessons? Don't fight the pain, work with it. Breathe! Breathe!"

"Let's get you to the hospital. Correct ladies," Mike smiled. He did not know all the players, but he did know that Shelley kept his patient calm. He suspected that with her physical condition and past injuries Mrs. Burns needed to be separated from Mr. Burns.

Mike stood up as he broke his first cardinal rule of non-involvement, "Mr. Burns, since you have your car. Why don't we let Shelley ride in the ambulance with your wife? You can follow."

"You won't leave her side, will you young man?"

"No sir. You don't worry about your wife or your baby. They will be just fine." Mike assisted the second attendant. They slipped their fragile cargo into the back of the ambulance.

"See you at the hospital," Mike waved to Mason as he slammed the ambulance door in Mason's face.

"Get rolling Ernie," was all Mason heard as the vehicle sped away. An afternoon breeze prevented Mason's hearing the driver's reply.

"OOOOH, Shell! It's terrible. My back hurts. Real sharp pains," Charlotte moaned as a burning pain shot through her body. " OOOOH NO! Here comes another one, OOOOOOH, Shell."

Charlotte began to jerk as she fought back from this alien inside her belly. She released an ear piercing scream. Charlotte released Shelley's hand as she was hurled into a blackness.

"She fainted. You've got to help her work through the pain, miss. It will be worse for her if she keeps fighting the contractions," Mike cautioned Shelley.

"We'll be at the hospital in five minutes. They can give you something to help," Mike told Charlotte reassuringly.

"How's her blood pressure? You've taken it three times already," Shelley demanded.

"Her pressure is a little high, but her vitals are stable. Try not to worry about your friend, miss."

"I appreciate your assistance Mike," realizing Charlotte had awakened Shelley whispered, "What really happened? I wasn't at a window so I didn't see anything. Did Mason hit you?" Shelley demanded although the tell-tell-tale evidence was glaring at her, the hand print on Charlotte's cheek.

"I fell... Mason told you," Charlotte snapped as she signaled Shelley to ask no further questions.

"That's a mighty bad bruise on your cheek," Mike joined the conversation.

"Yes. My husband told you, I fell," Mrs. Burns replied.

Mike was going to get no information.

On the journey to the hospital, the two women worked together through Charlotte's pains.

Mike could see that theirs was a special relationship, and it was none of his business. He also was aware by the way Charlotte Burns clammed up that more was going on than met the eye.

He felt sorry for the two women, but he had his own troubles. He tried not to get involved in others peoples problems. If he did, he'd go nuts. He would report to the doctors, his suspicions, but from then on, there wasn't much he could do.

The ambulance arrived at the Community hospital as nurses and attendants streamed out of the emergency room door.

"Hi Mike. What have we got here?"

"Mrs. Charlotte Burns took a fall about thirty minutes ago. Her vital signs are slightly elevated, and she is complaining on sharp back pains. Subsequent to the fall her water broke and she is in the early stages of labor. She says she's five weeks early."

"We'll take it from here. Anything else?"

"No!" Mike started to say something, but walked away. Whatever was going on wasn't any of his business. And here comes that creep of a husband.

"Don't look so scared, honey," smiled the large dark skinned woman, "Five weeks early is nothing these days."

"Has my baby been damaged by my fall? Will I loose my baby?" Charlotte forced the words out.

"Hush up, such talk. You and your baby will be just fine. Look how you are frightening your poor little friend with such talk. I'm gonna take good care of you. My name is Carla."

"Hi Carla! Please help me, it's too early for my baby to arrive," Charlotte begged.

"I'm gonna take good care of you. And as for this baby, they have a tendency to come when they're ready, not when their mama and are necessarily ready. You got your nursery fixed up nice and pretty?" Carla talked non-stop to keep Charlotte's mind off of worry.

"Yes, we've painted it white with a pink, yellow, and blue bear border. That's usable for a girl or a boy." "Well aren't you the practical one. You're all set for which ever the good Lord sends you," Carla smiled as she checked Charlotte's pulse.

Is this nervous man your husband, sweetie?"

"Yes, Mason, is my husband," Charlotte frowned.

"I was picking Charlotte up early." He repeated his story without being asked, "because Charlotte's been so tired lately. She fell coming down the steps. Madame Lorraine's Shoppe, where she works, is paying the bill. Right, Miss Branson?" Mason faced Shelley as he dared her to open her mouth.

"Oh course, we'll accept responsibility. Have your admissions clerk send the bill to our office," Shelley responded with all of the dignity she could muster.

"You folks will have to take that up with admitting. My only concern is my patient," Carla smiled down at Charlotte. "Family and friends may remain in the waiting room, after you fill out the admitting forms. They're such an aggravation, but hospitals run on paper work." Carla stated sympathetically as she wheeled Charlotte into a private cubby-hole. She called out, "I'll let you know when there's something to tell. Right now she needs quiet and rest."

Dr. Walker came in and examined Charlotte's chart, "Mrs. Burns, please try not to move. I know you are in pain, but you must let us examine you," Dr. Walker stated.

"I'm so sorry, but I hurt so terribly," Charlotte replied.

As the doctor turned Charlotte over the nurse suppressed a gasp. Her back, sides and buttocks were covered in bruises, not only fresh ones from today's accident, but old bruises, marks, and scars. This woman was obviously accident prone or a victim of abuse.

"Mrs. Burns, where did all of these abrasions come from?" Dr. Walker asked gently. "What abrasions?" Charlotte replied, "I am accident prone. Been that way all my life. Mother said I was the clumsiest child she had ever seen."

"Yes ma'am. Whatever you say," Dr. Walker replied.

Carla stepped away from Charlotte's side to consult with the doctor.

"This woman has been beaten, beaten often, and viscously. Mike felt she was afraid of her husband. Isn't there anything we can do? Report this to the police," Carla quizzed.

"Not unless she is prepared to tell the truth and to bring charges against her husband. My money's on him." Take good care of our patient, Carla."

"Yes, sir. With pleasure." Carla turned back to her patient.

"Oooh, please. Can't you give me something? The pains..." Charlotte cried.

"Yes ma'am. I'll give you something just as soon as the doctor writes the orders," the concerned nurse stated.

"Thanks. Where is Shelley?" Charlotte whispered.

"Shelley, that your husband?"

"No! Shelley's my friend. Please, may I see her. She's my coach," Charlotte implored. " Pl-ea-se!" A wave of pain tore through her body.

"Yes ma'am! I'd be happy to." Carla left the room. "I'll make my patient comfortable, one way or the other."

Nurse Carla joined the pair in the waiting room. She spoke softly as she made her story sound plausible.

"Well, our little mama is doing nicely. There is no need for you two to hang around losing sleep. Mr. Burns, why don't you go home and get some rest. Dr. Walker gave Mrs. Burns something to make her sleep. She'll be well rested in the morning. First babies normally take a long time. She's is in no immediate danger. Why don't you take our good advice? You'll need to be well rested. You won't be getting much sleep when the baby gets home. We'll call you if there are any changes."

"But can't I see her for just a minute?" Mason complained. "After all I'm the father."

"Oh course you are. Of course you are. You did the important part, planting the seed. Sorry sir. You're not needed until your little family returns home and you begin the two AM diaper change," Carla smiled brightly.

"Well okay, if you are sure. We live fifteen minutes away. Call me if I'm needed," Mason scowled as he walked away. He turned around, "You're leaving too, aren't you, Miss Branson?"

"Yes, I just need to speak to the nurse about the, uh insurance. You run along, Mr. Burns, I'll be right along," Shelley answered.

"No hurry, I'll wait. Have you eaten yet?" Mason pushed every situation to the limits. Maybe she could spring for dinner.

"Are you Shelley?" Carla asked.

"Yes," she whispered, "Where do I go to discuss the payment for Mrs. Burns accident?"

Carla pointed in the direction opposite to Mason.

"I'll call your house later to see if Charlotte has delivered. See you later, Mr. Burns, I must settle with admissions," Shelley walked down the hall and prepared to get on the elevator. Mason sadly realized that he had missed a free supper.

"Why should I have to pay to eat supper, just because Charlotte is injured. I'll go over to my Janie Sue's. She always looks after my needs," Mason complained to the night wind.

Shelley waited a few minutes to reassure herself Mason had left the hospital. She rode the elevator back to the maternity floor where she hoped to sneak past that nosey nurse.

"What is it? Is something wrong with Charlotte?" Shelley asked.

"Nothing. I'm sorry to have frightened you, but Mrs. Burns doesn't wish to be disturbed by her husband this evening. "After getting a look at her back with its old bruises and scars, I'm sure will agree that the heartless bastard should be kept miles away from her."

"You are her friend. Can't you convenience her to file charges against him."

"I've tried. She thinks she would have no place to go with the baby and all. But I want to thank you for your concern. She's been through so much," Shelley said angrily. Shelley, you'd better hold your tongue for Charlotte will never forgive you if you divulge too much.

"You have to be real careful in these situations. Can't accuse the wrong person.." Carla never finished her statement for Shelley interrupted.

"I've never understood why such a sweet person like Charlotte could settle for so little," Shelley's voice became more agitated.

"Well, we'll take care of her, the two of us. Come on." Carla led the way to the small white labor room. "She's in here."

"Hi!" Shelley stuck her head in the door. "Nursey asked me if I'd like to sit with you while she gets to get some good, major pain killer," Shelley grinned as she come to Charlotte.

"Shelley, this is the worst pain. If Mason hadn't hit me so hard. It's too soon for the baby."

"Lie still, you may have a concussion. Have they given you the results of any of the tests?" Shelley squeezed Charlotte hand.

"No, nothing yet. Carla has been great to me. Ooooh, Shell."

"Don't fight it, first babies take a long time. Work with the pain." Carla crooned as she returned to her patient. "The doctor has ordered this medication to take the edge off the pain."

Helping Charlotte sit up, Shelley assisted Carla readjust the patient.   "Thanks, Carla."

"You're quite welcome, Mrs. Burns."

"Please call me Charlotte."

"Okay Charlotte," Carla smiled. "This is going to be a busy night.

Full moon, or something. I have so many other patients to tend to. Shelley, would you mind staying with your friend?"

"Yes, I believe I might stay awhile."

"Good! You two visit. She'll be too busy for company later. See you girls. The buzzer is at the head of the bed if you need me."

Shelley held Charlotte's hand, oblivious to their surroundings. They talked, held hands tighter when the pains increased Shelley fed Charlotte ice. During the quiet time, Shelley brushed Charlotte's damp hair. Unable to stand Charlotte's pain Shelley would gently kiss Charlotte's lips..

Carla walked in during one of the kisses. "So that's what it's all about. How'd she ever let herself be bedded by a man," Carla thought as she stepped softly from the room. "Not my style, but seeing those two together, I've never seen greater devotion."

The hours dragged by as Charlotte continued with a long grueling labor. The pains were five minutes apart, then three. Charlotte jerked around the bed writhing with pain.

"Shell, get me some help. The pains are hot and long. I'm burning up. Help me," screamed the exhausted Charlotte.

"Help my friend, please. I don't know how much more she can stand."

"It shouldn't be much longer," Dr. Walker pronounced upon his latest examination of the patient almost 24 hours after she entered the hospital. "Miss, uh, Branson, if you are tired and would wish to excuse yourself, we'll understand."

"I'm fine, doctor. Thanks, anyway," Shelley responded with gritted teeth.

"Alright Mrs. Burns get ready for one last big push."

With that final push out popped Rebecca Jane Burns. Jane, for Charlotte's heroine Jane Eyre.

"We've already called the father. Shelley, you may want to leave before he gets here. Kiss the new mommy goodbye," Carla's statement surprised the pair.

Shelley kissed Charlotte.

"Night sweetheart," she whispered softly, "I'll see you tomorrow," the misty-eyed Shelley left.

"Thanks for your kindness, Carla. When will Mason arrive?"

"I had one of the other nurses call him, so I could make you comfortable. I'm giving you a sleeping pill, Doctor's orders," Carla stated in an innocent manner, "so you will probably be snoozing when he arrives. Sweet dreams," Carla said as she plopped a pill in Charlotte's mouth.

She was sleeping soundly when Mason arrived.

"Where's my son?" Mason bellowed.

"Your son?" Carla asked. "Didn't somebody tell you that you have a beautiful baby daughter?"

"Shit", Carla heard the expletive come from Mason Burns.

"Has she already named the kid without me, too?"

"I believe that she mentioned Rebecca Jane Burns, sir."

"She just had to get that name Jane in there somewhere. She thinks *Jane Eyre* is the greatest piece of literature ever written. Silly mush, as far as I'm concerned."

Mason Burns stalked out of the maternity ward and called back over his shoulder, "Let my wife know, I'll be back, if she wake's the hell up. Tell her that my ma will be coming up here too."

"Mr. Burns, don't you want to see your daughter?" Carla called to his back.

"Nope, I've got a lifetime to look at her. Next one better be a boy," Mason grumbled as he slammed through the hospital door.

Charlotte awoke in a room filled with the brilliance of the morning sun. In the distant she could see the skyline of Charleston. She ached everywhere. Charlotte was torn and exhausted, but strangely happy from the birth of her baby daughter.

"Charlotte, how are you feeling this morning?" Carla stood in the doorway.

"Have you ever awakened to the sound of tomtoms going off in your head? Or the feeling that you were run over by an eighteen wheeler, and then he backed up?"

"Yes, I have. That was the morning after the night before when I was dancing all night at Big Red's tavern. It's been difficult to get to work on Monday morning. My tongue has been a nasty green that tasted like the deep end of the garbage can," Carla frowned as she remembered several gigantic hangovers.

"I can not remember having a week-end party, but after all I've only had a baby," Charlotte giggled as she tried to envision her nurse's wild week-end.

"Well, you have given birth to a daughter. You have sustained two broken ribs and a cracked skull. If it wasn't for your hard head you'd have been in real trouble." Carla smiled. "Ready for breakfast? On yes, the Burns are on their way up. Sorry kid, I've held them off as long as possible."

"Well there's our new mommie." Nola pushed through the door.

"Hello granny," Charlotte returned the compliment.

"What did you say? Don't call me granny," Nola snapped back playfully.

"Hush ma. Where is the baby? I've got to see her sometime. When can we spring you? Ma cooked breakfast this morning, and I've been burping up a greasy taste all the way over to the hospital."

"When you get home it has been decided that you will go back to work, even if they are a strange sort. I'll keep the baby. Uh, Rebecca, is it?"

"I want to stay home with my baby. For a while, anyway. I'm her mother," Charlotte cried.

"What's wrong Miss Yankee, do you find me so incompetent that I may not care for your baby? I'm not wild about the idea, but face facts, you make the most money, Charlotte," Nola whined. "We're used to nice things again, my dear."

"Charlotte, we'll discuss it later, but you are going back to work," Mason stated firmly.

"But what if I plan to nurse Becky?"

"Forget it, even those people ain't gonna like it if you walk around their office with a leaking tit hanging out. Not very good for business," Mason laughed.

"Why couldn't we put a crib in the corner at work. Charlotte could feed Becky in the next room whenever she is hungry?" Shelley joined the conversation.

"Alright, the baby goes to work for a while. If Charlotte nurses her, we can save on the price of formula," Mason proclaimed, not happy losing to mere women.

"I can't hang around this fool hospital all day. I'll see the kid later. Ma, are you coming?"

"No dear. You run along. I'll see you back at the house."

"Goodbye Mason. I'll give your love to Becky," Charlotte replied.

"Charlotte, do you mind if we have a little chat while we wait for Rebecca. Miss Branson, you don't have to leave. I won't be staying long," Nola stated.

"Thank you, Mrs. Burns."

"I'm sorry, Charlotte, that Mason acted so badly about Rebecca's not being a boy. He's moody, bitter like his father. Been that way for as long as I can remember."

"I wish I had been able to get him to talk to me. I've never understood his anger," Charlotte replied.

"He is obsessed with the loss of the Burns family money. My baby boy believes in his heart that local politicians cheated his grandfather Burns out of most their land," Nola laughed. "We'll save that story for some rainy afternoon.

"Where's that granddaughter of mine?"

After Becky's birth Mason became unusually quiet about money. He continued to dream of the return to power that the Burns' family once enjoyed while a nervous Nola waited for the day that her disturbed son would explode.

Becky was about four months old when Mason approached Charlotte.

"Charlotte, why don't you change employment. A man has got his pride. He just can't have his wife working for weirdos like the Bransons."

"Why should I change, Mason? The money's great, and you're not bringing in a regular salary. Your mother enjoys pointing out that I make more money, and must I remind you that you are, again, used to nice things."

The subject of a job change was closed as Charlotte continued to work for Tom and Charles. She and Becky thrived on the attention from Shelley and the two men.

Mason kept his distance from Charlotte's friends. They suspected that he avoided them for fear of being prosecuted for the injuries that Charlotte had sustained in her supposed fall. It was Charlotte's fault, the bitch. She deserved to be punished. How dare she keep the secret that her weirdo friends Branson and Allgood owned Madame Lorraine. He'd keep an eye out for any shenanigans.

Becky's paternity never was in question for she was the spitting image of her father. Besides, Mason laughed, what could two old fags do with a woman?

Months rushed by as Mason become morbidly obese. Much to Charlotte's unhappiness his size so impeded Janie Sue and Mason's love making that Janie Sue lost interest. Mason stayed home and pestered Charlotte much to her chagrin.

In a local bar Janie Sue had been overheard saying, "what good is he to me, the fat is so deep you can't find his thing for a good ride."

Inevitably Janie Sue's remarks got back to Mason who was taunted by his barroom buddies. They offered to oblige Janie Sue if he could not manage. One friend suggested if Mason could not handle is mistress how in the hell can he manage a wife. During raucous laughter and guffaws another friend hollered, "The other night I found Mason in the can. He had pulled out a hair instead of his dick and peed down his leg.

Mason became so angry that his inevitable beatings of Charlotte became more violent as if he could punish her for the abuse he had taken at the bar.

Charlotte's life dragged on. The monotony of Mason's treatment ignoring her, beating, raping her interspersed with his wonderful pet names made time with him move imperceptibly. Charlotte was surprised when Becky began to talk that she did not refer to her mother as bitch or whore for good old Mason rarely referred to her in any other way. On the other hand, when Charlotte spent time with Shelley or was able to spend a glorious afternoon alone with Becky time literally flew.

Soon Becky would be celebrating her fourth birthday. Mason was afraid that she would be an only child, while Charlotte feared that there would be more.   She had discussed with Shelley the desirability of having her tubes tied, but thus far she had failed to take any action.

The morning breeze coming off the river was crisp and cold. There were crowds rushing about the city preparing for another busy day at work.   Frozen faced Charleston residents were recovering from Thanksgiving and anticipating the continuation holiday season.

"Christmas is coming soon.   Our Becky will enjoy the season better than before,"   Shelley stated.   She and Charlotte were enjoying a cup of coffee as they watched Becky play in their makeshift nursery.

"Yes, she has grown so much this year. Becky's no longer a baby, she's become her own little person,"   Charlotte replied.

"We've always decorated for the holidays, but this year we'll go all out."

"Mason seems to hate the holidays. I don't want it to rub off own our daughter," Charlotte replied wistfully.

"We'll have a big party and invite all of our friends," Shelley said, ignoring Charlotte's painful reference to Becky's parentage.

"I can hardly wait. Let me bake the fruit cakes. Becky will love helping us cut out Santa, Star and Tree cookies," Charlotte stated as she exploded in laughter.   "There is no way I can be a hum-bug with you around."

"Why do you always laugh at me? I just love Christmas."

"Oh, you are such a little minx. Your enthusiasm is so infectious," Charlotte replied.

Christmas down South was different from Baltimore Maryland. There was no snow piled along the edges of the house. Charlotte missed the winter wonderland of her youth. Her father's people had come from Vermont, and some of her fondest memories were of the sleigh rides. Someday she would carry Becky back home for a season of big snowmen, snow battles, and she, Becky, and Shelley would share a horse drawn sleigh ride.

Charlotte watched in amazement as the Branson house was transformed into a Holiday show place. Each year Tom and Shelley seemed to outdo all of the previous years efforts. The windows were ablaze with candlelight welcoming the holiday travelers.

"Do you realize life's joke was on me?" Nola grumbled as she begrudgingly walked to her neighbors festivities.

"How is that, ma?" Charlotte asked.

"I had dreamed of attending a finishing school in Switzerland, instead I stayed home and attended a Maryland University."

"Right, that's when you met dad, and got pregnant. Didn't they have birth control back then?" Mason asked as he watched his mother's face darken.

"Mason, don't be crude. Girls that took birth control were shunned. Please lower your voice, Becky might overhear. Remember, grandchildren should always have a high opinion of their grandmothers. Don't spoil my image, sonny," Nola chided.

"I'm crude, ma? If you had kept your knees together, you wouldn't have gotten pregnant. You could have been happily shipped off to Switzerland."

"Mason, after all of these years why don't you give it a rest just for one evening? It gets boring when you have heard about your lot in life hundreds and hundreds of times."

"Shush, you two. Somebody might hear you arguing. Be pleasant, this is the Christmas season," Charlotte scolded the pair.

"Don't shush me, for my poor manners. I assure you, Charlotte Burns, that my ancestors had the bluest blood in this area. Founding fathers and all of that." Nola turned up her nose in deepest offense.

"Ma Burns, we all know about your pedigree. If you had been a poodle we could have gotten AKC papers for you," Charlotte replied giggling. "Laugh all you wish, Becky has the finest blood flowing in her veins. And speaking of my granddaughter, why did she have to come over early to help these strange employers of yours?" Nola ranted.

"Oh, ma, don't be that way. She loves to help. The Bransons and Charles love our Becky, and would do her no harm," Charlotte replied.

"Okay, remember that I will be watching them in case a situation arises."

"What type of situation?" Charlotte challenged.

"Well, I hardly expect them to attack the child in front of their guests, but you never know," Nola answered.

"Don't be ridiculous. We're there, please behave, both of you."

"I've told you, I know how to behave, Charlotte." Nola snapped.

Charlotte held her breath for fear of other cutting remarks popping out of the mouth of her envious mother-in-law. Her first reaction to their invitation had been predictable.

"You don't imagine that I'm so bored that I must attend a Christmas party hosted by your weird employers?" Nola complained.

"Oh Ma, Shelley, Tom and Charles are sweet. You'd love them if you bothered to get to know them," Charlotte stated.

"Yeah, SWEET...That's what Mason and I are afraid of?"

"You're perfectly safe. You're not Tom or Charles type," Charlotte laughed.

"I may not be, but have they ever made any unnatural advances to you? I wonder sometimes, the way you are always jumping to their defense," Nola questioned as her hateful arrow struck its mark.

Charlotte turned her back on her mother-in-law feeling the color rise on her face. She was aware that her conduct would have to be more circumspect from this moment on if Nola Burns were to not realize the truth of Charlotte's true feelings.

"Come on Ma. It will be fun. They are nice people and excellent employers." "Oh pooh. I don't really want to go to their silly old party. Why do you wish to attend? We won't know a soul there," Nola complained.

"They have very interesting friends and business associates. A concert pianist from Europe will be there. I believe they know some famous writers, and an actress or two. There will be a gospel singer and an opera singer, Tommy somebody. He's from New York," Charlotte wheedled.

Entering the front door, they could not suppress their amazement over the twinkling multi colored lights adorning every archway. The chandelier sparkled in the living room. Pine cones could be heard crackling in the fireplace. Waiters from the catering service

circulated with large silver trays of champagne while others busily
served the lines of hungry guests.

Nola, of course, had to make her usual last sarcastic remark. "You
two may have dragged me inside this den of iniquity, but I thank my
maker that I won't have to pay the utility bills."

"Merry Christmas, everybody," Charlotte smiled as she reached
over to pick up her child.

"Merry Christmas, mommie, daddy, granny. Isn't it pretty?"
Becky's eyes danced with excitement.

"Yes it is darling," Charlotte replied.

"Merry Christmas, everyone," Nola nodded and she returned a
polite smile to her hosts.

"Merry Christmas, Mrs. Burns," Tom attempted to shake Nola's
hand. "How do you like the house?" He glanced about, "Aren't you
girls pleased that we hired the help so you could enjoy their own
party."

"Thanks Tom," Charlotte replied.

"Your decorations are beautiful, Mr. uh., Branson. It looks like
a ginger bread house."

"It is a ginger bread house, Granny. It was my idea," Becky
laughed. "Aunt Shelley asked me what kind of decorations I
wanted, and she created a ginger bread house just for me."

"How nice dear," Nola frowned, reacting this "aunt" business.
She'd talk to the child later, no need spoiling her holiday. Shelley
and Charlotte exchanged polite Christmas kisses, but an
undercurrent cracked throughout the room as their fingers touched.

"Come Mrs. Burns, let me introduce you to several of our other
friends. I am sure you will someone with common interest," Tom
replied as he guided her through the throng of merrymakers.

Winter dragged on, and in spite of the pleasant Christmas, the
warring Burns tiptoed about the house in their usual strained
atmosphere.

Each morning Charlotte trudged through the icy rain to the bus
stop as the numbing wind froze her face. She pushed her trembling
fingers inside her coat as a sudden whirlwind snapped at her scarf.
Charlotte enjoyed the winter wonderland created by the icy sleet as

the trees and bushes became frozen like crystal clear jewels. "Watch your step. The black ice is deceptive. You could fall", she thought. Charlotte hurried through the winter storm to the office filled with warm loving friends.

Suddenly the warmth of the sun covered the earth as tiny buds began to push their way through the barren soil. Baby birds peeking over warm nests chirped loudly as they announced their arrival heralding another spring, the promise of freedom for its winter prisoners.   "Charlotte, what are you doing home so early?" Nola demanded as she heard the door slam shut. "Out looking for a little excitement?" Nola chortled.

"I called home, Nola, because Madame Lorraine declared a half day holiday." "Half day holiday. Oh no, we live on a budget. How will we pay the mortgage?" Nola screamed.

"We could also use Mason's salary," Charlotte snapped as she faced down her tormentor.

"Mason does the best he can, you ungrateful girl. He needs all of his money to get his new business off the ground."

"What is this new business? Drugs, stolen goods," Charlotte attacked.

"How dare you say such a thing about my sonny," Nola retorted.

"Frankly Nola, I'll never understand why you so blindly defend Mason."

"Let's not argue. Be pleasant. Walk with me, Charlotte." Nola attempted to change the subject.

"How about apple pie for dessert? I'm tired of all of those vegetables. Veggie diets," Charlotte smiled at Nola's suggestion.

The neighbors were in shock as they gazed out their windows to see the Burns women strolling together as they appeared to enjoy the beautiful afternoon. Charlotte's thoughts kept straying to the sudden change in Nola's attitude. What was Nola Burns up to? She was actually attempting to make peace.

"What's Mason doing inside the carriage house everyday. He refuses to allow me to enter?" Charlotte asked.

"Mason," Nola called out to her son. "Supper is in an hour."

"Nola, what does he do in that carriage house?" Charlotte

pressed.

"I'm not sure. Knowing sonny as I do, I suspect your right. It's probably illegal."

"It bothers me that my mother's money might be being used to finance an illegal operation?" Charlotte turned to her mother-in-law. "After all of these years why are you suddenly being nice?"

"You're my son's wife. Family is family," Nola sighed as she picked a small flower and continued their stroll.

"Charlotte, you and Mason come from different backgrounds. Mason never trusts anybody. It's been so long, but he's still ashamed of his impoverished existence. How can a woman born with a silver spoon in her mouth possibly understand what motivates my boy," Nola seemed to be rambling on to herself.

"Silver spoon, me?" Charlotte protested.

"Sonny tried every way he could think of to improve himself. He spent hours pouring over every book in the library. He knew that education was his ticket out, but it never worked for my boy. He's too filled with hate and envy."

"Nola, why can't he trust me? I am his wife. Maybe I could help. I would be happy to listen to him, if nothing else," Charlotte replied, her voice filled with anguish.   "Oh I don't know. He never believed a woman like you could love him for himself. He's so angry, lashes back at everybody, everything. Nothing he tried seemed to work. I hoped a good marriage would turn things around."

"Nola, Mason's smart. I don't understand why he never found a good marketable skill. He's good with cars. Couldn't he have used my dowry to open a repair shop?"

"I know, I know. He thought his luck would change if he married a classy lady. I told him about my dear friend Peggy and her little girl. I always preached to him about good blood."

"Mason can be so charming, so interesting, I remember how he was when we first met. Why couldn't he have stayed that way?"

"He's sneaky, a great bluffer that son of mine. You scared the life out of him. Mason called me the night you met and he told me that he wanted to call the marriage plan off. He said you were much too fancy for him."

Charlotte deep in thought, as she too remembered their first meeting, and her dreams for their life together. Charlotte linked arms with her mother-in-law as she tried to understand the sad young man that was her husband. She listened intently to Nola Burns, but she knew it was too late for her heart belonged to Shelley. Mason had driven her into Shelley's arms, and she could never leave.

"Mason and his sister, Gladys suffered at the hands of my tyrannical husband," Nola whispered.

"Gladys? I don't remember hearing much about your daughter," Charlotte replied.

"Yes, my poor little girl. She died when she was ten."

"I'm sorry Nola," Charlotte squeezed Nola's arm.

"It was a long time ago. I'll show you her picture sometime, if you like. Rebecca looks a lot like her aunt Gladys." Nola smiled as she remembered her pretty little girl.

"Yes, I'd love to see Gladys's picture. You could tell Becky about her." "That would be nice. I believe you are never truly gone if someone remembers you. Rebecca can help keep my Gladys alive."

"How did she die? If you don't mind my asking?" Charlotte approached the subject carefully not wishing to drive another wedge between Nola and her.

"No, I don't mind. I'll always remember that day. Jim was in one of his dark moods. I tried to calm him down. The children could hear him screaming." Nola stumbled.

Charlotte attempted to steady her trembling mother-in-law.

Jim Burns' hateful words were branded on her brain. "Look what you brats have done to my life. I'm a college graduate and I can't get a job appropriate to my education."

"Jim, you know you don't mean what you are saying," Nola protested.

"I mean every word. Look what has happened to my life. I'm a hard worker, but the fates, you, the kids and the fates wrecked my life. I wish the two of them had never been born."

"Oh, Jim honey, you don't mean that. The children are our reason for living. You and the kids are everything to me."

Nola was reliving that terrible afternoon. "I remembered looking up into the sad faces of our children. Mason, Gladys. Dad didn't mean what he's saying; he's just tired. He spent another day looking for work."

Nola turned to face Charlotte, "The reason Jim couldn't get a job was he drank. When he drank, he beat up me and the children. Sometimes the neighbors became so disgusted with the screams coming from the house, they'd call the police. Jim would be hauled into the jail until he sobered up. He had to stay in jail because the family never had enough money to post his bail."

"Oh Nola, I had no idea." Charlotte impulsively embraced a startled Nola.

"It's sad to say, but the children and I enjoyed the peace and quiet while their dad was in jail. We would pack a picnic lunch and they would walk over to the meadow, spread the red checked table cloth; relax, and the children would run through the flowers with their dog Jolly. Oh, those were the good times," Nola smiled.

"When Jim got out we returned to the same frightened and miserable family. His meanness and fear infected us. Our lives seem to fall apart."

"I'm so sorry," Charlotte whispered.

"Me too. He knew how to be kind. He was quite the flatterer. Mason's like him, that way. But Jim was a drinker, and with a drinker there is so much uncertainty."

"Did you have nobody to talk with? A minister, AA, someone?"

"No back then you kept your family skeletons in the closet. Everything has changed today. People go on television to discuss their most personal problems. You just didn't do that back then," Nola's voice was strained.

"The day it happened," Nola cleared her throat, "Jim woke up in a good mood. He had won some money the night before, so he could afford to be generous."

"Nola, Mason, Gladys," Jim called out. "I feel good today. You know I did not mean those ugly things I said to you the other day. I was just tired. Nola my dear, pack plenty of food we're going on a picnic. We may stay all day. I do prefer your fried chicken and potato salad. Bring the dog."

"Not to eat, daddy. Jolly can't be our lunch," Gladys giggled. She always enjoyed picnics.

"Make lots of sandwiches. Remember I like bologna, also bring the bright red apples I picked up last night. Hurry, you hear me," Jim yelled as he swung wide the freezer door. He brought out two large bags of ice to fill the chest on the back steps.

"Before I fried the chicken, I suggested Jim put the ice back into the freezer. I knew it would melt before we could leave. A couple of hours later, the children and I packed the lunch and dog into the car and Jim drove to our favorite picnic spot. We spread a red and white checked table cloth, and lounged around on the deep lush green grass. We enjoyed the wonderful fragrances of the wild flowers. It was a perfect day."

"It sounded wonderful," Charlotte replied.

"It was. We munched happily on our favorite foods," Nola became silent. She was reliving that dreadful day.

"Mother, the chicken is good. The potato salad and sandwiches are best. Thanks dad for the apples. They're so chewy," giggled Gladys.

"Remember," Mason insisted, "you promised the leftovers to Jolly. He gets hungry, too. Remember ma."

Nola returned to the present, "The children were so young. They chose to believe that their parents were perfect. Of course, we were not, but that day we tried to be. It was a good day for mending fences."

"What changed?" Charlotte urged Nola on.

"Something so small, so insignificant. I was chatting with Jim. Talk, good talk, like the first days of our marriage. I felt so relaxed, but I made a mistake."

"What mistake?" Charlotte whispered.

"I mentioned that I had noticed a sign in the grocery store window. Help wanted. A clerk. Jim began to scream. He accused me of trying to force him into menial labor. He slapped me in the face, and ran for the car." A pale and trembling Nola began to cry.

"Please stop. Don't continue if the telling causes you such pain." Charlotte held Nola as she feared the story's outcome.

Nola continued, "No my dear, I'm fine. Jim told me he had enough of my nagging. Money was all I cared about. He couldn't take it anymore and he was leaving."

Nola placed her hands over her ears as she attempted to block out the nightmare.

"Jim jumped into the car. I could hear the engine start and the car speed away. There was a sudden thud, and Gladys screamed. I looked up in time to see the bright blue jacket fly up over the hood and heard the screech of brakes."

"Oh dear God. Your husband didn't hit his own child."

"By the time I reached by daughter she had ceased her whimpering. My baby was gone. Jim Burns could never hurt her again."

Charlotte held Nola until her sobbing ceased.

"The next few weeks were a living hell. Gladys was gone and everything in our lives changed. Guilt ridden, Jim dove into the bottle. He lost his part-time job. He was arguing with his supervisor again, and he was told to turn in his keys and leave the store immediately. Jim's life became unbearable so Jim simply quit trying."

"He left you?" Charlotte asked.

"No sweetie, he simply withdrew from life. This was worse than if he had run away and never returned. I stood by helplessly watching him die by inches."

"Nola, it must have been dreadful," Charlotte exclaimed.

"Oh it was. He moved us in with his father. He was probably the craziest old man I had ever known. He was so nasty that I'm sure he never had a personal relationship with a bar of soap," Nola giggled.

Charlotte joined in the laughter.

"We were forced to stay on that damned farm. The house was always filthy. Believe it or not, his place was worse than ours. There was furniture piled all over the house with stacks of

newspapers and mildewed magazines everywhere. The clutter was
a perfect breeding ground for all types of vermin. There were nights
we had to beat the roaches to the dinner table." Nola winced.

"Didn't you offer to help?" Charlotte asked as her face turned
crimson red. "Where was the farm?" Charlotte continued as she
attempted to change the subject.

"It's north of here," Nola replied. "Mason's stories are true?
There really is a farm in his family?" Charlotte responded in a
perplexed manner.

"There always was a thread of truth in my Sonny's stories. His
grandfather spent hours filling his head with old family tales of times
of greatness," Nola laughed.

"Grandmother Burns got sick of the story and shared the true one
with me. She told me that Mason's grandfather sold most of his
property for an outrageously pitiful amount of money," Nola
continued.

"Grandfather Burns invested his money in a more profitable
pursuit. Grandmother Burns recommended that he open a savings
account, but he refused. He would make a fortune in California, a
gold mine, the Lucky Lady.

"Wow! This is some story," Charlotte laughed as she tried to
blot out the death of young Gladys.

"Oh, that's only part of the story. You've not heard anything yet."

"There's more?" Charlotte asked.

"Grandmother Burns didn't understood her husband's dreamy
enterprise scheme plan until she found out that a young brunette
young lady from the red light district had convinced him to invest his
money. Turns out that Grandfather was one of her regulars.

Grandmother Burns permitted Grandfather to return to the family
home, but not her bedroom. Broke, his young lady gone from his
life, Grandfather Burns moved them into a farm. He was forced to
till the soil as a farmer on the land his family had owned for
generations." Nola thought dreamily as she imagined what her life
would have been like if the old man had not been led astray by the
lady from the red light district.

"The loss of the family money ate like a cancer destroying

Grandfather Burns, then my husband Jim. Jim's fate infected our son Mason. This folly of an old man corrupted the Burns family for generations. I'm a shrew and I know it. I'm nice now, but in a few hours I will revert back to my own selfish ways." Nola Burns cleared her throat.

"We still own a few acres with an old ramshackle house. Not much left of the days of glory. We may have to sell it. Almost couldn't pay the taxes this year."

"Maybe I can be of assistance. After all the land is part of my Becky's heritage."

"Maybe so, Charlotte. Let's get back to the house. Sonny will be waiting impatiently for his dinner."

Chapter 13

Water flowed down the sides of his face as he sought a shaded vantage point that would allow him to view the comings and goings of the house. He pressed his binoculars against his perspiration soaked face as he sought the visage that had haunted his dreams.

He sought the bedroom window as he fought back the painful image of his love in the arms of another. Sharing a room. A bed. What color is your room? What decor have you selected? Do you share a king sized bed or a full size for closer contact? These wandering thoughts made him insane with jealousy. If they had not had that terrible fight in New York how different their lives would have been.

He had become bored sitting in front of the television set of the local Holiday Inn. An occasional breeze caused the curtain to flutter. It was a hot afternoon, the worst heat wave in fifteen years; hot even for South Carolina.

A indiscernible force had brought him to Charleston seeking his quest. He must hear the voice, the voice of his beloved.

The stranger stood in his room with receiver in hand as the phone rang. Two rings, three, four times. The former lover picked up the receiver, he heard silence. "Hello, hello." he said, and the line went dead.

It was Charles' voice. Oh how Benjamin had longed to hear that voice again. The stranger felt a tight knot in his stomach. The time was near, the time of blissful reunion. Just a little longer.

The stranger returned to his vantage point, watching as a sudden gust of wind caused a tree limb to tap, tap, tap against the house. The stranger could feel Charles turning over from side to side in the huge bed as he reached for the evil one, the evil one that was not there, the evil one that must be eliminated.

The stranger knew Charles was in the house for a light came on in the bathroom. He leaned against a tree straining his eyes in the darkness. Someone was up, walking around the house. It must be his beloved for he was alone. The stranger watched as Charles pulled up the shade to check if the area was secure.

The stranger would succeed in his plan to rescue Charles for he was more intelligent than his adversaries. It never occurred to him that intellect was not the issue for he would succeed with his plan for the day of deliverance had arrived.

What had happened between the lovers the stranger had never understood, nor had he accepted the decision to part. Charles had been adamant that they go their separate ways, never to meet again. The stranger closed his eyes remembering his love. He released a deep sigh. It had been so long, but unlike the others he had met in that time, his love for Charles had been magnificent, sheer perfection.

"You're dead, Tom Branson. You never should have interfered," the stranger said to the night air. He stepped out into the moonlight and the roguishly handsome Benjamin Tracer walked confidently to his truck, "I must have you, again. It won't be long."

Benjamin Tracer called the local jaguar dealership, using Tom Branson's credit card number and leased a British Racing Green XJ-6 hoping that Charles would believe his companion was a spendthrift. Next he ordered six expensive sports coats from an exclusive men's store.

"You've always been with me, Charles. I will show you Tom is wrong for you," Ben whispered, as he swallowed hard remembering their brief time together. The ecstasy. The time in perfect unison. The perfect love.

Benjamin's family had rejected him due to his sexual orientation. Benjamin's father, super macho Police Sergeant Bubba Tracer was ashamed of his wimpy son. He wanted a real man. Bubba hated the snickering behind his back about his son's being gay.

The ultimate humiliation to Bubba Tracer was when his officers caught young Benjamin with three of his school buddies observing lovers lane couples entwined.

Friday afternoon Bubba Tracer persuaded a couple of the members of the local high school team to take Ben out Saturday night. Bubba paid them twenty dollars to find a woman to make his pansy a man.

Benjamin sat in the parked car staring at the floor board as his school mates reveled in the sexual activities around them. Mark, the captain of the team was taking perverse pleasure in watching the women squealing and writhing under the ministration of the disgusting males.

"Women, except for my mama, are all painted up whores. None of them are sincere or kind. They are universally unappreciative of what we males have to offer," Mark explained to young Benjamin.

"How do you know?" Benjamin asked as he suffered the laughter of his supposed friends.

Cal, the fullback, laughed the loudest "The women love the size of my privates."

"Cal is endowed as few men," crowed Mark.

Benjamin thought he was going to be sick as he watched as Cal began to masturbate in order to find release from the pressure in his groin.

"I'm not a voyeur. You invited me to join you at the malt shop. Let's go," the shamefaced Benjamin said, that terrible night. The teens had made themselves such a nuisance that one of the irritated couples left and telephoned the police.

Benjamin sat immobilized as he watched the blue light of the police car pull up behind Mark's car. He sat in stony silence during the ride to the police station.

Benjamin refused to speak to his father or any of his father's men.

"Sorry, Sarge. We found these guys jerking off in the bushes up on lovers lane," the first officer stated.

"Boys will be boys, don't you agree, Bubba?" the second officer laughed.

"We really hate to do this to you, but, uh..the boys had been making several of our citizens nervous. Peeking into windows, watching folks doing the dirty deed."

"Bubba, it's no big deal, but you ought to have a talk with Benjamin. He's awfully young to be running around with these jocks." "Too late for talk. I paid those boys to hire a hooker to show him how it's done...Well, I figure, I just wasted the money. He'd probably have thrown up the second she grabbed his jewels. Probably cried in the corner for his mama," Bubba Tracer replied.

"He's your only son, Bubba."

"Wish he wasn't. He's just another sorry, no good, flaming faggot. I can't believe a child of my loins could be so warped. I thought these boys might straighten him out," Bubba said with disgust.

"You've shamed me for the last time. If you won't listen to me, then you'll listen to this.

Benjamin stood frozen to the floor as his father produced an inch and a half wide cowhide workman's belt.

Bubba slapped young Benjamin across the face, knocking him off his feet. He slumped against the desk, tight-lipped and emotionless.

Bubba exploded in an angry rage, attacking, pounding, kicking his only son so viciously that it took two of his men to pull him off his battered boy.

"Sarge, stop it. You can't do this. You could kill him," one of the officers screamed as he grabbed the sarge's arm.

"You've brought enough shame on our family. You're a worthless piece of----." Bubba didn't finish his statement, as his men pulled him away.

Large, discolored, over lapping raised welts covered Benjamin's back, buttock and upper legs. Bloody cuts oozed a clear sticky fluid through his ripped shirt.

"Go home to your mama. She's spoiled you, made you a sissy," Bubba Tracer bellowed. "We'll finish this conversation later tonight." But, the conversation never occurred for that night Benjamin ran away, never looking back, never returning.

His mind drifted back to the past. He remembered his first encounter with another male, their next door neighbor, Mr. James Riley.

Mr. Riley was a gentle man who enjoyed the youthful enthusiasm of young Benjamin. They met several times a week in Mr. Riley's home where he taught the boy to fish and to build model boats. As their friendship grew he taught the young boy that it was important for Ben to be true to himself. Be yourself Mr. Riley would say, never follow mindlessly behind the herd.

The two spent many quiet afternoons sipping tea, reading sonnets and upstairs in the man's bed experimenting with their sexuality. Mr. Riley cared so deeply for Benjamin that he gave the boy a few dollars occasionally to help him purchase clothing.

After the beating in the police station, Benjamin left town is such haste that he failed to say goodbye to Mr. Riley. He wondered, for many years, what had happened to his dear friend. One night when his travels took him near his hometown, he chanced a visit to Mr. Riley's.

He found the house changed. The current occupants informed him that Mr. Riley had passed away two years ago. Benjamin visited the grave of his dear companion, but never attempted to contact his parents.

Guilty from abandoning Mr. Riley fueled the fire of his determination not to desert his beloved, Charles Allgood, in his hour of need.

Ben's thoughts returned to six months ago. It was in a small restaurant off Market Street. Benjamin gave the waiter his order. His gaze returned to the more pleasing sight outside the restaurant. The vantage allowed him to look upon a building. The building where his beloved, Charles worked.

Benjamin savored a bowl of French Onion Soup and salad while he watched Madame Lorraine's across the street. After twenty minutes of nibbling absentmindedly at his meal he heard the laughter of two men exiting the building. They crossed the street, Benjamin couldn't believe his good fortune, for they were entering the same restaurant.

Benjamin could hardly bear the exquisite pain focused in his loins, a hunger that had grown to madness since Charles had left New York. He poured another glass of Chablis from his carafe. " O h Charles," he whispered. "Why have you abandoned me? Do you not remember the sweet ecstasy we shared? How did I frighten you? All I ever wanted was to love you." Benjamin watched sadly as the object of his obsession was seated beside the interloper.

"You abandoned me for Tom. It's a good thing I still have friends in New York. Remember George and Harry. They spotted you two in the Big Apple recently. They told me about you and your old college mate Tom Branson. You must be made to understand what you have wrought. Punishment is the only way to salvation."

"Were you speaking to me, sir?" the waiter asked.

"No...yes. Bring me the bill," Benjamin snapped. How dare that man invade his thoughts,

"Yes, sir!" The waiter handed his customer the bill. "Hope everything was fine. It's been a pleasure to serve a fine gentleman like yourself," he smiled. His teeth flashed with spectacular highlights. Greed for a large tip read across his face.

"Fuck you, you jerk," Ben thought, but he replied, "Yeah, it was okay." Better leave this grinning idiot a good tip. He'll give great service. "Hope you will keep my table available. You give excellent service, young man," Benjamin answered as he returned the startled waiter's smile.

"Yes, sir! Just ask for Teddy, next time you're here."

Benjamin paused on the restaurant threshold seeking one last glimpse of Charles.

"It won't be long. Goodbye, Charles...for now."

Morning found the ever vigilant Benjamin waiting by the clump of trees. He heard the screen door slam. Charles was not alone, for sometime during the night Tom Branson had returned. Charles was smiling up at Tom as they prepared for their morning jog. The sound of a camera click came from the clump of bushes.

The neighborhood sounds echoed with laughter of children, the chirping of birds and the buzzing of bees. The clatter of garbage cans ricocheted against the driveways as the trash collectors passed by. The jogging shoes hit the asphalt in perfect cadence.

The aroma of sausage, bacon and eggs, and pancakes mingled from the various kitchens where breakfast was being prepared.

The sun was shining brightly, and steam raising from the pavement predicted another scorcher of a day. The morning radio reports announced (no rain in sight). The local weather bureau encouraged everyone to stay inside and keep cool. Charles and Tom refused to permit a slight elevation of the thermometer to put a halt to their activity.

Charles wore a blue and white jogging suit with a powder blue sweat band. It matches his eyes, thought Benjamin. He recalled telling Charles that blue was his best color.

Benjamin was tempted to call out to Charles, but he didn't want to do so with that man present. The man, Tom Branson, had kept them separated.

His knees trembled at the sight of Charles Allgood smiling to his companion as they jogged almost in unison past his vantage point. This caused Benjamin great confusion, because why would Charles appear so relaxed, so content, if he were held a prisoner. They would sort out all of those little matters after their reunion.

"It won't be long, My Bonnie Charlie, and we'll be together forever," Benjamin said, just as Charles wiped his forehead dropping the blue sweatband on the sidewalk.

"This is a sign," Benjamin stated, picking up the headband, wiping it across his face, mingling their sweat. "I can feel your body longing for mine," his thoughts returned to the destruction of his foe.

Ben followed the joggers in his blue panel truck. The rising temperature took its toll on Tom and Charles so they rested at their favorite cafe. As the couple chatted, sipping mineral water, Benjamin sent Charles a secret message. He put a coin in the juke box and played their favorite song, "Some Enchanted Evening." He was positive that when Charles looked up abruptly that the message was received and understood. The true lovers would be together soon.

Benjamin was content and happy with his sexual orientation, but, for him there was no peace, no happiness. He was driven by an obsession for his lost love.

Ben watched as the refreshed couple began their run home. They enjoyed the breath-taking scenery as they jogged along the Cooper River.

Charles suddenly sped up leaving a surprised Tom behind. Tom quickly followed suit. Their muscles ached as they stretched their legs in quickening pace as the two men joyously raced to the house they shared. Hearts pounded with anticipation of the quiet time in their kitchen and consuming fresh muffins which had been left by Charlotte.

Charles slowed his speed, feeling goose flesh rippling down his back. Somebody was watching him. He had felt this sensation before, those strange hidden eyes boring into his being. Shrugging his shoulders, he said, "My overactive imagination," and he dashed off to the house.

The rental truck pulled off towards Highway 17. He knew where Charles lived. Ben had learned his habits, his schedule. His search was over for he had found Charles Allgood, his perfect lover. The lover that had haunted his dreams since their time together in New York.

That afternoon the girls took a leisurely lunch break for sales were slow. Shelley's brother Tom was aware how much their afternoons meant to the couple.

Charlotte and Shelley strolled through the market area of Charleston. They enjoyed the beautiful things in the craft shops, and Charlotte was drawn to the simplicity of the grass baskets that outside of Charleston could only be found in Africa. The girls were fascinated watching the nimble fingers of the local women, weaving the baskets, an art form that had become almost extinct.

"Where will we have lunch today?" Charlotte smiled, allowing Shelley to take the lead.   "What do you think of Tommy Condon's Irish Pub on Church Street. We've not eaten there in weeks," Shelley replied.

"Oh that's a fantastic idea. I could eat my weight in the She-Crab stew topped off with one of their monster salads."

"I for one am ordering their Shepard's Pie and Fanny's Flowering Onion," Shelley stated.

"Let's go now. My mouth is salivating just talking of the fabulous food.

"Good afternoon, ladies," the friendly hostess greeted the pair. "Where do you wish to be seated. We have several excellent tables outside. Enjoy the spring breeze," she smiled.

"Could we have a table near the street?" Charlotte asked.

"Certainly," their hostess replied, "we have a table in the corner where you may watch the tourists and have the privacy and quiet time for good conversation. Your waiter will be Ken. Enjoy your meal," the hostess stated as she walked away.

"Afternoon, ladies. May I get your drinks while you check the menu?"

"Yes," replied Shelley, "My friend and I would like a glass of wine with our lunch. We would like two glasses of zinfandel, please. Does that meet with your approval, Charlotte?" she said as she looked up from the menu.

"Yes, zinfandel will be fine, but I also would like a cold glass of water."

"Alright ladies. Since you are ordering the same wine would you care to order a carafe?"

"That's an excellent idea. Don't you agree, Charlotte?"

"Yes, but, remember we still have be able to function when we get back to work," Charlotte replied.

I'll be right back with your drinks while you review the menu."

Returning with the carafe of wine and Charlotte's water, Ken proceeded to take their order.

"Have you decided what you will be having today?" Ken smiled.

"Yes," Charlotte replied, "I have been dreaming of a large bowl of She-Crab stew with one of your tasty salads."

"She-Crab and salad. Excellent choice. And for you ma'am?" Turning to Shelley, he continued to write.

"I wish to order the Shepard's Pie, also a small bowl of the She-Crab stew," Shelley stated as she handed Ken her menu.

"Would you care for an appetizer? I highly recommend the mushrooms stuffed with crab meat," Ken suggested.

"Oh Shell, it sounds great I haven't had stuffed mushrooms in ages."

"Alright, one order of mushrooms and two plates. How many mushrooms are in an order?" Shelley asked.

"Six mushrooms per order, ma'am," Ken replied.

"Just enough, but not too much," Shelley stated.

The couple sat and sipped their wine, reveling in the nearness of each other.

"One of the main reasons I patronize Tommy Condon's, except for the good food is that it's never so loud that you can't enjoy a conversation with your companion."

"I know that gentle breeze is refreshing and an aid to one's digestion."

The breeze was tossing Charlotte's hair. Shelley tenderly brushed a tousled curl out of her eyes.

"God, I love the nearness of you. I can smell you in my nostrils." A shiver ran down her spin.

"I live for these moments. It makes my other life almost bearable," Charlotte whispered.

Shelley and Charlotte relaxed. After sharing the food and their quiet time together, they glanced deep into each other's eyes, drawing mutual strength for the time of parting.

"Well Charlotte," Shelley finally said, "We've dilly dallied long enough. Sister or no sister, Tom will fire even me, if we don't get back to work."   "I'd be the first to go," Charlotte giggled.

"Don't count on it, sweetie. He and Charles think you are the greatest. I'm just family, they're stuck with me." Shelley leaned over to whisper, "if those two were straight, I'd have to fight them off for your affections." Shelley giggled as she watched Charlotte blush.

"Your modesty, after all that has happened to you is quite refreshing, my dear."

Shelley paid the bill, and then she guided Charlotte to the street. Shelley stopped abruptly, expelling an expletive. Her body stiffened and the color drained from her face.

"Charlotte, keep walking. Don't look back."

Charlotte stared into Shelley's terrified face.

"What is it, Shell?" Charlotte whispered, frozen with fear.

"There's a man behind us. No, don't look around."

"Who is he?" Charlotte's steps quickened to keep up with Shelley's steady pace.

"Oh lord, Charlotte, I can't believe he's tracked us all the way from New York. Listen carefully. We can't lead him to Madame Lorraine's and Charles."

"Please, tell me what's going on. You're scaring me, Shell."

"I'll explain later. We've got to split up. You take the long route and go home. I'll shake your hand as though you are merely an acquaintance, and walk away. If we are lucky, he'll follow me. You've got to get to a phone and warn Tom."

"Tell him I asked you to call."

"What do I say?" Charlotte asked, confused with the situation.

"Don't talk to Charles, not to Charles. Speak only Tom. Tell him that Benjamin has found us. Do you understand, Benjamin?"

"Isn't there anything further I might do to help?"

"No dear, just go to the safety of your home. Let us handle the matter. I love you," Shelley whispered.   "Please don't force me to leave you," Charlotte pleaded.

"You must, sweetie. Don't worry. He won't hurt me. The greatest help you can be is to call Tom. Scoot now."

Shaking Charlotte's hand Shelley said in a louder voice, "Enjoyed the luncheon.   Hope we'll be able to work together soon. Goodbye," Shelley gave Charlotte a quick wink of reassurance then she released Charlotte's hand and walked away.

Shelley Branson led away the dark ominous stranger. She hoped to keep Charlotte safe from anything that might develop.

Charlotte stood for a moment glued to the ground not understanding why her friends were in extreme danger. She headed for the pay phone.

Charlotte ran past the sweet grass basket display knocking over several of the baskets.

"I'm sorry," she said as she raced to the phone.

"Madame Lorraine's," Tom's voice sang through the wires.

"Tom, it's Charlotte."

"You two decided to enjoy a leisurely luncheon?" He laughed, "Charles and I enjoy young love in bloom."

"Tom, I'm scared. Shelley is acting strange."

"Strange how, my dear?" Tom inquired. "You two haven't had a disagreement, have you?"

"No Tom, we are fine."

"Tom, a man was following us, and Shelley went nuts," Charlotte said.

"Thought you two girls were cute, huh," Tom replied.

"Shell scared me the way she hurried me out of the restaurant. Shelley told me to get to the nearest phone, and call you, but not to mention the problem to Charles."

"Okay you've got me, sweetie. What's the message?"

"She said to tell you that Benjamin is in Charleston. Shelley said something about his following you from New York. What's this all about, Tom?"

"Shit". Tom whispered, "What does this Benjamin look like?"

"He's tall, a dark man with square shoulders and in his early thirties. Tom, he made my blood run cold. He's bold and impertinent. There is evil in his eyes. Will he hurt Charles?" Charlotte's shoulders shuttered as she spoke the words.

"How'd he find Charles?" Tom snapped.

"Tom, please, what's wrong?" Charlotte implored. "Tell me what's happening. You're scaring me now."

"Charlotte, don't come back to the shop. Tell Mason today's a half day. Tell him we are celebrating Weirdo Day. Tell him anything. You're better off at home. Don't worry. I'll take care of Benjamin. I've got to run. Charlotte."

"Yes, Tom."

"If he approaches you, walk away. Don't permit him to engage you in conversation,"

Charlotte heard the click of the receiver as the line went dead.

"He's gone to warn Charles. Wish I knew what this is all about."

Charlotte replaced the receiver and headed for home.

Late that evening, Benjamin Tracer returned to Charles favorite restaurant at the corner of Market and Broad Street. Benjamin knew he was close to his quarry. He had been unsuccessful in contacting Charles since his arrival in Charleston. He was haunted by those delicate features of this man. Benjamin moaned, his maleness hardened at the thought of Charles' smile, his slender fingers, and the salty taste of his skin. Benjamin adored the tender lips, the contour of his neck, and his delicate features.

Benjamin put his hand up to his forehead, covering his eyes as though they were light sensitive. In fact he felt exceedingly nervous, feeling a strange titillating sensation, a premonition, one might say.

Benjamin paid his bill and walked across the street to enjoy the beauty of the setting sun. Again, he closed his eyes dreaming of his beloved. Benjamin wondered how he had become so enamored with the pale blond man. Charles was everything he dreamed of in a mate.

Benjamin shook his head. Was he hallucinating? All of this time in search to find the object of his desire standing outside of a local restaurant. This was no hallucination, this truly was Charles Allgood.

Benjamin raced across the street, grabbing Charles's hand.

"Charles, it's me, Benjamin. It's been so long. I couldn't believe my eyes after all of this time to find you here in Charleston."

"I, uh, excuse me, Benjamin. I'm in a hurry," Charles said in a startled manner. "Nice to see you."

"What's the rush? I saw you leaving the restaurant," Benjamin said, "Didn't you notice my trying to attract your attention. I thought I saw you near the market yesterday, so I waited around. Welcome back into my life. It has been so empty since you left me and New York."

"I didn't see you," Charles said absentmindly, "Please excuse me, I'm late for an, uh, appointment."

Charles walked towards a nervous Tom. Benjamin followed, as he attempted to stop Charles's flight. Tom guided Charles into the market hallway.

"Benjamin, leave Charles alone. If you accost him again, I'll be forced to call the police."

"Accosting Charles, me? I was simply renewing an old acquaintance. We're still friends, aren't we?" Benjamin whimpered. "Charles, don't let this man speak for you. Talk to me. Why did you leave town? Was it something I did or said? You took the sunshine from my life when you left my world." Benjamin tried to pull Charles to him.

"Please don't," Charles spoke in a soft trembling voice.

"Why are you doing this, avoiding me? All I want is to sit, as old friends do, and talk," Benjamin pleaded.

"Please don't pursue me. I'm happy with Tom."

"Tom isn't the only person in the world. You were happy with me. Don't you remember, dear one?"

"Benjamin, let go. You're hurting me. Don't pursue this insanity you are hurting yourself."

"I'll take my chances. Goodbye for now," Benjamin declared with an unsteady laughter in his voice as he stood helpless as Charles and Tom hurried away.

Charles' rejection froze Benjamin's heart as his dreams were shredded to bits. Gazing through his tears, he stumbled backward off the curb as his mind swirled with disbelief.   "TomBranson, your life will become a constant nightmare. You will walk unceasingly through erratic situations until I get my revenge. No matter how you fight me, in the end, Charles will be mine." Benjamin thought with a firm resolve.

Ben's plan was to keep Tom Branson, his enemy, continually off balance.

Benjamin knew that Charles and Tom were dining out this evening so he drove toward the little house of St. Mary's. Two blocks over he parked the truck and skirted the edge of the trees as he worked his way to the house on the corner. He rang the doorbell, waited, rang again. There was no answer so he sneaked about until he found an open window, crawled in. Benjamin found himself in the dining room.

He crept up the stairs and found the bedroom his beloved shared with Tom Branson. He moved quickly first throwing a large sheet on the floor. Ben emptied each dresser drawer, and then he attacked the closet.

"Charles is so organized. This room is so neat and tidy," Ben spoke. "You shouldn't have gone off with that man. You've got quite a surprise in store for you. I'm sorry, you've made your choice, but now you will be punished. You must realize that I am serious."

Benjamin threw the heavy bundle out the window. Moments later he was back in the dining room. He stopped at a small desk, finding a sheet of paper, he wrote,

"Thank you generous citizens for your monumental contribution. We could not be a success without the charity of people like you. The note was signed, Sincerely, The Good Will."

Benjamin laughed as he left the house, and returned to his truck. He drove to a local good will drop box and poured his contribution inside.

When I'm finished with you Tom Branson, you will believe you are going mad. Just wait for the next incident.

In another part of town, Tom and Charles were enjoying a leisurely meal. They enjoyed each other's company and the beautiful Charleston evenings, but tension crackled through the restaurant.

"Charles, please remain calm. Let's enjoy our night out. Shelley will be late, so we can have some quiet time, alone. We could see a movie, if you wish."

Charles nodded no, his eyes glowing with anticipation. He did not wish to delay their intimate moments together.

Just then a young blond man walked over to their table.

"Tom, it is you. How on earth have you been? I've waited so long for you to phone me. Is there something wrong?" The young man could not take his eyes off of Tom.

Tom Branson sat speechless as the young man continued, "You promised we'd go out again for another delicious evening. It would be so tragic if you have forgotten," the young man pouted.

"Excuse me, but have we met?" Tom replied.

The young man finally seemed notice that Tom was not alone.

"Oh my dear, I am dreadfully sorry to have been so indiscrete. Please call me, Tommy when you have a free moment," the young man crooned as he turned and walked away from the startled couple.

"Who the hell was he, Tom," Charles asked as his face turned chalk white.

"I have no idea. He simply made a mistake. I've never seen that man before," Tom replied.

With hands shaking, Tom quickly paid the bill as he placed an affectionate hand on Charles'. It was the first time in their relationship that Charles pulled away.

Tom could see doubt written all over Charles' face. The two men left the restaurant, and drove home in silence.

Tom turned on all of the lights in the house they shared, for the night no longer looked lovely. Charles trudged up the stairs to their room.

"Tom! come here," Charles cried.

"What is it, are you alright?" Tom called out as he charged up the steps. "Look at our room. It's such a mess. Check the closets, I'm afraid to. I've already checked the dressers. All of our clothes are gone."

"I'll call the police," Tom screamed.

"Why bother, they don't care. Remember, we have no feelings. We're just weirdos, and they'll think we are just craving attention." Charles sank wearily onto their bed. "I'm just grateful that Shelley was out when the intruder broke in."

In another part of town Benjamin darted down the motel hallway without looking back as though pursued by demons. As he entered his room, Benjamin thought, "Charles you have no idea the void in my life. Now that I have found you, we will never be parted," he smiled as he remembered his night of mischief.

Tom paced back and forth like a caged tiger. "Who could be doing such dastardly things to us. All of the pranks, that damned sports car, then the expensive clothes that we were returning. Now I've got to pay for them."

"Not you, we've got to pay for the clothes," Charles corrected. "Why would anyone do this to us?"

"You know as well as I do Benjamin Tracer is our tormentor. We'll make extra precautions to prevent his becoming a greater pest. If I wasn't so mad, I could understand his obsession. He loves you," Tom smiled as he attempted to reassure Charles.

"Let's try to get some sleep, Tom. My nerves are shot. I'm not sure how much more I can endure."

Tom looked into the closet. "Well, our prankster left an old blanket. We can use it for a sheet," Tom turned around smiling, "and we can use our love to keep us warm."

The next day the two men searched the stores for replacement clothes.

"Let's drop by the shop and change clothes. A never could stand wearing clothes a second." Charles stated. "I agree. My hangup has always been dirty underwear."

After a quick trip to Madame Lorraine's, they attempted to blot out the unpleasantness of last night.

"Charles, can you believe it is lunchtime."

"Let's eat something special. I need a break from all the nonsense."

The two men walked to their favorite Irish restaurant. They sat sipping white wine and attempted to relax from the stressful day.

We've been scurrying around like frightened rabbits since Benjamin Tracer arrived."

"Tom, he's just lonely, and I can't believe that he's been these terrible things. He 'll never hurt me, or anyone I care for." Charles smiled up at Tom. "I told him I was happy with you. He's gone now, so lets enjoy our dinner. I'm starved," Charles babbled on nervously.

"Alright, my dear. Have it your own way. You have a more trusting nature." Tom patted Charles hand. "She-crab stew and a Caesar salad sounds perfect to me. I must watch my weight," Charles smiled.

"You never have to watch your weight. Your waist is perfect, Tom stated adoringly. "I will join you for She-crab stew and a Caesar salad. The change will do me good. What do you think of the new collection?" Tom attempted to change the subject.

"We have nothing to lose. It's a dynamic collection of afternoon creations, morning outfits, hats, sunglasses, shoes and stockings," Charles said.

"What can I say? We're about to become millionaires," Tom laughed happily.

The server brought the stew and salad as the couple chatted about their big fashion show. They both knew that they were unsuccessful in forgetting Benjamin Tracer. The tension caused by Benjamin's arrival was driving a wedge between the two lovers.

Benjamin proceeded down the motel hallway towards his room. Opening the door, he threw himself onto his bed. He was annoyed that his sabotage had not appeared to have worked. The two men still appeared to be close.

"I must be nuts," he cried out to the four walls, "Charles isn't the only fish in the sea. I can go out any night and find someone better, but for me there is no one else. He must be made to understand. What can I do to them now? I could contact bank examiners demanding that their company records be checked. That sounds good. Maybe I should make an anonymous call to the IRS. They're so suspicious, yes, I can use them," Benjamin smiled as he prepared for bed.

The next morning Charles entered his office to find a dozen yellow roses on his desk.

"Tom," Charles called out. "The flowers are lovely. Yellow roses are my favorite. What's the occasion?"

"They're not from me. Should I be jealous?" Tom asked.

"I wonder who?" Charles replied.

"Probably from Benjamin. He'll never give up."

"You worry too much. That business was over long ago. I am afraid that you are overreacting," Charles continued.

"I'm not as sure as you are. We have had blissful years before his interference."

"I'm not encouraging him. He just popped up, uninvited. He just appeared from nowhere."

"I hate his blasted impertinence, pushing himself in where he's not wanted. He acts as though he owns you."

"Please don't give him another thought. Tom, I care for you, you and nobody else. I hope you still feel the same. We're been through so much," Charles stated as though he were unsure of his place in Tom Branson's life.

"Charles, you are very important to me. Remember Benjamin Tracer didn't track us to Charleston to see, ME," Tom laughed sarcastically. "Damn it Charles, I don't trust him. He's capable of anything. You don't expect me to stand around helpless while that man makes goo-goo eyes at you," Tom stated. "Don't you trust me, dear?" Charles whispered, pain written over his face.

"Of course, I do. I don't trust Benjamin. He's trouble. I'm sure that he is the one doing all of the weird things to our lives."

"Please don't fret. It will all work out. My mistake was going out with him at all. It took no time for him to give me the creeps. He frightened me with his demands." Charles said.

"He's hoping that if he is persistent, you'll leave me."

"NEVER!" snapped Charles. "I'm sorry my poor judgment has put you in this position."

"You could always change your mind, and return to Benjamin," Tom said.

"Why should I change my mind? I love you, and our life." Charles stated. "With all of the harassment, I'm glad we share such a deep commitment."

Tom smiled without a reply as they left work and headed for home.

"What's this?" Tom asked.

"Oh no, your tires have been slashed.

"Let's call the auto club. They'll tow this thing away, and replace all four. We'll be right as rain in no time," Tom replied with feigned confidence.

"Should we report this incident to the police?" Charles looked worried.

"No, I'll mention it to Bill the next time I speak with him. Stop fretting, we'll go back inside, and call for assistance. Shelley can give us a ride home."

"I can hardly wait to get home and enjoy our new bedroom furniture," Tom smiled as he reached out to squeeze Charles hand.

"I know, my dear. We have saved a long time to be able to afford such a nice set," Charles replied.

The two men returned to their office where Shelley waited around while they called the auto club.

"Hello, is this the auto club?" Tom asked. We've been the victims of some mischief. Somebody has slashed all four of our tires. Yes, that's right. My name is Tom Branson. I'm at 211 St. Marys. Yes, that's right Charleston. You have the records. My Cadillac Allante is parked in front of Madame Lorraine's." Tom returned the phone to its cradle.

The Bransons' home was one place that Charlotte found peace and serenity. She enjoyed the peaceful mornings sipping coffee with Charles and Tom, and especially Shelley.

Tom and Shelley were away shopping so Charles and Charlotte were alone in the kitchen.

"Charles, would you care for a cup of coffee to go with these fresh muffins."

"Thanks, I would. You are thoughtful to shower our little family with your love and especially, your tasty blueberry muffins," Charles replied as he watched Charlotte closely. "You feel comfortable with us, don't you Charlotte." Charles continued.

Charlotte poured the cup, placed the warm muffins on plates, and joined Charles at the kitchen table.

"Having you here, being a part of this family is wonderful. Would you care for margarine?" Charlotte smiled as she passed the margarine to her friend. She warmed her hands on the freshly brewed coffee. "I always enjoy being with the three of you. It's so peaceful." Charlotte drew a deep breath as the scent of the blossoms drifted through the window weaving their hypnotic spell.

"You love being with Shelley." Charles stated.

"I love Charleston. I love the three of you. You and Tom are the gentlest men I have ever known."

"You are so kind, little one." Charles patted her hand.

"When I'm with you I don't miss so much." Misty-eyed Charlotte attempted to change the subject, "Shelley's flowers are lovely this season. I wash my dishes surrounded by their beauty."

"Shelley creates beauty everywhere, little one."

"You've found a special love with Shelley, haven't you?" Charles whispered.   "Charles, I've never known a person with whom I had instant rapport. Shell's kept my life together these last few years. You understand, don't you?"

"Oh, I understand perfectly," Charles smiled. "It is the same between Tom and me."

"Not the same. I'm married to Mason," Charlotte smiled.

"Why do you stay?" Charles asked, raising his brow.

"I must stay. I have my Becky to protect. Perhaps I was a fool to marry Mason, but I made the choice to..." Charlotte frowned unable to finish her thought.

The door bell rang. Charlotte waited while Charles determined the cause of the interruption. He found standing on the front porch a tall, lanky, pinched face, severely dressed man of about sixty.

Charles smiled. The visitor reminded him of the thin body, large nosed character, Ichabod Crane.

"May I help you?" Charles asked.

"Miss Shelley Branson, please," the visitor stated.

"I'm sorry. Miss Branson isn't in at the moment. May I be of assistance?"

"Oh dear, oh dear. My name is Chamberlain Goodbody of the Shady Rest Mortuary. This is most distressing. Miss Branson insisted that I be here promptly at 11 o'clock, this morning."

"Shelley mentioned no such appointment to me," Charles said, perplexed with the strange man.

"I am unaccustomed to making preparations for the departed outside my business, but since, Mrs. Branson, their mother is too infirmed to leave her bed..."

Charles stared at Mr. Goodbody in a disbelieving manner.

"No Mrs. Branson lives at this residence."

"OH DEAR! A practical joke. Mr. Thomas Branson has not gone to his great reward," Mr. Goodbody frowned.

"No! Mr. Branson is quite well. Thank you. As a matter of fact he has not gone to his great reward, he has gone to the grocery."

"Excuse the intrusion," the irritated Chamberlain Goodbody stated as he turned leaving the stunned Charles standing in the doorway.

He returned to Charlotte and repeated the conversation with Mr. Chamberlain Goodbody of the Shady Rest Mortuary.

"That was so weird. Who could have done something so cruel?"

"I don't know, but I tell you that gave me goose flesh, but this is not our first strange occurrence."

"Let's speak of more pleasant matters than death," Charlotte said as she attempted to draw Charles into better topics.

"That's fine with me," Charles stated as he stirred his cup of coffee.

"Charles, might I ask you a question?" Charlotte smiled at her friend.

"Of course. If it is too personal, I may not answer," Charles laughed strangely, still uncomfortable from the earlier visitor.

"How in this crazy world did you know that Tom was the one for you?"

"Still worried about your relationship with Shelley, my dear?"

"Somewhat. Someday I will be forced to leave Mason, but for now I must live on the fringe of Shelley's life. Am I fair to her?"

"She loves you, little one. Now you were asking about me. Tom gives me comfort, security. I miss him, his tenderness when we are apart."

"Have you never cared for anybody else?" Charlotte asked.

"Yes, but not the way it is with Tom," Charles continued.

"So Tom is not your first," Charlotte stated.

"No, we've been together for fifteen years, longer than most heterosexual marriages, wouldn't you say," Charles laughed. "We were separated for a short time several years ago when Tom was in Los Angeles. I was so lonely, I made a terrible mistake, but we don't speak of it."

"Then you did love others, not just Tom." "Yes, I have been with two others. They were kind and loving. But Tom holds my heart."

"Who were they? Do you mind telling me?"

"I shared my life with Alfred Collins during my teen years. He was my high school English teacher. He would sit on the porch swing and read to me. Shakespeare, poetry, it didn't matter, he had the softest voice."

"What happened to him, this dear man?" Charlotte whispered.

"He passed away years ago of a heart attack."

"I'm sorry. He must have been special," Charlotte said.

"He was. I lived with Perry Coleman for six months after college."

"That's all?" Charlotte's eyes flew opened.

"I'm not loose, Charlotte. I don't sleep around," Charles stated
indignantly.   "I wasn't implying such a thing, Charles. You've
been with less men than I have," Charlotte found herself strangely
laughing.

"Is that so?" Charles stated, raising his brow again, in that same
familiar manner.

"I was gang raped years ago. It was a nightmare, but I survived.
You could say my introduction to sex was that night under five
depraved men."

"My dear, I am terribly sorry. You must remember that we
become stronger when we survive adversity."

"As the saying goes, what doesn't kill us, makes us strong."

"There is a lot of truth in it, wouldn't you agree?"

"Yes, but back to Perry, that was his name, wasn't it? Why did
you break up with him?"

"Nosey, aren't you," Charles laughed. "His name was Perry
Coleman. But poor Perry didn't stand a chance. Tom and I had
gone to college together for a time. I had paid little attention to
Tom until he was injured in an auto accident. I almost lost my mind
with worry. I had enjoyed occasional sex with Tom, but after the
accident this fear engulfed me."

"The accident made you face the fact that you were in ...love?"

"Yes, it was like being struck by a bolt of lightning. I stayed in his
room day and night. When he woke up, he smiled and said your
place or mine."

"Your place or mine. After all that had happened you must have
been thrilled," Charlotte smiled her approval.

"It turns out that he had been semi-conscious, and he heard me
praying. I was so out of control. He heard me telling God how
much I loved and needed him. I went home and told Perry. It
seemed he had suspected from the start. Tom recovered, and
moved in with me. The rest is history."

"The End. Love triumphant," Charlotte smiled.

"Not the end. We fight. Nothing physical, just arguments.
People can't live together, without disagreements. Then we make
up. That's the best part."

"And there has been no one else since Tom."

"Nobody important.   One unimportant brief encounter. Remember, my dear, I'm a fool for a man that quotes Shakespeare."

"There was somebody. Was it Benjamin Tracer? Come on Charles, I told you my deepest secret," Charlotte smiled.

"I don't remember how it began. Tom was in L.A. and I was on a business trip in New York," Charles sighed. "I met him at a party. Ben was dark and scary. He had a way about him. Chills still run up my spine thinking about him. He had a way of staring with those dark piercing eyes that appeared to reach inside your very soul."

Charlotte sat quietly, absorbed in Charles' secret world. "Does Tom know?"

"Not everything. It's hard to talk about. Ben was life's forbidden fruit.   On the surface he appeared nice, but domineering. He convinced me he loved me, and he was a superior lover," Charles smiled in spite of himself.   "He knew where to put his hands, his lips, he could drive me over the edge with just one look," Charles shuttered as he remembered their blissful interlude in their shabby room.

"Charlotte, it was one of the most exciting, degrading times of my life. Ben was magnificent, not a huge man, but strong, powerful," Charles whispered.

"But he hurt you?" Charlotte asked as she stroked her friend's arm.

"He had been battered as a child. Ben's father was a macho cop. jerk. Knocked him around for being different. I suppose that's why he was always so angry. He walked through life like a time bomb ready to explode.

"In the early days, he had a wry sense of humor and quick wit," Charles related.

"Ben took me to superbly decorated restaurants. Nothing so provincial as sweet little Charleston. That's what he called us, provincial."

"Benjamin sounds quite interesting."

"Oh everybody thought he was. But, there was another side to him, a dark, secretive, moody Ben," Charles caught his breath as he continued he painted a picture of love, lust and terror.

"Benjamin Tracer was obsessive, possessive. If I wasn't where he thought I should be or he did not care for my explanation, he punished me," Charles stopped, deep in thought, "It sounds sick that I let him control me, punish me." Charles' voice was so soft Charlotte had to strain to hear.

"I suppose that was part of the attraction. He took care of me as though I was his beloved child. At night he would make love to me. Oh those slow hands. But, at other times, I never knew what would set him off. He'd slap me, knock me across the room. He would snap out of his dark mood. He would cry. Beg my forgiveness, swearing that it would never happen again. The loving after the fights were some of the best. Can you possibly understand my weakness, my obsession?" Charles shocked himself that he was sharing with Charlotte the ugly truth of their relationship.

Charles deep in thought remembered the feather light fingers so sensual moving across his body. His treacherous body, betraying him as Ben forced it to respond, to do unspeakable things.

"I've never told Tom the entire story. He would never understand the degrading power Ben had over me."

Charlotte sat quietly as she watched her friend reliving a time better forgotten. Charles Allgood bore his soul to her, and she must keep his confidence. For she alone knew of the wonderfully wicked time of his youth with the strong, enchanting, lusty Benjamin Tracer.

"When I look back, I recall that those were the most exciting, terrifying months of my life."

"What of Tom?" Charlotte asked.

"Tom is my life, my happiness. He is my stability. He is aware that I had an uncontrollable wild side. He loves me anyway. How's the family?" Charles smiled as he attempted to change the subject.

"Oh yes, the family," Charlotte laughed. "Nola and Mason are always the same. Becky, of course, is the light of my life. Sweet as ever."

"That Becky is a delicious angel, Charlotte. You've done a fantastic job."

"Thank you, kind sir!"

Charles touched his temples.

"What is it, dear?" Charlotte's voice was filled with concern.

"God! Charlotte, nostalgia can be tiring," Charles said sadly.

"Charles, are you all right? Your eyes are so drawn."

"I've one of those splitting headaches I get from time to time. I wonder what is keeping Tom and Shelley?"

"You go upstairs and rest. I've got to get back home. Today is wash day." Charlotte kissed Charles on the cheek and walked home.

Tom and Shelley arrived with their groceries. " G o o d morning, you two," Charlotte smiled stepping over to take Shelley's hand.

"Well, hello there," Shelley's voice crooned, "Join us for lunch?" Shelley asked, touching Charlotte's hand lovingly.

"No, I can't," Charlotte murmured. "I've got to get back to the house. Today is Saturday, and the dirty laundry waits for no man or woman," Charlotte laughed.

"Right. Has that mother-in-law of yours ever considered helping?" Shelley asked sarcastically.

"What? The demure Nola Burns, lift her hands in menial labor. We shouldn't be unkind. Nola's all right, she has her moments," Charlotte chortled.

"Something strange occurred while I was having coffee with Charles," Charlotte continued. "I wouldn't say anything to Charles. Just be aware. It may be someone with a sicko sense of humor, but it made me.." Charlotte did not continue for she felt a terrible shiver of foreboding run up her spine.

"What happened, Charlotte?" Tom urged. "What has so unnerved you?"

"We were having coffee, fresh muffins, and pleasant conversation. Charles was boring me, again, singing your praises," Tom smiled at the thought of his happiness with Charles.

"Go on," Tom encouraged.

"A strange man came to the door. He was a mortician, and he was making a house call, I guess you'd call it. He was inquiring about the death of a Mr. Tom Branson. Charles told him there was

some mistake, but it left me feeling creepy inside you know."
Charlotte frowned, "You should have seen Charles's face. It left
him with a migraine headache. I sent the poor thing upstairs after
giving him one of my headache tablets."

"Okay, I'll say nothing for now. Excuse me, I just want to run up
and check on him." Tom walked into the house.

"I hope I did the right thing telling Tom. He looked so worried."

"Charlotte!" called Nola Burns, "isn't it laundry day? You don't
have time to flitter the day away gossiping with our neighbors."

"I've got to go. My master or mistress voice. Let me know what
happens. See you later."

"Okay. I hate your going back into that damned house," Shelley
discretely rubbed her hand across Charlotte's breasts. "Lordy, I love
the smell of you. Will you come over, later?"

"Let you know," Charlotte whispered as her eyes caressed
Shelley. "They are going out tonight. I could send Becky along,
and feign a headache of my own," Charlotte giggled.

"I know how to cure what ails you," Shelley replied boldly.

"Shush. Don't, not so loud. You'll give everything away."

"If it wasn't for Becky, I would," Shelley stated.

"It's not very fair to you, this half life. You'd be better off with
someone devoting their entire life to you, not this fragment."

"Don't you talk that way again. A half life with you is better than
life without you. I wake up happy knowing you are in my world.
Run along before I grab you in front of that woman. Scat, you little
old heart breaker," Shelley smiled.

"What took you so long? What did that woman want?" Nola
snapped as Charlotte walked into the kitchen.

"She expressed her undying love for me, and begged me to run
away with her to a desert island," Charlotte replied sarcastically.

"Oh she did not," Nola retorted, unable to recognize the truth
when she heard it. "Must you be crude, you silly girl? What did she
really want?" Nola asked as she softened her tone.

"She was telling me that Charles Allgood had a terrible migraine.
Wanted to know if I had any good remedy," Charlotte shrugged.

"What did you suggest?" "I gave her a couple of my headache

tablets. I hope they help him, for I feel the beginnings of a headache myself."

"You always get a headache when we're about to visit Aunt Millie."

"That's not true. I adore Aunt Millie and Uncle Ralph. She is the most fantastic cook, and Becky loves his funny stories."

"Ugh! His ghost stories. I find them creepy," Nola shuttered.

"Well brave four year-olds of today simply find them funny. With all of those dreadful cartoons on the television today, nothing scares them," Charlotte grimaced.

"Lets get to the laundry. Want to help, Ma?" Charlotte called as Nola Burns retreated to her bedroom, and probably her bottle.

"No dear," she called. "I feel a swimmy head coming on. I must lie down. Maybe later," Nola called from the top of the stairs.

In another part of the city, Benjamin, dark and ominous, was busy with his plan. He was seated in a faded blue panel truck meticulously inspecting his supplies. "Let's see. I have the piece of carpet picked up from a goodwill store. I hated the way that old fool clerk smirked. He thinks he's better than me. I hate those kind of people. Man, will he be frosted when he sees his car." He began to laugh. "Slashing his tires made me feel better. It should have been his crummy face."

He fumbled with the contents of the bags. The drug store made it a piece of cake. They have almost everything; cokes, crackers and cheese, canned ham, potato chips, even small containers of soup, matches, flashlight, batteries, and several rolls of wide adhesive tape. He would have preferred the wide silver colored duct tape, but he would have had to find a hardware store to buy some. The adhesive tape would have to do.

He would use a large red handkerchief which he had used during his cowboy period. For a time all of the New York group dressed in western garb, and enjoyed line dancing in the local hangouts.

On the floor board he had placed a canteen, camp stove and lantern, with plenty of fuel. For the piece de resistance at the auto supply store he had purchased electrical tape and two spray cans of motor starting ether. The ether might help start a car, but he intended to use it in a far different role, to bring down a big man.

After the inspection of his supplies was complete, he drove toward the carefully chosen abandoned house on an isolated property.

He stopped at the local BP station near Patriots Point to fill up. Customers came and went. Hundred of families were rushing to their favorite spots. This area provided many attractions: the ships, the carriage rides, the picnic tables, and picnickers were everywhere. All ignored the dark shabby man in the blue panel truck.

He deposited the carpet and the bags of supplies on the porch upon his arrival. He searched over the doors's ledge and found the key he was assured would be there. The door opened easily.

Birds could be heard, squawking to the tourists for a tasty handout as they circled the river. The constant hum of tires on the highway in the distance reminded him that danger was always present.

Using a flashlight he was able to pierce the darkness as he placed a lantern on the table in the center of the room. He struck a match to light the lantern, and the flame drove back the shadows and signaled a welcome to the weary traveler. As he looked about he found a sad dilapidated house. It was in disrepair, dusty, and with an odor of old mildew permeating the heavy, oppressive air.

The room was Spartan in appearance with one bed, a table and a small chair. All had seen better days. Benjamin took a sip from his canteen and set about getting his supplies into the house. He stood the rolled-up carpet against the wall, and he tossed a blanket on the bed.

"I'll need to get plenty of rest tonight for tomorrow will change my entire life," a tired, but confident Benjamin whispered to the dark emptiness. Benjamin hung pictures of Charles all over the room. Below the largest portrait he hung a smaller picture of the two of them together. He placed a small table under the photographs, and on the table he placed a bowl of yellow roses with yellow candles on either side. Benjamin had carefully created a shrine to their love.

Ben's interference in their lives had forced Tom to work on

Sundays so he and Shelley left for work early to receive a special shipment. Charles was suffering from another migraine so he decided to sleep in. Charles was adrift in that nether land of sleep where half formed images drift in and out. He wasn't exactly dreaming because he could not later recall any single aspect of a dream.

His reverie was suddenly interrupted by a heavy weight and something over his nose and mouth. He couldn't move. He realized that someone was sitting astride him, holding him down. Whatever it was over his face was preventing him from breathing. He forced his mouth open against the pressure being applied from above and inhaled deeply. A pungent odor and a slightly acrid taste caused him to feel an even higher level of additional panic, but he had to breathe.

The pressure to his face had sealed his nose, and he could not identify the cause of the odor and taste. The panic of realizing he was being attacked and the suffocating pressure to his face caused adrenalin to pump into his blood stream in massive doses. His heart pounded.

The need for oxygen multiplied quickly. He must breathe at all costs. He gulped air through his mouth as rapidly as possible. Each breath was tainted with that odor and taste. Charles thought he had identified it, but his head began to swim. His ears rang with increasing volume and tempo. Suddenly, everything was gone, and the silent blackness closed over all of his senses.

What Charles did not know was that old anesthetic, ether, first used by a Georgia surgeon, Dr. Charles W. Long for surgery, had been used to send him into sensory oblivion. It was easy...

Benjamin had made a quick trip to the auto parts store for a couple of spray cans of engine starting ether. A long spray into a kitchen towel produced a "sleepy time mask". Ask his victim how effective it was.

Benjamin had planned to slip into the room where Charles lay sleeping, leap astride his beloved's body pinning his arms beneath his own body and the bedclothes, press the ether saturated towel over Charles face, and wait for the chemical to do its work.

It had gone perfectly, and as planned. Charles had soon ceased to struggle. Now Charles lay unconscious on the bed. He was still breathing, thank God, and he appeared to be asleep. The attack had not been noisy enough to alarm anyone else. Now the task was to get him downstairs and into the van.

After blindfolding him, Ben tied Charles' hands. Benjamin secured a croaker sack over Charles' head and arms. He rolled Charles gently off the bed onto a blanket. He pulled the blanket down the stairs without injuring Charles. Charles was next rolled up in the carpet which Benjamin secured with several lengths of stout cord. The open end of the carpet roll and the loose weave of the croaker sack material allowed Charles to breathe.

Benjamin jumped with a start when the phone began to ring, two rings, and three rings. "We'd better get out of here. That's Tom Branson, if I know human nature," crowed Benjamin Tracer, now an actual kidnapper.

Shock and the aftereffects of the ether had dulled Charles' senses. He could not move. The croaker sack was twisted about his neck, his wrists were tied, and he could feel something covering his eyes tightly. A terrified Charles felt that he was living in a nightmare as he was violently bounced around in a vehicle.

"Shit!" Benjamin muttered to himself. "Where did that cop car come from?"

Under the watchful eyes of the local police, Benjamin drove carefully not wishing to be stopped with his hot cargo in the truck.

He did not turn his head as the car pulled up next to him. He came to a full stop at the red light, almost in an angelic manner.

"I'll outsmart these mothers. The slickest thing I've done was while Charles was out cold, driving back to the Holiday Inn and having lunch. Right under all of their noses. Now just watch," Benjamin muttered under his breath as he turned and smiled at the officers.

"Excuse me, sir," Benjamin called out.

The officer rolled down his window. "Yes Sir, may I be of assistance."

"You sure can, officer," Benjamin who always enjoyed playing with fire, brazenly. He asked the officers, "How much further to Patriots Point?"

"Just a couple of miles to the BP Station, then you turn right. Just follow the signs," the officer smiled.

"Thanks. Have a nice day," Benjamin pulled away from the light as the police car turned left going about it's rounds.

"Stupid jerks. I told you I was smarter than you." Benjamin loved the feeling of superiority. The vehicle picked up speed continuing on its way.

After what seemed an eternity, the vehicle slowed, tossing Charles back and forth and then made an abrupt stop. The vehicle began a slow crawl through a grassy marsh. Charles could hear the scratching of overgrown vegetation as the truck passed over a drive which had not been cut in years.

At the house, Benjamin backed the truck up to only a couple of feet from the porch. When he let the tailgate down, it made an almost perfect bridge to the porch. There was only a few inches difference in height to handle. He was able to get the rolled carpet with Charles inside onto the porch by dragging it, one end at a time.

Benjamin had claimed Charles as if he were a prize he had just won in a game. Now he triumphantly dragged one end of the rolled carpet into the decorated room and unrolled his prize.

He had tied Charles' wrists in front of him. Charles's pajama top was torn and bedraggled. He had lost one of the bedroom slippers which Benjamin had so lovingly placed on the feet of his unconscious victim back in Charles' bedroom.

"Please, why are you doing this? What do you want?" A confused Charles hoarsely whispered.

His abductor did not respond.

Trapped in the croaker sack Charles labored for breath. His shoeless foot was a little bloody from a splinter courtesy of the old house's rough floor.

Benjamin had his lover inside the structure, and as rapidly as possible he removed the sack, and he gave Charles a drink of water from an old canteen. He pulled the blindfolded Charles over to the bed and released his wrists. Benjamin was taking no chances so he set about handcuffing each of Charles' hands to the headboard of the old fashioned iron bed.

Benjamin threw a blanket over Charles, and proceeded to clean his injured foot, gently pouring cool water over the wound gouged by the splinter. When he was satisfied that the wound was clean and contained no remnant of the splinter, he secured each of Charles' ankles to the foot of the bed with lengths of rope.

"What do you want?" Charles whispered, his voice hoarse from the effects of the ether. "Please answer me. I know you are there," his heart was pounding like a freight train.

Charles swallowed hard, persisting with his questions. "Where am I? What do you want? Please answer." Charles could hear the labored breathing of another person in the room, "I can hear you breathing."

There was a sudden loud thud, causing Charles to recoil.

"Don't get excited; I just tripped over a chair," the raspy voice of the abductor explained.

"Please tell me, why you have brought me here?" Charles jerked his head in a vague attempt at recognition. "I recognize your voice. We know each other, don't we?" Charles asked, his mind still muddled by the ether.

"Do we?" the abductor replied, attempting to disguise his voice with a hoarse whisper.

"I'm not sure, but there is something...If you know me, then you know that I'm not a mean person. Let's talk it out. Take me home. Tom and I won't prosecute. We'll get you help."

"What makes you think I need help?" The captor sat in the chair by the window staring at the horizon. He wore a rather stubborn, undaunted expression.

There was a light breeze, blowing across the vegetation. The abductor had needed a secluded spot, and, although he could hear highway traffic, no other person or structure could be seen from the house. If you didn't know exactly where to look, you would never find the overgrown driveway. The truck had now made four trips down the drive, but there was still no visible evidence attesting to its passage.

He was irritated listening to Charles slurred voice now muttering in prayer." "Will you stop your incessant whining? Have I hurt you?" the mocking abductor snapped.

There was a crashing of glass shattering against the wall.

"Sorry I lost control. I didn't mean to break the glass. Please stop the chattering, Charles, or you'll force me to gag you."

"Please don't. I'll choke. You don't understand, but I had my nose broken as a child and I have difficulty breathing. Stress makes it worse."

"Are you feeling stress? Are you afraid?" Benjamin continued to disguise his voice.

"Yes!" was all Charles could say.

Charles inhaled the lit cigarette the abductor was smoking. He must remain calm. Try to keep his wits about him. Remember every detail, but how could he? His brain felt as if it were full of large wads of cotton. Charles was having difficulty putting two thoughts together. He shook his head trying to force himself to think, and he wished he could get a breath of fresh air. He had enough presence of mind to realize that he must not antagonize his abductor.

The restraints were so tight. The blood slowly ceased to flow in his arms and legs which caused a tingling sensation. His abductor had secured the handcuffs and ropes tightly."

"Will you please loosen my restraints?" Charles asked. "They're cutting off the blood to my arms and legs," he sounded miserable.

Benjamin glanced away from Charles in anguish. The rescue was not supposed to be like this. Charles was to be happy with the reunion, but he was growling, and yanking at his restraints.

"Relax Charles, you'll hurt yourself."

"What do you care?"

"I do," Benjamin shoulders drooping walked into the kitchen to escape Charles' condemnation.

Tom was filled with concern when Charles did not answer the telephone. He must be worst, probably went to the doctor. He tore into the house like a mad man, his imagination running rampant as he charged through the house.

"Charles, Charles. Where are you?"

Tom charged up the stairs when no one answered.

He searched the house, unable to find Charles, and finding no note he sat down on the bed they shared. There was a strange pungent odor all about the spread. His worst fear had escaped from the deep inner recesses of his mind; it had suddenly become real.

All of his features seemed to slide as though they were made of wax on a hot day. Tom looked as old as time. His mind flooded with memories of Charles earlier in the week. What had been different? What could he have done to have prevented this tragedy? This very mortal and now feeling very ancient man, mechanically, reached for the phone and dialed.   "Charleston County Police Department," a bored voice said.

"This is Tom Branson. I live at 112 St. Mary Street. I have just come home to find my friend..."
Tom caught his breath, "My Significant Other is missing. Please send an officer."

"Your Significant, What?, oh yeah, your friend, did you say?"

"Yes, his name is Charles Allgood."

"How long has Mr. Allgood been missing?"

"Just a short while. The spread in our--his room has a strange odor. It reeks of ether."

"UH-HUH! Did you have an argument?"

"NO! We had no argument. Please send an officer, immediately," Tom was becoming hysterical.

"Sorry. But a person must be missing at least 24 hours before we can act."

"Give me your name. I want to speak to your superior, NOW!" Tom bellowed as angry spots of color flared in his cheeks.

"That won't be necessary, sir. An officer has been dispatched." The line went dead.

Ten minutes later, the screech of brakes heralded the arrival of the police. Tom raced to the door to admit them. Shelley and Charlotte arrived on their heels.

"Tommy, What's wrong?" Shelley asked, reading terror on her brother's face.

"Somebody broke into the house, Charles is gone," he blurted out.

"Oh, dear God," Shelley clutched Tom's arm.

"Alright who made the call?" The officer asked.

"I did. I'm Tom Branson."

"All of you live here?" the officer's tone heightened Tom's trepidation.

"I do. I'm Shelley Branson. Tom is my brother."

"And you, ma'am. Who are you?" The officer turned speaking to Charlotte.

"I'm Charlotte Burns. I live next door."

"Alright. Has Mr. Allgood been upset about anything? Could he be visiting a friend?" The officer scribbled in his notebook at the same time covertly studying Tom.

"No, Charles wasn't upset. He didn't go off with some friend. Please, you are wasting time. Go upstairs, check his pillow."

"I'll check the pillow, Steve," the other officer said. Shelley moved quickly to show the officer to Charles' room.

"Okay," Steve said and turned back to Tom.

"Have you checked with his friends? Co-workers?"

"No, actually all of us are co-workers. I smelled the strange odor and called you."

The other policeman returned.

"What do you think?"

"Smells like a strong hair tonic to me," The rookie officer replied with a smirk.

"Hair tonic. Are you crazy? That smell is ether," Tom cried out.

"Nonsense. He's probably gone for a walk. Who was the last person to see Charles Allgood?"

"I was," Tom snarled. "He was having a severe migraine headache. He said he hoped a nap would help. Poor Charles, He suffers terribly from migraine."

"Oh I'm sure he does," the officer replied sarcastically, unable to hide the revulsion on his face. "We'll file a report. Let us know if you hear from him. I will leave you my card. Afternoon, folks."

The two officers left as abruptly as they arrived.

"What do you think is really going on, Steve?" the rookie

policeman asked.

"Just a couple of pansies having a falling out. He'll show up sooner or later."

"You don't think we should investigate further?"

"No! Why waste manpower on a couple of deviates?" Steve laughed at the suggestion of the rookie. "Let's get back to real crime. I don't have the time or inclination to play referee to a couple of screamers." "They have feelings too, Steve."

"Yeah, sure.!" The older officer slammed his car door with unusual vigor as if he were protesting the statement.

Inside the Branson home, Shelley attempted to console Tom.

"What do we do now, Tommy?" Shelley asked.

"The police will be of little use," Charlotte chimed in.

"We'll contact our friends to begin searching, but first I'm going to call a police officer who will be sympathetic to our situation," Tom replied, pushing back his chair and stood up.

"Better make the calls from the shop. We should keep the door closed and avoid touching anything else. We can't afford to disturb any clues," Shelley stated.

"Come on over to our place. I don't think Nola or Mason are at home right now. Shelley, you'd better stay here in case the police call. The walk will help clear Tom's head," Charlotte said kissing Tom's cheek.

"Good idea, Charlotte. "I'll stay here. Charlotte will take good care of you." Shelley replied with encouragement. She waved as the couple charged out the door. goodbye.

Tom, with address book in hand followed Charlotte like a wounded puppy across the yard. He sat down at the Burns' phone and began to dial.

"Charleston Police," a honey-toned voice spoke.

"William Painter, please."

"One minute."

"Brownley".

"This is Tom Branson. I am trying to contact Bill Painter."

"Sorry Mr. Branson. He isn't in at the moment. May I be of assistance?"

"NO!" Tom thought, maybe I should tell this man what has occurred. "Ask Bill to call as soon as he can. Impress upon him the urgency of the situation." He gave the officer both his own and Charlotte's telephone numbers. Fear and disgust caused Tom to suddenly throw the phone across the kitchen floor.

"Sorry, I never intended to destroy the phone, but I had to do something. I feel so damned helpless Charlotte. Charles may be in mortal danger. In any event where ever he is, Charles is terrified."

Charlotte ignored Tom's apology. "Don't worry about the phone. Mason has given ours worse treatment. It takes a lickin' but keeps on ringing," she quipped as she gathered up the phone. "A little jolt occasionally is good for one of these things." Charlotte replaced the phone on its usual spot on the table.

I'm going back to the house," Tom explained, "I'd better be there when Bill Painter calls or if Charles...." his voice drifted off.

"Okay, Tom. I'll stay here for now. If he calls, I'll holler out the back door."

Tom waited in a paralyzed silence. He did not remember returning to his home, but he was being shaken by Shelley. Tom hated dropping his guard and permitting his sister to see his terror. The situation demanded that he keep a clear head. He had contacted many their friends that offered to assist in a search.

"What terror must Charles be facing? He must be feeling so alone, praying for help," Tom thought. "Stop it, Tom. This is not the time to fall apart," Tom commanded himself. "Charles needs your strength. Your strength in crisis is one of your most admirable qualities, so saith Charles. What time is it?" Tom asked as he nervously ran his fingers through his hair. "What time did you say?"

"A little after four," Shelley replied.

"Shell," Tom's eyes were large with shock and fear. "Do you think he's alive?" the whispered question cut through the layers of tension sending sparks reverberating around the room.

"Tommy, calm down. You will be no help to Charles if you collapse," Shelley whispered.

"I can't seem to help myself. Charles means so much to me. What if he's lying somewhere injured? What if at this very moment he is being tortured. Shell, he's my life," Tom screamed, his ruddy face was alarmingly pale.

Shelley watched her terrified brother, his eyes appeared to be those of a dead man crumbling under the stress.

Charlotte watched out her kitchen window for any sign of activity in the Bransons' household.

"Why the hell hasn't Bill returned my call? What could he be doing that is so important." Tom jumped as the phone rang.

"How you doing, buddy?" Bill Painter asked as he smiled, happy to hear from his friends. "Is Charles still pounding that new computer to pieces?"

"Charles has been kidnaped. I called your friends in blue to get some help, but it was to no avail. They sent a couple of bigoted assholes. They couldn't have cared less. They wouldn't investigate because Charles has not been missing 24 hours. The men probably won't do anything of a serious investigative nature, they believe we've had a lovers' quarrel."

"I'll be right there. Don't touch a thing. I know it's impossible, but try not to worry. We'll find him."

"Bill's on the way. I knew he'd listen. He's our only hope." Tom's pacing had a lighter bounce for he was feeling the first inkling of hope.

"Tom, who is Bill Painter?" Charlotte asked as she walked into the kitchen. She wanted so much to divert his attention temporarily from the appalling situation.

"He's a friend," Tom smiled.

"Is he gay?"

"Nope. Charlotte, all friends are not gay. He has a wife that he dearly loves and three gorgeous children."

"Where did you meet?"

"We met years ago during his brother's funeral. He was murdered by gay bashes. Bill, Charles and I became great friends. Charles was tutoring Bill in the use of computers."

"Don't say "was" like that. Charles will be back driving us all crazy about the importance of computers. He will continue attempting to drag us old fashioned bookkeepers, kicking and screaming into the twentieth century," Charlotte laughed.

Fifteen minutes later the mysterious friend, Bill Painter pulled up. He dashed up the stairs meeting the nervous Tom Branson on the front porch. They spoke for a moment and Tom led Bill into the house. Shelley hugged Bill upon entering the kitchen.

"Hi Shelley. How are you holding up?"

"I'm fine, Bill. Please bring Charles back to us."

"We'll find him. Right Tom."

"Right. Oh I've forgotten my manners. Bill Painter, this young lady is our dear friend, Charlotte Burns. She lives next door."

"Ms. Burns," Bill acknowledged Charlotte and turned to Tom. "From which room was Charles taken?"

"Our bedroom," Tom said simply.

"Show me."

Tom wearily climbed the stairs to the room he shared with Charles. He showed Bill their bed, and generally described what he had seen, earlier. The odor of ether was still evident, although now, it was somewhat subdued - not fresh, not as pungent - but to an experienced nose, it was still ether. Bill flipped down the coverlet, and there was the dish towel that had been saturated with ether earlier in the day. He also noticed that there was only one bedroom shoe at the foot of the bed.

"Tom, you wait downstairs with the ladies. I'll holler if I need help. We'll talk when I've finished."

Tom returned to the kitchen and dropped into a chair. With head in hands he rocked back and forth.

"Tommy, please! You have got to get control of yourself. You are scaring me," Shelley pleaded.

"I've never known such fear, Shell."

Suddenly Bill Painter came charging down the steps spouting very colorful language.

"Tom, where's the phone?" Bill was holding something wrapped in a bath towel.

"Charleston Police."   "Yeah! This is Lt. William Painter. Connect me with Lt. Brownley."

"Brownley."

"George. This is Bill Painter."

"Hi, Bill. What's up?"

"Send me a full team to Tom Branson's house, 112 St. Mary's Street. I'm taking over the Charles Allgood investigation. When I've got time there are two officers that will receive one damned good tongue lashing. Such stupidity, such incompetence."

"Why all the excitement, Bill? The original investigators reported nothing. Just another domestic disagreement between a couple of...." George's statement died on his lips, as he remembered Bill's brother. "Sorry, man."

Ignoring George's stupidity, Bill continued, "Well, if those two assholes had bothered to look under the bed they'd of found what I did."

"What's that?"

"A can of engine starting ether."

"NO SHIT!

"Yeah, NO SHIT."

"Their report indicated a container of something they thought queers used for kinky sex. I'll send the team immediately."

"You do that thing personally. Don't you dare send back those two assholes. I'm mad enough to shoot them myself."

Bill Painter slammed the receiver into its cradle. "Incompetent bigots."

Soon the house was filled to standing-room-only capacity with the local police. They dusted for fingerprints and searched the house and grounds for the spot the abductor entered or any other evidence.

"Most of the prints will probably match those of the four of you, Tom, since you are its occupants," Bill Painter stated.

"The perp entered from this back window, Lt. Painter," one of the officers returned to the kitchen. "Probably wore gloves. Only those without televisions fail to wear gloves these days."

Chapter 14

The rear door slammed shut as a sudden gust of wind blew through the house. Outside, lightning crackled across the sky like a bull whip attacking the thick black clouds. Blinding rain, accompanied by hail the size of golf balls, pounded the tin roof.

The driving rain poured in through the window drenching Benjamin's face. His devilish youthful smile returned as he mopped his brow with an already soaked rag. It began to rain harder as he averted his face to avoid further pounding.

"What's happening?" Charles demanded.

"The heat wave is over, my friend," the kidnapper answered. His mouth twitched upward with pleasure, the sheer pleasure of being with Charles.

The stormy night continued. Unpredicted thunderstorms, and gusty winds ripped the coastline. Cell after cell formed, transforming the heat of the day into wind, rain, hail, lightning, and the thunder that followed. Finally, the storm dissipated and left the stage to make room for the next cell to form and perform. The waves swelled angrily pounding the beaches.

Charles, blindfolded and hogtied to the creaky bed, lay helplessly listening to the sounds of mother nature's rage while he raged inside with his own personal storm.

Charles dropped off into a semi-sleep with his mind still in a state of muddled confusion. Why couldn't he think clearly? I'll get some rest, he thought, and try to put the pieces of the puzzle together later.

The sound of a loose limb striking the side of the house awoke Charles. "Hello! where are you? What was that sound?" Nobody answered. "Oh Dear God in Heaven, I'm alone."

Extreme fatigue flooded over Charles. He drifted off pretending that he was back home in his own bed in the arms of Tom. "Oh Tom", was all he could say. Charles awoke with a start. His limbs felt stiff and heavy as he twisted around the small bed. There was a humming in his ears as vehicles in the distance passed his prison. He dreamed of a warm bath, soaking his weary body in his own tub.

He missed the fragrance of his favorite soap. Tom occasionally joined him during this quiet time.

Charles drew in a deep breath as he remembered Tom's strong hands massaging the taunt muscles in his neck. Tom always sensed the onset of another migraine. Charles needed Tom's tender ministration relieving the throbbing pain he was enduring. He longed for the security of Tom's body against his.

The captor laughed as he slid over, drawing Charles close, tickling his victim's ear with his tongue.

"Don't do that. When did you get back? I didn't hear you come in," Charles snatched away. "I need to use the bathroom, please."

Ignoring Charles' question his captor began to assist to the facility. "Okay, I have to help you. Don't worry, you are safe for now. I won't touch you until you beg me."

He began to disconnect the ropes that held Charles' legs to the foot of the bed. Benjamin attached a lead rope to the restraint on Charles left ankle, then he released the handcuffs at the head of the bed. Thus fettered and still blindfolded, he was sure that Charles would remain helpless for the trip to the bathroom.

When they returned from the facilities, the abductor returned Charles to the bed and reconnected his bonds. Finally, Benjamin covered him carefully with the blanket.

"Just lie there like a good boy. You'll begin to remember and soon it will all become clear. Sweet dreams."

"I can't rest. My back hurts." Charles whispered, shaking his head as he attempted to clear his head.

"I watched you and Tom the other day as you frolicked in the water."

"What? Oh yeah. Where were you?"   "Observing from the bushes. You have the most glorious body," Benjamin continued, attempting to carry on a conversation. "You're a great swimmer. I made your picture to immortalize the moment."

"Immortalize, huh. You are wrong about my abilities. Tom is strongest. He won several trophies in college."

"Do you have any trophies?"

"No. I can just keep my head above water."

"I saw you floating with your arms and legs spread out like a beautiful sacrifice to the sun god," Benjamin smiled at the memory.

"Me? I don't think so."

Benjamin found it impossible to accept the change in their relationship. Time had changed each of them, but soon they would return to the same comfortable familiarity that Benjamin remembered.

"I sat in the corner of your favorite restaurant watching you eat lunch."

"Where was this?" Charles asked as he tried desperately to make sense of the situation.

"Oh, a place off Broad. You were eating a bowl of soup. It looked so good I asked the waiter to bring me the same."

"Did you enjoy the soup?" Charles asked. He wanted to laugh at the absurdity of the conversation.

"There's no soup tonight. Just a couple of sandwiches."

"I'm not really hungry. Thanks," Charles responded almost too politely.

The room felt stifling as Benjamin mechanically prepared sandwiches for their evening consumption. What is wrong? This is not the reunion he had dreamed of.

"Try some cold chicken. I'll bring it to you. You must eat. Now do like the doctor says," Benjamin attempted some levity in the stilted conversation.

Charles ate the dry sandwiches and drank the hot coffee. His abductor watched quietly as the sleeping potion took effect on Charles. His prisoner asleep the kidnapper could run some errands.

Lt. Bill Painter waited impatiently in the hotel lobby until a young employee approached him.

"May I help you?" the clerk asked.

"Yes. I'm Lt. Bill Painter, Charleston Police," Bill said as he flashed his shield. "Do you have a Benjamin Tracer of New York staying in this hotel?"

The young man flinched at the sight of the badge. He wasn't having any trouble with police on his shift.

"I'll be happy to check for you, lieutenant."

Looking through the files the young man said. "Room 214. You may call Mr. Tracer on the house phone across the lobby."

"No thanks, and don't you call him. Understand?" Bill headed for the elevators.

Bill Painter walked briskly down the hall to room 214.   "Yes, may I help you?" a baritone voice called through the door.

"Lt. Bill Painter, Charleston Police. May I come in?"

"Of course, I've been expecting you, I'm just a little surprised to see you so early. But, please, do come in," Benjamin said as he stepped aside permitting the officer to enter.

"You say that you have been expecting me, why's that?" Painter asked, ignoring Benjamin's attempt to engage him in pleasant conversation.

"I assume you are here because of Charles Allgood. His friends were upset with me. Said they would contact the police because I have been attempting to contact him since my arrival in Charleston,"Benjamin stated as his voice trembled with disbelief.

"Go on," Painter encouraged Benjamin to speak.

"I attempted to engage Charles in conversation several days ago. He actually dashed out of a restaurant. I don't understand it. We used to be such good friends. You know what I mean, officer?" Benjamin smiled.

Everything was going along as planned. "This cop doesn't have a clue. I only have to continue my naive act. If you only knew how stupid you really are," Benjamin thought as he continued his most sincere smile.

"He's dirty, through and through," Bill Painter thought. Then he spoke, "I'm afraid, I don't. Why do you think he overreacted to a innocent conversation?"

"I do not know. He seemed terribly distraught," Benjamin stated sadly, "I suppose his lover isolates him from the outside world."

"When was the last time you and Mr. Allgood spoke?" Painter ignored Benjamin sarcastic remark.

"In New York, about three years ago. I was so thrilled to see him again that I forgot myself and rushed up and attempted to draw him into conversation. He literally bolted for the door as though some evil apparition was pursuing him. It was very strange," Benjamin, the wide-eyed innocent threw his arms into the air. "Very strange indeed. Since we had been so close years ago."

"Close, you say. Uh huh," Painter replied.

"Didn't Charles explain? We lived together for a time."

"It didn't last?" Painter asked.

Hit the mark... Benjamin looked stricken, "No, we grew apart as couples often do." He hardly had the time to discuss his life with the klutz of a cop. Charles was all alone in that old house and he was impatient to rejoin him.

"I'm terribly sorry he and his companion are angry. I suppose Charlie never told him about us."

"Charles is not angry, he's missing," Painter interrupted, as he watched Benjamin's reaction.

"What happened? I can't imagine why our brief encounter would cause him to bolt and run away from his family. He does have a family. Doesn't he?" Benjamin said as he dropped into a nearby chair.

"Damn it, but you are good," he thought, "don't overplay the scene. This detective is just another publicity seeking, arrogant, flat foot."

"Yes, he has a family, and they are devastated." Painter replied.

"Can you account for your whereabouts between 7:00 am and noon today?" the lieutenant asked.

"I was in my room most of the morning, except for breakfast. Room service brought up a light meal about 7:15 am. Fruit, toast and coffee."

"Alright that covers breakfast. Then what?"

"I sunned myself by the pool, then I napped until lunch. I ate in the hotel restaurant about 1:00. The server should remember me. I am embarrassed that I lost my composure when he served me improperly grilled Red Snapper."

"You didn't care for the chef's culinary art?" Bill Painter asked sarcastically.

"Culinary art, you call it. The man is a barbarian. He's fit only to work for one of those fast food greasy spoon. The gall of the man calling himself a chef," Benjamin stated as he turned his nose up in disgust.

Establishing an alibi had not been so difficult. Benjamin had to create a scene in the restaurant while Charles was softly snoring, hogtied and rolled up in the carpet in the back of the blue panel truck.

"Watch it. You must focus on the present. Don't let your mind stray," Ben thought.

Benjamin was so sure of himself, so sure of his performance. People were so stupid. If they only knew. If he could tell them how they had been used? Of his genius. He pulled off the rescue of Charles under the noses of those silly, brain-dead morons.

While he was busy congratulating himself, the annoying police officer jerked him back to reality.

"Did the chef correct your problem?" Painter inquired.

"Yes, I relaxed over a pleasant glass of zinfandel while my replacement fish was being prepared," Benjamin smiled again, remembering the afternoon.

"Where did you go after lunch?"

"Back to my room for a short nap."

"A nap?"

"Yes. I have been recovering from an illness, and my physician recommended a vacation in the sun. Hey, why all of the strange questions. I told you I'm sorry. When Charles returns I'll call him immediately and apologize. I don't understand why he became so nervous and took off. Tom Branson probably knows little of our relationship," Benjamin stated, his voice filled with emotion.

"Charles Allgood isn't just missing. He's been kidnaped," Painter stated coldly convinced that he was currently speaking to the kidnapper.

"Oh Dear God NO! Not Charles, not dear sweet Charles. Lieutenant Painter, no one would do such a terrible thing as harm Charles. Everybody loves him," Benjamin moaned.

"Well he's gone, and everything points to a kidnaping," Painter stated without expression.

"Have you any suspects in this heinous crime against dear

Charles?" Benjamin asked imploringly.

"We've got a few leads we're working on," Painter replied.

"You can't possibly think he's met with foul play?"

"Only time will tell. As I said we have a few leads. We're currently interviewing his co-workers, friends and acquaintances."

Rising to face the lieutenant, Benjamin requested, "Please keep me posted on the case's progress. If I can be of any assistance, I will do whatever is in my power. You understand, that with our previous history, I did not want to contact Tom Branson. Please call me when you form a search party." Benjamin escorted the detective to the door and carefully closed it behind Lt. Bill Painter.

"You're real slick, but you're dirty. Just how dirty only time and good police work will tell," Bill Painter thought as he left the hotel room.

Lt. Painter arrived at the Branson house while another investigator was interviewing Tom.

"Is Mr. Allgood the sort to disappear without leaving word?" Officer Parker asked. "No, of course not." replied Tom.

"Mr. Branson, has Mr. Allgood been suffering from mood swings lately?"

"Mood swings? no," Tom snarled as he answered the officer's pointless questions.

"Does he have any close friends he might have gone to visit?"

"What's all of this fool talk about mood swings, visiting friends?" Tom demanded.

"He lives in this house with you and your sister?" Parker continued.

"Yes, what of it?"

"Has your relationship been--uh cordial the last few months?"

"Of course our relationship is cordial. We've disagreed as any couple would," Tom frowned as he replied.

"Did you have a disagreement today?"

"No! They did not," Charlotte interjected.

The officers turned to face a livid Charlotte Hamby Burns.

"Charles and I were having morning coffee in this very kitchen just moments before he disappeared. We talked about how happy he and Tom were."

"He told you that he and Mr. Branson were happy?" the officer asked as Bill Painter joined them.

"Was it unusual for him to make such a declaration?"

"No, not really. He's been nervous lately," Charlotte frowned.

"Nervous, did you say?"

"Yes, weird things have been happening lately," Charlotte continued.

"Charles received a dozen of yellow roses. The next week he received a dozen dead roses."

"Dead roses?" Charlotte, why didn't you tell me?" Tom demanded.

"Charles didn't want you to worry, so we decided not to tell you," Shelley stated as he joined the conversation.

"Anything else?" Bill asked.

"Weird things have been going on. Last week someone broke into our house and stole all of our clothes. Then someone delivered an expensive car that we had not ordered," Tom recalled. "He's been getting a lot of hang-up calls. There was one phone call several days ago. A whispered voice asked him to leave Tom alone." Charlotte added.

"What? Who the hell was it? I'll bet it was that damnable Benjamin Tracer," Tom snapped.

"Shelley, did Charles recognize the voice?" Bill asked.

"He said that there was something familiar in the voice," Shelley stated. "I am positive that our mischief maker is Benjamin Tracer."

"Charles told me that several weeks ago he began to have the strange sensation of unseen eyes watching him," Charlotte added.

"We had a nutty occurrence last week," Tom chimed in, "I received about fifty letters from women agreeing to marry me. Somebody thought it was a great joke to place an ad in the newspaper offering marriage to woman from a gay man."

"Did you contact the newspaper to see who placed the ad?"

"I contacted the newspaper and the only record they had was that the customer paid cash."

"Is that all you can remember?" Bill Painter asked. "Try not to worry, my friend. We'll find him. You have my number, call me if any of you think of anything else."

"Sir, call us. Anytime you remember something new, no matter how small. We want to get Mr. Allgood back into his home as soon as possible," the other officer stated, extending his hand, "Goodbye, you'll be hearing from us."

"Lt. Painter, what do you think?" Officer Parker asked after they had exited the house. "I'm afraid that we'll find the poor bastard floating in the Cooper River."

"You believe that he's another victim of a hate crime," Bill Painter conjectured.

"Yes sir, the world is full of nuts that don't need an excuse to hate. They do not care that just because some people have a different lifestyle it doesn't make them evil. The Bransons seem like real nice folks," Parker stated.

"They are. I've known them for several years so I only pray you are wrong about Charles."

"By the way, sir, how did you fare with that Benjamin Tracer character?" Parker asked.

"I just came from his hotel room. He couldn't have been more co-operative. A little too co-operative. Remembered too much. How many people do you know that can recall minute by minute their daily activities?"

"Yes sir. I don't like the smell of this. They all agreed that Mr. Allgood was afraid of Mr. Tracer," Officer Parker stated.

"Yes. He and Tracer met in New York several years ago. Tracer told me that they had been lovers for quite a while. On the other hand, I know that it lasted only a short while. Charles didn't want to see him. For some reason he was terrified of Tracer," Bill replied.

"Parker, contact the NYPD and see what they've got on him. You can run a routine NCIC check. He's a slick one, but I'm sure that he has slipped up somewhere. He has to have a rap sheet out there somewhere. You should have been there. Yes sir, that man gave me the creeps. He's dirty, and too slick for my taste," Painter said, his brows knitted with concern.

"We'll have to keep an eye on this one. He's a powder keg who could explode."

"He sounds like a hard case. We may never make him crack."

"I bet my last penny that Benjamin Tracer is a severely disturbed person. He's quite the actor. A con man, a real loose cannon. Tracer appears to be crafty as a fox. We ought to grab that fox, and put him our darkest cell and see how long it takes to make him crack." Parker stated.

"A quiet cell. I prefer a 9 mm bullet in his brain, now that would make Charleston a safer place."

"I'm concerned that we'll not find Charles alive. Tracer's a big fruit cake," Bill Painter stated as he wiped his worried brow.

"Lieutenant, you are the best in the state. You'll find him, if anybody can." Parker stated, his voice filled with reassurance. "Have you ever misread a perp, Sir."

Years ago this one kid fooled me. I listened to his words, not his actions. I believed nobody was that evil. He was a bright boy, much like Tracer... This boy had strange tantrums. He listened to voices. But we lived in an era when children belonged to their parents. His parents appeared to be loving, supportive folks," Bill paused, then continued,

"It turned out their idea of family activities was to whip him, beat him, kick him, and burn him with cigarettes. One day they really got out of hand attacking him, and even pulled out his hair in small bunches until he lost consciousness."

"My God, Lieutenant, what finally happened?" Parker asked as his face blanched.

"That night while they were sleeping, he listened to the voices, and tiptoed downstairs, got his father's shotgun and blew his parents in half."

"What happened to the boy?" The rookie asked as his pallor turned into a greenish tinge.

"The neighbors called the department after they had broken in the back door. They reported not having seen any activity for several days. They found the couple sprawled on their beds, blood everywhere. The stench was so bad that a couple of the neighbors run outside. We brought our cigars to smoke, helps to cut down the odor. Keeps you from puking."

"Did you ever find the boy?" Parker pressed on in a hushed voice.

"We found him in his bed covered with cuts, bruises, dried caked blood. The shotgun was on the floor. After finishing off those sadistic bastards he called his parents, that poor pitiful child, placed the shot gun in his mouth and blew himself away. You'll learn more on the streets than you did at the academy. Learn the street and you may be around long enough to retire."

"Yes sir, Lieutenant. I'll do the best I can, but I'm no hero," Parker replied. "We'd better handle Benjamin with kid gloves. Can't push him too far, if we want Allgood back in one piece."

" Don't try to be a hero. Heroes get themselves killed. Let Tracer continue to believe that he's fooling us,"Lt. Painter turned to the young officer. "He's not our only problem. We're going to be dealing with Commissioner Crowley."

"Why's Commissioner Crowley getting into this kidnaping? He hates gays? Crowley's not running for mayor?"

"Crowley knows that this kidnaping is a real hot potato since the gay community has been demanding police action. It's to his best advantage to publicly appear concerned. If we don't find Charles Allgood soon we'll be combing picketers out of our hair."

"Yes, he's trouble. He was giving the men one of his famous lectures about the bleeding heart press. They are always yakking about Gay Rights. Wouldn't surprise me to find his name on the ballot next year," Parker laughed.

"He won't get elected dog catcher with his track record of brutality and intolerance," Bill Painter replied.

"He'd better hire a PR man, or person willing to put up with his chauvinistic crap. Somebody has got to teach him the current politically correct terminology."

"It will never happen. He's not that smart," Bill laughed.

Chapter 15

Benjamin put his hand across his forehead, covering his eyes as though they were light sensitive. In fact, he felt exceedingly nervous. He must return to the old house and check on Charles, but he had to be careful in case the police were trying to follow him. Benjamin had found it impossible to sleep because he was either worried about avoiding discovery or anticipating a final delicious reunion, reunion in every sense of the word, with Charles.

Benjamin slipped out of the hotel in the wee hours of the morning. The blue panel truck turned onto Hwy. 17 carrying its driver to his rendezvous with Charles Allgood. The downpour impeded his drive north towards the small dilapidated house. He was not displeased because the night and the weather provided him with a great deal of protection from prying eyes. Benjamin drove five miles past the turn off to assure himself that he was not being followed.

He turned around by driving through a large parking lot which allowed him to be more certain that he had not been tailed. After turning around, he proceeded with great haste the five miles back down the highway to check on the well-being of his guest.

He never saw Bill Painter's small car following him through Charleston. Unfortunately for Bill the weather was so bad Benjamin Tracer lost him.

Charles was asleep when Benjamin entered the room. He was pleased to see that the sedative in the drinking water had been effective. Benjamin tripped over a chair and the resulting commotion shocked Charles into consciousness.

"Who is it? Please answer. Is someone there?" Charles pled.

"It's just me," Benjamin replied softly.

Charles appeared confused. The range of emotions playing against each other in his head left him totally bewildered. Charles was relieved that someone, anyone had come to his private prison.

He was finding it extremely difficult being alone, blindfolded and handcuffed. The isolation and the situation were driving him mad.

He could not understand why he felt such relief at the sound of his captors voice. He hated this person who had stolen him from all that was familiar.

The intruder sat near Charles. He ran his hand through Charles' hair, disturbed that the beautiful locks were now wet, matted, dirty, and emitted a terrible stench.

Charles drew away from his captor feeling a sudden dizziness and a threatening wave of nausea.

"What do you want of me?" Charles asked. "If it's money you want, we're not wealthy, but if you contact Tom Branson he will pay you for my safe return."

"Have I mentioned money?" the intruder whispered.

"No, you haven't. But please, it's so dark and terrifying. Won't you take off the blindfold?"

"No, not yet," the intruder replied.

The intruder checked the restraints, "You understand, if you try to escape, I'll be forced to kill you."

"I need to relieve my bladder. I've held it all day," Charles replied ignoring the intruder's threat.

"Okay, okay, I don't want you peeing all over the bed. This place stinks enough."

The kidnapper went through the ritual of freeing him from the bed. This time, however, his hands were handcuffed together behind his back before he was escorted to the tiled floor. He felt his captor unsnap his pajama bottoms, dropping them to the floor.

The kidnapper could not control himself as he slid his hands slowly down Charles' bare buttock. He pulled Charles against his broad chest. He nibbled on his victim's ear as he hungrily flicked his tongue around Charles' neck.

"Please! Please don't! You mustn't do this." Charles cried.

"I must. I need you. Your exquisite body. Relax, dear heart. I won't hurt you."   Benjamin slowly moved his hands over Charles quivering body. With a giddy school-boy gasp of delight, he pulled Charles closer to him. Benjamin squeezed his hand as he continued nibbling the ear and neck of his victim. He folded Charles into his arms as their mouths joined over and over Benjamin sucked at the juices from his former lover. He stroked Charles' thighs as he moved a trembling hand down to his genitals. As Charles attempted to separate from his capture Benjamin moved his hand up the back of his head and pressed him closer.

Charles managed to free his lips as he tried to pull away. He was shocked by his captors wild passionate behavior. Exhausted from his time of captivity, Charles slumped against his kidnapper.

"Please, I'm tired and confused. Please let me relieve myself." Charles cried out.

"Liked it didn't you. Alright don't cry. I won't touch you again, for now. If we had a working sink next to the toilet," Benjamin laughed, "a little trickling water might inspire you."

Charles tried to relax so he could urinate, but with the stress and his body's betrayal, he found it impossible.

"Calm down. I promised to behave. Sit. It will be easier this way."

Charles could not suppress a nervous laugh at the obscurity of the situation and finally, a tentative stream freed itself from his body.

"May I wash?" Charles asked. "I feel so dirty."

"Later. Now we 're returning to the bedroom."

"Then what?"

"That's up to you, Charlie," Benjamin said as he nuzzled his face against Charles.

"Don't! I said no. When may I remove the blindfold?" Charles complained with an exasperated sigh as he attempted to change the subject.

"No matter what the situation you never loose your manners, do you Charles?"

"No Benjamin. I don't."

"So you knew it was me." "Of course, Benjamin. "You should have kept me doped up. As soon as my head cleared, I recognized my kidnapper, Charles stated coldly. Did you think I could ever forget your deep voice? Those strong hands caressing my body. Don't touch me again, Ben. I belong to Tom. "You are guilty of kidnaping, don't you realize it. I loved you once so I don't want you to go to jail."

"I'd go to jail anyway, Charlie." Benjamin replied softly as removed the blindfold.

"Not if you released me. I won't press charges," Charles, his eyes surveying his surroundings insisted in a scratchy voice.

"Charles, listen to me. Do you remember when you left New York?"

"Yes. I remember."

"After about two weeks of being alone, I began to see you in the face of every young man with whom I came into contact. One night I was taking a late stroll when this handsome young man came out from between two buildings," Benjamin frowned as he remembered.

"It was an area filled with old dilapidated buildings. The alleyways were lined with homeless derelicts, homeless that is if you didn't count the small area of the alley or the heating grate that each now called home. I gave him my best smile. He looked at me with the most alarmingly innocent eyes. You know what I mean, eyes that were inviting and promising. We both knew what the other wanted. With few words, we walked to the nearest hotel."

Benjamin smiled, as went on, "I believe that his name was Scott. He made me a cup of coffee. It wasn't good, kind of weak, but he talked. He had left home for the bright lights of Broadway but his money ran out."

"What did Scott look like? Do you even remember?" Charles asked.

"He was a tall brunette with a small moustache. Oh Charlie, he had the softest doe-like brown eyes just made for sin. We lay on the bed eating fruit and exchanging confidences."

"It sounded quite pleasant," Charles interjected. "He pulled down the shade to darken the room. He began to undress and laid back down on the bed. His eyes promising a exquisite evening.

Between kisses he told me that he had been beaten and robbed of his rent money. His delicate body still had ugly bruises from the assault. I longed to kiss the pain away. Instead, I took a fifty-dollar bill from my wallet and laid it on the table. Scott was immediately offended."

"I'm no whore, Bennie," Scott said, those exquisite doe eyes leaking with shame.

"We're friends aren't we? I asked him".

"Yes, Scott replied."

"We all need help on occasion. Take the money."

"Oh Benjamin, you were right to help," Charles said, as he began to feel a strange protectiveness of his former friend.

"Charlie, You know how it feels to be so damned lonesome. I needed a pair of caring arms around me, to comfort me," Benjamin whispered in deep remorse.

"I sat on the bed looking at his fine young body. It was different from yours."

Charles could not suppress a smile.

"Please don't be offended, but you outweighed him a good fifteen pounds," Benjamin stated, searched Charles's eyes for any sense of anger, but his prisoner remained silence.

"He squeezed my hand, squirming about the bed with great anticipation. Oh, Charlie, I felt so cheap. I just felt used. But I was so alone. No one cared. Suddenly he snaked his long slender legs around my waist. We made love over and over. I closed my eyes pretending he was you." Benjamin looked off into space as he relived that evening.

He reached out, calling my name, embracing me, and suddenly I freaked."

"Bennie, what did you do?" Charles whispered.

"Oh, I don't know. I was out of my body, floating above the bed watching this crazed entity as he choked the life out of the young man. I felt something in his throat pop like one of those ripe grapes we had been eating, and then he was dead," Benjamin shivered.

"I regained my sanity and dressed. I shoved the fifty into my pocket, a dead man did not need money, and left the hotel. The next day I began my quest for you."

"I'm sorry. What happened to the young man, Scott? You didn't just leave his broken body in that dark room?"

"If he was dead, there was nothing I could do. I had to get out of that hotel without attracting attention. I searched the papers for weeks, but there was never any mention of any unclaimed young white male missing or dead in the area."

"Bennie, please. You've got to get control of yourself. Our time together was a mistake. Tom and I are happy together. You must understand."

Benjamin embraced the handcuffed Charles as he slipped his hand inside his captive's pajamas.

"I saw you entering the restaurant several weeks ago. I tried to attract your attention. I saw you near your home, so I followed you. Welcome back into my life," he stroked Charles' face. "I've missed you so much," Benjamin kissed the pale cheek of his true love as he stroked his shoulder.

"Please, don't," Charles replied his voice sounded hoarse and dry. "Why are you doing this?" Charles whispered.

"I was alone, so alone. I missed you terribly. After you I could find no special friend," Ben stated softly as he fondled Charles' thigh. "God, you always had the tightest looking ass."

He waited for Charles to move, fight, respond in some way, but he was frozen, immobilized with fear.

"We'll be safe together. They will forget about you and go on with their lives. They'll abandon you in time, and then we will together, forever!" Benjamin whispered into Charles' ear.

He tried to hold Charles tenderly in his arms, but he lay there like death itself.

Charles was aware of the arousal of his abductor. But he lay still, hoping he would awaken from this nightmare.

"Tom! Oh Tom, why was this happening? Where are you what are you doing? You'll never forget me, you promised," Charles moaned.

"I know you're awake. Talk to me. Lets enjoy our quiet time together."

"Please do not talk to me anymore. Just take me home, and we will forget that this ugly thing ever happened," Charles pled.

"Ugly..what ugly thing? We are destined to be together. Our love is ordained by the stars," the confused abductor stated.

"No! If you love me why are you making my life so miserable. Tom was right all along. You have been responsible for all the weird things happening to us."

"Yep! The missing clothes, and fancy sports car. How'd you like the beautiful young man I sent to your table? Did he tell you about the jet skis I ordered?"

"No! Please...you are wrecking my life."

"You are lucky, I considered trashing your house. Remember, Charles, better not make me angry. Scott made me angry, and in the end he was sorry, but he'll never make me angry again."

Benjamin tried to blot out words he did not wish to hear. Benjamin did not wish to understand Charles' words. He quietly walked into the kitchen to make sandwiches for dinner.

Deep in more pleasant thoughts, Benjamin congratulated himself on his performance with the police. He had done it. He had shown his superiority by beating them at their own game. He was better at head games than most people. Benjamin knew how stupid the authorities would feel if and when they found out how brilliantly he had outsmarted them.

In Benjamin Tracer's confused mind he thought he'd have a pleasant evening with Charles. He hoped that he would spend the remainder of the night making love to Charles. He must convince Charles that they belonged together. They would share a supper of sandwiches and soup, and speak of happier times, in New York. Reminisce about the good old days.

Benjamin watched Charles as he sipped his clam chowder soup. He seemed so preoccupied, probably dreaming of Tom. The tension could be cut by a knife.

"Charles, is the soup to your liking?" Benjamin said, continuing to watch his captive. "Try one of the ham sandwiches. They're surprisingly moist for a canned product. I purchased a bottle of vodka. Care to join me?"

"Not now. The soup is fine, Benjamin. I'm not hungry. I'm stiff and sore from lying around on this bed all day and night."

Benjamin filled a small juice glass with vodka and drank it quickly. He refilled the glass and took another drink. "Please eat. You must keep up your strength. When we have eaten, I promise we will take a stroll, work out all of those kinks," Benjamin smiled.

He thought, nervously, "Life is a play, but there is something wrong with this scene. I am not feeling what I thought I'd feel. I'll take Charles for a walk. He always enjoyed the late night air.

"Charles, how can you just sit there as though I'm a stranger? You act as though we share no history. We shared a wonderful experience, and in time your true feelings will return," Benjamin smiled triumphantly.

Charles slammed his spoon into the bowl, bringing Benjamin back to the reality.

"I don't give a damn about your fool sandwich. Benjamin, take these ridiculous restraints off my wrists and let me go home," Charles demanded.

"You are home, my dear. We're together, again," Benjamin exclaimed as he pointedly ignored Charles' outburst. The forlorn Benjamin drained his glass of Vodka and poured another.

"We're not together, damn it. We'll never be." Charles never had spoken to Benjamin in such a rude and forceful manner.

"But I care for you. I've waited so long to be with you," Benjamin replied.

"Please, put down that glass and try to concentrate," Charles demanded.

"You want to talk. That's wonderful," Benjamin smiled, red eyed, as he attempted to concentrate through his alcoholic haze.

The harshness of his face melted as Charles was confronted by his jubilant abductor.

"Bennie, please think about what you are doing. We were friends once, but, damn it man, you tried to rape me. You are confused. You drink too much. Remember the love we once shared. Let me help you." Charles' demeanor changed. He spoke to this young man, tenderly, gently in tones used by a benevolent father.

Benjamin finished the last sip of his drink, placing the glass on the table. "Alright, I'm listening."

"You loved me once, didn't we Charlie?"

The brevity of sleep and small intake of food combined with the alcohol and worry to cause Benjamin to weave back and forth. His smile was filled with lust. He was drunk with desire as well as alcohol. Desire for his lost love overcame any rational thought he might have had.

"Benjamin, please. I'm begging you, please concentrate. If you will just take me home. Nobody knows what has happened, and it will remain our little secret. We can always say we went fishing."

"Take you back. What's the hurry. You just got here," Benjamin replied.

"Bennie, this whole thing is all wrong. Can't you understand, you will get into trouble?" Charles pled.

"Trouble. No, there'll be no trouble. We'll stay here. I'll cook for you. When you are rested, we'll talk. Then you'll realize... His voice tapered off as
the drink was taking its toll.

"We'll go outside tomorrow. Catch a few rays. You look pale. You just need a little rest." Benjamin led Charles back to his prison bed and reapplied the restraints.

In Benjamin's confused alcoholic state it never occurred to him that the stress he read on Charles' face and the disheveled appearance was his doing. He stood watching as Charles finally drifted off to sleep.

Benjamin re-entered the Holiday Inn before dawn. He made it to the elevators unnoticed. Sleep eluded Benjamin as he tossed back and forth consumed in his own nightmare. He was tortured by the vision of Charles handcuffed to the bed, but his only hope for salvation was the cleansing redemption that Charles could receive.

On late night news Benjamin Tracer listened to a boring interview with Police Commissioner Dennis Crowley. "Commissioner Crowley, can you tell our viewers how the investigation of Mr. Charles Allgood's abduction is progressing? Do you have any suspects? The gay community is up in arms about the apparent lack of interest from you, and the police force," Marsha Mayfield of a local TV station asked.

"Why little lady, I do not know where you get your information," the commissioner paused to catch his breath before he continued, "it is my intention and of every man in our department to find this young man and return him to...uh his loved ones."

"It has been charged that because Charles Allgood is gay your department is dragging its feet. Sir, how do you wish to respond?"

Marsha pointed her microphone in the commissioner's face.

"These reports are absurd. We no longer live in the dark ages where people are frightened of those that are different."

"You are saying that gay people are no longer persecuted in our fair city."

"If you can prove to me that one man in the police department deals unjustly with gays, I will deal with him personally."

"Only men, Commissioner Crowley. What about the police women?"

Commissioner Crowley faced the camera crimson faced and silent.

Marsha Mayfield turned to face the camera, "The commissioner appears to have no response. Only time will tell. This is Marsha Mayfield broadcasting outside the Charleston Police Department. Back to you in the studio." Commissioner Crowley walked away. He hated interviews with reporters for they constantly misquoted him. The news conference was the mayor's idea to bolster the community's confidence in the Charleston law enforcement. Besides, if Crowley wanted to run for mayor, he had to publicly take a stand in support of gays.

Dennis Crowley was an a politician in every sense of the word. Voters were fickle, of this he was sure, but he knew the rules. Crowley worked hard taking action on popular causes such as clean air and clear water. He never supported controversial issues such as blacks, gays, or women's libbers for they had their own lobbyists. His main goal was for the voter to remember his name when they go to the poll.

Alone in the motel, Benjamin's thoughts turned to Charles. Was he alright hogtied in that cold lonely house? The long hours without sleep, and the alcohol had muddled his thinking.

The time had come when he and Charles would have to discuss their future. It had become obvious that all Charles wanted was to put as many miles between Benjamin and himself as possible. Benjamin dropped off to sleep exhausted from the days of extreme tension.

Early the next morning, Benjamin was seated at his regular seat in the Holiday Inn Restaurant. He enjoyed their complimentary breakfast. There usually was an excellent buffet, not some foreigners idea of a breakfast tea and toast.

He munched on eggs and bacon, with sweet rolls, juice, and coffee. His server, Shirley remembered that her customer always requested catsup on his eggs so she had discretely placed a bottle on his table.

"Would you care for another cup of coffee?" Shirley asked.

"No thanks, I'll just nurse this one along. Shirley, I want you to know that your smile brightens an otherwise dreary day." Benjamin rose, feeling benevolent he left the startled server a big tip. "Oh hell," Benjamin Tracer thought, "she could probably use the money."

Benjamin smirked to himself. He wondered if Shirley noticed that when he departed at least two or three undercover officers left the restaurant. He would have to shake them before rejoining Charles.

Benjamin had to do some shopping for their supplies were running low. He was tired of serving sandwiches and soup. He thought a quiet evening at home was just what the two needed. Cocktails were an excellent way to begin the perfect meal. Benjamin dreamed of grilling a couple of two inch thick steaks, the aroma drifting carelessly on the evening breeze. Then he would serve baked potatoes, steamed broccoli, and rolls. Unfortunately, the steaks would have to wait for tonight, his small Coleman stove would heat up a can of beef stew.

Benjamin was amused as unmarked police cars followed at a discrete distance while on his right he was positive that the jeep was party of the convoy. He enjoyed all of the attention. The police must have decided that he was a man to be reckoned with for moments later a motorcyclist joined the surveillance team.

Benjamin made it through a crowded intersection just as it was blocked by a stalled truck. A series of quick left and right turns assured he that he had given his shadows the slip. While they cooled their heels ensnared in late evening traffic, Benjamin made a dash for the Hwy. 17 bridge.

He drove as quickly as the traffic would allow for at the end of the journey was his love.

Benjamin was alone in a violent world not of his choosing. He was secure enough to go his own way, but these days everything he touched had gone sour. As he crossed over the bridge, the water was dark and nearly invisible below. Between the clouds overhead and the mist on the water almost all reflected light was swallowed up.

"Charles has changed," Ben frowned. "Once we could read each others' minds. Soon we will be together in perfect sync."

"I'm home, Bonnie Charlie. Thought I'd see to your comfort before shopping for our dinner," Benjamin called out, as if he were returning home from an ordinary day at the office.

Charles did not respond. Exhausted from another day in shackles, he was in no mood to chat with his captor.   "Charles, don't be that way. I'll fix you a nice pan of cool water to soothe your fevered brow."

"I have no fever, but I'm sweaty, dirty, and would give almost anything for a toothbrush and toothpaste. Do you have any notion how scratchy ones teeth get after several days of zero personal hygiene," Charles responded.

"How would you like a thick steak for dinner? Doesn't it sound fantastic?"

"For now, Benjamin, may I have a glass of water? I ran out several hours ago, and the humidity is atrocious this evening," Charles stated as Benjamin walked about the small house seemingly ignoring Charles' request for water.

"Please. It's been so long," Charles complained.

Benjamin finally returned to the bed with a glass of fresh water. He asked, "Are you alright? What do you wish for dinner? Would you enjoy a hamburger, fries and coke? I'm tired of sandwiches and soup. What do you say?"

"I would love to use the bathroom facilities, as primitive as they are. You don't suppose you could handcuff me to a bath tub for a soak in warm water. Several days with you, my pioneer friend, and I have developed a great appreciation for simple creature comforts, such as bathing and wearing clean clothes."

"Don't be difficult, Charles. I have had a difficult day," Benjamin pouted. "To tell the truth, your dear police buddy, Lt. Bill Painter has been questioning me. Grilling me, I believe is the term."

"So, Bill Painter has been assigned to my case?" Charles smiled. He knew Benjamin had bit off more than he could chew for Bill was the best police officer east of the Mississippi.

"You needn't look so happy. He questioned me about your whereabouts as tenaciously as a terrier attacking my leg. He's smarter than those other cops."

"Yes, Bennie. He is one of the finest. You'd better watch your step, or Bill will put you behind bars and throw the key away."

"You'd love that wouldn't you?" "Bennie, I don't want you to go to jail, but I do want to go home to my real life."

"Your real life is with Tom," Benjamin replied, his face drawn with pain.

"This was a mistake. We can never go back to what we once shared. Our lives have gone in separate directions."

Finding no pleasure in the direction of Charles' conversation, Benjamin moved slowly across the kitchen. A premonition of danger was sending nervous tension radiating through his entire body. His eyes narrowed as they attempted to penetrate the darkness.

"What's wrong?" Charles asked as he sensed Benjamin's irritation.

"I don't know. Something is not quite right."

"What do you see?" Charles whispered.

"I thought I saw somebody out back."

Benjamin glanced nervously about the wooded area.

"Nothing." Benjamin began to open the last of the saltines. "These peanut butter crackers will have to hold us until I go shopping. This weather stinks. On again, off again rain."

"I know, the sound on the roof has driven me half crazy. Makes you want to go, even when there's no need."

"Yes, inspiration!" Benjamin laughed. "Just like a baby on the potty. Makes you nuts, huh."

"Yes, but you have had modern facilities available when you need them. All I've had was a once a day trip to the toilet," Charles complained.

Again ignoring Charles' complaint Benjamin asked, "Do you

remember our time in New York?"

"Of course. What about it?" Charles replied.

"Remember the fourth floor apartment. That long climb could cause a heart attack if you were out of shape," Benjamin smiled as he fantasied about the experiences that he and Charles had shared.

"That was a long time ago," Charles answered.

"I enjoyed shopping for our meals. We were always broke, but we got by. Remember the night I blew our entire bankroll on a special dinner."

"I remember Bennie, you've never been practical," Charles laughed, the past seemed to fade away like a thin veil floating to the floor. I could have murdered you wasting all that money just for one meal."

"You certainly savored those two inch thick steaks, baking potatoes, broccoli. Remember how you always raved over my steamed broccoli."

"Yes steamed, never soggy, just right. Then you poured a special cheese sauce across the top. You never did tell me your secret ingredients."

Benjamin laughed as the tension in his face washed away. Charles was suddenly afraid of the direction this conversation could lead for he read the look of hope across Benjamin's face. He must not give his captor hope of reconciliation.

"That was a long time ago, Benjamin. I've moved on with my life. It's time you moved on with yours," Charles said firmly.

"You forgot about the lobster," Benjamin pressed on. "You loved the lobster, once you recovered from the sight of that large grocery bill." Benjamin walked closer to Charles. He reached out to stroke Charles' hair. "You haven't forgotten our life together, no matter how you fight the memories. They were good times."

"Yes, there were good times, but I also remember the bad times," Charles reminded Benjamin.

"Now don't be mean," Benjamin pouted, "this is a night for remembering happier times."

"Benjamin, you have selective memory," Charles challenged.

"I don't know what you mean?" Benjamin replied innocently.

"You lost job after job. Do you remember?"

"Not really."

"Well, I do. Your temper, your mistrust. Do you remember that poor guy in the sushi bar? He was just talking to me while I waited for you to get off from work. Remember?" Charles demanded.

"Yes, but he looked like a mugger," Benjamin demanded.

"A mugger? A mugger, you say. Bullshit! In the middle of a restaurant? Get serious. He had simply asked me the time. The man was lonesome. You attacked him! Broke his nose, for nothing."

"I did not like the look of him. He was trying to pick you up. I could see it in his eyes. He could have been dangerous," Benjamin defended his actions.

"Dangerous! Pick me up! He was showing me pictures of his grandchildren. He simply wanted someone to talk to. He missed his family."

"Why are you being so judgmental? Everyone can make a mistake. We're all human. Remember the saying, 'To Err is Human, To forgive Divine'," Benjamin cried.

"To err. Right. If that one encounter was all there was, but you did everything to isolate me. You followed me to work, and when I went to the laundry. You must have thought I was sneaking out to meet our laundryman."

"I loved you. I wanted to protect you. You were everything to me."

"You enjoy quotes. I've got one for you. Love is like a delicate bird held in your hand. Hold it gently, give it room to breathe, and it will survive. Hold it too tightly and it chokes and dies. Your obsession, your lack of trust choked any feeling I had for you. I'm sorry, Bennie," Charles said sadly.

Benjamin hung his head, "I love you more than life, Charles," he whispered.

While the two former friends continued their strange conversation inside the house, the conversation in another part of town was different.

Chapter 16

"I can't believe it. That damned SOB has stolen from me," Mason screamed as he slammed the kitchen door.

"Mason, what on earth has you so upset?" Charlotte asked.

"I thought we were friends and he stole my frigging tool box. We've been playing pool for the last few weeks," Mason whined.

"Please calm down. Have you searched the garage? Maybe you should check again, I'll be glad to help? Come on, dear," Charlotte took his arm and guided him to the garage.

They searched every nook and cranny, but the tool box and Mason's best lantern were gone. Someone had been in the garage recently. Mason was famous for keeping his treasures, his grandfather's and his father's keepsakes but now they were thrown everywhere.

"I'm calling the cops. That bastard won't get away with this act of betrayal," Mason shrieked.

Mason Burns pushed Charlotte aside as he charged out of the garage. Charlotte hurried behind him.

"Let me talk to anybody in charge of theft," the crimson faced Mason found it difficult to catch his breath as he yelled at the person on the other end of the phone.

Lt. Bill Painter recognized the address of the caller. He picked up his microphone informing the dispatcher that he would answer the call. If there was a problem in the Burns he thought he'd better take the call.

"A car has been dispatched," the operator stated.

Mason replaced the receiver in its cradle.

"They're sending somebody. I hope they know their job," Mason dropped into a kitchen chair to await for the police.

In a matter of minutes a car pulled up at the Burns' house.

Charlotte was surprised to see Bill Painter walking through the door.

"Is there a problem, Mrs. Burns?" Bill Painter asked Charlotte.

"Mason is... Lieutenant., I'm sorry. This is my husband Mason Burns. Mason, this is Lt. Bill Painter. He's the one working on

Charles Allgood's kidnaping."

"He's probably just another screaming fruitcake who's run off with another screamer. He'll show up after he's gotten his fill of what ever those weirdos do," Mason replied with disgust.

"You reported a theft, sir," Painter stated as he tried to ignore Mason's commentary.

"He stole my tool box and lantern."

"Mr. Burns, who stole your tool box."

"He did. We sat in the bar, played pool and shared a couple of beers and talked about our past. He listened to me and appeared to be interested."

"Who stole from you?" Lt. Painter pressed. "Who did? Please try to think. What's his name? The name of your pool buddy."

Somewhere in the deepest recesses of his mind, Mason was jerked back to reality.

"Charlotte I told him about everything, even how the government stole from my family," Mason moaned. "I told him about our land. The crooks did not steal everything we owned. I told him about our small house," Mason muttered incoherently.

"Please think, Mr. Burns. What's the man's name?" Lt. Painter pushed.

"Bennie, his name is Bennie. Bennie betrayed our friendship. He stole from me," Mason cried.

Charlotte had never seen Mason so angry, so out of control.

"Mr. Burns, please start at the beginning," Lt. Painter requested.

"I met a man in the pub on Market Street. We talked. I thought we were friends. I told him personal things, about our lives, our family.
He supposedly told me about his. We did some work together in the carriage house." "What were you doing in the carriage house? You never let anybody inside, not even me?" Charlotte asked.

"Well I invited him to the carriage house and look what happened."

"Exactly what happened?"

"I let him inside and he took my rope, my grandmother's quilt, tool box and a lantern. I just can't believe that Benjamin would do that to me."

"What did you say?" Charlotte asked.

"I told you. If you would listen to me, Charlotte, it wouldn't be necessary for me to repeat myself."

"I'm sorry, Mason. Did you say his name is Bennie? Bennie, who?"

"Benjamin Tracer from New York City, or so he said. He loved quoting Shakespeare. "The evil that men do live after them..." He liked that sort of stuff. Thought he was sad and lonely for he talked about his lost love."

Recognition spread across her face, as she looked up at the policeman.

"Mason, his lost love, did you say?" Charlotte quizzed.

"Yes, he followed some woman from New York. He never mentioned her name, but he confided in me that his life was empty without her."

"I wonder what happened between Bennie and his friend?" Charlotte continued.

"I don't know. He said they had great sex, that she was his soul mate. Then one day she disappeared. He's been searching for her ever since."

"What was the name of his love?" Charlotte pressed.

"I don't know. I didn't ask. Why are you concerned about her name. I've been robbed," Mason complained."

Could Mason somehow have met Benjamin Tracer? Have Charlotte and Bill Painter accidentally found his hiding place?

"Do you think?" Was all Charlotte could manage to say.

"I don't know, but we are going to find out now," Bill Painter's face shone with hope.

"Could he have been under our nose all this time?" Charlotte whispered.

"Where's this house, Charlotte?"

"North of Charleston, past Patriot's Point."

"Charlotte give me the directions to the Burns property. I pray that our captive and friend is inside." Bill Painter proudly stated.

Charlotte gave him detailed directions to the little house.

"Thank you, my dear," called exhausted officer as he charged out the door.

"Don't tell Tom until we know for sure. I'll call the second I know something."

"Where the hell is he going? He didn't even take a report," Mason complained.

"Be patient, I think you may get your tools back tonight," Charlotte stated.

Bill Painter tore out of the drive, as he radioed his men to meet him at the Hwy. 17 bridge.

"What's up Bill?" His partner asked.

"I think we're about to solve a kidnaping, and return a friend to his home and loved ones," Bill smiled as a tear slid down his face.

His men were prompt, and they assembled to receive the orders being issued by their superior officer. The gentle breeze crackled with electricity. Excitement filled the night air. Men that laid their lives on the line daily checked their equipment, preparing to rescue Charles Allgood.

It took the police about thirty minutes to reach the Burns property. Bill Painter slowed his car as he took the turnoff and stopped only a short distance from the highway.

"We'll stop here. I'm afraid the sound of our motor would tip our hand. Get the men in place?"

"Yes sir," his partner replied.

"Tell everybody to lay low. Don't do anything until I give the signal. We going to do this one by the book. Anything goes wrong it could cost that poor SOB his life. Got it."

"Got it, Lt. Painter." "Lieutenant, I'm going to get a closer look at the occupants of that house."

"Lieutenant Graham waited as Bill Painter did a recon. He listened to the snapping of every twig, and he anxiously awaited Lt. Painter's return.

"Lt. Painter," Graham whispered as he heard the snap of a branch.

"Hold your fire," Painter crawled into view face to face with another police revolver.

"Can you see or hear anything?"

"Yes. I heard two male voices from inside. Couldn't get too close. Didn't want to risk being spotted."

"How do you want to handle it?"

"We'll take it slow. Keep the perimeter secure, and if you see an opportunity, move in to rescue the hostage."

"Painter, mind my asking how you found out about this place?"

"A little bird told me," Painter laughed. "Got a tip from an unexpected place."

"Holy shit! What's going on?" Graham growled. "This ain't no damned parade ground.

"Shit! It's Police Commissioner Crowley. That mother's been monitoring the calls. He always was the type to let others do the real work, and step in for the kill."

"Jesus Christ, Painter! What's that asshole think he's doing?"

"Hostage situations are dicey enough without a bunch of desk jockeys butting in. I'm surprised that he didn't bring along a big brass band."

"He did," Graham pointed to the road.

"Holy Mother of God. That jerk's allowing that television truck inside the perimeter.

"We're taking over now, lieutenant. Return to your men. When you're needed, we'll let you know," Commissioner Dennis Crowley was standing there bold as brass dressed in military garb, and he was wearing shiny military boots. "Good thing there's a cloud cover, Painter. Those boots are better than a neon sign."

"Yeah, I'm just worried about that poor schmuck inside," Graham quipped. With a half-ass commissioner taking charge, anything can happen," Painter stated angrily.

"We're got to get in that cabin. There is no telling what that crazy bastard has done to Charles Allgood."

"Yes! With our beloved commissioner in the drivers seat, we may find Charles chopped into small pieces," Bill Painter replied as the color drained from his face.

"Sorry! I keep forgetting you two are friends. This has got to be a hard one," Graham replied.

"Yes, it is. Wanda and I have been friends with Charles and Tom Branson since my brother passed away. Those three men were close, and I sort of inherited them."

"It's a strange relationship, your not being gay, and all."

"Like everybody else I had preconceived notions about the homosexual community, but those two men have shared a longer relationship than most heterosexual marriages. I'm afraid of what will become of Tom if Charles does not come out of this mess alive."

"Two men, that way. It's not my style," Graham replied.

"Mine either, but they don't force themselves on others. And my friend," slapping Graham on the shoulder, "I'd trust them with my life."

"No shit?"

"No shit!"

"A couple of years ago I was driving through the outskirts of the town when I was broadsided by a drunk driver." Bill began the story.

"I must have been lying in my car for about an hour, my life's blood pouring from my body. Somewhere behind me I heard this little voice whispering, you've got to fight. Tom's gone for help. It seemed like an eternity, but it was probably a few minutes, Tom brought the paramedics. Charles had stayed with me because Tom thought he was better at first aid."   "I never heard that story."

"You understand why I owe those men my life."

The group assembled outside awaiting the final orders. The officers waited impatiently. Their fingers were itchy to pull down on the perpetrator inside. It would be a sure way of rescuing the captive.

"Painter," Commissioner Crowley called.

"Yes sir."

"Who's our best marksman?"

"Higgins. Officer Higgins," Painter replied.

"Okay! Get me Higgins."

The young officer stepped into view.

"You called for me, Sir?" Officer Higgins asked.

"Son! I understand you're our best sharpshooter."

"Yes, Sir!" Higgins replied enthusiastically.

"Find your best vantage. If that perp inside causes trouble, take him down," Crowley bellowed his command.

"Higgins."

"Yes, Lieutenant."

"When you start firing, make sure you're aiming at the perp, and not the hostage," Painter interjected.

"You bet sir," Higgins replied softly as he left to take his position.

"Graham, get back to the van. You'll find two men there. Tell them to bring the camcorders. I need to document this hostage situation."

"Yes sir," Graham shook his head as he moved away from this travesty.

Commissioner Crowley rubbed his chin while deep in thought. "Damn it. This started off with our department having to placate a bunch of fairies. I could parlay this into heavy political advantage if I play it right. The voters are hot for strong law-and-order candidates. If I'm a little rough on this perpetrator who's gonna care if a damned fairy gets hurt. No matter what happens I'll look good on camera. Benjamin nervously looked out the window. There it was again. That sound. The sound of snapping twigs. The police. Their refuge had been discovered.

Inside the cabin there was only the flicker from a single light.

"Bennie, what's happening?" Charles whispered. He was terrified at the stricken look on Benjamin's face.

"Police, they're everywhere," Benjamin replied, his voice strangely cold.

"You must give up. There is no place to run," Charles cried. "No one is hurt, so far."

Ignoring Charles' plea, Benjamin leaned against the wall attempting to regain his composure. He concentrated on regulating his breathing. "Breathe slowly. There is no time for emotional paralysis." Sweat poured down his face and neck collecting on his shirt and soaking it through and through.

Benjamin moved about the house like a wounded animal.

Benjamin Tracer began striking hysterically at the pictures on the walls the source of his torment, Charles Allgood, his beloved.

His fingers, their knuckles white from the tension, held a knife in a death grip. He worked the knife up and down, side to side. First scratching the sides, and then gouging holes in the pictures that had been placed on the wall so lovingly a short time ago. He continued dragging the knife, causing multiple cuts on the portraits.

Suddenly as though awakened from a nightmare, he ran from the vandalism he had caused. He fell exhausted on the bed beside his prisoner, and he began weeping inconsolably.

He cried because he was feeling more dejected, more unloved and uncared for than he had ever felt before in his entire life. His life, his entire reason for being had been a total lie. How could he face life? The absurdity of the situation was totally beyond his ability to deal with.   His stomach felt as if a washing machine's agitator were churning the contents into a froth. His throat burned with the acid from the contents of his stomach bubbling up, and threatening to cause regurgitation on a massive scale.

Benjamin's head was spinning, and he was experiencing the sensation that his mind was disconnected from his body. He began to pace back and forth. His exhausted body felt as though he was walking through soft beach sand with invisible fingers dragging his feet down with every step.

Benjamin retreated into a world of his own design.

"They will separate us. This place is not well designed. No emergency way out. The ancient castles of Europe had priests holes and hidden tunnels extended far outside the walls, in case the place is attacked," Benjamin continued muttering incoherently to himself.

"Why did those fools not build a tunnel in this place?" Benjamin continued mournfully as the horrified Charles watched while helplessly handcuffed to the dingy bed.

A dozen men surrounded the cabin with guns drawn. Police cars, unmarked cars, and jeeps barricaded the dirt road. There was an emergency medical team standing by. A second news truck was attempting to get through the blockade. It's occupants were yelling something about their constitutional rights being violated.

The confusion at the police road block was worse than expected. There were frightening rumors echoing through the community causing police brass to come out of the wood work. Within the first hectic moments of arrival you would have thought they had discovered a psycho mass murderer rather a love stricken young man.

This was the cabin in which Charles Allgood was being held. There was a feeling that the very air was charged with electricity, and the sounds of the massive police manpower buildup reverberated throughout the wooded area. The kidnapper of Charles Allgood was about to receive a sample of swift justice.

Benjamin's plan had failed; the police had found them. It must have been that Lt. Painter. He was the only one smart enough to understand his relationship with Charles. He prayed that Painter was in a leadership position among the throng of men assembling for the assault upon his refuge or his life would surely be forfeit before this night was over. Painter was a man, the rest were incompetents.

Benjamin was defeated for everything he touched had gone sour. He remembered his exhilaration the day he arrived in Charleston. The euphoria had long passed, for Benjamin Tracer was no longer the rescuer, he was a hunted criminal.

"Hit the lights," the commissioner shouted. The flood lights came on along with those from six police cars.

"This is the police. Benjamin Tracer, we know you are in there. Release your hostage, and come out with your hands held high."

There was total silence from the cabin, only the occasional sound from the soft drizzle landing pat, pat, pat on the tin roof. There was the sudden crack of twigs as the men moved cautiously through the wooded brush. Police officers crouched behind every car, shrub, tree, anything that afforded protection from the violence that the evening might bring.

Benjamin crawled across the kitchen floor to Charles side. Tonight was the time of deliverance. Benjamin anxiously considered his prospects for survival. He was, after all, a murderer, and now a kidnapper.

"We'd both better lay low," Charles whispered.

"Why did it have to be this way? Our time together is nearly over," Benjamin replied.

"Those trigger happy police might shoot us before the night is over. That bunch of red necks do not care what happens to either or us, they just want some big headlines. Well I'll just give them some." "No Benjamin, NO!" Charles screamed as Benjamin snatched up an oil lamp from the table and slammed it against the wall. The flame from the wick of the broken oil lamp sputtered and then produced a whooshing sound as it ignited the oil from the broken reservoir which now saturated the torn curtain. Moments later the room was engulfed in flames.

Charles could not longer see Benjamin through the dense grey smoke which quickly filled the room, but he felt and heard the snapping sound as the other end of the handcuff dropped to the floor.

"Goodbye, beloved. Stay close to the ground, and go outside. Your rescuers have arrived," Benjamin whispered from somewhere within the smoke, "I've always loved you."

With his heart in his throat, Charles Allgood stumbled onto the front porch in hasty compliance. His eyes were stinging, and his was head pounding, but he made his escape. He could hear the distant cries of "Fire! Fire!" He felt the assistance of strong hands drawing him to safety.

Charles blinked, frozen in terror at the number of men surrounding the cabin. He turned, staring at the blazing building in search of Benjamin.

"Bennie! Where are you?" There was only the sound of crackling flames consuming the cabin.

"Charles! Can you hear me? It's Bill, Bill Painter."

Charles staggered unassisted into the arms of Police Lt. Bill Painter.

"Bill, is it really you?" Charles laughed as he suffered the unexpected embrace of his worried friend.

"Yes, it's me. Are you alright? You look like shit."

"Thanks, I'd look better if I had a bath. Benjamin's resort had few of the amenities. Bennie, did you find him?" Charles pleasure suddenly turned to sadness.

"Sorry old man. He didn't get out."

"He's gone. Bennie was a tortured soul. Maybe he'll finally find the rest in death he couldn't find in life," Charles whispered with a heavy-heart. "It's an awful way to go, Charles, but there was no way you could help him. Benjamin was beyond help, but my friend, lets get you to the hospital. Let's not think of death; let's think of those back home waiting."

"How's Tom? I don't need a hospital, I want to go home."

"He'll be better once he sees you. We'll call him and have him meet us at the hospital," Bill placed his coat about Charles' shoulders.

"Bill, what about Benjamin?" Charles asked as he look back to the place of his former imprisonment.

"We won't know until the fire cools and we can sift the ashes. Come on, let's get out of here."

"Okay Bill, but I'm going home," Charles spoke in ragged terms as he looked up unseeing into Bill's misty-eyes.

"Okay, pal. It's home for you," Bill Painter, hardened detective replied as the two men walked to the awaiting police car amid the cacophony of the fire and crime scene.

The house blazed out of control in the murky dimness. The hellish flames, crackling through the night's air, forced the exhausted rescuers to step back to a safe vantage. The fire's intensity caused heavy perspiration to bead up on the faces of the men, and sweat dampened their clothes.

Tom Branson sat looking out of the kitchen window in silent meditation. What horror was Charles experiencing? Was his abductor torturing him, abusing him? Was he afraid?

Shelley burst into the house and threw herself into her startled brother's arms.

"It's over, Tom!" she cried as tears cascaded down her face.

"It's over?" Tom asked.

"Yes! It was on the television."

"What?" was all he could ask.

"The local television station sent a truck with the police and they filmed Charles' rescue," Shelley squealed.

"Was he hurt?" Tom whispered.

"I don't know," a breathless Shelley replied.   T w e n t y minutes later, an exhausted Charles walked into the house followed by an equally weary Bill Painter. Charles and Tom embarrassed and without conversation walked hand in hand up the stairs, while on the other side of the lake the water was lapping on the beach, a friendly welcome, as the exhausted stranger crawled ashore. He glanced over his shoulder watching as the column of smoke changed from black to white.

Half an hour later, Tom came down the stairs.

"He looks much better after a bath and shave. I convinced him rest was the best medicine."

Shelley Branson and Bill Painter were joined by Charlotte Burns for coffee and conversation in the comfortable kitchen.

"How is Charles? Was he hurt? Should be contact a physician?" Charlotte asked.

"He'll be fine, thanks to you," Bill replied as he cooled his hot cup of coffee.

"What do you mean, thanks to Charlotte?" Tom asked.

"Charlotte found Charles for us. That's all," Bill stated as he smiled brightly.

"How did you find Charles for us, Charlotte?" Tom replied.

"I had gone home to await word of Charles when Mason came in," Charlotte began her story of Mason and his missing tool box. Charlotte repeated to her captive audience the saga of Mason and his friend Bennie from New York City.

Life seemed to get back to normal with the rescue of Charles. Charlotte Burns and the Branson family had been reunited with Charles Allgood. There were smiles, tears and lots of squealing.

It had been only a few days since Charles' return when he entered the kitchen saying,"Life is getting back to normal. Let's celebrate with a party."

"A party? What kind of party? You are still weak,"Tom asked.

"I may be but let's have a day to remember," Charles declared.

"Let's have a picnic. We can visit the pretty boats," squealed

Becky as she and Charlotte entered the kitchen door.

"Darling, only you could call the 'Yorktown Aircraft Carrier' a pretty boat," laughed Charles.

He was haggard from his experience, but with the love of his companions, he would regain his strength in no time.

"If we picnic, it must be in the back yard," Tom declared.

The group dashed about the kitchen preparing for a back yard picnic. The house too long quiet now rang again with laughter.

Charlotte halted her picnic preparations. "I have an excellent idea. Becky has wanted to visit my hometown, Baltimore so why don't we pretend we're there and have our very own clam bake."

"Oh mommie, a clam bake like when you were a little girl," Becky squealed.

"Yes darling, we'll have everything. Clams, corn, potatoes," Charlotte laughed. "We're going outside for a backyard clam bake."

"A clam bake? Okay, sounds enchanting. I'm game, but what do I wear?" Charles said laughing.

"Dress casual," Charlotte giggled, feeling like a kid again. "Things that you don't mind getting wet."

"If we're not going to a beach, how are we going to catch little fishes?" Tom asked.

"Oh Uncle Tom, don't be silly," Becky stated as she giggled, "mommie might let us jump in the sprinkler and pretend to catch fishes."

"I'll bring my appetite," Charles said as he joined in the merriment.

"Charlotte, I've not heard you sound so happy in months. It's great to hear you laugh," Shelley stated.

"No really happy more at peace. This day is Charles'," Charlotte suddenly needed reassurance. She caressed Shelley's arm as she used her best smile.

"I know, and we will make it a day he'll never forget," Shelley agreed. "Granny Burns, we're having a clam bake," Becky called out to her grandmother as she noticed her in the backyard. "We're celebrating Uncle Charles' rescue from that silly ole man."

Everyone stopped what they were doing and stared at the child. They had taken great pains to shield Becky from Charles' kidnaping, but she appeared to know more than they suspected.

"What do you know of the silly man, Becky?" Charlotte asked.

"I watched it on television," replied the proud Becky.

"Why didn't you tell us?" Charlotte continued.

"I was too busy praying for a super hero to come and rescue him."

"Thank you darling," Charles hugged the small girl. "All of our prayers were answered. God sent us a super hero and his name is Bill."

"Ma," called Charlotte, "We'd love it if you joined us."

"I'll be glad to attend. I've never been to a backyard clam bake. What shall I bring?"

"Bring your appetite, Granny. That's what Uncle Charles is bringing," Becky giggled.

"Shelley, lets make this party the best. Nobody will spoil this day," Charlotte smiled as she turned to Nola Burns. "Oh by the way Ma, where's Mason, ma?"

"He's visiting Janie Sue. I'm sorry to say," Nola replied,

"If we were going to have a clam bake, what do we do first?" Nola smiled as she began to help."

"If we were back home we'd find the rakes and put them in the car truck. I've told you the story of your Uncle Charlie, my mother's brother, using our rake to mix the cement to widen his walkway?" Charlotte explained to her adoring wide-eyed child.

"I remember. Do you still have the special rake, mommie?" Becky giggled.

"Oh you're such a silly goose," Charlotte kissed Becky on the forehead, "that one fell apart years ago."

"Okay. What else would we do?" Shelley asked.

"There would be big pots to steam the crabs and lobsters," Charlotte continued. "Since we don't have lobsters, we'll serve shrimp."

"Where's the silverware?" Shelley asked.

"We're bringing it. We'll set up the picnic table," Tom called out as he and Charles hauled out the table and chairs.

"You have forgotten, we may not need silver. Fingers were invented before forks and knives," Charles joined the merriment.

"Next we would have put our hammers in the trunk," Charlotte continued.

"What would you do with your hammers, knock me in the head if I try to nibble off your plate?" Shelley said teasing.

"Nope, but I would teach you to build your first bonfire, and to fill the pots with water and so we can steam the clams."

"How would you get lobsters and crabs, mommie?" Becky asked.

"The younger folk would use their boats to set the crab and lobster traps in the bay. They would be very careful, one of our teens fell out of his boat when I was a child, and nearly drowned."

"Clam bakes could get dangerous, if you don't know what you are doing?" Charles asked, seemingly more interested.

"Back home the average child of ten knows all about clam bakes. They put out traps attached with floating milk cartons on them. Years ago we used big corks, but they were harder to see."

"Well you learn something new everyday," Tom laughed.

"Becky, next we put out the knives. If we were actually going to the beach we would put them in the trunk.?"

"Mommie this is fun, but tell Uncle Tom you don't let me play with knives," Becky called out to Charlotte.

"I'm glad it's fun, but must you hollow so loud. I'm not deaf, and I'm standing next to you,"
Charlotte enjoyed the merriment.

"Charlotte, I'll run back home and get some potatoes and corn," Nola said as she took the child's hand. "Come on Becky and help Granny."

"We bring Turkish towels, paper towels, butter," Charlotte continued as she watched her happy child skipping along beside her grandmother.

"We need a table cloth," Shelley said, retreating into the house.

"Better bring plenty bug repellent, and a couple of blankets."

"Blankets!" Charles yelped as he fell over a bag of potatoes contributed by Nola.

"I see I'm too late to help. But maybe not, I have brought the important stuff for the Clam Bake," Bill Painter called out. "A keg of beer, and of course, diet cokes for the ladies."

"Hey Bill. Welcome to our South Carolina clam bake. How did you find out about our party?" Charles shook the newcomers hand.

"Tom invited me and my partner."

"Bill, this is my mother-in-law, Nola Burns. And this little minx is my daughter, Becky."

"Nola, Becky, this is our friend, Bill Painter," Tom introduced his guests.

"Oh I know who you are. You are our super hero that saved Uncle Charles from that bad man," Becky giggled.

"Someone is bound to want coffee, for those that don't care for beer, or cokes," Charlotte replied, turning her nose up at the thought of smelly beer.

The picnickers stood around a large tub, with great enthusiasm as they waited for the water to begin boiling. The only thing missing was the ocean and sand, but no one seemed to care.

"Don't you folks remember a watched pot never boils," Nola said, as she dropped her contribution into the gurgling water.

"Mommie, may I please put in the corn. I'll be careful."

"Certainly Becky. I'll help you," Charlotte took her daughter's hand as they carried corn cobs to be added to the pot.   After their bellies were full from their afternoon feast, Charles went to his room to rest while Shelley and Tom cleaned up. Charlotte lay on a blanket with Becky enjoying the beauty of the afternoon. Nola uncomfortably observed the mother and daughter reveling in each others company.

"Nola, I don't know why, but today for some reason, I miss my mother. That flighty little lady that never grew up. Would she understand what is happening in her daughter's life?" Charlotte asked.

"Probably not, but I think it matters not. You must make the choices right for your life."

Charlotte watched a cloud that appeared to be a feathered winged creature soaring through the clouds racing to meet its destiny. After all that had occurred, could she survive? Did she wish life without Becky? She might not have a choice.

Charlotte's heroine, Jane Eyre survived Edward Rochester's

betrayal, but I am the betrayer. I have betrayed everything I was raised to believe I was told.

"Mother, Are you up there in the clouds? Can you see me?, hear me?"

Charlotte rolled over grabbing Becky, "Always remember that I will love you as long as I live. Remember, my sweet child. Your mommie loves you."

"I'll remember, Mommie. I love you too," Becky said solemnly. Charlotte rolled away so Becky could not see her tears.

"Look Becky. Look at the clouds. They have all kinds of shapes. Wouldn't it be fun if we could climb up on the clouds. We could bring a bat and use the smaller clouds as balls. We could bounce from one cloud to another."

"I see them, Mommie. I see them."

"Becky, those clouds far to our left look like rows of Christmas trees dotting the mountain terrain. Look at that extra fat one straight ahead. It's soft and squishy. It could be our trampoline."

"Mommie, look over there. That one looks like a furry bear."

"Yes darling, I see."

"It's getting late," Nola turned to Shelley. "Becky, Charlotte, I'm going home. Thanks Ms. Branson for a wonderful afternoon."

"Bye Aunt Shelley," Becky yelled as she ran toward her yard.

"Talk to you later, Shelley," Charlotte stated as she watched Becky walking hand in hand with her grandmother.

Charlotte drew a sigh of relief. She took a quick glance one more time into Shelley's strangely compelling eyes. This had been a special day that everyone enjoyed. "Imagine," Charlotte smiled, "a backyard clam bake."

Becky's voice soothed her mother's exhausted mind. Fear vibrated through Charlotte's body. It was late afternoon. Mason would be arriving soon, and the happy atmosphere would evaporate.

Chapter 17

Mason made an interesting discovery one morning while searching for money in Charlotte's dresser. He found his wife's birth control pills, and he went charging over to her place of employment.

"Charlotte, where the hell are you?" Mason jerked open the door to her office and found her kissing, not another man, but a woman, Shelley Branson.

Mason began to roar with laughter. "You silly fool, this is one I never thought of. I warned you years ago about people like this; they rob men of their women. Now look at you, breathless with passion, foundling a woman. Well shit, Charlotte, her tits are bigger than yours. Maybe we can share. Two women. A little here and a little there, " Mason could hardly control his hysterical laughter.

"Mason, must you always be crude. Let's go home where we may talk quietly, calmly," Charlotte ignored Mason's vulgarity, as she adjusted her blouse. "Why have you visited my office? Run out of money so soon?"

"No, I've got everything I need now that I know your nasty little secret. Tell me wife of mine, does she have bigger balls, or do you play the part of the man? You've tried hard enough to wear the pants in our family. Oh man, if this don't beat all," Mason through back his head in laughter, "two women making out in the middle of the day."

"Mason, the only pleasure I find in life is Becky and of course, working at Madame Lorraine's. You've been a vile, filthy beast ever since we married. Is it any wonder I turned to Shelley for kindness?" Charlotte accused.

"Oh you love to work for Madame Lorraine's. I'll just bet you do. Well ladies," Mason continued his laughter ignoring Charlotte's indictment. "What ever you are? If you wish to continue seeing each other, who am I to complain. You have each other, and I have Janie Sue. She likes what I give her. But if you make it worth my while, I keep quiet."

"What do you want, Mason?" Shelley asked. "Charlotte has the right to live her life as she chooses. Now that you know, she and

Becky will leave your house and move in with me and my brother."

"I want to live a pleasant life without interference from the likes of you," Mason replied. "Well you've enticed my wife into a life of depravity."

"Charlotte and I don't care for our sake, but before you publicly condemn her, you better consider the effect our relationship would have on Becky," Shelley challenged.

"You two should have thought of the consequences before you started fooling around. Besides, what if I don't choose to live under your rules?"

"I'll take Becky and leave. We are still young enough to start over again. Your mother never wanted me in the house," Charlotte stated.

"You slut. Go where you please, but when you leave, my daughter stays with me," Mason said, eyes flashing like warning signs across a railroad track.

"I am the child's mother. She belongs with me."

"You will stay with me to keep Becky. No court in the land will give an innocent child to a bull dike and her lover. Get your coat you ungrateful slut, we're leaving, now!" Mason left the office without looking back.

Charlotte was staring helplessly at Shelley. Shelley could see the pain in her tear brimmed eyes. "I can read it in your face. You have made your decision. You will stay with him." Shelley cried, "Don't leave me, Charlotte. I'll give him the money. That's all he wants. He doesn't love you. When are you going to break away from that animal?"

"I mustn't cost you everything that you and the others have worked for. Our love would turn to hate, if you give up everything. I don't know what to do. I just can't think straight," Charlotte whispered.

"It's alright baby. I'll think for the two of us. Trust me, I'll make it work," Shelley pleaded.   "I must go for now, for Becky's sake. There is no other way, for now I'll stay with Mason. I can't take the chance," Charlotte said, all of her resolve drained from her trembling body.

"Leave him, divorce him. Times are changing. No judge in his right mind will give a small girl to a depraved man like Mason. We'll show the courts the kind of man he truly is."

Mason opened the door. "Charlotte, come here. I told you we are leaving."

"Mason, I'm sorry for you. We share a child and no matter what happens, you will always be her father," Charlotte said as she tried to be as civil as possible.

Mason stood in the center of the room watching Charlotte shrug on her coat and follow him to his car.

"You've brought this down our all our heads. Mine, Ma's, and Becky's," Mason said as he looked straight ahead driving to his house.

"What? What did you say, Mason?" Charlotte replied. She had been deep in her own thoughts.

"You have done this to all of us. Nothing this disgusting has ever happened in my family," Mason lowered his voice in an ugly growl.

"I never pretended with you," Charlotte replied as she attempted to touch her husband's arm. "I'm sorry things turned out this way."

"Shut up slut. I always wondered what was wrong. I know what you are and you...and that female lover of yours. You have broken my heart, shattered my life until I have nothing left."

"I'm sorry, Mason," Charlotte whispered. "I never intended to hurt you. We were never meant to be together."

Charlotte's body shook as though she was sitting in the middle of an icy blizzard. She couldn't speak without bursting into tears.

"You don't understand," Charlotte finally said. "I am the way that nature intended me."

"Oh, I understand, alright. You, and weirdos like you, use this nature intended me to be this way. Just a sorry excuse to try to make me look bad. You use excuses to justify you're trashy weirdo ways.?" Mason screamed so loud the sound shook the automobile.

"Do you wish me to leave?"

"I don't know? At first, I wanted to kill you. Shaming me this way. But for now I've got a better idea, you and that whore will support me. Now that idea has great possibilities." Mason laughed, slapping Charlotte's thigh.

"If you feel this way maybe Becky and I should go."

"I don't give a damn where you go, but Becky stays with me. No court, when it learns of your depravity will award a young girl to a weirdo couple."

"You're just angry, hurt, you don't mean what you are saying. I'm her mother, and a girl needs to be with her mother.

"Never as long as there is breath in my body will you get my child, Charlotte. You'd better start getting use to the idea. I can imagine Becky being raised to be a weirdo. Who would take her to pee? You in the ladies room or Shelley with the guys or is it interchangeable?" Mason said disgustedly as he pulled the car into the yard.

Charlotte ran from the car to the safety of her daughter's room.

"Mama, are you playing tag with daddy?" Becky asked.

"Tag, darling?" Charlotte hugged her child tightly.

"You ran so fast," Becky giggled.

"No Becky. I was just in a hurry to see your sweet face," Charlotte said as she smiled into her daughter's hair. "Oh your hair smells so good."

"Granny Nola washed it. She says it's squeaky clean," Becky replied, picking up her brush. "Will you brush my hair for me Mama?" Becky handed her mother the small pink brush Shelley had given her for her fourth birthday.

"Oh you are growing like a weed. You're no longer a baby. You're mother's big girl."   "I'm so big, I'm gonna go to school soon. Right, Mama," Becky replied as she wiggled in Charlotte's lap.

"Yes dear," Charlotte replied. She enjoyed the sight and smell of her young child.

"What's for supper, Mama? I'm starved," Becky jabbered.

"Shall we go down and see what tasty morsels granny has whipped up," Charlotte replied as she placed the brush on the dresser. She followed Becky down the stairs.

Charlotte sat at the dinner table more like a victim going to her own hanging rather than a family dinner. She anxiously searched her mother-in-law's eyes for some sign of knowledge of this afternoon's happenings.

Mason smiled nervously as his eyes shifted first to his mother and then to his wife. He looked like a cat that had swallowed a canary as he quietly hummed between bites of the evening meal.

"Ma, the green beans and chicken are super. The corn bread is the best I can remember," Mason suddenly stated.

"Thank you, dear. The receipt is Charlotte's, not mine."

Charlotte looked up startled from the rare moment of praise.

"Don't look so surprised, Charlotte. I always give the devil its due. What's wrong with you two anyway? You've been real skittish all night."

Charlotte nibbled at her meal unresponsive. "It's just been a long day, Ma," Mason replied as his dark brooding eyes challenged Charlotte in silent battle. "Charlotte and me, we're going to bed early tonight. You can handle the dishes, can't you?"

"Yes!" Nola grumbled. "Becky, you can help granny. Can't you darling? Then you can put me to bed."

"Oh boy, daddy. That's great. Granny, needs my help."

"Oh alright. Becky and I will clean up."

Becky hopped around the room with great anticipation. "I won't drop anything. I promise. I promise," Becky squealed as she grabbed a dish towel.

"Becky, careful! You might break something. Good night you two," Nola laughed at her grandchild. She watched a subdued Charlotte hangdoggedly climb the stairs with Mason close on her heels.

A familiar sound came from the couple's room. The night would be filled again with the loud drunken voice of Mason Burns lecturing his wife on her shortcoming.

Nola didn't understand the turn of the conversation, if she wanted to call the brow beating by her son, conversation. She caught drunken snatches of slurred speech about Charlotte and somebody. What in the world was happening? Nola was aware that Charlotte worked such long hours she had little time to dally around with another man.

Sometimes in the wee hours Charlotte let out a cry and suddenly the bed began the unmistakable sound of bodies swaying in the throes of passion or violence.

Nola laughed. There those two go again. If Mason gave Charlotte a full load, she could present Becky with a baby brother in nine months. Nola rolled over in the bed and fell into a deep sleep.

Inside the room it was a different story for Charlotte lay like a corpse in the middle of the bed.

"You stupid whore. What have I done to deserve this treatment? A woman. Cheating on me with some damn queer woman. Speak to me, you slut," Charlotte's seemingly lifeless body lay in his hands as Mason shook her like some bedraggled rag doll. "Say something, or by God, I'll kill you."

"What do you wish me to say?" Charlotte responded in a hoarse whisper.

"Haven't I fed you? clothed you?"

"Yes."

"Haven't I kept a roof over our heads?"

"Yes."

"I've been generous in bed. Haven't I?" Mason thought he heard his wife expel a laugh.

"Did you laugh? You think this situation is funny?"

"Nothing about my life has been funny, Mason," replied the exhausted Charlotte.

"You have pushed me too far, Charlotte. Tonight you must be punished," Mason slapped Charlotte's face as he tugged violently at her gown. "I always loved these tits, but they are not as big as Shelley's. Wanna call her over and join us," he muttered, nipping her breasts with his tobacco stained teeth.

Charlotte began to moan, not from pleasure, but from the pain he was causing.

Mason consumed with anger jammed his ugly throbbing member into her body. She screamed as he covered her mouth with his. He rammed his tongue into her throat, Charlotte gagged, struggling with all of her might as she looked into Mason's dark twisted face.

Charlotte thought of Becky, and of Shelley as she closed her eyes and sank into oblivion.

She lay motionless beside him. No! Charlotte couldn't be dead. Death would have freed her from life's pain. He would not allow her easy release.

Charlotte moaned as she moved a sharp stabbing pain shot through her rectum. Charlotte ached everywhere.

"Good! you're awake," Mason said. "You were so still I thought for a minute you were dead."

"I'm awake. You haven't killed me yet," Charlotte whispered as a shiver shot through her body.

"Good, I hate fuckin' a corpse. We're doin' it again. I done your ass while you were sleepin' like a baby. Roll over, this time you're gonna be awake," Mason snatched her up by her hair as he forced Charlotte to her knees.

Charlotte's heart hammered with fear. She clenched her teeth so she would not cry out as he mounted her. She felt bile building up in the back of her throat. Oh God! He was ripping her to pieces, and with one last jab he fell away spent.

Moments later the room was filled with the sound of snoring. Charlotte's eyes, heavy with fatigue, closed, and she dreamed of another world. A world of her creation, of Becky, and Shelley living in peaceful happiness. For Charlotte there was no happiness. Nightmares filled her life with Mason. They even managed to invade her dreams.

The noise of the local tom cat on the back fence yowling to his lady love caused Charlotte to wake with a start.

"I better clean up. I feel so dirty," Charlotte muttered.

She stared into the mirrored imagine of someone she did not know. Charlotte saw the face of a girl that so many years ago had been raped by those vermin. Her eyes appeared dead. Dead eyes, dead soul. Her face was scratched and bruised. Mason had even ripped out a chunk of her hair. Charlotte's lip drooped to the side split from a violent blow. Her eye lid was oozing blood. "Do I need stitches? I'd better get Becky to a safe place. If he hits me again, he'll kill me."

Charlotte tiptoed to Becky's room, wrapped her sleeping child, and left the house of horror.

In moments she aroused the Bransons household. A light came on and a startled Charles opened the screen door.

"Holy Mother of God!" he shrilled, as Charlotte came through the door. "What happened to you? What has that man done to you? Your poor face. Your clothes are in pieces."

Placing her carefully wrapped package into his arms, Charlotte whispered, "Shush, I'm alright. Don't wake Becky. Mason's gone mad. I had to leave for fear he would kill me, and what would become of my little one."

"I'll take her upstairs. You sit, rest. I'll tuck her in bed. We'll have some tea and talk. Want me to wake Shelley?"

"No! She'll have enough to deal with in the morning."

"You're sure. Rest, I'll be right back."   Charlotte laid her head on the kitchen table and sobbed. She began to shake with the realization of the primeval attack she had survived.

A moment later Charles returned with Shelley and Tom on his heels.

"I'm sorry Charlotte, but they heard the movement in the kitchen," Charles apologized.

"I was afraid of something like this. I never should have left you," Shelley moaned, afraid to touch Charlotte for fear of causing more pain.

"Shelley calm down. Help me get her upstairs." Tom said. He gave orders as though he were a general commanding his troops. He assisted the quivering Charlotte to Shelley's room. Over his shoulder he called out, "Charles, call Dr. Bailey. He's discrete."

"Alright. I'll prepare Charlotte some tea after I make the call."

Charlotte stared fearfully at the strange man as he entered the bedroom. Shelley had glued herself to the chair by the window as she guarded her dear one from further harm. He stood by her bed, his eyes saying, "Oh my dear, who has hurt you?" Instead he smiled, taking both of Charlotte hands, and said, "I am Dr. Bailey. Mrs. Burns, is it?"

"Call me, Charlotte," she attempted a smile through her bleeding split lip. "Oh..," Charlotte blotted her lip as fresh blood began to ooze.

"Let's see what we've got here. Relax, I'll try not to hurt. That's a mighty bad cut. We'll fix it up. Miss Branson, would you mind waiting outside with your brother for a few minutes?" Doctor Bailey turned to open the bedroom door.

"May I stay?" Shelley asked.

"I'll call you in when Mrs. Burns and I are finished," Doctor Bailey stated firmly as he escorted Shelley to the door.

"I'll be alright, Shelley. Do as the doctor says," Charlotte replied asa she smiled to her companion.

"I must examine you to determine the extent of your injuries," Doctor Bailey stated tenderly as he touched the offended areas.

"My husband.." was all Charlotte could bring herself to say.

"I'm sorry, dear. You might be better off in the hospital. I'm just a country doctor. I might have missed something," Dr. Bailey corrected himself.

"No! I want to stay here with Shelley. I'd be terrified in the hospital. Mason, Mason could find me and rape me again."

"Yes, I can see. You sustained much damage in the vagina and anus," Dr. Bailey stated as he discussed the offended area. "You've got several severe lacerations. You could benefit by a few stitches. Did he use a foreign object on you?"

"Yes," Charlotte whispered as her face turned white. "He had a night stick he kept for protection. So he said."

"Okay, don't worry. The worse is over. I'll give you a shot. We'll take a stitch or two, and with time, rest and lots of TLC you'll be fine physically."

"Thank you Doctor."

"It's quite alright my dear, and if you will permit, I'd like to contact our local rape crisis center. Have someone come by, discuss your options. The Bransons' love you. They mean well, but you need professional assistance," Dr. Bailey stated. "Alright, you think on it, but for now you must be a good patient and remain in this room. Do not walk around without assistance. Call me if your condition worsens."

"May Shelley come back in."

"Sure, I'll be glad to get her," he stated as he opened the door. Dr. Bailey faced three frightened people.

"Well all of you, come in. I believe you are just what the doctor ordered. You visit while I run down to my car to fetch a few extra items. Tom, I'll leave our patient a mild sedative," Dr. Bailey left the room as Shelley returned to Charlotte's side.

"Remember it is important for you to remain in bed," Dr. Bailey stated.

"I recommended that Charlotte contact the local rape crisis center. She declined."

"Charlotte," Shelley pleaded, "they can help you work through this mess."

"Shelley, I'd rather not. Maybe later."   "I'll drop by tomorrow. Remember, call if she get worse," Doctor Bailey waved as he closed the door.

Tom and Charles followed the doctor to the kitchen.

"Alright, Doc. The girls are upstairs out of ear shot. What did that bastard do to Charlotte?" Tom demanded.

"Bastard's a good description. He beat, raped and sodomized his own wife. When he was finished," Dr. Bailey stopped, wiping the sweat off his brow. "When he was finished, he jammed a night stick up her rectum, tearing her to pieces."

"Dear God. How can she stay with a person that treats her so badly?" Charles asked.

"I don't know, Charles. I've been in practice for more than twenty years and...Oh, I've seen it all. I never get use to it. Charlotte ought to be in the hospital. She says she won't go for fear her husband will find her. You know, somebody ought to castrate scum like Mason Burns."

"Tom, you're awfully quiet. Don't get any bright ideas of revenge. You can be no help to Charlotte Burns from a jail cell."

"I know, Doc. I've just seen a lovely women with a beautiful heart and spirit defiled by an animal. The irony is that the law won't lift a finger to protect she and her daughter."

"Let me get you the medication. She'll be in considerable pain.

Give her one every four hours, two at most," the doctor stated.

Dr. Bailey returned from his car. He would leave the medicine that would aid in the physical damage to Charlotte Burns' body, but what of her mind.

Upon his return he asked the two men, "Will Mrs. Burns be staying here for the time being?"

"Yes, she will. She'll never return to that monster if I have anything to say about it," Charles cried.

"Mason Burns inflicted immeasurable damage to our Charlotte's body, but I am most worried about the violation he inflicted to her mind," Tom stated.

"Encourage her to contact the rape crisis center. They can help."

"We will. And Dr. Bailey, thanks for coming so quickly," Tom continued as he escorted the doctor to the back door.

"The next couple of days will be rough. Follow my instructions to the fullest," Doctor Bailey firmly stated.

"Thank you doctor," Charles called out.

"Call my office at the end of the week for an appointment. See that she takes all of her antibiotics."

"We will. That's a promise." Charles replied.

"Night, folks."

"Good night." Tom answered as he returned to Charles in the kitchen.

The two men stood helplessly as Shelley trudged up the stairs preparing for her long vigil.

A few days later after having had a quiet afternoon followed by a nice nap Charlotte decided to attempt to make peace with Mason. She had spotted him outside and thought she would appeal to him for the last time.

"Mason, you must listen to what I have to say. It will be for the last time."

"Get away from me you whore, you slut. You spawn of Satan."

Mason was afraid, she could feel his terror. He had avoided this confrontation with his wife. He refused to accept the truth. Charlotte watched Mason as he shuttered, and then a light switch seemed to flash on in her head, she understood.

"Mason, you're scared to death of being ostracized by your illiterate cronies. What's the matter, Mason? A man can cheat with another woman and nobody thinks the worse of them. Society winks its collective eye. The members of the zipper club, you good old boys stick together no matter what," Charlotte interjected angrily.

"Shut up you no good bitch. Who do you think you are, lecturing me? You're a whore. Have you no pride, Charlotte? Have you sunk so low that you can't make it with a man, any man?" Mason demanded as his eyes jumped with furtive motions.

Charlotte broke through the defensive wall, from which he had so successfully hidden. "The one thing you really hate is when the world finds out our dirty little secret."

"Secret! What secret, Charlotte? What the hell are your talking about? You don't make sense," Mason snapped.

"Your family and friends have always judged a man by his ability to control a woman. Beat her into submission, if necessary. You're not only lost your wife, but lost her to another woman. That's got to kill you. For the first time in our marriage, I truly feel sorry for you."

"Don't you dare. Don't you dare pity me. I'm on my way for a little quickie with Janie Sue. Sorry to disappoint you. Were you expecting me to plead with you to stay?"

"I don't know why I should care, but what will you do? Mason, will you hide out in the house with your mother?"

"Hell no. Tomorrow my house goes on the market, but for today I'll pleasure myself with Janie Sue. She's more woman than you are. If she gets dull I'll find another sexy woman. Someone who is not an iceberg like you," Mason said smugly.

"What do you think, every woman is out to jump your bones? You're not all that good and I'm in the best position to know," Charlotte laughed.

"That's one weirdo woman's opinion." Mason retorted in a contemptuous manner.

"Mason, you are pathetic. You wouldn't recognize love if you fell over it," Charlotte stated sadly. "You can't love anybody else because you can't love yourself."

"I'll never know where on earth you have gotten your nutty ideas? Love myself. When you're tired of that woman, and run back to me, crying, Please love me again. I can't lose you. Don't expect me to take you back."

Charlotte left the pathetic man rambling on to an empty yard. "I'll pay you back, slut," Mason screamed as she walked away. She was out of his life forever.

That night he went bowling with his buddies. The next day he took Janie Sue to lunch. Everyone smiled too brightly when facing him, but behind his back there was laughter or worse, pity.

No matter how busy he kept himself, every waking moment he could not erase the memory of Charlotte in the arms of Shelley Branson. He knew that his friends laughed about the fact that he could not keep his wife satisfied at home. He had lost her to a woman. He would make Charlotte Hamby Burns rue the day she had set eyes on him.

"What's all of the commotion out there?" Shelley asked.

The trio had been unsuccessful in their attempt to keep Charlotte lying flat in bed until her body healed. She was perched across soft pillows enjoying the evening breeze.

Shelley was busy preparing supper as the door chimes rang out its welcome. Tom greeted a strange pair at the back door.

"Tom, what's going on?" Charlotte called out but there was no response. She climbed out of bed and proceeded down the stairs.

Shelley and Tom were facing an officer and an unfamiliar woman who had just entered the kitchen.

"Mrs. Charlotte Burns?" the officer asked as he faced Shelley.

"No, I'm not Mrs. Burns. I'm Shelley Branson, her friend," Shelley replied.

"Where's Mrs. Burns?" the woman asked.

"I'm Mrs. Burns" Charlotte stated as she descended the stairs. "Is there something I can do for you officer?" Charlotte asked, as Shelley stepped forward to stand beside Charlotte.

"What are you doing? The doctor warned you about your walking down the stairs," Shelley complained as she assisted the wobbly Charlotte to a comfortable chair.

"Yes, ma'am. I am Officer Luther Roland. This is Ms. Brenda Morrison of South Carolina Child Protective Services. She and I...we're here with a juvenile court order to take the youngster, Rebecca Burns into protective custody.

"In custody of the juvenile court? Why?" the confused Charlotte asked. "Rebecca is in immediate danger from you and your, uhh, companions. Her father alleges that due to your peculiar life style you are an unfit mother."

"Unfit. Sir," Charlotte faced the officer. There must be some mistake," Charlotte retorted. "I'm an excellent mother."

"I'm sorry, ma'am. We are here to carry out the court order, not try the case."

"In what way am I unfit?" Charlotte asked. "This must be a joke."

"This is not a joking matter," Brenda Morrison stated as she looked at Shelley as though she were the worst kind of vermin.

"Exactly what do you think you are doing? We're guilty of nothing," Charlotte demanded.

"I have total authority and the responsibility to carry out the order of the Court. The court will determine the validity of the charges that are being brought against you. In the interest of the safety of the child, the Court has ordered that the child be removed from the home pending that determination of validity of the charges. But believe you me if you do not co-operate your child may be placed in another part of the state and you may never see her again," Ms. Morrison smirked as she seemed to enjoy the pain she was inflicting.

"Rebecca Jane Burns has the right to proper moral training and an example of a normal home environment. Mrs. Burns, your husband accuses you of leaving his marital bed for an unnatural relationship with another woman," Ms. Brenda Morrison answered, her voice obviously filled with disgust.

"But, Charlotte is a good mother. The best mother. The father, Mason Burns, is an animal. She and Becky have been treated terribly by this abusive man," Tom said, attempting to read the document held by the officer.

"This can not be happening. She has a legal right to her daughter. They belong together," Shelley cried.

"Sorry, uh ma'am. I'm afraid that's for a court to decide. "Becky and I, we're the victims," Charlotte pleaded. "My husband is a monster."

"Our office understands otherwise. Now ma'am, I hope this doesn't become unpleasant," the officer added, "for the sake of your daughter."

"Ladies, fetch Rebecca. Let's not have any trouble," the policeman stated as he squirmed. He was extremely uncomfortable being a party to this situation.

Brenda Morrison stepped forward as though she would grab Charlotte. She thought better of it and backed off. "Where's Rebecca?"

"Can't you see that Mrs. Burns has been ill? She can not stand much more stress," Shelley stated as her faced turned a deep crimson.

"Sorry Miss," the officer replied, "we must take the child. It's the law."

"We're not dangerous criminals..." Shelley stated.

"Where is the child?" Brenda Morrison again demanded.

"She's in her room with Charles impatiently awaiting her dinner," Charlotte replied.

"Please fetch her, sweetie," Tom said tenderly.

"Rebecca Burns will be placed in foster care until the hearing," Brenda Morrison stated proudly.

"Ms., uhh, why can't my baby stay with me? I have not deprived Becky of anything," Charlotte whispered.

"Your husband has issued this complaint, so we have no choice," the social worked smiled.

"Why must Mason be so cruel?" Charlotte cried. "He said he would punish me. He said he didn't mind stacking the deck, in his favor."

"Mason's got an order from juvenile court. Please, my dear try to stay calm for Becky's sake." Tom said.

"Tom's right, Charlotte," Shelley said. "We'll hire the best lawyer money can buy. This is only temporary. Surely the court will allow Nola to have temporary custody. Nola will look after her." "I don't know who this Nola is, but are you bunch of weirdos in for a surprise. Rebecca is in the system now." Brenda Morrison stated. Then she thought as she laughed to herself. "These queers have no normal feelings. Why are they acting up so?"

"No, please don't do this. Haven't I suffered enough?" Charlotte backed away. "Shell, you promised if we came with you nothing bad would happen," Charlotte accused.

"Must you do this, sir?" Shelley asked, brows knitted together apprehensively. "Didn't you investigate the charges?"

"Since the charges are considered serious in this jurisdiction, the child must be protected while any investigation is conducted," replied Officer Roland. "She is enjoying their misery," the officer thought as he watched helplessly as Brenda Morrison gave the other two women a big knowing grin.

"Knock it off, Ms. Morrison," Luther Roland wanted to say.

"Ma'am, I'm sorry. I am not the judge, but this court order will be carried out. If you truly love your child, you'd better adhere to the order. Fetch the child," Officer Roland stated decisively.

"Shelley, I've lost my home, and my child. What will become of me?" Charlotte asked as she slumped into the kitchen chair.

"It could get nasty, Charlotte, if we don't comply," Tom stated. "We'll have our attorney explain the true nature of Mason Burns. I'm sure we'll get our girl back soon."

"It never ceases to amaze me how vicious Mason can be?" Charlotte moaned. "No matter what he has done to me in the past, I always thought he loved Rebecca."

"Uh, if he did, he wouldn't put her through this ugly mess," Tom said, patting Charlotte's shoulder. "Go get, Becky. It must be done."

"I hate, Mason Burns. I'd love to see him dead," Shelley stated.

"Shell, he's not worth the bullet it would take to blow his sorry, no good ass off this planet," Tom growled. Charlotte   trudged sadly up the stairs to Becky's room where she quietly waited with Charles Allgood. Shelley stood, arms folded tightly as she watched helplessly as her world collapsed.

"Now baby, you will be visiting with your papa and Granny Nola," Charlotte chattered on as she and her child joined the others. "Granny will give you your supper tonight and read you your favorite bedtime story."

"May I take my Little Puppy book? Granny reads it funny. She makes me laugh," Rebecca smiled. She was doing her best to get through a situation she did not understand.

"That's right, darling. Wear your warm nightie, and remember to brush your pretty little teeth. Promise?" Charlotte said.

"I promise, Mommie. I'll be a good girl. Can't you come? Can't Aunty Shelley, and Uncle Charlie, and Uncle Tom Tom come. We can sleep on the pallets," Becky giggled.

"Now why would want them to sleep on the floor?" Charlotte asked, squeezing Becky's hand.

"We could have a pajama party."

"That would be neat, darling." Charlotte hugged Becky. "This nice man is a friend of Mommies', Officer Luther Roland. He is going to take you to Granny's house." Charlotte explained as she pointedly ignored Ms. Brenda Morrison.

"He is not taking you to Granny's house." Brenda Morrison snapped.

"No Dear, I am going to take you to visit a nice lady's house." Officer Roland responded in a soft tone.

"What nice lady?" Becky asked. She was not happy with the intrusion of the strange people.

"Her name is Mrs. Carson. She had a little girl just your age that needs somebody nice like you to play with," Officer Roland replied.

"Okay, Mommie," Becky answered, never taking her eyes off her mother. Rebecca Burns sensed her mother's fear and attempted a smile as tears welled up in her eyes. The terrified child had suddenly forgotten about her puppy book.   "Say your prayers, precious child. God will take care of you," Charlotte called.

"I will, Mommie," replied the nervous child. "See you in the morning, Mommie. Don't let the bed bugs bite," Becky looked unsure as she waved goodbye.

Mason had over played his hand. He had thought Becky would be given to him, but he had thrown his family into a maze of horror. There would be no justice for the accused. An accusation these days was all it took and lives were destroyed in the name of protection.

Rebecca Burns was so terrified that she showed little resistance as the strange man took her hand and led her towards the big police car.

"Let's get moving, Ms. Morrison," Officer Roland stated. This whole thing bothers me, even if it doesn't you."

Luther Roland had heard about Mason Burns. He was a mean SOB if he had heard right. He hated taking this innocent little girl away from a descent parent just because of her sexual orientation.

Charlotte sat in the Branson house, positive that her life was over. Charlotte's only child had been taken and was being placed in foster care until the court rendered its decision to give custody of Rebecca to Charlotte or Mason. "Those two lesbos are getting just what they deserve," Brenda Morrison said with disgust.

"What's a lizard, Mr. Luther?" Becky asked.

"A lizard is a nice green animal, sweetheart." Luther replied. "Watch your mouth Ms. Morrison, remember little pitchers have big ears."

"You are so funny. Pitchers don't have ears, Mr. Luther. You put water in it," Becky laughed, "Hey mommie! You didn't pack my rabbit."

Luther Roland watched as Becky dashed past him into the Branson house.

"Stop that kid, Roland, where is she going?" Ms. Morrison snapped.

"Be right back, Mr. Luther. I don't sleep without "Bunny Elizabeth."

Minutes passed and Becky did not return. He looked at his watch. She's been gone five minutes. What could be keeping her? Luther Roland was not concerned because he could see the reflection of the two women through the window.

"Better check on Becky. See what's the holdup?" Ms. Morrison asked.

"That woman yaps and yaps like a bluejay when she's after her quarry." Luther Roland thought.

"I'll check myself. You act like these are nice people, not lawbreakers," Ms. Morrison snapped at the officer as she opened the kitchen door to find Tom and Charles wearing the robes that the two women had previously been wearing.

"Where the hell's the kid?" Ms. Morrison bellowed, "Officer Roland! they're gone."

"There must be some mistake. Mrs. Burns isn't the type to break the law," Officer Roland replied as he slowly opened the screen door to survey the situation.

"Good luck ladies," he whispered to the moon. "Oh how I hate wife beaters. What you can't rule you destroy."

"Roland, these men swapped clothes with the women to buy them time," the red faced social worker screamed, "tell us where they are or we'll arrest you."

Charles and Tom looked at each other with blank stares.

"Why Officer Roland, we thought they were upstairs searching for the stuffed rabbit. You certainly are not implying that we would be party to anything illegal?" Charles asked.

"Think of our reputations. Our standing in the community," Tom's voice dripped with sarcasm. "Charles, don't over react. The officer isn't suggesting that we've done anything wrong. Are you, Officer?"

With Charlotte, Becky and Shelley having made their escape from the authorities the intruders had nothing to do but rushed out to the police radio and make their report.

Mason Burns left the Bransons' home madder than a sidewinder that's been stepped on. He couldn't believe that two stupid broads like Charlotte and Shelley could run off with little Becky right under the noses of the police. His face was deep purple when he came around demanding to know there whereabouts.

"I know I'm better off without Ben, but did he have to die so violently. Tom, I did remember to tell you that Shelley will contact us when she and Charlotte find a safe haven."

"My sister has been an independent character for as long as I can remember. She'll be fine."

"Our luck has not been all bad. The local authorities have finally closed the case of Benjamin Tracer. Charlotte, Rebecca, and Shelley are safe so we can get some rest," Tom stated.

"Tom," Charles whispered, "you did remind Shelley to contact us when she and Charlotte reach their safe haven, didn't you?"

"Yes!, I told Shell to place an ad in the newspaper personals saying, Tom-Tom, lets have a clam bake. Love, Sea Shell."

"Tom, we can rest now that our girls are safe. I know I'm better off without Ben, but did he have to die so... Tom, I'm feeling quite weary. I'm going on upstairs to lie down. I feel a migraine coming on," Charles frowned.

Weariness engulfed his body. Charles' shoes felt like fifty pound weights about his ankles. He had aged a hundred years in the last week. Charles knew he would be changed forever.

How could he speak of his abduction? How could he make any one understand his strange sadness? His feeling of grief?

Ben was not totally evil. Charles and Benjamin shared many wonderful times, but worst of all was his final memory of Ben. His death. Such a awful way to die. Charles grimaced as he replayed that terrible moment over and over in his mind like some cheap B-grade movie. Charles' mind would forever be haunted by Ben's screams. Ben's last words. "I always loved you, Charles." When Charles Allgood reaches his bedroom he will find in the center of the white coverlet of his bed a fresh, long stemmed yellow rose.

Chapter 18

Six blocks from the Branson house, Shelley stopped her car as a blue light appeared in her rear view mirror. Two policemen appeared at their window with their hands on their guns.

"Step out of the car," one of the officer's demanded.

"What's the problem officers?" Shelley asked as she rolled down the window. "Out of the cars ladies," the officer demanded as his partner appeared on the passenger side.

"Out of the car," the officer demanded again.

"Sorry baby," Shelley whispered as she patted Charlotte thigh.

Shelley and Charlotte did not move. There was a faint cry from the terrified Rebecca as she crouched in the backseat.

"Mama, what do these men what?" "Don't worry, baby. There has been some mistake," Charlotte crooned to her daughter.

"We told you two to get out of the car," the officer snapped as Charlotte stared down a gun barrel.

"What's this all about officers?" Shelley asked as she slowly exited the car.

Charlotte slid out of the car drawing Becky out the other side.

"You two are being arrested for the kidnaping of one Rebecca Jane Burns. Turn around please."

Charlotte's face turned ash as she heard the click of the handcuffs.

"Kidnaping? Kidnaping my Becky. There's been a terrible mistake, officers. We're no kidnappers. I'm Becky's mother. Darling, tell the nice policeman who you are," Charlotte pleaded with her small frightened child.

"Mr. Policeman," Becky whispered, "I'm my mama's little girl."

"As I stated earlier Becky is my daughter," Charlotte added. "Please removed the handcuffs, you are terrifying my baby."

"Can't do that. It's the law. Suspects must be cuffed."

"Officer," Shelley whispered, "Mrs. Burns has been ill. Please try not to be so rough."

"Yes ma'am. I'll do my best, but we must get going."

"Mama is no stranger. Aunt Shelley is not a stranger. They told me not to talk to strangers when they were not with me," Becky attempted a smile.

"Ma'am, we've got an APB to be on the lookout for grey Chevy with South Carolina plates RJR791, two female Caucasians with a four year old female child answering to the name of Rebecca."

"But, I am Becky's mother," Charlotte cried.

"Sorry, but we're not paid to try cases in the streets," the first officer stated, "Get in the car."

"You two better call a lawyer." The other officer continued, "kidnaping, even if it's your own child is serious business."

The trembling Charlotte and Shelley were placed in the back of the police car.

"Sit up here with us sweetie. We'll have you safe and sound with your daddy and grandmother in a jiffy," the officer smiled brightly.

The sullen Becky climbed up into the big police car as she heard the click of the seat belt.

"Remember Becky, we must buckle up for safety," the second officer stated.

It seemed a lifetime as the two women sat in the small cell. The cement walls had absorbed the acrid odor from the toilet. Charlotte gagged from the stench that permeated her nostrils. The odor spoke of old sweat, vomit, stale urine, excessive flatulence, and feces.

Charlotte and Shelley had no privacy because they were under a suicide watch.

"Why do you suppose they assume that we will commit suicide," Charlotte whispered.

"Because lesbians are unstable. Remember we can't handle pressure," Shelley could not refrain from laughter.

"Did you notice that the guards withheld our belts? Probably thought we'd hang each other," Charlotte attempted a chuckle.

"I am quite annoyed that they confiscated our shoe strings. My shoes keep falling off my feet. I hate to put them on these cold floors. We don't know what's been on them."   Night fell and Shelley and Charlotte found solace in each others' arms   until exhaustion overcame them.

They were awaken suddenly by the snickers of the guards.

"Oh my, isn't this sweet. Two lesbos locked in an embrace. Can we come in and join you?"

The next few days began and ended with the laughter of their captors.

The third day they were informed that they must appear in court at 8:00 am. They were dressed in jump suits as were the other prisoners. Charlotte and Shelley leaned against the wall to avoid falling as they marched chained at the ankles as they were transferred in the prison van. The crackle of electricity shot throughout the courtroom. The onlookers craned their necks with anticipation to get a glimpse of the arraignment of the two lesbians. They had caused much embarrassment to a fine local boy and they wished to see justice done.

Charlotte and Shelley pled "not guilty" to all charges. They were asked if they had an attorney. Both women replied "No." Shelley informed the judge that they would not require a public defender. She stated that her brother Tom Branson was making arrangements for representation.

After the bond hearing, Tom and Charles used their home as security to bail them out of jail.

As they left the court house Charlotte complained as she leaned on Charles' arm, "These last few days have been the most humiliating of my life."

"It's going to get worse," Charles stated.

"What's wrong, Tom?" Shelley demanded as she nervously tugged at her hair.

"You haven't been in a position to know, but some of our local good old boys tried to set the house on fire. It was dreadful," Charles replied to Shelley's question.

"You'll be staying with Bill Painter and his family. We thought it would be the safest place for now," Tom stated as he led his sister to the car.

"He's such a dear. Always ready to help. Do you think his wife objects to the possible danger?" Charlotte asked.

"Wanda Painter is a gutsy lady. She might haul out her baseball bat if anybody bothers you," Charles laughed.

The thought of the four foot ten Wanda Painter hurling a bat made the four burst into laughter. Charlotte had been positive that she would never laugh again. This moment of levity was good for her.

"How's my Becky?" Charlotte asked.

"She's just fine. Mrs. Burns brought her out in the backyard for a visit. We were a little surprise at her kindness," Charles replied.

Chapter 19

Robert Travis, a large man wearing an ill-fitting suit paced back and forth in the Painters' living room as he awaited his new clients. A woman cracked the door and said something to someone behind her.

"Travis," Bill Painter entered the room shepherding two women that he assumed were his clients, "thanks for coming by. We sure need your help."

"Let's be seated, Bill, so we can sort out this mess. Ladies, I'm Bobby Travis a longtime friend of this big lug," Attorney Travis spoke as he extended his hand to his startled clients.

"Thank you, Mr. Travis," Shelley smiled as she took his hand, "we were beginning to believe that there was no one in this town that cared."

"Oh you'd be surprised. Now ladies, lets get some background. I'll need your help in understanding the complete picture. Mrs. Burns are you from Charleston?"

"No, I'm from Baltimore."

"And you Ms. Branson?"

"New York City. If it makes any difference, my legal name is Michelle Elizabeth Branson. I'm called Shelley by friends and family."

"I'll make note of your legal name. Thank you," Travis answered.

"Mrs. Burns, what did you do in Baltimore?"

"I worked in the Mitchells' Bookstore several blocks from my childhood home."

"And you Ms. Branson?"

"I worked at Madame Lorraine's which is run by my brother Tom Branson and Charles Allgood, his, uhh, companion."

"A gay couple, I presume?" Travis asked.

"Yes, you got a problem with it?" Shelley snapped. She shivered with apprehension, expecting disapproval.

"What people do in the privacy of their homes is no concern of mine," Bob Travis replied and quickly changed the subject. "Mrs. Burns, what does your husband, Mason Burns, do for a living?"

Charlotte laughed, "as little as possible."

"How did you meet? How long have you been married?" Travis asked.

"We've been married six years. My mother-in-law, Nola Burns was my mother's oldest friend. They felt our marriage would be a good match, but I always felt I was sold off to a depraved man to remove me from my home. With dead, mama had a boyfriend and she wanted me out of the way."

His face blanched, Robert Travis sat mesmerized as the tiny Charlotte Hamby Burns relived her life of terror and abuse with Mason Burns.

Shelley Branson sat as close as possible as she held Charlotte's hand. Her face was red with anger as she listened to Charlotte's story .

Several hours later Mr. Travis halted the meeting.

"I believe I have enough information for the moment. I'll contact Mr. Burns to see if there is any compromise in the offing. I'll call you in the morning. You two try to get some rest. I'm sure you'd like to forget the last few days. Good night," Robert Travis stated as he walked with Bill Painter to the front door.

"What do you think, Bobby?" Bill asked.

"If they were not a lesbian couple Mrs. Burns would have a chance. I don't know, there is no way to read people these days. The odds are really stacked against them," Travis replied as he closed the door.

Shelley and Charlotte had left the room absorbed in their own thoughts.

"Poor things," Bill said to the empty room, "you two don't stand a chance."

Robert Travis left the Painter driveway and turned towards his home. He drove in deep thought wandering the best way to approach Mason Burns.

He picked up his car phone and dialed the Burns household.

"Mason Burns, please," Travis said.

"This is Mason Burns. Who the hell are you?" bellowed Mason.

"Mr. Burns, my name is Robert Travis. I am representing your wife, Charlotte Hamby Burns, and her friend Michelle (Shelley) Branson," Travis deliberately omitted any pleasantries.

"So my long suffering wife as hired a lawyer," Mason laughed. "You don't seriously believe a jury of my peers would give a bitch and her bull-dyke lover my innocent child," Mason's detestable laughter ripped through the cellular phone.

"You have retained an attorney, haven't you, Mr. Burns?" Travis asked.

"You're damned right, and tell the dyke bitch that I will see Rebecca dead before she and that bunch of weirdos get their hands on her."

"Thank you, Mr. Burns. If you will give me the name of your attorney I will contact him."

"His name is Herbert Shoemaker. Are you impressed? You didn't think I could afford such a high powered mouthpiece," Mason laughed again.

"Herbert Shoemaker, thank you. Good evening," Travis disconnected the call without comment.

Herbert Shoemaker would be a rough adversary. He ate lawyers for a snack. A real heartless bastard. Robert Travis felt a shiver race down his spine.

Robert Travis trudged into his ranch brick home. As he sat down on the bed and looked at his sleeping wife Penny, he was glad she was asleep. He was not prepared to discuss his new case with anyone, even Penny. Bob Travis quietly disrobed and slid into his bed.

He stared at the ceiling for hours unable to get those two women out of his mind. What would be the best advise he could give them? This case could take months, even years. These type of cases usually took about two years, and manages to destroy all of the participants.

"Oh," Bob sighed, "What will become of that innocent child? The children are the real losers."

Robert Travis turned on his side and attempted to get some rest. He woke with a start.

It was morning and the mist had rolled in covering Charleston like a protective blanket. He could smell the aroma of fresh coffee Penny prepared each morning. Bob laid back on his pillow listening as she sang her favorite song.

The telephone broke into his restful trance.

"Bob, it's Bill Painter. Hope I didn't wake you."

"No. We're up. What may I do for you this morning? Nothing's happened to the ladies?" Bob Travis asked as he sat straight up.

"Everybody's okay. But some jackass put a couple of rounds through my front window. I wanted to shoot those MF's but Wanda stopped me."

"You sure everybody's fine?"

"Yeah! But I have a house full of nervous people. The kids are terrified."

"I can imagine. First, the destruction of Tom's car. Then the fire at the Branson house, and now this, bullets through your windows. What are you going to do?"

"I'm not sure, but those scum are not running me out of my home," Bill responded. "Wanda is taking the kids to her parents and then coming back. I feel like pulling rank on her. If I were smart I'd demand she stay with her folks where she'll be safe."

"Now Bill, Wanda will never leave you to face those terrorists alone. That's quite a gal you've got."

"You're telling me. When I made the suggestion she informed me that she was not a child and could make up her own mind. Then she reminded me that this was also her home."

"What did I tell you."

"I didn't care for the report I received about the increase in "hate" crimes. There were three cases last night where some of our good old boys beat up several men coming out of the Other side. You remember that's a gay bar. Worst of all, Bob, oh shit. People and their narrow-mindedness."

"What's happened, Bill?"

"One thing I haven't told those poor souls is that last night some piece of shit burned down Madame Lorraine's."

"NO! Was anybody in the building?"

"The watchman had left to get some fresh coffee."

"I suppose Tom and Charles know."

"Yes I told them before they left. This is another reason leaving town is desirable."

"I hoped things would not get this nasty. Hold down the fort. I'll have breakfast and be right over. We need to discuss strategy. Bill, we'd better do something fast before somebody really gets hurt."

"Yeah! See you soon."

About an hour later Robert Travis appeared on Elm Street. The sky had turned an eerie black overcast. The silence was deafening. The yard always appeared to be a bee-hive of activity at the favorite neighborhood home of Bill and Wanda. But this morning no one was outdoors since the shoots of last evening destroyed the apparent safety of the neighborhood.

"Morning Bob," Bill greeted the attorney.

"Bill, good to see you. Where are the ladies?"

"They are in the kitchen finishing breakfast."

"Good morning, Mrs. Burns. Ms. Branson. Where are the gentlemen?"

"They left before we woke up. They're trying to rent a car."

"I think Tommy is feeling claustrophobic. My brother must have his wheels," Shelley stated.

Bob Travis sat down in an oversize kitchen chair. Shelley sat beside Charlotte. The black mist poured through the thin, white blinds. Travis, avoiding the inevitable looked out on the river where the boats and ships navigated down the Ashley River.

Shelley bit her lips and Charlotte held her breath as they waited the decision of their attorney. Robert Travis was unusually quiet. He shifted his eyes toward the two women and stared for a moment.

"Shelley. Charlotte. I don't want you to panic, Tom and Charles are alright."

"Please, what's wrong?" Shelley asked, her eyes stricken with terror.

"I'm sorry Shelley, but last night somebody burned down Madame Lorraine's."

"Oh no!" Charlotte cried out.

"Who! why!" Shelley moaned.

"It's all my fault. If I had not left Mason none of this would not have happened."

"You can't blame yourself solely, Charlotte. You knew what you wanted and I wanted it too. We knew the risks we were taking," Shelley murmured. "It was my idea. We knew it wouldn't be easy," Shelley continued as she hugged Charlotte tightly.

"Don't blame yourself. You're not responsible for Mason's being a narrow minded creep."

"Charlotte, I'm sorry but we must move quickly. You must face a trial, but it will be a long time coming. The first order of business will be to find a safe place for you to start over."

"To start over," Charlotte cried, "What about my Becky?"

"You are now in the limelight. Everybody is waiting for the next chapter of your war with Mason Burns. You have done nothing but protect yourself and your child. Unfortunately, your leaving your husband for a woman has put you on the front page of the newspaper."

Charlotte turned ashen as tears cascaded down her thin face as she whispered, "I can't leave Becky."

"I'll play the devil's advocate," Travis said, continuing to smiled softly toward the two women. "You said you left your husband, a hard working man for a woman. You and your innocent daughter live with a gay couple. What kind of example are you to an impressionable child?"

"But Mason is a beast," Charlotte cried out.

"Maybe so, but an alternate life style has not caught on in the nineties yet. You must leave Charleston now. I'll keep working on your case. If anything changes you won't be too far away." "I don't know," Charlotte whispered.

Shelley pressed Charlotte's hand, kissed her cheek, and left the room. She walked upstairs to pack.

"Charlotte Hamby Burns, you'd better start thinking about somebody besides yourself. Tom or Charles could have been killed in that fire. You are just an oddity, but they are in real danger. Women don't get beat up, but men do. Sometimes they get killed."

Charlotte cried. She knew that everything Robert Travis had said was true.

The late afternoon grew darker and darker through the thick storm clouds. The blue sky like the happiness that they had shared disappeared. Familiar places began to appear, as the four grew more apprehensive of their future.

"Starting over at our age. Tom, where will be live?" Charles asked.

"We will stay with friends in Atlanta."

An eery silence fell over the grey rental car as Tom drove Charles, Shelley and Charlotte toward the Georgia border. They were unable to talk for fear of bursting into tears. Three hours later, the only voice heard was Tom's directing Charles to the Ansley Park house and their new future.

Charlotte remembered little of the next few weeks. She moved about the house like a sleepwalker, eating little, doing little as possible. Clouds of gloom hovered over their Ansley Park house with an oppression that filled every corners. She fell asleep during a spring rain.

Charlotte woke with a start. "Who is it?" She was in no mood to talk to any of Tom and Charles' friends. She was in no mood to listen to idle gossip.

Charlotte had asked Shelley to let her spend a quiet afternoon alone. She was so weary that she was unaware when Shelley came to bed. Charlotte gave no response when Shelley stroked her shoulder.

Late in the morning, Charlotte rose alone. Shelley had left early for work. Charlotte bathed, dressed and brushed out her hair. She had some breakfast and sat in the back porch swing. All of her energy and excitement had been drained from her body. After a short while she dragged herself to her room.

"Oh Becky, how I miss your sweet little face," Charlotte moaned. "I wish I could talk to you. How I long to put my arms about you, my sweet Becky." Charlotte's heart pounded from the loneliness as the pain shot down her spine and then up to her head. She felt faint as she lay back. Shelley opened the door bringing Charlotte back to reality.

"You've got to snap out of your doldrums. Nola is taking care of our Becky. She's safe," Shelley assured Charlotte. She squeezed Charlotte's hand as she challenged her love to fight back.

"Let's go downstairs, sweetie. The guys have found a small shop, but let them tell you about it. Show some interest. Pretend, for their sake. Come on. You need some fresh air. You've been up here too long."

Charlotte nodded. The two women went down the stairs. Charlotte embraced Tom and Charles.

"Sorry guys. I've been a real pain in the neck."

She joined the others on the couch as they happily explained the possibilities of the new shop.

"We have found the sweetest little place in Ansley Mall. It's at the corner of Piedmont and Monroe Drive," Charles exclaimed with unbridled emotion.

"Shell, you and Charlotte can return to your afternoon strolls. Piedmont Park is close by," Tom chimed in.

"Tommy, it sounds delightful. Don't you think so Charlotte?"

"Let's check out the store. What do you say? How much space do we have, Tom?" Charlotte asked.

Charlotte wanted to be strong, but she was shaken with the realization that when ever life became too difficult she ran. Nobody ever said life was easy. It was filled with pain. The greatest pain was the loss of Becky. One day, maybe someday she and Becky would be reunited. Until that day she would live and love those around her. Together she and Shelley would build a home in which any little girl could thrive.

Shelley and Tom laughed. They found Charlotte's excitement infectious.

"Charles, come on, Charlotte wants to see our shop," Tom called.

The four piled into the rental and headed toward Ansley Mall. They made their way through gigantic magnolias heavy with creamy, white blossoms. Dogwood trees dotted the streets. This was the most beautiful season in fifty years. Everybody's yard was filled with tulips, crocus, jonquils and blue bells of Scotland. Azaleas were exquisite, their branches thick with pink, red or white blossoms.

Tom opened the car door and stepped out as he gazed proudly at his future. The shop was a two story. The second story opened up onto a back porch. Tom had thought, "cleaned up, it would make an excellent place to sit and rest. The inside was similar to their shop back home in Charleston."

"Stop it Tom," he whispered. "You have got to stop thinking about Charleston as home. Atlanta is now our home. It is a beautiful city that anyone could enjoy."

"Come on. Let's see what we're going to need," Charles said.

"I can make curtains," Charlotte stated.

"Curtains are certainly needed. The walls need cleaning. We must paint everything. The previous owners did not believe in soap and water," Tom smiled.

"Well my friends, let's get to work," Charles stated.

After six months of hope and prayer Mason Burns called.

"Charlotte, hi this is Mason."

"Yes Mason. How is Becky?"

"Must you sound so brittle. Oh she's fine."

"Mason, get to the point. What do you want?"

"I have been wondering if it would be convenient for Becky to come for a visit? I haven't been fair to you."

"What? Are you joking?"

"No, I'm not joking. Just because we can't get along doesn't mean you are a bad mother. I am sure you have missed her. She misses you."

"Of course, I want to see my baby. When may she come?"

"She can come this Saturday. We'll take advantage of the weekend rates."

Charlotte could not believe what she was hearing. Something must have happened in the last few months for him to become so generous. He's probably tired of babysitting. What ever the reason, Becky would be with her this weekend.

Tom whipped the car through the parking deck almost striking another car.

"I can not believe there is so much traffic," Charles complained.

"The Atlanta Airport sure is big. You can get lost wandering about this place," Tom complained.

The four bolted out of the car and headed inside for their reunion with the angel girl. They came to a sudden halt as they saw long lines at the security check point.

"Oh no! We'll miss the plane," Charlotte moaned, "she'll be walking around wondering where I am."

"Charlotte, calm down. Someone from the airline will stay with Becky." Tom stated calmly.

"Oh I hope so."

The four walked single file through the checkpoint.

"Excuse me. Which is the speediest way to Delta flights?" Shelley asked.

"Go to the first escalator. Take the trams to Concourse A or B. Do you have the flight number?" the guard asked.

"It's my daughter, Becky," Charlotte's face lit up like a Christmas tree. "She's coming for a visit. She's coming in at gate B-14. Flight 1201 from Charleston, SC. It arrives at 4:21."

"Take the tram to Concourse B. Good luck ma'am."

"Thank you," Charlotte called out as she raced to the awaiting tram.

Charlotte and Shelley were exhausted from the hasty redecoration of Becky's room. They had kept the fourth bedroom hoping this day would arrive.

Shelley, Tom and Charles worked cleaning and sprucing up the room while Charlotte attempted to purchase a white spread and window treatment. They had thought Barney was popular, Winnie the Pooh was a classic. They had decided to have pink walls trimmed with small pink and white roses.

Today the harried group were fidgeting as the tram seemed to take forever. Suddenly they could see the numbers of the gates.

"Did anybody remember Becky's teddy bear?"

"I've got the bear," Charles laughed. "I've been receiving interesting looks all through this airport."

"This way. We're just a few gates away," Charlotte squealed.

"The passengers have already disembarked. We'll have to find an agent to assist us," Tom stated.

"Excuse me", Charlotte pulled at the sleeve of a ticket agent. We're looking for my daughter. She was supposed to be on this plane."

"What is her name?"

"Becky! Rebecca Jane Burns."

"I'm sorry, but we have no passenger named Rebecca Jane Burns. Maybe she'll be on a later plane."

"Mrs. Burns, Mrs. Charlotte Burns," Charlotte heard a soft voice behind her.

"Yes, I'm Charlotte Burns. Do you have information about my Becky?"

"I was asked to deliver this box to Mrs. Charlotte Burns. May I see some identification, please?"

"Identification, yes. I have identification," Charlotte replied.

Satisfied, the stewardess handed Charlotte a small box and envelope.

Years of mistreatment had taught Charlotte to be wary of Mason. Charlotte hands shook uncontrollably as she opened the envelope.

This is all of Becky you're ever gonna get. Enjoy your weirdo life. You can't corrupt my girl anymore. Becky caught pneumonia two weeks ago. She couldn't be saved, here's your share of her ashes."

Mason.

Shelley caught the box as Charlotte dropped to the floor into oblivion. Charlotte shuttered as a black emptiness engulfed her heart. She tried to be as invisible as possible. Charlotte was a stranger cut off, cut off forever from her beloved child.

Turning his head back and forth Charles strained to hear the slightest sound. Gooseflesh spread across his skin, every nerve end tingled causing a stinging sensation. He felt helpless to give aid to Charlotte. Beside him he began to hear Shelley moaning in disbelief.

"This can't be. Becky is gone," Shelley cried out as she pressed her face into Charlotte's hair.

"Shell, get yourself under control. You must be strong for Charlotte," Tom demanded.

Charlotte lay in her arms as the hysterical airline attendant called for medical attention. The airport supplied a wheelchair and an attendant assisted the stunned Charlotte to their car.

Several weeks passed as the inconsolable Charlotte lay in her darken room. She refused to allow anyone to open the drapes. She had turned her back on the world. Charlotte was positive that God had taken her child as a punishment for her lesbian lifestyle. The doctor came everyday. He kept her heavily sedated because he feared she would loose her mind.

The telephone rang, and Shelley picked it up.

"Yes? I don't know. She's not doing well. I'll ask," Shelley responded. "Charlotte," she squeezed Charlotte's lifeless hand, "It's Nola she wants to talk to you."

"No! I won't talk to her," Charlotte whispered as she rolled away from Shelley.

Shelley returned to the phone, "I'm sorry," was all she could get out as Nola Burns began to beg.

"Please, let me speak to Charlotte. I have no one now. Please."

Shelley pressed the receiver into Charlotte's hand. "I have never heard anybody sound so pitiful. You tell her you have lost all of your charity. I won't turn her away. Shelley Branson left the room in disgust. The Charlotte she had loved was gone. She did not know this selfish stranger that shared her bed.

"Nola?" Charlotte whispered tentatively.

"Yes Charlotte, this is Nola. I can hardly hear you."

"I'm here Nola. They gave me something. I can't think."

"Have you been ill?" Nola asked.

"Have I been ill?" thought Charlotte. My child is dead and she asks if I have been ill, Charlotte laughed at the absurdity of her question. "How are you? How is Mason?"

Why did she ask after Mason? She did not care about Mason Burns. He had destroyed her life. I must be making polite conversation, Charlotte thought.

"Oh Mason, I suppose he's alright. But right now I don't much care. Sonny always had a cruel streak. You remember when others crossed him he would become incredibly belligerent. He'd set out on a campaign to hurt and discredit his enemy real or imagined. Since you left he's become worse. He's even turned on me." Nola caught her breath.

"I'm sorry Nola. You have always been devoted to him," Charlotte replied. She understood Nola's pain.

"I'm so lonely and worn down. It's become so terrible I've had to hide in my own room. He's been like a stick of dynamite ready to explode."

Shelley tiptoed back into the room and sat down gently on the bed.

"Nola I wish I could help. I'm so sorry that your life has become so difficult," Charlotte smiled as she patted Shelley's hand.

"Charlotte, remember my cat Precious?"

"Yes, I remember. Mason called her fur ball."

"He got so mad one night that he poisoned Precious. Then he set her body on fire."

"He killed your cat? That must have been dreadful for you."

"Oh it has been a nightmare. All of the responsibility has fallen on me. And now Mason's run off with Janie Sue. Good riddance. I gave up my life for him. Sacrificed everything. Now I'm all alone."

"Is there anything I can do to help you?" Charlotte asked.

"Yes dear, when are you coming after Becky?"
